A BOUNDARY OF STONES

Millie Thom

To Mike,
Best Wishes
from
Millie.

Copyright © 2024 by Millie Thom

The moral right of Millie Thom to be identified as the author of this work has been asserted in accordance with the Copyright, Designs and Patents Act 1988.

All rights reserved. No part of this publication may be reproduced, stored in a retrieval system, or transmitted, in any form or by any means, electronic, mechanical, photocopying, recording or otherwise without prior consent of the publisher.

Contents

One	5
Two	25
Three	42
Four	52
Five	62
Six	81
Seven	92
Eight	102
Nine	114
Ten	127
Eleven	140
Twelve	155
Thirteen	175
Fourteen	185
Fifteen	207
Sixteen	225
Seventeen	238
Eighteen	251
Nineteen	265
Twenty	285
Twenty-One	292
Twenty-Two	302
Twenty-Three	312
Twenty-Four	326
Twenty-Five	337
Twenty-Six	351
Twenty-Seven	358
Other Books by Millie Thom	379

One

Derbyshire: Wednesday July 2 1664

Catherine Mompesson shifted the chuntering one-year-old to her right thigh and rubbed her left back to life as she focused on her husband, sitting opposite with their young son. 'Elizabeth is becoming increasingly cantankerous, William, and is likely to be screaming her head off before long. Would it not be permissible to disembark for a while?'

Holding him in a pleading gaze she took a breath. 'We've been inside this coach for the past five hours and although George seems happy to watch the scenery pass by, I am sure even he would enjoy a breath of fresh, country air.'

'Can we, Papa… please? I'd like to see if the sheep run away when I get close to them. If they don't, I want to know what their furry coats feel like.'

'Their coats are wool, George, not fur, and they are timid creatures so would most certainly run away before you got anywhere near them. We *may* manage a short stop, but only if I see a suitable place to do so.'

'Why can't we just stop here? Look at all those sheep over–'

William's forefinger before his son's nose brought his pestering to an abrupt end. 'If you say another word, we most definitely won't be stopping. Is that clear?' The boy nodded and resumed his survey of the sheep through the coach window.

Sweating beneath the high-necked black suit of his Anglican calling, William would have loved to step outside and savour the cooling breeze on his face. But he doubted that time would allow it. He smiled at his disgruntled wife and the way a single blonde curl had broken free of her bonnet. 'I fear we must reach Eyam by four o'clock, my dear, and we still have some miles to cover. Had we been obliged to continue our travels overnight instead of staying at that comfortable lodging house in Doncaster, we would probably have reached our destination some hours ago. But the journey would have been very hard to bear, even for you and I.'

Realising his words had placated neither his wife nor his tiny daughter, he reached across and lifted Elizabeth to his own substantial lap. 'Perhaps a change in our seating arrangement is in order for you, little girl?' he cooed. But his light-hearted words were not appreciated by the tired and irritable child and she opened her mouth to let out a piercing scream followed by a series of pitiful wails.

William promptly tapped the coachman's window behind him with his cane. 'I agree, Catherine, a short break in the fresh air would be beneficial to all.'

It was almost five o'clock in the afternoon when the coach pulled up in front of the impressive parish Church of St Helen's on Church Street, the main road through the Derbyshire village of Eyam. Heaving a sigh of relief that the long journey was over, William stepped down to the road, squinting in the glare of the late afternoon sun as he helped his wife and children to alight. As arranged, the previous incumbent of St Helen's was there to welcome them and William turned to shake his hand.

'Good afternoon, Reverend Stanley. I'm pleased to—'

'You're late,' Stanley snapped, the proffered hand ignored.

One

'Your letter clearly stated you would be here by four. I've wasted over an hour of my time waiting for you, becoming more uncomfortable by the minute in this insufferable heat.'

Taken aback by the man's brusque reply, William shrugged, his upturned hands outstretched. 'For which I sincerely apologise. I can only say that travelling any distance with two small children is not to be recommended. We were obliged to make a short stop in order to placate both our tiny daughter and our four-year-old son.'

Stanley grunted. 'Then we'd best get on with what needs doing so I can go home and rest. Your wife and children can make their way to the rectory to meet Mrs Chapman, your cook. The rectory gardener will also be there to introduce himself to you. As myself, they have been wating for over an hour to welcome you. I know for a fact that Mrs Chapman has been baking most of the day in order to provide you and your family with refreshments.'

William turned to his wife, whose face revealed her indignation at Stanley's uncivil tone. 'Take the children along to our new home, my dear.' He pointed in the direction of the rectory, a stone's throw from the church. 'Reverend Stanley and I have a few matters to discuss, but I'll be along shortly.'

Catherine flashed a caustic look at Stanley, then turned and headed to the rectory, Elizabeth in her arms and little George trotting at her side, his small hand clutching her long skirts. William watched them go before refocusing on Stanley in his dark green doublet with its oversized white collar and cuffs and equally green breeches. His wide-rimmed, black hat sat atop long, grey-steaked brown hair.

Before William could say anything further the former rector resumed his disgruntled tirade. 'Your belongings arrived yesterday as arranged, Reverend Mompesson. But I hope you realise that the people of Eyam are of the Puritan persuasion as, indeed, am I, so your presence here will not be welcomed. I suspect you will not wish to remain in this village for long, especially with the happiness of your family to think of.'

Not wishing to show affront at the man's cold directness, William simply nodded. He already knew his work here would not be easy. Unfortunately, Catherine's health was delicate at the best of times and he hoped her consumptive condition would benefit from living inland, away from the bitter North Sea winds that swept across their previous home in Scalby on the North Yorkshire coast. But he had no intention of sharing that with this abrasive and rude man. William still hoped that once the villagers had met him and his family they would simply be accepted, despite their Anglican faith.

'I have had many years of ministering to the people of this parish,' Stanley went on, his outstretched arm and raised eyebrows indicating they should make their way to the church. 'We remained loyal to the Puritan faith during the Civil War and the years when Lord Cromwell was in power. But following the Restoration of Charles II, I was dismissed from my post and replaced by Shoreland Adams, a member of the Church of England, as yourself. As rector here, he was lax and inefficient, and extremely unpopular with the villagers.'

Determined to keep his demeanour affable, William met Stanley's derisive words with a nod and a benign smile as he opened the church door to allow the older man to enter first.

One

'I know nothing of Reverend Adams,' he said, placing his bags inside the door. 'But since you say he *was* disliked I assume he simply left.'

Stanley shook his head. 'He died earlier this year. I merely stepped in to fill the gap until a new Church of England rector was appointed. And here you are...

'Believe me, I love the people here and want them to be happy. They have seen many changes over the years and are feeling extremely unsettled. I would have liked to continue my ministry in Eyam until my deathbed called but the bishops in the Church of England would have none of it.'

Stanley sighed. 'I shall not interfere with your running of the parish, Reverend Mompesson, but do not expect me to assist you in your work. I have acquired my own small cottage a short distance inside Eyam's boundary and will be keeping myself to myself in future. Few people even know I'm still living in the village and I'd like to keep it that way.'

'You have no family in Eyam?'

'My wife died almost two years ago and we were never blessed with children. I am now quite alone, although I do hire people to cook and clean for me. And a farmer's lad keeps my garden tidy.'

'Then I wish you a peaceful retirement. But now I need to have a wander around this lovely old church.'

The two clerics spent some time discussing various aspects of the church, which enabled William to see where everything he might need was located. He noted the simplicity of the church's interior, completely devoid of colour and religious icons. The walls were simply painted white and the window glazing was clear. William knew such bareness was suited to the Puritan faith whereas, since the restoration of the monarchy four years ago, his previous church in Scalby once again boasted glorious colour. Daylight streamed through colourful, stained-glass windows, and walls displayed brightly painted frescoes with images of Christ and the apostles. The church even housed an organ and a statue of St Laurence, its patron saint.

And yet, as William wandered around St Helen's, the bareness failed to mask the feeling of sanctity and peace he felt. But he kept that thought to himself for fear of inciting Stanley to spouting further contempt of the Church of England.

'Thank you for your time, Reverend Stanley.' William gave a curt nod as he turned towards the door. Another moment in the company of this sour-faced cleric would be a moment too long.

—

William spent most of his first Saturday in Eyam at his desk in the rectory's large study, preparing his service for the following day. Engrossed in searching through the Anglican Book of Common Prayer, he hadn't heard Mrs Chapman enter the room and her voice made him jump.

'Pardon me for disturbing you, Rector, but I wondered if Reverend Stanley mentioned that the villagers will not accept hymns or prayers from your Anglican prayer book.'

William gazed up at Lydia's earnest face. 'I was aware that the book as a whole was not acceptable to Puritans, but I was hoping you had adopted some of the well-known hymns and prayers.'

'We are only permitted to recite the psalms.'

'What about prayers? Surely, *The Lord's Prayer* can be said by us all?'

Lydia shook her head. 'We believe that particular prayer was never intended to be spoken aloud but used as a guide on how we should conduct our everyday lives. As with the psalms, we are only permitted to recite our own prayers. Could you, perhaps, choose one or two psalms for tomorrow and allow the congregation to say them together? We have our own versions of many of those, too, you see.'

'I suppose I could do that for my introductory service,' William said, a small frown furrowing his brow. Allowing his congregation to continue their Puritan form of worship during his service seemed a betrayal of his Church of England beliefs. 'I have no wish to cause discontent amongst the villagers the first time I meet them.'

Lydia held out her hands, shoulders hunched. 'I cannot advise you on how to introduce Anglican prayers and teachings into your services, Rector, although I do understand that you have no other choice than to try. I would hate to see things become as bad for you as they were for Reverend Adams.'

William had no intention of allowing Lydia's warning to daunt him although, he realised, he would need to tread carefully for the first few weeks. He decided to open the service with Psalm 23, *The Lord is My Shepherd*. Surely, none of the congregation would object to that?

—

'It has been my favourite psalm since I was a girl,' Catherine declared as they ate the delicious beef stew that Lydia had prepared for their evening meal. 'I imagine it's a favourite of many people and I'm sure your congregation will enjoy singing it tomorrow. I just wish I could be there to enjoy your first service with you. But Elizabeth is too young to sit on my lap for long without disrupting the congregation by howling at the top of her voice.'

'Our daughter will not be a babe for ever, my dear, and there will be many more Sunday services for you to attend. As for tomorrow, we'll only be reciting Psalm 23, and that will likely be in a way that you and I are not familiar with.'

Catherine's eyebrows rose, her knife and fork motionless in her hands. 'You intend to permit Puritan versions of the psalms to be recited in St Helen's?'

'Merely as a means of easing my way into Anglican teachings.' William shrugged. 'Lydia tells me that Puritans believe even *The Lord's Prayer* is not to be recited. Her words made me realise how little I know of their faith… something I should have rectified before accepting the position of rector here in Eyam.'

He pushed his empty platter aside and eyed the strawberry tarts sitting on a side table ready for dessert, then focused on his wife. 'The bishops are expecting me to steer our parishioners towards acceptance of the Church of England as soon as possible. But I fear it might take some time to achieve that goal. As for tomorrow's service, I'm hoping the people of Eyam will, at least, be willing to give me a chance to get to know them.

'But at this moment, Catherine, my mouth is watering at

One

the prospect of consuming some of those delectably appealing strawberry tarts.'

—

On Sunday morning, William left the rectory with a spring in his step, thoughts of holding his first service in St Helen's filling him with joy. It was another still, hot day, and despite the coolness of the old building's interior, he had chosen to wear his long black cassock and white surplice without his usual black suit beneath. Atop his head of collar length dark hair perched a simple black, beret-style hat.

As he entered the church, the fragrance emanating from the vases of colourful wildflowers that Catherine and George had picked yesterday brought a smile to his face. He drifted from vase to vase, savouring their heady scents, their vibrant colours and the wide variety of structure and shape. Spiky, sky-blue cornflowers, pincushion heads of pale pink scabious and sunny, orange marigolds nestled between the taller, dark pink foxglove bells and frothy clusters of creamy-white meadowsweet flowers with their abundance of deep green leaves.

William thanked God for creating an earth of such beauty for all to enjoy, then turned his attention to the preparations for his service. Having already located where Reverend Adams had stacked several dozen copies of the Anglican Prayer Book, he placed them at the ends the pews in readiness for distribution. Although surprised at the newness of the books, he was relieved he wouldn't need to order more for some years.

Excited at the prospect of becoming acquainted with some

of his congregation, William stood at the church door as they arrived. But he was greatly disheartened when most of them ignored his tendered hand and cheery 'good morning'. Dour-faced, they filed past without so much as a word or nod, as Stanley's warnings of the villagers' unwavering Puritan faith filled his head.

Having no intention of appearing weak and easily swayed by their uncivil behaviour, William pasted a smile on his face. Responsibility for the spiritual welfare of these people was now his and he vowed to do all in his power to help them enjoy his services and take an active part in them. No matter how long it took.

He followed the last person to arrive into the church and took his place in the pulpit. With his arms thrown out wide he gazed round at the closely packed congregation that filled both the north and south transepts as well as the nave.

'I must open my first service in this wonderful old church by thanking you all for attending today. It is truly heartening to see so large a congregation before me. I also need to introduce myself and after the service I will gladly stand outside the church door to enable some of you to introduce yourselves to me.'

'What for?' a male voice called out. 'We already know who and what you are. Reverend Stanley told us.'

Encouraged by the caller's nerve, other villagers joined in – men and women alike.

'We don't take kindly to Anglicans in Eyam, Reverend *Mompesson,* so you might as well pack your bags and go!'

'And take your Anglican prayer books with you. And your flowers!'

One

'We don't allow decorations in our church. Including flowers.'

'And our ministers don't wear fancy dresses like a woman!'

'You're no better than the last fool who tried to turn us against our Puritan beliefs.'

With that, the congregation erupted with a cacophony of more scathing yells demeaning William's faith, followed by chants of, 'We want Reverend Stanley!'

William stood his ground, waiting for them to settle. 'Now that you've got that off your chests, I'll start again. And since you already know my name, I will further add that no matter what you say, or what you do, I am here to stay.'

He waited for the ruckus of discontent at that declaration to die down before continuing. 'I am not here to antagonise any of you, or force you to accept a different religion to your own. We are all Christians here, are we not?'

No one replied to William's question, although around the church, several heads were nodding. 'The way I see it, we simply express our devotion to God in different ways and some of our everyday customs are a little different.'

He paused, just long enough for them to think about what he'd said. 'Over the coming weeks, I hope to learn a little more about the way you practise your faith, and I am sure you are all adult enough to learn a little of how I practise mine. I think you will find we are basically, just the same.'

'Then it's a pity them high-up bishops in the Roman Catholic and Anglican churches can't see that and stop persecuting us,' a woman called out. 'Who needs bishops anyway? We don't have them in our faith.'

'I have no answer to any that at present, but I can tell you this: I have no intention of persecuting any of you. I simply hope to find a way in which we can work together and make our devotions here, in this beautiful church.'

No one remarked, and William went on, 'I am told that you accept nothing from the Anglican Book of Common Prayer other than the psalms. I also believe you have your own versions of those.'

'That's right, we do,' another woman sneered. 'And seeing as you don't know what they are, Reverend Mompesson, I'd say you'd best move straight to your sermon and we'll say one of our own psalms before we all go home.'

Having no intention of allowing anyone to dictate how he ordered his service, William beamed round at them. 'We will open our service by you all reciting your own version of Psalm 23: *The Lord is My Shepherd*. Is there anyone amongst you, or perhaps a small group of you, willing to lead everyone through the psalm so it can be recited in unison?'

From her place on the front pew, Lydia rose to her feet. 'We'll do that, Reverend… that is, my husband, our daughter and I. We know that psalm well, as do we all.'

'Thank you, Lydia, I appreciate that. Would you mind stepping forward and facing the congregation.'

As William listened to the recital, he realised that the wording of the Puritan version of the psalm was almost the same as the Anglican one, except that many lines were repeated, so it took longer to say. To his Anglican ears that sounded odd, but he was relieved that by allowing his parishioners to recite one of the psalms in their chosen way, he had averted further antagonism. For now.

The stillness and silence of the congregation as they waited for William to deliver his sermon was in sharp contrast to their loud, animated response to his initial presence. There and then he decided to forego the sermon he had planned on 'New Beginnings' and make reference to the vases of lovely wildflowers supplied by his thoughtful wife.

'Summer is upon us once more and we have only to stroll along the lanes, or across the fields around our pretty village, for our senses to be assailed by such colours and scents as those that fill our church today.' He paused, long enough for people to gaze round at the vases full of summer blooms. 'Who amongst us can fail to delight in the blue of the sky above and the warmth of the evening sun? Who cannot admire the majesty of our great trees, the splendour of the colourful blossoms, or the sweet birdsong that fills the air?

'Very few of us, I imagine,' William answered himself. 'And in the coming weeks, the harvest will be upon us, when God blesses us with bounty enough to ensure we do not starve during the long, cold months of winter.'

As William had hoped, no one booed or made further objection to having flowers in the church. He smiled round at them, their faces holding a wariness as they listened to his words.

'So why does God provide us with this bounty? It can only be because we are His children and He wants us to prosper. You may then ask why He sends storms to those at sea, or holds back the rain so that droughts ravish the land. Why does He inflict disease upon us, or allow accidents to happen if, as we believe, He loves us?'

An aged, kindly looking man close to the front of the nave rose to his feet. 'I'll tell you why the earth is filled with beautiful things, Reverend. The Lord created them to remind us of His own beauty and perfection, and that of His only son, Our Saviour.'

William smiled at the old man. 'Thank you for your explanation, Mr…?'

'Fryth, Reverend. Henry Fryth.'

'You have given me something to think about, Henry. Does anyone else wish to share their thoughts on this?'

A pretty young woman sitting at the far side of the south transept raised her hand and rose to her feet. 'My name is Agnes Sheldon, Reverend. We are taught that we are born evil and must live our lives constantly striving to be better people – as perfect as the things in Nature that the Lord created. Yes, He rewards us with the bounties you mentioned, but He also punishes our wickedness. That is why we have such things as storms, famines, floods and diseases.'

'Well, Agnes, you have given me further insight into Puritan beliefs and I heartily thank you for that. I will add that, if we truly regret our sinful ways, and are willing to forgive those who have sinned against us, God will forgive us.

'So now, let us all put our hands together and say our own silent thanks to God for the many blessings He bestows upon us.'

As promised, after the service William stood outside the church door beside Lydia and her family, as members of the congregation filed past. He was pleased at how many of them

One

nodded their thanks although, as yet, none had stopped to introduce themselves. He realised it could be some time before he was truly accepted.

But William was a patient man and, at only twenty-eight, he had years ahead of him to achieve that goal.

—

Friday, August 8 1664

'Morning, Mrs Mompesson,' Lydia called, closing the rectory door and placing the basket of provisions at her feet as George charged across the hall to greet her. Lydia laughed and gave the boy a hug. 'It's good to see you, too, young man.'

'Can you make some more of that shortbread, please, Mrs Chapman? My tummy loved it!'

Lydia laughed. 'Oh, I'm sure there's enough shortbread left for a day or two, but I'll be baking some currant buns as soon as I've unloaded my basket and washed the breakfast dishes. So, tomorrow, you'll have a choice.'

'George! You know better than to pester Mrs Chapman the moment she walks through the door.' Catherine's smile belied the chastisement in her words as she came downstairs with Elizabeth in her arms.

'You look hot, Lydia. Is it that warm outside already or are your cheeks flushed after carrying that heavy basket?'

Lydia smiled as she pushed the auburn curls clinging to her moist cheeks beneath her coif. 'A little bit of both, I think. It's certainly hot out there, and it's not yet ten o'clock. And not a breath of wind. I dread to think what it will be like by this afternoon.'

Catherine nodded. 'It's been far too warm all night. It makes it difficult for anyone to sleep, so we'll probably be yawning all day. We need a good storm to clear the air.'

'My poor Samuel needs to be out of the house by five every morning to get to the lead mines for a five-thirty start. He was up and down all night, trying to cool himself with cold water, so he'll likely nod off in his chair once he gets home this evening. I'm guessing he won't be the only one who'll be glad when autumn comes.'

'I can't say I enjoy hot weather either, Lydia. But like your husband, William can't tolerate it at all, especially when he has a busy day ahead of him.'

Lydia bent to retrieve her basket. 'If the Lord sends us hot weather, it must be for a reason, so we'll just have to make the best of it. But now I'd best get these supplies somewhere cool. The butter will be completely melted before long if I don't. The market was heaving this morning, probably because no one wants to be out and about later on, when the sun gets really hot.'

'Then it was just as well I didn't come with you this week, although I really missed seeing everyone. Has Mary Rowe had her baby yet?'

'Oh yes… I knew there was something I meant to tell you. She had a little boy at four o'clock on Wednesday afternoon. I called in to see them all on my way home yesterday and I'm glad to say that both mother and son are doing well.'

Lydia ruffled George's dark hair. 'As for you, young man,

One

be good for your mother and play nicely with your sister or there'll be no more cakes and buns for you.'

George's dark eyes twinkled. 'I'm always good. It's Elizabeth who doesn't know how to play nicely. But I always get the blame when she falls over and cries.'

Catherine stifled a laugh. 'Remember, I'll be watching you, too, and I'll certainly report any misbehaviour to Mrs Chapman.'

She watched Lydia's retreating back, thinking what a godsend the woman had been since their arrival in Eyam. Although almost fifteen years Catherine's senior, Lydia seemed to possess boundless strength and vitality. How else could she cope with running the rectory kitchen so efficiently in addition to managing her own home? Catherine felt blessed to have her as a friend as well as an employee.

—

The following week seemed to fly as William and his family settled into what had become the regular rhythm of day-to-day tasks and activities. On most mornings, when not required to officiate at a marriage, baptism or funeral, William spent time alone in the church. The tranquillity he felt in the presence of God enabled him to think more clearly whilst planning his service for the coming Sunday.

But for today, he decided a change was in order.

'Aren't you going to St Helen's this morning?' Catherine asked as she came into the sitting room after breakfast to see her husband lounging on the sofa between George and Elizabeth.

'I thought you'd be in the study gathering whatever you need for working in the church… Are you feeling unwell? Perhaps you ate too many of those lovely sausages that Lydia cooked for breakfast.'

'I am quite well, my dear. I simply thought I'd spend some time with the children today whilst you enjoy yourself at the market with Lydia. It will be much easier for you amongst the crowds without Elizabeth in your arms and keeping an eye on this young rascal beside me.'

George's small face scrunched with indignation. 'I'm not a rascal, Papa! I just like to be *doing* things, and standing with Mama and Mrs Chapman while they talk to everyone at the market is just so *boring*.'

William struggled to hold back a chuckle. 'Be that as it may, running around making a nuisance of yourself is not permitted, especially when people are trying to buy their supplies. So, you and Elizabeth will stay with me this morning and we'll try to find something to do that doesn't make you bored.'

George's face lit up. 'Thank you, Papa. Can we–'

William's forefinger beneath his nose put paid to George's request, whatever it was. Catherine smiled and bent to give her husband a kiss on the cheek, then bestowed one on each of the children. 'That's very thoughtful of you, William, but I hope you realise that these two will expect you to play games with them. At very least you will have to read them stories, preferably from an illustrated book. Elizabeth loves the pictures, especially those of animals and birds. But don't let her grab at the pages and rip them.'

William patted his wife's hand. 'Don't you worry about

One

any of that. I have several things in mind to keep them both happy. Now, go and see if Lydia is ready to head out.'

—

'Let's hope the market isn't as busy as it was for you last week,' Catherine said as she walked beside Lydia along Church Street to the village green, on which Eyam's weekly market was held.

'It's no cooler today, so it probably will be,' Lydia replied, her outstretched arm urging Catherine to stand flat against one of the cottages edging the road as a horse and cart rumbled past, far too close for comfort. The animal left a heap of steaming dung in its wake, not two feet away from where they stood. The stench of it hung on the warm August air, masking aromas of bacon and freshly baked bread that drifted through the open windows and doors of family homes.

'I swear, some of the folk driving wagons and carts along here come too close to the sides on purpose.' Lydia grimaced. 'Perhaps they think that watching people jump out of their way is funny. The road is easily wide enough for them to keep further out. This loose dirt surface is bad enough to walk on at any time of year. When we've had rain, muddy shoes and skirts aren't funny and after dry weather it's nothing but dust, as it is now.'

Catherine smiled at the look of affront on Lydia's face. 'I couldn't agree more, though I don't think we can do anything about the road surface. But I could ask William to remind cart drivers to give walkers a wide berth along here during his service next week. Whether they'll take any notice is a different matter, of course.'

They walked on, their chatter turning to what they needed to buy. Like them, a number of women were heading to the market, the large white collars and cuffs on their dresses and the coifs on their heads, distinguishing them all as Puritans. Others were going home, struggling to carry well-laden baskets whilst clutching the hands of whingeing infants for whom the market held little appeal.

Catherine loved the feeling of being a part of this happy and thriving community. She admitted to herself that having the popular and respected Lydia Chapman at her side had given her the confidence she needed to chat to strangers and make new friends. And what better place in which to do that than somewhere that attracted women to it like bees to a honeypot?

The market had fascinated Catherine since the first time she'd visited soon after moving to Eyam. It was primarily a place of business where, both inside and out of the small market hall, farmers' wives set up stalls to display their produce. Milk, butter, eggs, cheese and poultry drew the villagers without fail every Friday. Seasonal vegetables could also be purchased here. But to Catherine, the market was more than a place of buying and selling. She delighted in the hustle and bustle, which transformed the quiet Derbyshire village into a hive of activity.

They wove their way between the stalls, acknowledging Lydia's friends and acquaintances with a smile and a genial greeting. The constant buzz of barter, combined with the laughing and chattering of groups of women as they caught up with each other's news, made Catherine feel alive. And it warmed her heart to think of herself as one of them.

Two

Mid-November 1664

William sat back in his comfortable chair in the rectory's sitting room, watching his wife teaching George and Elizabeth the words of some well-known rhymes. A log fire crackled as it burned in the hearth, adding brightness and cheer to the dark November evening. The grandfather clock, tall and elegant against the chimney breast wall, chimed eight o'clock, announcing the children's bedtime. But in no mood for sleep, the youngsters were presently chanting the words of *Ding Dong Bell* while pretending to tug on the bell ropes.

George's big brown eyes fixed on his mother's blue. 'Can we do *Humpty Dumpty* now, Mama? *Ding Dong Bell* is just *boring*.'

'How, exactly, would you "do" Humpty Dumpty, George?' William asked, eyebrows raised.

'Well, first I'd pretend to sit up on a wall. Like this, Papa…' The boy perched upright on the edge of the sofa, legs dangling from the knees, arms bent a little at his sides and his chin tucked in, making him appear to be lacking a neck and looking decidedly more egg-like.

'Well, that's a good start,' William said, smiling at the sight of his small daughter attempting to emulate her brother's pose while perched on her mother's knee.

'So, if everyone's ready,' Catherine said, 'let's show your papa how this rhyme should be done.'

'Humpty Dumpty sat on a wall…' Catherine and George

chanted together, while George assumed his stance for sitting on a wall.

'Humpty Dumpty had a great fall...' Catherine continued, as George hurled himself onto the Persian rug that covered most of the floorboards, his twisted limbs spread out as though he'd been broken into pieces. Not to be outdone in the activity, while George began his 'ride' around to room to mimic the arrival of 'all the king's horses and all the king's men', Elizabeth flung herself from her mother's knee to the floor in an effort to imitate her brother... only to land badly on her shoulder and start wailing.

But it seemed to William that George instinctively knew what to do. The sturdy four-year-old picked up his little sister and swirled her round. Within seconds, she was giggling her head off, the fall forgotten.

'You were an excellent king's man,' Catherine complimented the boy, very smart and devoted to your duty. Wasn't he, Elizabeth?'

The little girl gave her brother a sloppy kiss on the cheek, which he rubbed off when she wasn't looking. 'George certainly put this little Humpty together again,' Catherine added, hugging her children to her. 'But now, it's time for bed.'

Unfortunately, the children still seemed wide awake and George pestered his mother for more rhymes to enact.

'No more rhymes for tonight, and that's final,' Catherine declared. 'It's well past Elizabeth's bedtime, so we're going upstairs right now. While I'm gone, George, if you ask your papa nicely, he might tell you one of his bible stories.'

Knowing his son to be an intelligent and thoughtful child,

Two

William decided his wife's suggestion was a good one and chose to tell George the parable of *The Wheat and the Tares*. At the end, he explained that the tares were weeds which an enemy of the farmer had put to grow between the good, healthy wheat plants.

George fixed William in a questioning gaze. 'Why didn't the farmer just pull the weeds out as they grew?'

'Because he knew that pulling up the weeds could cause some of the wheat plants to be pulled up with them, or become damaged in some way.'

George frowned. 'So, the weeds were just left there to grow?'

'They were. But once the ripened crop was gathered in, the weeds could be sifted out without damaging any of the wheat, and burnt.'

'But what does the story *really* mean, Papa?' George persisted with a sigh of exasperation that made William smile. 'You said that a parable is a story which has another meaning to the one being told.'

William nodded, impressed by his son's memory and eagerness to learn. 'Well, young man, you already know that the parables were told by Jesus, so they must carry important lessons for us.' George nodded. 'So, if we think of the farmer's field as the Earth, and the wheat plants as the good people living on it, as what should we see the weeds?'

'The bad people,' George replied, needing no time to think about that.

William noticed that Catherine had come downstairs and was waiting to take George to bed, so he quickly finished his explanation. 'Like the farmer with the field of wheat and weeds,

God allows bad people to live on Earth because removing them might hurt some of the good people around them. And, like the weeds that are taken away and burnt after harvesting, when bad people reach the end of their lives, they will not be taken into Heaven with God but will burn in Hell for evermore.'

'That's a strange story, but I enjoyed listening to it, Papa. I wouldn't like to be burnt as a weed, so I'll try to be good, like the wheat.'

'Then you can start right now and go straight to bed. And I don't want to hear any arguments with your mama as you climb the stairs.'

William waited for Catherine to return, his heart swelling with love as he thought of his little family. They had settled well into their new home and surroundings. Thanks to Lydia and visits to the Friday market, Catherine had already befriended some of the women of the community, including Mary Hadfield, who lived on the other side of the church, and Elizabeth Syddall and her eldest daughters, Ellen and Emmott, who lived opposite the Hadfield's. And although the villagers resented William for his faith, most were now at least pleasant when speaking to him. Yet they remained resolutely silent when he asked for responses to the prayers and lessons from the Anglican Prayer Book.

Lydia was a blessing to the rectory. Her cooking was superb and she made sure the kitchen and dining room were always spick and span. But William was concerned that despite all the help Catherine got from Lydia, she was left with the rest of this large house to clean, as well as having the children and parochial duties to attend to.

Two

By the time Catherine came downstairs after tucking George into his bed, William felt more than ready for bed himself. But he had something on his mind that needed to be voiced.

'I have only one thing to mention tonight,' he said, as Catherine perched on the edge of the sofa, a smile on her face as she faced William in his armchair.

'I have nothing of importance to say tonight, William, so considering the fact that you've been yawning for the past hour, I'll be happy just to hear what you have to say.'

William nodded. 'The main thing that concerns me at present is our need of a housekeeper. I hate to see you struggling to scrub and polish while the children pester you to play with them. At very least, we need someone to do the cleaning in this large house and tomorrow, I intend to ask Lydia for the names of any village women she thinks would be suitable.'

Catherine's face reflected her delight. 'Thank you so much, William. If you're certain the extra outlay is within our means, another pair of hands would be very helpful. Having someone to help in the house would leave me more time with the children. Teaching George to read is quite time consuming.'

'Then that settles it, my dear. I'll be happy to follow any recommendations made by Lydia. I know how highly you value her friendship, and having lived here all her life, she knows most of the families in Eyam.'

The short, dark days of November galloped by, and although it seemed that summer had only just taken its leave, December duly stepped over the threshold. And with it came the Advent.

Following a word of warning from Lydia, William decided to forego decorating inside the church until a few days before Christmas Eve, and merely mention what Advent meant to Anglicans during his first service in December. Unfortunately, on doing so, the scowling silence of the congregation served to verify Lydia's words regarding the Puritan abhorrence of Christmas.

William quickly moved on with his sermon on the importance of kindness. But it seemed that even so simple a theme evoked objections from the puritanical congregation.

'Kindness is all well and good, Reverend, but we are taught that piety, hard work and honesty are more important than kindness.'

William nodded. 'I cannot disagree that those qualities are important, Anthony, since they are amongst others that we must strive for in ourselves. But in my opinion, kindness should walk alongside them.'

He smiled round at the faces as they listened to his words. 'Kindness is a gift that we must freely give to others. It can be bestowed in many ways, from helping someone at a time of need to consoling a crying child who has tumbled and grazed his knees, or merely offering a cheerful smile and encouraging word to lift someone from a downcast mood. The list is endless. But I believe that kindness should be a part of our everyday lives… a part of who we are and how we behave.'

No one disagreed and William finished his service with a prayer for Advent:

Be with us in this Advent moment
as we come together to celebrate this season of waiting.

Two

We ask this in the name of Jesus who draws near,
who lives and reigns with You and the Holy Spirit;
one God forever and ever.
Amen.

The prayer was received in flinty silence, so William thanked them all for attending and, without a sound, they departed.

—

During the second week of December, winter's icy fingers gripped the land, bringing the first covering of snow to the Derbyshire hills. Catherine gazed through the sitting room window, mesmerised by the beauty she beheld across the rectory gardens and the churchyard beyond. It was snowing again, a gentle fall of feathery, white flakes that she longed to catch in her hands. But she knew she could never do that. The piercingly cold air would aggravate her lungs and worsen the consumption that made her feel so weak.

Yet Catherine refused to let ill health get her down, despite missing her weekly visits to the market with Lydia. On a positive note, she considered, sitting down to hear her young son read whilst Elizabeth took her afternoon nap, her confinement indoors meant she had time to do the things she loved. And since the third week of November, her leisure time had been further extended by the daily visits of a cleaner in the form of the pretty, fair-headed Joan French.

'You work with such diligence, Joan,' Catherine said, glancing up as George reached the bottom of a page and smiling at the slight young woman polishing a delicate glass vase. 'I confess, I've never seen anyone scrub and clean a house with such zeal. I'm so glad Lydia persuaded you to work for us.'

'I love working here, mistress, making sure the rooms are clean and fresh and all your lovely ornaments are bright and shiny. And Lydia didn't need to persuade me. If truth be told, I jumped at the chance. My husband doesn't earn much as a quarryman, you see, and the coin I earn here has been a boon these past few weeks.'

'I'm glad to hear that because I love having you here to talk to, though I do realise you will need to finish work once you have a child of your own. I shall just have to enjoy your company whilst I can.'

'We've been wed for over a year, mistress, and I'd hoped to be with child by now. But we haven't yet been blessed.' Joan gave a coy smile, the dimples in her cheeks pronounced. 'Robert says that's probably just as well until we can manage to save a little coin to fall back on when I finish work. Although I know he's right, I can't help feeling broody. It's so hard when I see other women carrying their little ones around.'

Catherine directed George's attention to the next page in the book. 'Read the following three pages to yourself. You can tell me what you've read about when Joan and I have finished talking.'

George nodded and did as he was told.

'Feeling broody is a condition that affects many women at times, Joan, including me.'

'I know that, Mistress, and for now, I am content to be here and able to make life a little easier for you. I realise you

Two

need to rest often and keep warm by the fire in winter. And dusting this big, old house is not for anyone with lung problems to cope with.'

Catherine wanted to hug the young woman for her kindness and understanding. 'Having you and Lydia here every day means more than I can say, Joan. I even have time to do a little embroidery now and then, something I've loved to do since I was a child.'

'I never learnt to embroider, mistress. My ma didn't like any kind of needlework, so I had no one to teach me.'

Catherine smiled. 'That can soon be rectified. If you like, tomorrow I'll bring a few spare pieces of linen, my sewing needles and embroidery threads, and show you how some of the stitches are worked. I'll sketch a few simple flowers on the cloths and you can use the stitches you learn to embroider each flower differently.'

'Thank you so much, Mrs Mompesson,' the young woman gushed. 'Lydia was right when she said that you and the reverend were lovely people to work for.'

—

At eleven-thirty on Christmas Eve, William donned his thickest coat and prepared to leave for the church. 'I'm hoping most of the villagers will come to this service, Catherine. Midnight Communion is always a moving affair on Christmas Eve. I'm also impatient to watch their reactions when they see how lovely the church looks with the Nativity scene in place. And, of course, the candles will be lit throughout the service.'

'Considering the church is never locked, night or day, William, I'm sure some of them will have already seen the crib with the infant Jesus, Mary and Joseph – not to mention the shepherds and the three kings with their gifts. It's always a wonderful sight, with the crib full of straw and the bright star above.'

'It is a beautiful sight, my dear, and you're right in thinking that some of the villagers might have seen it by now. In fact, it wouldn't surprise me to hear that everyone in the village has been in the church to look at it.'

'And you know what Lydia told you about the Puritan view of Christmas. The way they reacted to the mere mention of Advent was bad enough.'

'Oh, I haven't forgotten, but I am hopeful that after attending my services for the last few months, some of them will realise that not every Anglican – or Roman Catholic for that matter – sees Christmas as nothing more than a time for gluttony, drunkenness and debauchery.'

Catherine's eyebrows rose. 'I think you'll be sorely disappointed. They will have had that view of an Anglican Christmas drummed into them for years by that cheerless Reverend Stanley.' William nodded, knowing she was probably right. 'They'll see the crib and Nativity figures as symbols of idolatry and the pagan practises that go with it,' she continued. 'And we both know that many people of our faith *do* use the season as an excuse for wantonness.

'I could never be a Puritan, William, but I can understand how such behaviour could make Puritans shun our faith and the festivals we uphold.'

Two

William gave a tolerant smile. 'I cannot give up trying to win them to our faith, any more than I can prevent some non-Puritans turning to licentiousness at Christmas. I've already refrained from hanging holly and other greenery in the church due to their links with pagan revelry, but I refuse to back down over the Nativity scene. It will remain in St Helen's for the rest of the Christmas season.'

'Which means that no one will come for a single service until it has gone.'

'I can only hope you are wrong, my dear. But whatever the outcome tonight, I am obligated to make the effort to steer the villagers towards the Anglican faith. Now I really must be going, and you need to curl up in our nice warm bed. I'll try not to waken you when I return.'

With that, William picked up his little oil lamp and stepped out into the snowy night, heading for St Helen's.

The glow of several lamps became visible as soon as he reached the side gate into the cemetery from the rectory garden. The bobbing lights seemed to be outside the main church door and he smiled to himself, happy that at least some of the villagers had come for the Midnight Communion. But as he drew close, the throb of voices could not be missed. He halted, long enough for him to make sense of what it could mean. His perusals did nothing to appease his pounding heart. What he was hearing were the raised voices of an angry mob.

'Here he comes!' someone yelled as William drew close. 'Wait 'til he gets here before you say anything.'

The mob went quiet and William had no other choice than to keep moving towards them. If he turned and ran, there was a possibility they'd chase after him. And he had no intention of appearing a coward to people he viewed as his flock.

He stood before them and estimated over a hundred people, most of whom were men. 'Tell me what you have to say, then either come into the church with me for the communion or be off to your homes. Your present actions compare to the rowdy, drunken, Christmastime behaviour of the Catholic and Anglican mobs you claim to abhor.'

'We aren't drunk, Reverend Mompesson, and we apologise for being rowdy.'

William nodded at the man he knew to be a blacksmith. 'Apology accepted, Richard, but it doesn't take much to see that something is troubling you all.'

'I think you know what we're bothered about, Reverend,' Richard Talbot continued from the front of the crowd. 'We've been telling you for weeks that Puritans don't celebrate Christmas. Nowhere in the Scriptures does it say on which day of the year Christ was born.'

'And to put idolatrous images in our church makes a mockery of our beliefs,' another voice added.

'I assure you, Matthew, I have no intention of mocking any of you, or your beliefs. But on the same note, I don't want you to make a mockery of mine.'

'We know that, Reverend Mompesson,' an ageing lady at the front of the gathering said. 'But you putting those images and sculpted figures in the church got us all angry. It means that none of us can come to Sunday service until you take them away. And if we don't come to church, our souls will be damned.'

Two

'It is your choice not to come to any services, Mrs Fryth,' William replied. 'All I can say is that the Nativity scene will stay in the church until after Christmas. It is my duty as a minister in the Church of England to celebrate the birth of Christ.'

'Then you'll celebrate it on your own, Reverend. All we can ask is that you pin notices outside the church gate to let us know when Sunday services start again.'

William's resolve weakened as he viewed their troubled faces. He heaved a sigh. 'I am prepared to remove the crib a day or two after Christmas Day, Richard, so that a service can be held on Sunday, the twenty-eighth of December. I can offer no more than that. Under normal circumstances, the Nativity scene would remain in place until Twelfth Night on the sixth of January.'

William waited while they spoke amongst themselves.

'Thank you, Reverend,' Richard Talbot said. 'We realise you've made the compromise on our behalf. We'll let our neighbours know what you've agreed to.'

The group headed for the main gate, while William returned to the rectory. He wondered what the bishops' reaction would be if they knew how he'd pandered to the belligerence of the puritanical villagers of Eyam.

Spring 1665

Snow lingered long on the hills and moors but by the end of March, all traces of it had gone from the village. The air had lost its penetrating bite and Catherine soon felt well enough to venture outdoors. At first, she simply strolled around the rectory gardens, enjoying the warmth of the April sun whilst admiring the year's fresh growth and chatting to Joseph, the friendly gardener. Within a week, she declared herself strong enough to resume her visits to the Friday market.

William was overjoyed to see his wife looking and feeling so much better. 'I will gladly stay with the children this morning, my dear, in order for you and Lydia to browse the stalls in peace.'

'Thank you, William, that is kind of you. I'm longing to see some of the women I know and catch up with all that has happened in their lives since we last met.'

William smiled at the image of groups of gossiping women. 'It will do you good to be out and about, amongst others again, and Lydia has remarked on how much she looks forward to having your company again. Let us hope for a few months of sunshine ahead of us, so you can enjoy many more Fridays with your friends.'

—

William rubbed his tired eyes. It was Saturday evening on the ninth of May and, once again, he was seated at his desk, staring down at a blank page, racking his brains for a suitable theme for his service tomorrow. In truth, he felt such a failure, as well as a traitor to his faith. Since coming to Eyam, he had allowed his congregation to continue saying their own Puritan prayers and versions of the psalms. Yes, he'd managed to keep

Two

his sermons on themes acceptable to all, and people happily listened to them – which was, at least, something. But that alone did not make him feel any the less defeatist, or any the less guilty. He had been sent to Eyam to steer the Puritans towards the Anglican faith, yet in the first ten months of his ministry, he had made little effort to do that.

Choosing to overlook the celebrations of Easter, in addition to those of Christmas, had heightened William's fears of God's punishment. His failure was putting peoples' souls at risk of being barred from Heaven, as well as his and his family's. And that failure weighed heavily upon him. So much so, he had felt the need to fall to his knees every night, beseeching God for forgiveness.

Yet after the villagers' reactions to his attempted Christmas Communion, William feared that riots may ensue if he insisted on an Easter Service. Instead, he would merely include the crucifixion and resurrection of Christ within the context of a service on the forgiveness of sins… or perhaps on loving thy neighbour. In that way, the events of Holy Week would not be assigned to any particular date, nor even a time of year.

Additionally, William had recently foregone delivery of a service dedicated to the welcoming of spring for fear of inciting further antagonism against pagan revelry. Recollection of a conversation he'd had with Catherine as they'd taken a stroll with the children two weeks ago, brought a smile to his lips. As thoughts of his lovely wife usually did…

'If you don't wish to celebrate the onset of spring in your service, William, perhaps we could just have a maypole erected on the green? The May Day festival on the first day of the month is traditionally part of our welcome to the new season.'

William's smile widened as he recalled her words. 'There are plenty of young women and girls in Eyam who would probably love to dress up with flowers in their hair and dance around the maypole. I'm also sure there are a few flute or pipe players in the village to provide the music.'

William had stared at her, aghast. 'My dear, dancing around the maypole is rooted in pagan tradition which goes back hundreds of years! It is often linked to the Roman custom of offering gifts to Flora, the goddess of flowering plants. I'm afraid that even mentioning maypole dancing would greatly anger our villagers, let alone having a maypole on the green.'

Nothing further had been said on the subject.

William's thoughts returned to the task in hand. Perhaps he could preach of the joys of family life. Having touched on this subject before, he knew that Puritans were governed by strict principles of prayer, obedience and work. Even young children were given daily tasks to do in the home. Villagers' comments had given William insight into how their home lives were organised, which he hoped would help him to better understand them, and their faith, without being overtly critical.

He contemplated what his bishops would say to that and, once again, grimaced at his own cowardice. After almost a year, the only parts of William's services they would listen to were his sermons – excluding those involving the celebrations of Advent, Christmas, Lent, Easter and Whitsuntide. Unfortunately, the fundamental beliefs of the Anglican Church revolved around those very celebrations. Yet the only way that William could speak of them was at times in the year that were not attached to dates assigned by the Roman Catholic and Anglican Churches.

The bishops had not given William a time limit in which to gather the people of Eyam into the Anglican fold, but he knew they were hoping for speedy results. Worse still, if they discovered that William had not delivered the two foremost Anglican celebrations, he could be facing immediate removal from his position in Eyam.

With thoughts of his failings filling his head, William picked up his quill and wrote his title, *The Joys of Family Life*. But after staring at it for some moments, he crossed it out and replaced it with, *Parental Responsibilities*. He would convey his own views on this issue and hope his congregation's response would simply open the door to sensible discussion. He heaved a sigh, knowing full well that the Puritan way of bringing up their children was vastly different to his own and their comments would likely be scathing. Once again, he drew a line through the title, wondering if Lydia might know of a suitable topic for tomorrow's service.

Three

Saturday, July 11 1665

Thirteen-year-old Jonathan Cooper whistled as he sauntered home from work on Saturday afternoon, happy it wasn't Monday morning when he'd be heading in the opposite direction. He tugged at the neck of his shirt, which clung to his sweaty skin like leeches to a wound. He hated working the land, especially during the summer, with nothing to shield him from the glaring sun. But he'd put up with it until he was the one in charge of his pa's land instead of that miserable old manager his mother had hired following his father's death last year.

After a hard week, Jonathan looked forward to having Sunday to himself. He couldn't miss church in the morning, of course. Ma would make sure of that.

'If you don't go to church on a Sunday, you'll be putting your soul at risk and be barred from Heaven,' she had said so many times.

Jonathan had still to decide how true that was. And if he was barred from Heaven, where would he go instead? He'd heard Reverend Stanley saying that sinners would burn in Hell for all eternity when they died, and he didn't want that to happen to him. But he couldn't see the harm in missing a few services, especially when the reverend was that Church of England prat, Mompesson.

The man had been in Eyam a year now and still didn't seem to understand that no one wanted him here. He just kept that

Three

silly smile on his face and continued with his services as though everyone enjoyed them. How come he didn't notice that no one sang the hymns or said the prayers he came up with from that prayer book of his?

Jonathan decided that once he'd had time to cool off, he'd call round to see William Thorpe. As next-door neighbours, he and Will had been friends for years. Even if Will was a year older than him and a bit on the wild side, he was fun to hang around with. It was always Will who came up with ideas for how their little gang of six could enjoy themselves. Some of the crazy things they'd done would've landed them in hot water if their pas had found out. But, for the fun times they had, Will's pranks were worth taking that risk.

As it turned out, Will must have seen Jonathan walking along Church Street and passing his house, and charged out to meet him.

'You're home early today,' Jonathan said, watching Will's face crease into a grin. 'You don't usually get home for an hour or so after me.'

'Mr Wood let me leave a couple of hours ago. He had no more shoes to sole and heel, and we'd had no customers all day, so we packed up early. Said he'd pay me for a full day's work, so I'm not complaining.'

'Lucky you, I've been stuck in the fields all day.'

'I can see that by your face.' Will grinned. 'I haven't seen it that red since Annie Lowe plonked a kiss on your cheek at last year's Wakes.'

'Very funny. She was only congratulating me for winning that one-legged race, as well you know. Anyway, I'm guessing you dashed out of the house to tell me something.'

'I did, as a matter of fact, but seeing as you need to get home and let your face cool off it can wait 'til we meet up with the others tonight. I've told 'em all to meet us at eleven o'clock in the usual place in the cemetery.'

'Eleven o'clock! Ma won't allow me out at that time.'

'Your ma doesn't have to know, does she?'

'So, you're asking us all to sneak out like a gang of thieves?'

'I wouldn't quite put it that way. There'll only be me doing any stealing. And it wouldn't really be stealing, anyway.'

Jonathan stared at him. 'You're not making sense. Stealing is stealing, as far as I know.'

'I'll be taking a couple o' flagons of claret from Pa's cellar. He's got dozens of 'em down there, so he won't even notice two have gone walkabout.'

'I just hope you know what you're doing.' Jonathan shook his head. 'Whether it's from family or not, taking things that aren't yours is still stealing.'

Will shrugged. 'If you want to be such a goody-goody, you don't have to drink any of the wine. In fact, you don't have to come out at all. There'll be more wine for the rest of us if you stay at home.'

'I didn't say I wanted to stay at home, did I? It's just that stealing isn't right.'

'Well, I reckon taking summat from your own family isn't stealing. If I were a couple o' years older, Pa'd probably be giving me a flagon or two to share with me friends, So, are you with us tonight, or not?'

'That depends on what we'll be doing after we've drunk

Three

the wine… or is that all you've got planned?'

'Nah, I've a good plan for tonight, Johnny boy. And I think you'll want to be with us when you hear what it is.'

'I'm listening,' Jonathan said, wondering how he could sneak out of the house a little before eleven o'clock without his ma or stepfather hearing.

—

The heat and mugginess of the July day continued into the evening and, as the hours ticked by and weary folk fell to their beds, towering black clouds rose from the heated earth, threatening a storm before morning.

As midnight neared, a small group of lads, emboldened by sharing a couple of flagons of rich, red claret, braved the oncoming storm to hasten to the pasture along the Lydgate Road. There they threw bridles of rope about the heads of three of Isaac Wilson's milch cows as they lay chewing the cud, seemingly oblivious to the strengthening wind. Careful not to cause the cows to bellow their presence to the sleeping village, the lads led them back along Church Street, across the cemetery and into the Church of Saint Helen.

'Get them bridles off 'em and leave 'em free to move about,' Will whispered. 'The stink of cow dung all over the place will give that smiley faced rector summat to think about when he comes to do his service tomorrow.'

The other five lads nodded, keen to be away from the scene of their crime.

'Aye, let's get home while the coast's clear,' Will said, starting the retreat. 'It'll seem like all hell's broken loose in Eyam tomorrow, so you need to act like you know nowt about any cows and try not to look guilty. We'll be for it if our pas learn the truth.'

The lads closed the heavy church door behind them, leaving the cows to do their work.

—

At nine o'clock the following morning, Catherine left the rectory for St Helen's in joyful mood, the fragrance of summer greenery and that earthy smell after the heavy rain filling her with delight. Young George skipped along at her side, enjoying the warmth of the summer morning and the glint of puddles along the path.

'Here we are,' Catherine said, placing the basket of flowers by her feet while she opened the church door. 'We'll soon have these lovely blooms in vases for everyone to enjoy while your papa gives his service.'

As soon as she pushed the door open, the overpowering stench of manure wafted out. On the verge of retching, George took several paces back. 'Stay there while I peep inside to see what's causing that dreadful smell,' Catherine ordered, covering her nose and mouth with her hand. She stepped inside… and gasped at the sight before her, battling the urge to bring up her breakfast to add to the appalling, trampled mess. Seeing a way out to the open air, three cows trotted towards her, their udders dripping milk.

Catherine backed out and closed the door. 'Dear Lord, I

beseech you to forgive whoever wreaked such desecration in Your house,' she prayed, then picked up her basket, grabbed George's hand and fled back to the rectory.

—

One glance at the faces of his wife and son, and William's cheerful mood plummeted. 'Whatever's wrong?' he asked, urging them both to sit on the sofa. 'Has someone said something to upset you, or stopped you entering St Helen's?'

Catherine shook her head. 'It's what they've done inside the church. Just thinking about it makes me want to retch.'

'The smell made my tummy poorly, Papa, and I thought there must have been dead people in there. But there couldn't have been because I could hear noises.'

'Go and lie down until you feel better, George.' William reassured him with a smile. 'Your tummy should be well again soon.'

He waited until George's bedchamber door clicked shut and glanced to check Elizabeth was busy with her bricks before turning to his wife. 'So, what is it that smells so awful? It must be something quite repugnant to cause you both to feel so sick.'

'Someone has put some cows inside the church – three of them, from what I saw – and they appear to be in great need of milking. How could anyone do such a thing?'

William overlooked his wife's question as he glanced at the grandfather clock, aware of the need for haste. 'I must get them out of there before it's time for the service. I'll ask Joseph to help me. I'm sure he wouldn't mind losing an hour of his

Sunday when I explain what has happened. I'll also pop along the road to see if John Syddall could lend a hand. One of them might know of somewhere we can pen the animals until we find out who they belong to.'

'Removing the cows is the least of your problems, William. By the amount of manure in there, I'd say they've been locked in the church all night.'

'Manure…?'

Catherine nodded, her nose wrinkling at the thought. 'And the cows have trampled it everywhere – along the nave and transepts, and even into the chancel. It will take a long time to clean it all out and the stench will make you heave. I suggest you tie a piece of cloth around your nose.'

'Then there'll be no service today.' William choked on the thought that some villagers must truly hate him to have done such a thing. 'Even if we manage to clear the dung in time, the reek of it will likely linger for some time. I'll write out a couple of notices, explaining the situation and pin them outside the gates.

'I just hope the stink doesn't linger overnight. I have a baptism booked for tomorrow morning.'

—

The Hadfield/Cooper household: Wednesday July 15 1665

'How could you even *think* of doing such a thing, Jonathan? You were brought up to be polite and considerate. If your father were still alive, you'd be feeling the weight of his cane across your backside instead of me yelling at you. Edward Cooper was not a man to tolerate disrespectful behaviour.'

Mary Hadfield shook her head, at a loss to understand what had prompted her normally sensible elder son to take part in such a shameful act as locking cows in the House of the Lord. 'Goodness knows what your stepfather will think of you after this. I asked you to make a good impression on Alexander and you have done the complete opposite!'

She thumped the breakfast table with the side of her fisted hand. 'Look at me when I'm speaking to you. You won't find a credible reason to warrant pulling such an outrageous prank written on your platter. In fact, nothing in this world could warrant such a wicked act.'

Unable to face the look of hurt and betrayal in his mother's eyes, Jonathan stood to get ready for work. 'We thought you'd all be pleased that –'

Mary's gasp cut his explanation short. 'I can't believe you just said that. No one I know could ever condone what you've done, for whatever reason. You were brought up to treat others with *respect*. What you did last weekend was the height of *dis*respect, not to mention being thoughtless and utterly appalling.'

'I'm sorry, Ma,' Jonathan said as his mother wiped tears from her eyes. 'We thought it was a good way of making Mompesson realise we don't want him in Eyam. Nobody likes him, and –'

Mary raised her hand. 'Don't say another word against Reverend Mompesson. He's a good man, even though he isn't a Puritan, and he's tried hard to make his services acceptable to us all. When you get home from work this evening, you will come with me and apologise to both him and Mrs Mompesson and promise you will never do anything like it again.'

Jonathan scowled. 'Why should I say sorry to her? It's her husband who's causing everyone problems in Eyam.'

'It was Mrs Mompesson and their young son who found the cows and the filthy dung they'd trampled everywhere. Lydia said the poor lady was very distressed that anyone could cause such sacrilege in a church. And by all accounts, the stench made the little boy sick.'

'But it wasn't just me that did it! Why should I be the one to apologise for everyone?'

'I'm not expecting you to apologise for anyone but yourself. And don't try to make light of your part in this wicked deed by blaming someone else for proposing it. I don't have to think too hard as to whose idea it was, but that doesn't make you innocent. You agreed to go along with it.'

'How did you find out it was us?'

'You were seen coming out of the church, that's all I'm saying. Who it was is for me to know and you to wonder at, my lad. As far as I'm concerned, it's a good job you *were* seen, or goodness knows what you'd have got up to next!'

'I'm sorry Ma, I really am. I knew it was wrong when I agreed to the plan, but I didn't want to be the only one in our group to object to it.'

'Then you can tell Reverend Mompesson that this evening and hope he'll forgive you. In future, just remember, it's a question of having the courage of your own convictions and not allowing anyone to talk you into doing something you know to be unjust, dishonest, disrespectful, or just plain wrong.'

Three

Jonathan hung his head as Mary watched him. 'Before you go to work tomorrow, you will walk over to Isaac Wilson's house and say how truly sorry you are for causing distress to his cows. You have no need to name the other lads involved in this shameful escapade. I'm sure Mr Wilson will know who they are by now.

'And don't even consider not going, and lying to me when you get home. I've known Isaac and his wife all my life and I'll be checking with them tomorrow. Now get yourself off to work.'

Four

The Church of St Helen: Sunday August 23 1665

William smiled round at the congregation now that his sermon had come to an end. 'I don't need to remind anyone that next Saturday, the twenty-ninth of August, marks the start of Wakes Week in our village. It is a time of year we look forward to, and I hope you all enjoy the events and festivities that accompany the week.

'On Saturday morning the fair will arrive and set up its tents and stalls on and around the village green. I must point out that although the green will be the focal point of the fair, as usual, tents and booths will also spread out along one side of Church Street. This will leave enough space to enable carts and wagons to pass through. I'm told that donkey rides and the three-legged races will take place along the Lydgate Road. Which means that anyone wanting to travel in either direction on that road will be asked to wait until a particular ride or race has finished. Longer races on foot will again take place across the fells.

'And please remember that Saturday morning will be a time of preparation for the fair folk, so do not try to visit until noon at the earliest. Tumblers, jesters, bards and ballad singers will be warming up ready to perform, and animals required for rides and races will need to be made ready for a noon start. I also believe that one of the main attractions that hasn't been seen in Eyam before is that of a dancing bear.'

Four

William waited until the buzz of excited chatter died down and held out his hands. 'I'll say no more about the fair, but before you all leave here this morning, I want to say a word about the deeper meanings of Wakes Week. Of course, every town and village that celebrates this week has its own reasons for doing so, but I'll focus on what the week means to Eyam.

'Firstly, in our prayers we must remember St Helena, the patron saint to whom this beautiful old church is dedicated. Her feast day is on the fifteenth day of this month, so our celebrations are partly in honour of that. As one of the earliest Christians, hundreds of years ago, St Helena's story is an inspiration to us all and is something I've addressed in several of my sermons over the past year.

'Secondly, we must bless the wells that provide our village with abundant supplies of fresh water. At ten o'clock next Saturday morning, I shall lead the procession to the Townhead and the first of our wells to be blessed this year. I ask all those who wish to take part to congregate outside the main gate of St Helen's, where we will organise ourselves into a long procession of no more than four abreast before we move off. If anyone wishes to lay flowers around the trough as a sign that it has been blessed, it would be greatly appreciated. I know that my wife intends to place a bunch at every well that is blessed. Which could well leave the rectory garden without a bloom in sight.'

William's jest was appreciated and gentle laughter filled the church, so William took his cue to end his speech. 'I look forward to seeing as many of you as possible next Saturday.'

—

A Boundary of Stones

The Hadfield /Cooper household: Wednesday, August 26 1665

'Something arrived for you a few moments ago,' Mary said as the young journeyman tailor, George Viccars, came into the cottage's kitchen-cum-living room from the workroom beyond. She adjusted her coif to ensure no stray hair could escape whilst she baked and gestured at the large wooden crate sitting against the wall. 'It has come from London, so I imagine it's the cloth my husband ordered.'

'Thank you, Mrs Hadfield. Better late than never, I suppose.' George stepped around three-year-old Edward, who was rolling his leather balls across the stone-flagged floor. 'What with everything we had in stock used up on orders for Wakes Week, we had nothing left for latecomers. But if we manage to make a couple of extra garments before the Wakes start on Saturday, it will be better than nothing.'

George heaved a sigh and sank onto one of the dining chairs.

'Are you still enjoying life as a full-time tailor?' Mary asked, aware that something was bothering the usually cheerful young man.

'Well, I'm enjoying making gentlemen's waistcoats and breeches.'

'But…?'

'But the variety of gowns that ladies ask for, especially the wealthier ones, can be quite a challenge.' George grimaced and held out his hands. 'There are so many different shapes and designs, I don't know if I'll ever learn all of them.'

Mary focused on the pleasant young man, whose genial

Four

features were framed by his wavy, collar-length, brown hair. He had come to Eyam to complete the final eight months of his two-year training as a journeyman, working alongside master tailor, Alexander Hadfield. Since his arrival a couple of months ago, he had already become a part of the family.

'Well, George, that's because no lady wants to bump into someone wearing an identical garment to hers. Even Puritans like us want to feel unique, especially when we dress up for the Wakes. Surely a Buxton lad like yourself did the same?'

'I suppose I did. Ma always made sure I had a new shirt to wear. But at that time what the ladies wore from year to year always looked the same to me. Now I realise that ladies are fussy about such things.' He shook his head. 'How can I keep up with it all?'

'You're aware of such things now, lad, because you've changed. You know your trade and can tell one style and cut from another. And you'll keep on learning as you go on. As for keeping up with everything, you must make it your business to know about new fashions and designs coming out of London. Mr Hadfield will tell you, he's researching such things all year round.'

George seemed lost in thought as Mary continued rubbing in the pastry for the chicken pie to be served at the evening meal.

'Are you planning to go to the Wakes, George?'

'I am, Mrs Hadfield. Jonathan and I have arranged to go together on Tuesday. The farm manager has given him that day off and I have Mr Hadfield's permission to be off the same day. It will be good to have Jonathan's company and I know he loves the races. I might even enter a race or two myself. My ma always said I could give a hare a run for its money.'

Mary chuckled at the image. 'That is nice to hear. I know Jonathan loves your company, and I'll be happy knowing he isn't getting up to mischief with that little group of friends he has.' She grimaced as the incident with the cows came back to mind. 'I believe there'll be a longer run across the fells again this year, although there'll still be the shorter races. You could also test your skills by entering one of the donkey races. Jonathan is intent upon doing that. There'll be sports and games aplenty, and stalls with foods and drinks on offer. And let's not forget the blessings of our wells.'

'I hope to attend at least one of the well blessings, perhaps during the opening ceremony this Saturday.'

'Edward, stop that noise!' Mary called to her small son as he beat a loud, monotonous rhythm on his drum. 'Play with something quietly while George and I are talking… How about building a big, tall tower with your bricks?

'Sorry about that, George. I was about to say that most of the villagers try to attend a few of the blessings, but there'll be crowds of us enjoying ourselves at the fair for the whole week. The wealthier folk will be showing off their finest clothes, many of which, I'm happy to say, were made by Mr Hadfield.' She gestured at the young man. 'And this year, you've made a number of them, which gives you every reason to be proud of yourself.'

'Thank you for saying so, Mrs Hadfield. This is my final position with master tailors like your husband, and once I've finished, I hope to return to my hometown and set up my own business. Mr Hadfield has taught me so much already, and I've loved working with him. I'm also grateful for the room you have allowed me to rent in your home. Most journeymen I've known had to find their own lodgings elsewhere.'

Mary carried her chicken pie across to the small stone-built oven alongside the hearth, placing it carefully inside and closing the heavy, iron door. 'Since you wish to return to Buxton, you must really love the town.'

George smiled. 'I have many memories of a happy childhood there with my parents, and when I return, I hope to rekindle some of my early friendships.'

'I sincerely hope you succeed in life, George. You've already become a valued member of our family and I know my husband has enjoyed working with you these past two months. Between you and me, he'll likely grumble about your leaving for weeks after you've gone.'

They laughed at that before George headed back to the workroom, intending to open the crate of cloths once his work was over for the day.

A hearty meal was enjoyed by all and a short time later, young Edward was settled into his bed, to be followed an hour or so later by his older brother, Jonathan. Mary left George in the kitchen to open the crate and removed her apron before disappearing into the workroom so that Alexander could show her the garments already paid for and awaiting collection.

Mary gazed at the man she had come to love dearly as well as admire. Dark-headed, stylishly dressed and well-groomed, he was a perfect advertisement for his trade. She felt proud to have found such a diligent husband after the death of her first husband, Edward Cooper, father of her two sons. But it was Alexander's kind, considerate nature that made her love him the most. Their marriage five months ago had done much to ease the heartache and loss that had overwhelmed her following Edward's death the previous year.

She surveyed the array of garments Alexander had laid out for her inspection, admiring the sophisticated gowns created for the wealthier ladies of Eyam and the simpler designs and muted shades for the less well-off villagers. The selection of men's garments was also impressive, from breeches and coats to shirts and waistcoats.

'What a wonderful collection,' Mary complimented. 'Which of them were made by George?'

Alexander singled out a few of the garments, including two of the more simply styled ladies' dresses, plus a gentleman's shirt, a waistcoat and two pairs of breeches. 'George has done an excellent job with these in the short time he's been with me. The different designs he's mastered here will stand him in good stead in future years.'

'I'm so glad to hear that. George is such a pleasant young man and it will be strange not having him around when his time with you comes to an end.'

'It will, but he still has another six months with me yet. George is an astute student and once we've worked through a few more intricacies of our trade, he'll be as competent and qualified as any master tailor I know, and ready to set up his own business.'

Alexander yawned widely. 'Time for bed, I think. I want to make an early start tomorrow on one of the new cloths and

Four

I need to feel wide awake to do that.'

Mary nodded. 'I'll just say goodnight to George and see if he's finished unpacking the crate. He'll need an early night, too.'

—

'Unfortunately, most of the cloth feels damp and smells quite musty,' George said, a bale of it over his arm when Mary returned to the living room. 'It needs a good airing before it can be used. Would you mind if I draped it over the dining chairs overnight? Mr Hadfield wants to get a garment or two cut out from some of it in the morning.'

'I know he does, and I don't mind you using the table and chairs at all. They aren't needed until breakfast. But now, Mr Hadfield and I are off to bed, and you need to head upstairs soon or you'll be yawning all day tomorrow. Let's hope the cloth will be well-aired by morning.'

Alone downstairs, George lifted the individual bales from the crate, unfolding them and giving each a good shake before examining their colours and textures. His mind's eye pictured the different garments to which each cloth could be suited, smiling as he realised how much he was looking forward to working on the different designs. Eventually, he draped them all over the high backs of chairs.

At the bottom of the crate, he was surprised to find half a dozen, previously worn, ladies' dresses, which he shook out before studying the designs and stitching. After what Mrs Hadfield had said earlier, he realised that if the garments had been made in compliance with recent fashions in London, Mr Hadfield would doubtless be pleased to use them as patterns for his own creations later in the year. The dresses from London could then be offered to villagers as second-hand goods, at a reduced price.

Eventually, George laid the dresses across the table to air with the cloths. The fire in the hearth still gave off its warmth as he headed upstairs, knowing they'd be able to start work on those extra garments in the morning.

—

Saturday August 29 1665

'Will you be joining us in the procession to the Townhead, George?' Mary continued to clear the breakfast dishes from the table as she spoke. 'There'll be few folk working on the first day of Wakes Week. Even Mr Hadfield likes to take part in the opening parade and the blessing of the first well.'

'I'd love to walk with you all, thank you, Mrs Hadfield. These things are always more enjoyable when you aren't alone. And I can help you to keep an eye on little Edward.'

'I'll hold you to that.' Mary chuckled. 'Edward might be three, but he doesn't like walking too far. He'll likely want to be carried by the time we reach the village green, if not before.'

George grinned. 'My arms are strong, but Edward can ride on my shoulders, if he wants.'

'Then all I can do is thank you for offering. I just hope you don't regret it. Now, we'd best get ready. I can't walk in the procession in my workaday dress.'

Mary smiled as she thought of the day ahead. 'I hope you've got something special you can wear for this morning, George. Mr Hadfield has a fancy shirt and waistcoat he keeps for special occasions. Even Jonathan and Edward have a smart shirt apiece.'

'I have a shirt my ma bought me when I became a journeyman. She had it made by a master tailor in Tideswell. I haven't worn it yet so it's still brand new. I also have a new pair of breeches.'

'Good. That means we're all set up to have a happy day and, of course, a happy week. Let us hope that nothing comes along to spoil it.'

Five

Wednesday, September 2 1665

George awoke a couple of hours before dawn, shivering so much his teeth were chattering. He'd never felt so cold, and despite the thick blankets of his bed, he could not get warm. To make matters worse, every muscle in his body ached, so much so that movement became an ordeal. He tried to lie still but, eventually, he forced himself to rise and dress. He shuffled downstairs, aware of the need to work on the waistcoat he'd cut out yesterday.

As he entered the workroom, Alexander glanced up from his stitching. 'Morning, George, another pleasant day for the Wakes.'

'Good morning, Mr Hadfield,' George replied, sinking into his seat opposite the master tailor at the work table. 'The sun is shining, but the air is cold for so early in September.'

Alexander pulled his threaded needle through the half-made breeches and stared at him. 'You think so?'

'I do, but it's probably just me. I woke up aching and shivering and I just can't get warm.'

'You missed breakfast, so perhaps you should go and see if Mrs Hadfield has kept any bacon warm for you. You might feel better with food in your belly.'

'Thank you, but I don't think I could eat anything just yet. I'm afraid I am quite out of sorts this morning. I'm hoping I'll feel better as the morning goes on and I can take off this jerkin. It's far too bulky to work in.'

'We can close the widow if the cooler air is bothering you. The room felt overly warm earlier with the sun shining in, but I know how feeling cold can take the pleasure out of working.'

'I would be grateful for that, if you are sure, Mr Hadfield.'

'I am,' the master tailor said, closing the offending window and returning to his seat. He rubbed a forefinger up and down his nose, the motion one that George recognised as something he did when he was thinking. 'Let's hope you just have a passing chill and it will soon be gone.'

It wasn't long before George knew he couldn't continue working. 'My head is throbbing so much, I can barely think, Mr Hadfield. And my stomach is churning as though I'm going to be sick any moment.'

'Then bed's the best place for you, young man. I doubt we'll see any more customers for Wakes Week attire at this late stage.'

On unsteady legs, George mumbled his thanks and withdrew from the room.

—

George was not at breakfast the following morning. More than a little concerned, once Mary had served her husband and sons their bacon, she headed upstairs and knocked on his bedchamber door. 'Could you drink a mug of cocoa, George… or perhaps just some warm milk?' The response was little more than a groan, which prompted her to ask, 'Are you still feeling unwell?'

Unable to make sense of George's muffled replies, she

opened the door, pushing it far enough back to enable her to slip into the room. Expecting to find him sitting up, probably rubbing his eyes after oversleeping, she was surprised to see him huddled beneath his blankets. The room had the stomach-churning stench of unemptied chamber pots.

'Are you still feeling unwell?' Mary repeated. Another mere murmur caused her a further stab of unease. 'Do you need a potion from the apothecary to ease your aches and pains?'

The young tailor shuffled beneath the blankets but said nothing and Mary grew increasingly fearful he was severely ill. She sped downstairs. 'Could you spare a moment to check on George, Alexander? I can't get anything from him but shuffles and groans.'

Within minutes, Alexander came down, gesturing that Mary should follow him into his workroom. 'Push the door to, my dear. I don't want Jonathan to hear what I say.'

Mary's heartbeat quickened. 'What is so awful that Jonathan mustn't hear?'

'George will not be rising from his bed today. He is extremely ill and I fear he may never recover.'

Mary stared at him, dreading to hear him confirm what she already suspected.

'You know that London and a few other towns south of here are presently tormented by bubonic plague?' She nodded, wishing with all her heart she wasn't hearing this. 'From what I saw of George's body just now, the symptoms he has are those of plague.'

'Are you sure that's what it is? As far as I know, no one else in the village has it.'

Five

Alexander shrugged and held out his hands. 'Unfortunately, the symptoms speak for themselves, though I have no idea where George could have contracted the disease. He admits to feeling pain in all parts of his body and is extremely nauseous. By the look and smell of his nightshirt and bedsheets, I'd say he's suffered diarrhoea for some hours. On top of which, his nose and fingertips are black, and there are some of those ugly, red swellings in his armpits – symptoms which, I believe, appear in the later stages of bubonic plague.'

'Poor, poor George,' Mary croaked as the tears welled. 'If that's the case, he won't have long to live. We must pray with him and ask God to forgive his sins and accept him into Heaven. Oh, Alexander, I've heard that plague is so contagious that anyone living in the same household will catch it.'

'We can't allow ourselves to think that way. George is in our care and it's our duty to see he's made as comfortable as possible and hope he'll recover. But we must ensure that Jonathan and Edward don't enter his room, especially Jonathan. If he mentions to anyone there is plague in our house it would cause an uproar.'

Mary swept the tears from her eyes. 'You're right, I'll speak to him as soon as he gets home tonight. But as you rightly say, George is in our care and I could never allow him to lie in the filthy condition you described. I'll make time this morning to wash him down and change his clothes and bedding.'

Alexander nodded, the flash of fear in his eyes not missed by Mary. 'I'm sure being clean and dry will help George to feel much more comfortable. You may well have to wash him and change his clothes more than once today, unless the apothecary can give us some form of medication. I'll walk over to see him as soon as Jonathan has left for work.'

—

As Humphrey Merrell pulled back the bedsheets on George's bed the overwhelming stench of loose excrement almost caused the two men to retch. Having already experienced this earlier, Alexander managed to compose himself quickly.

'It is not something anyone should ever have to see, is it Humphrey?' he whispered, as they stared at the repellent sight before them.

'It certainly isn't,' the portly apothecary mumbled through fingers clamped across his nose and mouth. But he pulled himself together and lifted George's clothing with a short cane he'd brought with him for that purpose.

'May the Lord preserve us! I've known what the symptoms of bubonic plague are for years, but never in my wildest dreams had I imagined them to be so hideous.'

'Are you sure that's what it is…?' Alexander's words echoed those of Mary earlier.

Humphrey nodded. 'I wish I could say otherwise but, together with the other symptoms, there's no doubt in my mind that the ghastly buboes are indicators of bubonic plague. George also appears to be covered in flea bites, although that isn't surprising at this time of year when rats infest every nook and cranny of our homes… How in Heaven's name has this disease reached our village, Alexander? Have you been in contact with anyone who has it?'

'I have not, nor has anyone else in my family. We have no idea how plague came to our home.'

Humphrey's face reflected his deepest fears. 'No one else in the village must hear of this or there'll be pandemonium. Once fear and panic take hold of people, riots can soon follow. They will know that once plague strikes a small community such as ours, it could wipe it out. I've heard that thousands of people have already died in London this year.'

'Mary and I both know all that and have already had this discussion. I came to you only for some potions to ease George's suffering or you would have known nothing of this, either. We could not just leave the boy to die in pain.'

'No, and I commend you for that. But since no one knows how plague spreads amongst people, you and your family could now be at risk.' Humphrey's normally ruddy face paled. 'As could I, and my wife and son.'

'Indeed,' Alexander said, knowing no way of allaying the apothecary's fears. 'As far as I've heard, no physician in this land has a cure for plague. I also realise that all we can do for George is to keep him as comfortable as we can and hope he recovers. Mary will be coming in to wash him and change his clothes and bedding once we are finished. She insists he can't be left in this filthy state until he dies.'

Humphrey nodded. 'Mary's right. Keeping George dry, warm and comfortable is the only thing we can do for him now – although it could be at great risk to yourselves.'

'I know, and the thought fills me with dread. But we cannot allow that possibility to thwart our responsibility. We are all George has and we cannot fail him in this.'

'I'll leave you a few of my remedies which will reduce the sickness and fevers the young man exhibits. I'll also leave one or two balms to soothe, and perhaps reduce, the swellings. I will, of course, advise you on how to administer them all. If you find any of them of help with George's condition you can always come to me for more once they are gone. Either that, or purchase the ingredients and make the remedies yourselves. The receipts are on the containers, if that is what you decide.'

The apothecary delved into his large leather bag and placed a number of jars and bottles on a chest of drawers beside the door. 'Since George displays several effects of plague, you will need to counter each in order to bring comfort to what may well be the young man's last days on God's earth.' He singled out two of the bottles. 'Both of these will help to stop the nausea and accompanying diarrhoea that presently overwhelm him.' He tapped the cork on one of the green bottles. 'This contains water of scabious into which various plants have been infused, including endive, rue, white dittany and petals of red rose. A small amount needs to be drunk three times a day. You will see that the full list of ingredients is written on the container, as it is on them all.'

Alexander glanced at the list and Humphrey tapped a shorter but stouter green bottle. 'This potion will counter feverishness and chills when drunk at least twice daily. Try to alternate it with the scabious water. It simply consists of barberries that have been steeped in warm water before being beaten, powdered and mixed with strong vinegar and a little salt.

'If George continues to shiver uncontrollably and constantly feels cold, the barberry potion can be made with

Five

strong wine. I've given you some of that, too, which is in… let me see… yes, this bottle.' Humphrey pointed to a similarly coloured and shaped bottle but with a label stating, Barberries in Wine. 'It is best to serve this one warm and, needless to say, George himself must be kept warm and away from draughts.'

Alexander felt a little overwhelmed by all this information and Humphrey patted his arm. 'I know it sounds a great deal to take in, my friend, but I'm sure that Mary has a good understanding of caring for the sick and will probably be willing to make more of these potions herself.

'Now, there are several remedies to ease the pain of the buboes, but I thought it best to try one of the simplest first. I must stress that this balm is by no means any less effective than other treatments for buboes, some of which require parts of live pigeons, hens, or frogs in order to make them.'

'Then I shall be glad to try this balm first.'

Humphrey nodded 'It consists of bay leaves, rue meal and salt, all mixed with enough egg yolk to make a thick paste. Simply spread it onto a piece of leather or stiff cloth and apply to the sore. It will effectively draw out the infection.

'I will pray that this disease stays within these four walls, Alexander, and that no one else in your family succumbs to it. But if the Lord has chosen to inflict plague upon our village as punishment for the hostility we have shown to our new rector, I dare not think what the consequences will be. Within a few months, most of us could be dead.'

'The wrath of the Lord is, indeed, something to be feared,' Alexander replied. 'We must hope He hears our prayers and forgives us, but only time will tell if He does. Thank you for the potions, my friend. I'll make payment to you in my workroom downstairs.'

—

No further remedies from the apothecary were required. The following day, George Viccars' suffering came to an end. It was Friday morning on the fourth of September, the day that Wakes Week finished. Sounds of last-minute festivities rang out from the village green and crowded streets before the stallholders and fair packed away and left later that afternoon.

Mary blinked back her tears and stared through the window at the front of her cottage, thankful that her cherished garden set the cottage some way back from the road. The sadness she felt was at odds with the merriment of her friends and neighbours outside and she thanked the Lord that George had, at least, managed to attend the blessings of two of the wells and enjoy the fair with its many activities earlier in the week. With this in mind, she left Edward playing with his bricks and headed upstairs to George's chamber, where Alexander had escorted Reverend Mompesson on his arrival to say prayers and blessings over the young man's body.

Not wishing to intrude, Mary slipped into the room and remained at the door, intending to simply observe, unless she felt the need to speak. She had washed George down and dressed him in a clean set of clothes earlier, using a bedsheet as a shroud, as the reverend had instructed. The young tailor, with all the promise of a successful life ahead of him, now lay silent and still whilst Reverend Mompesson said the final prayers

Five

before the funeral, the location and date of which had yet to be decided. Alexander knelt by the reverend's side, joining him in prayer. In the short time he'd lived in Eyam, George had attended church every Sunday. He had also befriended several other young people in the village, and would be sorely missed.

Once the final Amen had been said and they had risen to their feet, Reverend Mompesson turned to face Alexander. Spotting Mary at the door, he beckoned her to join them. 'Do you have the address of George's closest relatives to whom you can write with this sad news?'

Alexander nodded. 'George was born and raised in Buxton, and his parents are still there. I imagine they'll want their son's body returning to them for burial. I have their address in my workroom.'

'I'm afraid I cannot permit George to be taken from this village, Mr Hadfield. The risk of the seeds of plague being carried to Buxton on his body and clothing is too great. George will be given a Christian burial here in Eyam, as soon as possible. Of course, you must still inform Mr and Mrs Viccars of this.

'I have a christening this afternoon, so I'll instruct our sexton to prepare a grave for tomorrow morning. A simple cross will be erected with a few necessary details scratched into it to mark the site, should George's parents wish to visit at some future date.'

The reverend's gaze moved between Mary and her husband. 'I imagine there will be few mourners at the graveside when the cause of Mr Viccars' death becomes known.' He took a breath to continue, but paused, and Mary could see that whatever he wanted to say would not be easy for him.

'Most of the villagers will have heard tales of the deadly plague spreading from London and other afflicted towns,' he continued eventually, 'and I sincerely hope they do not turn against your family when they learn the truth of George's tragic death. I doubt we'll ever know the reason why he should have been stricken by plague, miles away from any of those towns, but I will pray daily that no more of our villagers are similarly afflicted.'

Alexander heaved a sigh. 'If we are treated with animosity, Reverend, we'll have no other choice than to take things in our stride. There are as many causes of plague being bandied about as there are remedies to cure it, so no blame can be laid at our feet – or anyone else's, come to that. Unfortunately, once someone is stricken by this disease it spreads like wildfire, taking the lives of anyone in its path.

'But now I must head to the carpenters to buy a coffin. I don't want George buried in just the shroud and Robert usually has a few coffins ready for immediate purchase. I'm sure he'll have one that will be suitable; George was not of uncommon height and build.'

'That is generous of you, Mr. Hadfield,' Reverend Mompesson said, 'and it tells me how much young George meant to you. Your family will be uppermost in my thoughts and prayers. It has been an upsetting time for all of you. Edward is too young to understand, but Jonathan is not. He will doubtless feel the impact of George's death, as well as realising the possible consequences to his family.'

Mary's heart was heavy as she retreated downstairs to do her chores, considering what a sad little funeral such a lovely

Five

person as George Viccars would be given. She was also very aware that the future welfare of her own family now hung in the balance.

—

'It was probably a blessing that only our family attended George's burial yesterday, Alexander. I would have found it too difficult to speak to anyone.' Mary nodded in agreement with the words she had already voiced several times and patted her husband's hand as they sat together in his workroom. Alexander was finding it hard to resume working alone after enjoying George's company for the past two months. A second pair of hands had greatly eased his workload, the convivial conversation making the time pass both quickly and pleasantly.

'I felt it my duty to inform our closest neighbours of George's death, and the cause of it,' Mary went on. 'They would have seen the coffin being carried to the wagon and we would have had to explain who had died and why, sooner or later. I wanted to assure them they need not feel obliged to attend the funeral, though they would be welcome to do so if they felt comfortable in doing so. But I did say they would be well received in our home afterwards to share our food as a way of celebrating George's life. I was so pleased to see them here. After all, I've known the Hawksworth, Thorpe, and Syddall families for many years and we've shared some happy times together.'

'You did the right thing, my dear, and it was good to welcome them to spend a little time with us. Besides, the funeral could never have taken place entirely in secret. Any number of villagers could have wandered past St Helen's and enquired as to whom was being buried. I don't doubt that several people will have done so, and our neighbours would probably have mentioned George's death to others.'

Mary rubbed her aching brow. 'In which case, everyone in Eyam will now be aware of what has happened and we'll be shunned. Just as Reverend Mompesson feared.'

—

Thursday, September 17 1665

'My head still hurts, Mama.'

Little Edward Cooper sat in his bed while Mary perched next to him ready to tell him one of his favourite bedtime stories. The boy had eaten little at the evening meal, nor had he touched his bedtime mug of milk, and Mary hoped his headache would go with a good night's sleep. She smiled and wrapped him in her arms. 'Well, you did fall off that tree stump when you were playing in the garden today, didn't you?' The little boy nodded. 'Are you sure you didn't bang your head when you landed?'

'I hurt my chin,' he insisted, jutting it out to display a small graze, whilst keeping to the story he'd told her at the time. 'Now my head hurts. Here,' he added, rubbing his brow.'

'Well, that's probably because you're tired,' Mary said, taking his hands to stop him from scratching the flea bites he'd acquired a few days ago. 'Shall we put some balm on those nasty bites?'

Edward nodded and Mary scurried downstairs, returning with one of the pots that Humphrey Merrell had left here for George. 'Here we are,' she said, forcing a cheerful smile on her face. 'This should calm that awful itchiness and help you to stop scratching yourself all night. So keep still while I rub it in.

'Now, close your eyes and think about something nice,' she ordered when she'd finished. 'And tomorrow, when we've done all our tasks, we can go for a walk along the footpath up the hill. There'll be lots of fallen leaves there for you to kick about, and you can help me to pick some blackberries for a nice, juicy pie.'

'I'd like that, but only if my head feels better.'

Mary eventually left the room, saying a silent prayer that it was just tiredness causing her little boy's headache. The thought caused the problems presently tormenting her family to flood back to mind and she rubbed her own aching head. It would probably be many weeks before villagers felt able to trust that the Hadfield household harboured no seeds of plague. Even her husband and elder son had been avoided by people in Eyam, including a few once-close friends. George's burial was only eight days ago, but Mary was already willing the weeks away until the time came when their fears could be put behind them.

By the following morning, Mary had no need to insist that her younger son stayed in his bed. The now ashen-faced child felt too poorly to rise and constantly drifted in and out of sleep. Edward had called out for her several times in the night, complaining of tummy ache and being cold to add to his continuing headache. Mary dared not dwell on the possibility that his aches and pains could be the early symptoms of plague, convincing herself that her little boy must have bumped his head harder than he'd thought, causing him to feel quite nauseous.

As the afternoon wore on, Edward lost control of his bowels, and by the time Mary was alerted by the smell, excrement covered his small nightshirt and bedsheets. Determined to keep her child clean, she washed him down on three occasions during the afternoon and early evening, a clean nightgown and bed sheets being needed each time. Her thoughts turned to Jonathan, who would probably spend another night deprived of sleep if the situation with Edward continued. With that in mind, she and Alexander carried the truckle bed downstairs and Mary laid fresh bedding on it. It would be better all round if the ailing child slept downstairs, and Mary would be on hand, dozing in an armchair.

Mary was distraught, though she refused to believe that a child as healthy and robust as Edward would be unable to shake off these early symptoms of plague. As the boy drifted into the deep sleep of the ailing, Mary fell to her knees before his bed.

Dear Lord, I beseech you to look kindly upon this child and help him to conquer the disease that is slowly bringing his young life to an end. He is innocent of all sin and will be reared to become one of your faithful servants. Amen

Mary fervently hoped that if she kept her beloved child clean and free of all faeces, the seeds of the horrendous disease would simply wither and perish. But despite her many prayers and constant nursing, during the evening and through the night, Edward became increasingly distressed when blood streamed from his nose and mouth and Mary couldn't contain

Five

her tears as patches of blackened skin appeared at the ends of his nose, fingers and toes. Poor George had experienced the same, such a short time ago. But the thought of losing one of her own beloved sons was too much for Mary to bear.

While inside she was screaming, for Edward's sake, Mary knew she must stay calm and appear to be cheerful. She smiled as she coaxed him to swallow the remedy to ease the sickness and diarrhoea and put soothing balm on the buboes that swelled in his armpits and groin. Over the next three days, her constant care seemed to be working. Edward did not display any new or worsening symptoms, other than ever-increasing fatigue.

But, on the morning of Monday, the twenty-first day of September, Mary watched in anguish as the small boy's eyes closed for the very last time. Despite knowing that few people ever recovered from the plague, she had clung to the hope that God would not allow so young a child to depart this Earth.

'He has gone to the Lord,' was all Mary needed to say to Alexander as she poured warm water from the kettle in the hearth into a bowl and gathered cloths with which to wash and dry Edward's small body before re-dressing him. As she finally gathered up the soiled nightshirt and bedsheets, her only thought was that she would probably be the next victim of this most cruel of afflictions.

But at this moment in time, that did not seem to matter.

—

Alexander hurried from his workroom to answer the soft rapping on the door, wondering who it could be. He, Mary and

Jonathan had only returned from Edward's funeral a short while ago and Mary was too overcome with grief to speak to anyone. Jonathan was also distraught, and had returned to work to stop himself from weeping. He had adored his little brother.

'Won't you come in, Mrs Hawksworth,' Alexander said to one of their next-door neighbours. Jane was a friendly and generally cheerful young woman with a small boy of fourteen months. Only last week, she had joyfully confided in Mary and Alexander that she and Peter were expecting their second child the following spring. But today, her face was pale and drawn and Alexander didn't have to look too hard to see that she had been weeping.

'I won't, thank you, Mr Hadfield. I only wanted to let you know that my husband passed away this morning. I'm not sure if you know my mother, Scythe Torre?'

'No, I'm afraid I don't, although Mary may well do.'

'Well, my mother's been staying with me since Peter fell ill a few days ago. She's looking after little Humphrey this afternoon, though she'll be going back to her own home in Stoney Middleton the day after Peter's funeral. I'm on my way to see Robert about a coffin now.'

With that, the tears welled and Jane sobbed. Not knowing how to comfort someone he'd known for so short a time, Alexander stood for some moments, wishing he could call Mary. But he would not disturb his wife in her grief-stricken state.

Jane blew her nose and swept the tears from her face. 'I don't know why I'm telling you all this, Mr Hadfield. I suppose I feel so confused, and overwhelmed by what has happened to us.'

'You have no need to explain yourself to me, Mrs

Five

Hawksworth. Mary is similarly distressed over losing young Edward so soon after the death of George. And struggling to cope with my own grief, I feel at a loss as to how to comfort her. I can only repeat what Reverend Stanley always told us about dealing with bereavement. Time will heal. Am I correct in thinking that Peter's death was due to plague?'

Jane nodded. 'It seemed to come so fast. He only complained of feeling unwell a few days ago. He's been so ill since, especially once those dreadful swellings appeared. After what Mary said about George's suffering, then dear little Edward's, I can only wonder how many others in our village will succumb to this cursed disease. Only today I learned that our neighbour, Thomas Thorpe, has been ill these past few days. I've heard nothing to confirm he has the plague, but that is more than likely what it is.'

'I agree,' Alexander replied, 'which leads us to wonder how this disease is carried and passed on to others. Many believe it to be a miasma in the air, and since we all breathe air into our lungs, I suppose that could be true. But how this foul air can be cleansed, no one seems to know.'

Jane's brow creased in thought. 'Perhaps not… though I've heard say that many women in London rely on sweet-smelling flowers and herbs to protect themselves. Some of them even hold pomanders filled with flowers, or herbs and spices, to their noses whenever they leave their homes. I believe the men prefer to smoke tobacco in their pipes to keep the miasma at bay.'

Alexander shrugged. 'But since no one can be certain that plague is caused by a miasma, it is impossible to safeguard ourselves from it. There are so many forms of protection talked about, most of them stemming from London, but who knows if any of them actually work? I, for one, could never put my trust in nostrums, charms and cabalistic signs, although many people do. They are all hocus-pocus to me. And although I agree that many herbs are effective for relieving pain, I doubt they could provide protection from plague.'

'It is hard to know what to do for the best,' Jane agreed with a sigh. 'And many of us have our families to consider. I have little Humphrey to think about, as well as our unborn child. Peter has a brother in the village and he and his wife have children of their own. Then there are my parents and siblings in Stoney Middleton…

'But I must go about my business and leave you to your own grieving. Would you be so kind as to tell Mary that she and her family are in my prayers, and that Reverend Mompesson has agreed to officiate at Peter's funeral tomorrow? I don't expect any of you to attend at this unhappy time and I shall pray that my husband's death will be the last in our village.'

Alexander closed the door, praying that the three deaths to date were not the beginning of an epidemic of far greater proportions. He was also very aware of the likelihood that he, Mary and Jonathan could succumb to this appalling affliction before long.

But he would keep that thought to himself.

Six

It was Wednesday, the last day of September, and Catherine stood beside her husband in the cemetery of St Helen's as he prayed over the grave of young Sarah Syddall, the second of his parishioners to be buried that day:

O Merciful God, the Father of
our Lord, Jesus Christ,
who is the resurrection and the life;
in whom whosoever believeth shall live, though he die,
and whosoever liveth and believeth in him,
shall not die eternally…

An air of sorrow and desolation hung over the gathering like a heavy, dark cloud that even the unseasonal warmth could not dispel. This morning had seen the funeral of Mary, twelve-year-old daughter of Thomas Thorpe, whose burial had been but four days ago. Catherine was heartbroken that six villagers had died over the course of a mere three weeks. Nor had she failed to note that all six had been close neighbours who lived little more than a stone's throw from the church.

Fear and dread rippled through Eyam. No one knew who the plague would take next, or the source from which it would come. Catherine had visited the homes of bereaved relatives to offer her condolences, as well as assisting with household chores. She also tried to support her husband as much as she could at this time, knowing how the deaths of six of his parishioners weighed heavily upon him. Feeling helpless to do anything to alleviate the pain of stricken families other than to pray with them, Catherine knew that William was also greatly worried about how many more would die before the disease left the village.

Tomorrow was the first day of October. Trees around the village and hillsides were already shedding their leaves, a sign that the year would start drawing to a close. William assured her that the onset of the cold, winter weather would generally bring a marked drop in the numbers of plague victims. But, at this point in time, Catherine had seen little lessening of the heat that had been a constant test of endurance throughout the summer.

—

Mary was pondering on whether to make cocoa for Alexander and herself or the new drink they called coffee, when there was a knock at the door. Since Edward's death, Mary had found it hard to talk to anyone, knowing they would offer their condolences and the same old advice of allowing time to heal her grief. Though she knew that to be true, having dealt with such pain after her first husband's death, the death of a beloved child was too much for any mother to bear. But Alexander was in his workroom, busy working on a gentleman's coat that needed finishing by tomorrow, and she would not disturb him.

She opened the door to find her neighbour, Jane Hawksworth, standing there with her little son, Humphrey in her arms. Her red eyes told Mary she had been weeping.

'Whatever's the matter, Jane? Do you need someone to look after Humphrey for a while? I know your mother went

Six

home the day after–'

'My mother's dead,' Jane spluttered as tears streamed down her face. 'She died this morning, barely a fortnight after we buried Peter. And I don't know how to cope with it all.'

'I'm so sorry to hear that. Scythe was such a lovely woman. The Torre family was always kind to Edward after he bought some of their land to extend his farm… But where are my manners? Come in and share a drink with us. I was just about to make one for Alexander and I.'

'I won't today, Mary, if you don't mind. I don't mean to be rude but I need to get back to my work. I just wanted to tell you that Sythe, too, died from plague. She was such a kind woman to everyone, so why did the Lord choose to take her?'

'Oh Jane, I don't know anyone who could answer that question. My grief is still raw over little Edward's death and I'm not sure my heart will ever mend. Often, his smiling face comes to mind and I find myself weeping like a babe. I'm sure both Reverend Stanley and Reverend Mompesson would tell us that the Lord works in mysterious ways, so who are we to question who He chooses to take into Heaven? But I know how hard that is to take in.'

'Thank you, Mary, your words have brought me some consolation. Maybe we'll meet those we have lost when the Lord takes us into Heaven, too. My mother will be buried tomorrow. As you know, Reverend Mompesson likes to have the funerals of those who die from plague as soon as possible after their deaths.'

'I know,' Mary said, as she watched her friend walking to her own house next door.

Saturday, the tenth of October dawned warm and sunny and, as he did on most days after breakfasting, William left the rectory for the church, intending to spend some time mulling over ideas for his service the following day. But on arrival he was taken aback at the sight of none other than Reverend Stanley, on his knees in prayer. How the former rector dared to show his face in Eyam following his banishment from the village, William couldn't guess. He waited until the ageing cleric rose to his feet and turned to face him.

'Good morning, Reverend Stanley. I haven't seen you in church since the day I arrived in Eyam. In fact, I haven't seen you at all.'

'No, you haven't, nor would you have done today had I come at my usual time during the hours of darkness. I have no intention of participating in Anglican services and certainly did not lose my faith on your arrival here.'

William stared at the man whose bitter words and scowling face gave him little incentive to engage in cordial conversation. He took a breath, feeling it his duty to at least try.

'St Helen's is open to all who wish to pray, as you know Reverend Stanley. But considering you shouldn't even be living in Eyam, I can understand why you visit at a time when you are unlikely to be seen. And before *you* say anything, I can assure you, I have no intention of revealing your presence to the bishops, or to the Earl of Devonshire. No matter what you think of me, I have no desire to see you hounded from the village. I'm sure you're aware of the Five Mile Act?'

Stanley snorted. 'I know of it and I can assure you, it means nothing to me.'

'You might see things differently if you are arrested and imprisoned as an ousted cleric, living within the five-mile boundary.' William sighed. 'But, as I said, if you are apprehended, it will not be because of anything that has passed through my lips.'

Stanley stared at him. 'Don't expect me to thank you for that. If your patron had not conspired with the Earl of Devonshire to ensure your placement in this parish, I would still have been rector here. And, unlike you, I know how to guide the people through this time of disease and death in a way appropriate to our faith.'

William did not dispute the misinformed beliefs of the belligerent Puritan, having neither the time nor the patience to do so. Had Sir George Savile and the Earl of Devonshire not recommended William for this position, the Church of England bishops would have found another Anglican cleric soon enough.

'My gardener tells me that twelve people have already died of plague in this village in little more than four weeks,' Stanley went on. 'It is evident to all that something is seriously amiss which, I must assume, you have overlooked. I can only hope that in your future services you will encourage the people to pray to the Lord for forgiveness of their sins. We are being punished for some great wrong that has been committed here – whether communal or by a single person – and the vengeance of the Lord is terrible to behold.

'Remember that when you hold your service tomorrow,

since whatever you are presently preaching is having no effect. Good day, Reverend Mompesson.'

With that, Stanley strode from St Helen's, leaving William gaping after him – and having no intention of stressing any such thing in his services.

—

Morning service the following day started as a sombre affair. Sitting at the rear of the church with her little ones, Catherine was able to observe her fellow villagers' reactions to William's teaching and assurances of God's abiding love. As a rule, people listened attentively to his sermons, but today, most were too lost in their own worries to pay attention. Several struggled to hold back their tears and fear of the coming days seemed to emanate from each of them, like sweat from the skins of workers on hot, summer days.

Catherine watched as William glanced around at the bowed heads. Even from the rear of the church she could see that his normally straight, broad shoulders sagged and the expression on his face held such sympathy and love that Catherine wanted to take him in her arms and hold him close.

Overwhelmed by thoughts of the terrible possibilities for the whole of Eyam, Catherine held George and Elizabeth close, as though shielding them with her loving arms was enough to keep the seeds of plague at bay. She thought of the bereaved, grief-stricken families, her pity going out to them. Amongst them were the Thorpes, neighbours of Mary and Alexander Hadfield. Young Will Thorpe, who was buried on Wednes-

Six

day, was the fifth of that large family to succumb to plague's far-reaching tendrils.

Catherine could not help wondering if God was punishing the Thorpes for the part Will played in putting those cows in the church in July. She resolved to visit the family during the coming week to offer not only her condolences, but a helping hand around their cottage while their grief was still raw.

As his sermon ended, William said, 'Let us bring our hands together in a final prayer for all those who have lost loved ones to the plague.' Once again, his voice rang out:

Almighty God, Father and giver of comfort:
deal graciously, we pray, with all who mourn,
that in casting all their care on you,
they may know the consolation of your love,
through Jesus Christ our Lord.
Amen

No one joined in the final 'Amen' and for a moment, the church was silent. Then, pent up fear and anger erupted and mayhem prevailed, the bitter words aimed at William…

'There'd be a lot fewer mourners in Eyam if you hadn't come here!'

'The Lord is punishing us because *you* say prayers from your Anglican Prayer Book.'

'We need to renew our covenant with the Lord every time we pray.'

'We pledge obedience to Him in our prayers so we can be freed from our sinful beginnings: *Be merciful to me a sinner, for this I am by nature and practise.*'

'We want Reverend Stanley to help us through this plague!'

'Take your Anglican ways somewhere else and leave us Puritans alone!'

With that, the aisles emptied and Prayer Books stacked at the end of pews were swept to the floor.

Catherine's heart pounded as she hugged George and Elizabeth, knowing they'd be trampled underfoot if they left their seats. How *could* these people hurl such harsh words at William, when all he wanted was to help them through this time of suffering and loss? Her husband loved the citizens of this village and their actions today would cause him immense pain. Yet still, after fifteen months, they continued to hold his ministrations at bay in the deluded hope that Reverend Stanley would return.

But Catherine knew that William would never cease trying to win their trust. No matter how much they distanced themselves or fired callous words at him, he would continue to take care of them, offering his help and friendship to all.

—

On Monday morning, William spent an hour in the church, beseeching God for guidance in his task of bringing comfort to the panicking villagers. From their outburst during yesterday's service, together with Stanley's accusations the day before, it was evident that the people he loved so much blamed his Anglican teaching for the outbreak of plague in their village.

The thought that they truly believed that to be true stabbed at William's heart. He'd tried *so* hard to make his services accessible to all, and the realisation that they despised him hurt more than he could say. Perhaps even worse, their vicious accusations had given him cause to question the Anglican doctrines he'd lived by all his life. He'd spent most of the night wondering if those doctrines could, in fact, be misguided, and that Puritan dogmas conveyed the rightful, Christian path.

By morning, William's mind was no clearer, although his hour of solitude and prayer in St Helen's had left him with a sense of peace and calm.

On leaving the church, he headed to Church Street, needing a stroll in the fresh air as his contemplations continued. By now it was late morning and the street was quiet, most folk either at work, or indoors, tending to children or household chores. Their wounding accusations had lodged in William's head, strident and unruly, although the stabbing pain they had induced in his chest had eased. He now felt able to consider the charges they voiced and strive to find a way of alleviating them.

It would seem that the villagers' fears stemmed from one vital difference in the way prayers were said during Sunday Worship. They believed William ignored the fact that they needed to renew their covenant with the Lord every time they prayed. That covenant involved them declaring their sinful state at birth and renewing their pledge of obedience to God in return for His forgiveness of those sins as they journeyed through life.

But, he argued with himself, didn't The Lord's Prayer – spoken by him during many Anglican services – contain a similar plea: *Forgive us our trespasses as we forgive those that trespass against us?*

To Anglicans, The Lord's Prayer was intended to be spoken, whereas to Puritans, it was a guide on how to conduct their everyday lives. Surely it was suitable for both? William reasoned, though he had no intentions of voicing that opinion in his next service.

The villagers also claimed that William always insisted on being the one to lead them through the prayers, most of which were from the Anglican Prayer Book. Knowing that to be only partly true – since he had permitted them to say their own prayers on many occasions – William felt he was being judged unfairly.

Intending to mull over the best way to deal with the villagers' assertions as he walked, William continued along Church Street. His first thought was that he should remain true to his Anglican calling and allow no room for compromise. And yet… in allowing them to say their own versions of psalms and prayers, hadn't he been making compromises since the day of his very first service in Eyam?

Could he, then, at this time of great uncertainty and fear, allow them even greater freedom in the way they worshipped – just enough to help them to believe that their prayers were being heard?

Of course you can't! his own voice sounded inside his head. *You've given in enough to their demands already.*

William knew that to be true, and it filled him with guilt. After fifteen months of his ministry, the Puritan villagers were no closer to accepting his faith, or his Prayer Book, than they had been before his arrival.

And yet, his conscience reminded him, *in the face of raging plague, that should be of little consequence. Concentrate on gaining the people's trust, even if it means making further allowances in your services. If you permit things to continue as they are, you could be facing far greater protests than that in the church yesterday.*

William's musings were brought to an abrupt halt by the sight and sounds of a large, yellow coach careering through the village. Strapped to its roof casing was an assortment of travel trunks and general baggage. The coach was followed by a covered wagon, of a type suitable for a few people to sit inside as well as carrying further baggage.

William's first thought was that it was merely some wealthy folk passing through on the way to visit friends or relatives. Then he noticed the crest on the carriage door. It was that of the Bradshaw family. He could only deduce that they were leaving Eyam and, by the amount of baggage they were taking with them, probably for some time. Despite being one of the few families in Eyam able to control the way in which things were done, especially in times of crisis, the Bradshaws were fleeing from the plague-stricken village, and would likely remain away until the plague had well and truly left it.

He wondered how many other influential or landowning families had already done the same.

Seven

Thursday, October 15 1665

The knock on the rectory door at one-thirty in the afternoon could mean only one thing. Someone was here to report another death.

'It's Mrs Syddall again, Reverend,' Joan said, peeping round the study door. 'She's very upset and I'm sorry to say, I think another of her children may have died. Shall I show her into here?'

'I'll bring her through myself, thank you, Joan.'

'Come through to my study, Elizabeth,' William said, his pity going out to the sobbing woman perched on a chair in the hall. This poor lady had already lost her husband, John, and two of their seven children to the plague. John, had only been buried yesterday.

'It's Ellen, Reverend, our eldest,' she started, once they were seated in the study. 'She died this morning. She was twenty-three, and such a delightful young woman.'

'She was indeed,' William agreed, recalling Ellen's lovely face and sweet nature. 'And a credit to her parents.'

'Ellen had been ill for the past three days,' Elizabeth croaked, knuckling further tears from her eyes. 'But although we knew it was the plague she'd caught, just like the others, I somehow thought that… that the Lord would spare her because she was to be married on the last day of the month. She and Adam were already betrothed when the plague struck Eyam and they decided then not to wait any longer.'

'I have that Saturday marked in my diary, Elizabeth. Ellen's death is, indeed, a tragedy.'

William waited whilst Elizabeth composed herself again. 'I'll come and say the blessings over Ellen in about half an hour, if that's convenient for you. I'll also call on our sexton and arrange the burial for ten o'clock tomorrow morning.'

'Both times are suitable, thank you, Reverend. I've already washed Ellen and dressed her in clean clothes.'

Elizabeth stifled a yawn and William guessed she'd had little sleep for days, especially with her youngest son, eighteen-month-old Josiah, to care for as well as coping with her aching grief. 'I'd best get home,' she said. 'Emmott is sitting with the three younger ones, so I can't be away for long. Josiah is always cranky when he's tired and due for his afternoon nap.'

William nodded. 'I quite understand. I'll see you to the door and, as I said, I'll be along shortly to say the blessing.'

—

With little Josiah heavy in her arms and her younger sisters, Lizzie and Alice, quietly sobbing at her sides, Emmott Syddall blinked back her tears as she watched their mother toss the first handful of earth back into the grave of Ellen, her beautiful elder sister. Elizabeth's actions were followed by Adam, Ellen's devastated betrothed, as he scooped a handful of earth from the waiting mound and dropped it onto the lonely coffin.

Elizabeth relieved Emmott of Josiah, enabling her three daughters to participate in the initial refilling of Ellen's grave.

Emmott's heart was heavy and her mind refused to contemplate life without the sister she loved so much. Ellen had been Emmott's constant companion when they were growing up. The two had happily helped their mother about the house, often caring for their younger siblings, allowing Elizabeth time to rest, or sit quietly with her sewing.

But at this moment, with her sister lying cold in her grave, Emmott's pain engulfed her and she strove to draw comfort from the fact that Ellen had been dearly loved by so many.

The sexton returned the first shovel of earth into Ellen's grave while Reverend Mompesson recited a prayer for the dead:
Unto Almighty God we commend the soul of our departed sister
and commit her body to the ground;
earth to earth, ashes to ashes, dust to dust...

Eventually, the mourners departed, with Adam returning to his own home. For him to accompany Ellen's family to a 'plague house' was deemed unthinkable by his parents.

—

It was a small gathering in the cemetery of St Helen's two days later, despite the number of friends and relatives that Jane and Peter Hawksworth had in the parish. Few risked attending funerals for fear of being stricken by the seeds of plague that still hovered around the afflicted corpse. Yet Mary was determined that her young friend and neighbour would not stand alone at the burial of her fifteen-month-old son, Humphrey.

As the coffin was lowered into a tiny grave next to that of his father, William prayed for the child:

Seven

*We have come together to worship God,
to thank Him for His love and remember the short life
of Humphrey; son of Peter and Jane Hawksworth.
We share their grief and commend Humphrey to the
eternal care of the Lord.*

Already fragile and tearful due to the ongoing sickness of early pregnancy, the torment of losing little Humphrey, so soon after the deaths of her husband and mother, was too much for Jane to bear. Mary held the young woman in her arms while Alexander stood by, ready to support them should grief cause Jane to collapse. But Jane stood her ground as tears rolled down her face.

October was well underway and a coolness hovered on the air, bringing a welcomed respite from the oppressive heat of summer. Leaves fluttered silently down to swathe the cemetery in autumnal splendour, a few coming to rest on the tiny coffin about to be buried. Yet Mary knew that, blinded by her tears, the beauty of the season would be lost to Jane.

—

As October ticked by and trees grew bare, smiling faces became a rarity in Eyam. Few days remained unscathed, and groups of grieving families gathered in the church almost daily to say goodbye to their loved ones.

By now, the early symptoms of plague were known by most in the village, whether they were pounding headaches, overwhelming fatigue or nausea and loosening of the bowels. They also knew that, in a matter of days, those early symptoms would rapidly worsen until the blackened extremities, bleeding from the mouth or nose, and hideous buboes would appear. Eventually, the voracious jaws of death would reign supreme.

In the early afternoon of the twenty-seventh of October, Mary's elder son, thirteen-year-old Jonathan Cooper, took his final breath. Despite having constantly nursed and bathed him for the last three days, watching him grow weaker and weaker, Mary had clung to the hope that he would recover. But all her prayers and perseverance with Humphrey Merrell's remedies had been in vain. By yesterday, she had faced the awful truth that her son would eventually die. It was simply a matter of time.

Mary washed Jonathan's body and dressed him in his best set of clothes before she and Alexander wrapped him in a shroud. Later that afternoon, Reverend Mompesson recited the prayers and blessings over his body, just as he would over any deceased man, woman or child. Tomorrow, her son would be buried in the cemetery of St Helen's.

'You have my sincere condolences, Mrs Hadfield,' Reverend Mompesson said. 'Only time and your faith in God can help you through the weeks ahead. October has been an unhappy month for Eyam and I pray daily that once winter fully arrives, the number of deaths from plague will considerably drop.'

Mary momentarily hung her head, overcome with grief, and her tears flowed freely down her cheeks. 'I pray for that, too, Reverend. Losing both of my sons is hard to bear and I don't know how I'll cope for the next few weeks. But I shall put my trust in the Lord and hope I find a way to go on living without constantly weeping. I have Alexander to think of and I owe it to him to be strong.'

'You must allow yourself time to grieve, Mary. We all need to do that after the loss of someone dear to us, as I'm sure Alexander will understand. Having lived with your sons for some months now, he will feel some grief, too. I know how he grieved over the death of George Viccars, and he had only known that young man for a matter of weeks.'

Mary nodded. 'Alexander is a kind and caring man and I shall pray to the Lord to keep him safe.'

—

The deaths of Elizabeth Syddall's two youngest daughters, Lizzie and Alice, within two days of each other during the last week of October, almost brought her to her knees. She had lost not only her beloved husband, John, but five of their seven children to the plague, and the pain of it all left her weak and constantly in tears. If not for the support of Emmott, her pretty and kind-hearted second child, Elizabeth knew she would never have coped, especially when little Josiah was in a cantankerous mood.

Elizabeth and her husband had been delighted when Emmott announced her betrothal to Rowland Torre, son of a prominent family of millers in Stoney Middleton. Then this cursed plague had come to Eyam and taken away any chance of happiness from so many of them.

It was mid-afternoon on Friday, the thirtieth of October, and mother and daughter were enjoying an hour or so of peace whilst little Josiah took his usual nap. Elizabeth glanced up from the embroidery that had become her means of blocking her mind from the pain and worry. Emmott had wandered across to the window and appeared to be staring at the cottages opposite. 'Is everything all right, my love?'

'I'm fine, Mama, just thinking.'

'A penny for them…'

Emmott came to sit beside her mother on the sofa, a small frown shaping her face. 'It just occurred to me that, with a few exceptions, all the deaths from plague in Eyam have been in the three houses across the road, and our own.'

Elizabeth twisted round to face Emmott, guessing she had more to say.

'In Stoney Middleton, Rowland's Aunt Scythe and Uncle Humphrey, as well and three others in their household, have also died of plague. And all of them became ill after Scythe had spent a few days in the stricken Hawksworth household across the road from us.' Emmott held out her hands. 'Surely, Mama, that must tell us something about where the plague is spreading from.'

Elizabeth laid her sewing on her lap and took Emmott's hands in her own. 'I can't deny that the same thought has crossed my mind and I'm sure others in Eyam will be thinking the same. But we cannot hold anyone responsible for spreading the plague since no one knows where it came from in the first place, or the means by which it travelled.'

'But George Viccars in the Hadfield house was the first to die of plague so –'

'And no one knows where he got it from.' Elizabeth's words

curtailed Emmott's speculations. 'George had lived with the Hadfields for two months by the time he became ill, so he didn't bring the plague here with him.'

Elizabeth heaved a sigh. 'What we must remember is that the families across the road are our friends, and are just as heartbroken at their losses as we are at ours. So, we must keep our opinions to ourselves on this or we, and our friends, may be subjected to harassment, or even physical abuse – especially if the plague continues to spread.'

Emmott's eyes opened wide then she seemed to accept her mother's counsel and changed the subject. 'Rowland hopes to visit me in a few days, if you have no objections.'

Elizabeth frowned. 'Don't you think Rowland is taking too great a risk by coming to Eyam while the plague is still rife? I realise his family has also suffered losses but we've lost six in this house and many other people in the village have died.'

'Rowland says he's prepared to take any risk in order to see me. I know that sounds overly romantic but neither of us know what tomorrow will bring. Look what happened to Ellen! She was due to be married tomorrow and now she's gone. The way I see it, Rowland and I could both be dead in a matter of weeks.'

'Don't say such things, Emmott, it's tempting Providence!' With that, Elizabeth burst into tears and Emmott threw her arms around her.

'I'm sorry for sounding selfish and inconsiderate, Mama. Our family has lost so much already and, deep down, I know you're right about Rowland coming here. Next time he comes I'll tell him not to do so again until the spring. Reverend Mompesson has let it be known that plague is a summer disease and he hopes the cold, winter months will be enough to bring it to an end.'

Elizabeth returned her daughter's embrace. 'Thank you, Emmott. It's for the best.'

—

Rowland did not appear at Bagshaw House until three days later. As Emmott stood in the doorway with the man she loved so dearly, she pleaded with him to stay away from Eyam until the plague was over. In the silence of the ensuing moments, Emmott watched him, wondering if his love for her would withstand the long months apart. Rowland's handsome face was blank and he seemed far away, in a world of his own. His old cheerfulness had gone and he had listened to Emmott's words without interruption.

'I couldn't bear to spend that long without so much as a glimpse of you,' he said, at last. 'Couldn't we meet somewhere midway between our villages? Just seeing you and knowing you were well would be enough until this disease has gone. We could keep some distance between us and simply talk.'

Emmott's spirits rose. 'What about Cucklett Delph? It's such a pretty place and would be easy for both of us to reach.'

'It would, and we could stand on either side of the brook to talk.'

'It will break my heart to see you and be unable to hold you in my arms, but at least I'll know you are safe. If you came to my home, or just into Eyam, you could catch the plague and I could never live with myself if you did. My mother and little

Seven

brother are all I have left and I simply can't lose you, too. How can the Lord allow people to suffer so much?'

Rowland shook his head and Emmott could see the sadness in his blue eyes. 'I have no answer to that, my sweet. I just know we must stay strong and follow the advice of those we trust to lead us through this awful time. The plague will leave us one day and we must pray that day is not too far away.'

There seemed nothing more to say without bringing them both further distress. But before he turned to leave, Rowland said, 'Promise you will meet me in Cucklett Delph every Saturday afternoon until next spring.'

'Of course I promise.'

'Then unless the weather is far too cold, or heavy rain or snow would make our meeting impossible, we will both be there a little after noon. Is that agreeable to you?'

Emmott nodded. 'It's the best thing to do until we can be together again.'

Eight

Friday November 6 1665

Lydia popped her head round the door of the rectory's sitting room. 'I'll be off to the market now, Mrs Mompesson. Are you sure you don't want to come with me this week?'

'I'd love to come,' Catherine said, cradling two-year-old Elizabeth in her arms on the sofa whilst George perused a book at her side. 'Unfortunately, William is too busy to stay with the children this morning. He has a wedding to do tomorrow, so he wants to prepare his Sunday service today. Besides, Elizabeth is feeling poorly and William wouldn't know how to deal with her if she was sick, or started bawling her head off as she usually does when she's unwell.'

Lydia stepped into the room, a small smile on her face. 'My husband was just the same when our daughter was little, as I'm sure, are most men. Well then, I'd best get off. I heard there'll be a fish stall this week and thought a nice bit of fish would make a pleasant change for you from meat this evening. I believe Peter Morten's been fishing in the Derwent, so I'm hoping he's caught some trout.'

Catherine's face brightened at the thought. 'Oh good, we haven't had fish for months, and we all love it. Trout would be wonderful, but we'll have whatever you can get.'

'From what I hear, the Derwent's well stocked with many kinds of fish at this time of year, November and December being particularly good for trout. So we might just be lucky.

Eight

But I won't pull my nose up at whatever Peter's got. I'm just thankful the snows haven't arrived yet and he managed to go fishing in the first place.

'Now, I really must be off or all the stalls will be empty and we'll have no meat, never mind fish. I shouldn't be long.'

As usual on a Friday, Eyam market was packed, although it didn't take Lydia long to realise that few customers were smiling. Most were purchasing their goods and moving on, keeping themselves to themselves. Some carried that haunted look of grief and loss.

Lydia headed straight to the fish stall, thankful that although Peter's trays were running low, there was still enough of the trout she had set her heart on. She soon completed the rest of her purchases, feeling particularly pleased to have acquired three brown trout for the Mompesson's meal later today. About to head back to the rectory, she spotted a small group of her friends and decided to join them for a general catch up and chat.

'I don't know about all of you, but I'm scared to death of catching this plague,' Annie Stubbs was saying, the fear in her dark eyes reflecting her words. 'They say that few folk ever recover from it. Once you've got it, it just gets worse and worse until your skin goes black and them ugly bubies appear. Then you only have a day or two to live. John says I should stay in the house and keep away from crowded places like the market.' She shrugged. 'I don't know if he's right or not, but how am I to buy our food, or milk from the farms, if I stay home all week? John'd soon grumble if he didn't have a good meal to come home to every night. Besides, he goes off to work at the lead mines every day, so you're not telling me he keeps away from people.'

'The swellings are called bub*oes*, Annie, not bub*ies*,' Lydia corrected the younger woman. 'By all accounts they're extremely painful, and horrible to look at. John has a point, though, hasn't he? The plague must be spread somehow, so it's up to all of us to avoid anyone or anything that is likely to be carrying it.'

Lydia held out her upturned hands. 'The trouble is, no one can be certain how plague *is* carried and spread, although everyone seems to have their own views about it. For a start, no one knows how it came to Eyam in the first place, so John could be right in saying that plague is caught by mingling with people who carry it. But that doesn't explain how George Viccars caught it when no one else in Eyam had it. And he hadn't been out of Eyam for a couple of months.'

Mary Skidmore nodded. Short and plump with a smile that could bring cheer to the dreariest of days, Mary always spoke her mind. 'I've heard that plague's carried in the air, and if that's true, none of us is safe anywhere, even in our own homes.'

'I'll remind John of that the next time he starts on about me going out,' Annie replied. 'And if he thinks I'm going to walk round all day with a flowery pomander stuck under me nose, he can think again!'

They all laughed at the thought, bringing a moment's relief from talk of disease and death. Then young Joan French piped up and the women once again faced the grim realities of the present. 'What I want to know is why this is happening to us. My Robert says that plague is always a punishment from God.

Eight

But what have we done in Eyam that was so bad?'

Lydia put her arm around the young woman's shoulders. 'Don't let anyone tell you that the people of Eyam are bad, Joan. We've had our share of thieves and drunkards over the years like anywhere else, but most of us are honest, hard-working folk who try to lead good lives and go to church on a Sunday, even if our new reverend isn't of the faith we've followed for years. But I believe he's a good and kind man who means well, and –'

'But he's not the reverend we want – or need – in Eyam!' Mary Skidmore's face wrinkled with distaste as the other women nodded agreement. 'Mrs Mompesson is a lovely, kind lady, and no one could find fault with her. But her husband has no idea how services were held by Reverend Stanley and he's no intention of finding out. He's just another rigid Anglican, like that Shoreland Adams before him.'

'That's true,' Annie agreed. 'And it served him right that we all stormed out of church a few weeks ago. If any of us are to survive this plague, he needs to let us pray to the Lord ourselves in our Sunday service.'

'As a matter of fact, Reverend Mompesson has worked hard to understand our faith,' Lydia informed them. 'And don't forget how he's allowed us to recite the psalms in our own way.'

She took a deep breath and exhaled slowly, saddened by the expressions of scathing doubt on their faces. 'All I am saying is that we need to give Reverend Mompesson a chance. Not everything he preaches goes against Puritan beliefs – as you know from listening to his sermons. He means well and cares about us all. And, as we all agree, you couldn't meet a nicer lady than Mrs Mompesson.'

Lydia smiled at the nodding heads. 'So, Joan, if God *is* punishing us, it's for the sins of a mere few.'

'Perhaps it's because those silly boys took cows into the church and left them there to foul the nave back in July,' Annie said, shaking her head at the thought. 'What an awful thing to do in such a sacred place as the Lord's own house. Didn't Reverend Stanley teach us that the wrath of the Lord is terrible to behold? As you said, Lydia, perhaps we're all being punished for the sins of just a few.'

'There are folk in this village who will tell of hearing Gabriel's Hounds howling in the air over the moors on dark nights.' Joan shuddered at her own words. 'Some people say they're the souls of unbaptised children, and their howling is a sign that death or misfortune is coming. Then there're folk as say they've seen white crickets in their hearth, and that's another sign that doom is coming.'

Lydia picked up the heavy basket of provisions which had lain by her feet whilst they chatted, and made to leave. 'I've heard those tales too, Joan, but I've yet to hear any howling or see any white crickets jumping around my own hearth, or in the rectory. Have you?' Joan shook her head. 'Then I suggest we don't panic about such things until we witness them for ourselves.

'As for seeking the Lord's forgiveness for our sins, we can all do that when we say our prayers each night,' she added, by way of rounding things up. 'Asking God to "forgive us our trespasses" is written in The Lord's Prayer, after all, so declaring our own wrongdoings would let God see that we know we've done something wrong and are sorry for it.'

Eight

Lydia smiled round at her friends, acknowledging the nodding heads. 'But now, I've stood here chatting for long enough and need to get back to the rectory. I'll see you there in an hour, Joan, and the rest of us will see each other in church on Sunday.'

—

Once the children were tucked into their beds that evening, William and Catherine settled in the sitting room in order to share their thoughts for the day. Perched on the sofa to face William in his armchair, Catherine said, 'I have no requests to make today, but I wondered if you'd heard the latest news from the village.'

Smiling, William held out his hands. 'I won't know whether I've heard it or not until you tell me what it is.'

'Well, I don't need to tell you that many of our villagers are panicking about catching the plague. Their fear is understandable, of course; I am greatly worried for our own family. But did you know that a goodly number of Eyam's residents are leaving… fleeing to other towns and villages? Most of them are poor and unless they have relatives to take them in, how do they expect to live in a strange town, especially as winter is almost upon us? They will not find shelter without the coin to pay for it, and without paid work they will never have the coin. Without food and shelter, they will surely die.

'Oh William, dying of plague is not a death to be wished upon anyone. But being frozen to death, out in the open, would also be dreadful.'

William rose, seated himself beside his wife and took her hand. 'People have been leaving Eyam since the earliest cases of plague became known in September, Catherine. And since none of them has returned, I can only assume they found homes somewhere and a means of earning a living. But I do take your point regarding those leaving the village now that winter draws near.'

Catherine nodded, seemingly thinking about that.

'Of more importance, perhaps,' William continued, 'is the fact that news of the plague in Eyam will doubtless have spread throughout Derbyshire by now, perhaps even further afield. It may well be that most of the poor folk choosing to leave now will find that nowhere at all will give them shelter, or employment. We know that some of the larger settlements in this region have posted guards around their boundaries to turn away anyone they believe to be from Eyam. We also know that news of Eyam's plight has reached at least fourteen miles from here. I am told that the citizens of Sheffield have even erected barriers, and their guards are particularly hostile to strangers at their gates.

'I fear that some of those turned away may end up living in caves, or amongst the rocks on Eyam Moor, or merely in fields out in the open. To their way of thinking, anywhere is preferable to staying in a plague-ridden village.'

William heaved a heartfelt sigh. 'Sadly, I am not in a position to stop anyone from leaving. I am only the rector here, and my authority comes a lowly second to that of titled residents and wealthy land or mine-owners. I'm hoping that when winter becomes really bitter and the cases of plague drop, people still in this village will be prepared to stay here, and that anyone trying to survive on the moors will come back.

'Now, is there anything else you wanted to add, my dear?'

'Only that you do not seem to have heard that the Bradshaw and Sheldon families were amongst some of the wealthier families to have already left the village.' Catherine shook her head, her face contorted in disdain. 'They evidently felt no duty or compulsion to remain in control while plague takes the poor villagers one by one. Selfish and irresponsible is what I call it. It goes without saying that rich folk often have second homes to flee to or, at least, equally wealthy families and friends willing to take them in.'

She glanced at William as though anticipating rebuke for her scathing judgement of others. 'I'm sorry if my opinion of those people is uncharitable, William. It's simply that I am extremely concerned about the number of our villagers dying, and being helpless to do anything about it. Seeing the rich people leaving makes me even more concerned for the poor who have no other choice than to stay. But running away to other towns, or ending up living on the moors in the bleakness of winter, will not keep death at bay.'

'I understand how you feel and I know you don't make judgements of people lightly, Catherine. But wherever plague strikes, so many people die that those able to flee will do so, whether they are rich or poor. I do know that the Sheldons were amongst the first landowners to leave Eyam. They have a second farm on the edge of the moors to the north and decided to live there until plague left the village. And I witnessed the Bradshaws leaving myself, three weeks ago.

'Self-preservation is inborn in all of us, my dear. I've heard that the high numbers of wealthy people who left London when plague struck the city – including King Charles himself, I might add – were instrumental in carrying plague to towns as far away from the city as Norwich, Yarmouth and even Derby. Since I cannot recall any Londoners, or folk from any of the stricken towns, coming to Eyam, I can only wonder how the plague travelled here.'

As he and Catherine headed upstairs to bed, William decided he would not pursue his intention of writing to his uncle in Sheffield. He had hoped that the kindly man would agree to permitting Catherine and the children to stay in his home until Eyam was free of the plague. But after listening to his wife's low opinion of the wealthy folk fleeing from Eyam, he knew she would never, willingly, agree to go.

Perhaps best to leave things as they are. For now.

—

By the end of the third week of November the lingering warmth of autumn was rapidly curtailed. Harsh winds swept in from the east and the air became intensely cold. Once again, snow draped the hills, moors and villages with a mantle of white, and nights grew cold enough to create patches of glassy, slippery ice from the many puddles along the uneven, dirt roads of Eyam.

'I swear, we're more likely to die of a cracked skull or a broken back than plague before the ice on our roads has had time to thaw of a morning,' Lydia said to Catherine as they carried the mutton stew and root vegetables through to the din-

Eight

ing room for the evening meal. Lydia returned to the kitchen for the bread-and-butter pudding for dessert while Catherine arranged the drinking glasses in the correct places.

'It's a good thing you're staying indoors now that the weather's turned, Mrs Mompesson,' Lydia continued on her return. 'Going outside would do your condition no good at all. Best to stay where it's warm and teach your little ones all the things they'll need to know when they're grown up.'

'I do that every day, anyway, but that doesn't stop me yearning to be outdoors for a short time each day. Oh, don't mind me, Lydia. I'm like this every winter. Being cooped up makes me depressed, especially when I can't even stroll around the rectory garden because it's so cold. And I would have liked to pay my respects at Annie Stubbs' funeral today.'

'There were few mourners there, despite Annie having many friends in the village. It was the same at her husband's funeral yesterday.'

Catherine nodded and Lydia added, 'I can't help wondering if it could have been Annie's husband who took the plague back to their home from someone or something at the lead mines. After all, John died the day before Annie, so he could have caught it first. But it serves no purpose to apportion blame… Ah, here come the rest of your family.'

'We could not ignore the wonderful aromas coming from this room for a moment longer,' William said, grinning. 'We thought you'd never call us, so here we are, quite uninvited.'

'Well, I'll be off home, then,' Lydia said, laughing as she ruffled George's hair. 'Enjoy your meal, and I'll see you tomorrow morning, provided I can stay upright on those icy roads.'

As William had predicted, the number of plague deaths dropped rapidly with the onset of the frigid winter conditions and villagers began to feel hopeful that the disease would not return until the spring, or preferably, not at all. But for Catherine, the winter meant she was once again confined to the rectory. She devoted her time to teaching the children and was delighted with their progress. Even little Elizabeth, now nearing her third year, knew many of the letters in the alphabet and could identify most of the animals and birds shown to her, as well as most of the items in the rectory.

As Christmas drew near with the start of Advent, William made the decision to place the Nativity scene in St Helen's again.

'I couldn't live with myself… my guilty conscience… if I neglected my duty to the Anglican faith,' he explained to Catherine as they enjoyed their breakfast with George and Elizabeth. 'It's my duty to celebrate Christmas, and that includes placing the Nativity scene in the church. I had hoped that some of the villagers, if only a mere few, would come to the Christmas Eve Communion.'

Catherine shook her head. 'From what Lydia tells me, I'm afraid you'll be sadly disappointed. The people of Eyam remain very much against Christmas being celebrated. I fear you will face hostility and even abuse over this issue, William. They made their views on the Nativity scene and Christmas celebrations clear to you last year, so what makes you think things will be different now?'

Eight

William looked downcast and Catherine reached out to take his hand. 'I think only of your safety, husband. I couldn't bear it if you were badly hurt, and would rather you didn't incite them to protests in the first place. You have admitted yourself that converting Eyam's citizens to our faith could take many years. I am sure your bishops would understand if you explained the situation to them. Besides, I doubt they'd remove you from your position here while the threat of ongoing plague hangs over us.'

'I believe you're right, my dear. They'd be unlikely to find anyone to take my place at this time. But nothing can persuade me to abandon Anglican traditions at Christmas.'

'Why is Christmas any different to Easter? Surely, Easter is the foremost of Christian celebrations, yet you abandoned all thoughts of celebrating that with the villagers earlier this year for fear of provoking the same reaction they'd displayed at Christmas.'

William was silent for some moments whilst he thought. 'You're right. I suppose it's because my parents loved Christmas and our celebrations of it were always joyous. It became a special occasion for me, too.'

He sighed, deeply. 'You have given me much to think about, Catherine. Perhaps it would be better all round to continue normal services in St Helen's throughout the Christmastide. I have no right to put our parishioners' souls at risk by denying them weekly prayers and sermons. We can celebrate Christmas ourselves, here in the rectory, and create our own little nativity scene.'

'Then I suggest we allow Lydia and Joan several days off. With full pay, of course.'

Nine

During the first few weeks of 1666, William remained hopeful that the plague had been halted by the piercing cold of winter. Between the beginning of November and the end of February he recorded only twenty-nine more deaths, and a dozen of those had been from the usual winter ailments and old age. Throughout those months, his worries over bubonic plague had become surpassed by concerns for Catherine's health. Yet again, he admitted to himself that the Derbyshire winters were no less harsh than those along the North Yorkshire coast.

With consumption keeping her weak and prone to illness, Catherine could not cope with such cold. Without the help and support she received from the sweet Joan French and their wonderful cook, Lydia, William knew his wife would not have coped with their second Derbyshire winter. As it was, Catherine had no need to leave the rectory for several weeks.

As the new year progressed and spring hovered in the air, William was filled with the ever-constant fear that with the return of warmer weather, bubonic plague would return to the village. And with it, the number of deaths would soar.

—

Late March 1666

Mary Hadfield held her distraught young neighbour in her arms as she sobbed. Only three days ago, Jane Hawksworth

Nine

had celebrated the birth of a tiny daughter, whom she named Alice. Earlier today, the babe had died.

'Oh, Mary, I have lost everything – my husband, my parents, my little son, and now my daughter. I have nothing left in this world to cherish as my own.'

Mary gently pushed her neighbour to arm's length and wiped the tears from her cheeks. 'Take heart in the fact that you're still a young woman, and a pretty, thoughtful and loving one at that,' she said, by way of giving Jane hope and reassurance. 'Once this plague has left us, there will likely be several young men in the same position as you. You will find someone who will love and cherish you, just as much as Peter did. And although I know you cannot bear to think of it so soon after losing little Alice, you have many child-bearing years ahead of you.'

'Thank you, Mary. I shall think of your words when grief threatens to overwhelm me. I knew in my heart that Alice would not survive. She moved so seldom in my womb, as though she sensed how I was struggling through the long winter months on my own, and the bouts of coughing I endured. She was such a tiny, sickly-looking babe compared to Humphrey. I realise that all newborns are different to others, but Alice looked unwell from the moment she was born. Yet I accept that it was the Lord's will, and she will be cared for in Heaven.'

—

As March drew to a close, William thanked God that no more than six of his parishioners had died that month, bringing the total number of deaths since the end of the previous October to thirty-five. But as April progressed, his hopes for an end to the plague became clouded with uncertainty. Although the number of deaths had risen by very little so far that month, a continuation of the fall in numbers had not occurred.

Life in Eyam continued as normally as possible. People pursued their everyday work and William held his weekly services in St Helen's. Funerals for the departed and baptisms of the newly born still took place, as did weddings. One marriage William had conducted gave him particular pleasure, since one of the families concerned had suffered more losses to plague than most in the village. As he'd gazed upon the congregation, it had warmed his heart to see smiles on the faces of the Syddall family for the first time since last September…

Emmott Syddall stood with two-year-old Josiah and a few close relatives in the Church of St Helen as Reverend Mompesson joined in marriage her widowed mother, Elizabeth, and John Daniel, a widower and a foreman at the quarry. It was Saturday, the twenty-fourth of April and outside, the trilling of nesting birds and the hues and scents of spring, added to the joy of the occasion. For a couple of hours those gathered were able to forget the horrors of plague.

The match was a good one, and although Emmott still grieved for her father, she was happy to see her mother wed to a kind and gentle man and be able to smile again. It had been a difficult six months since John Syddall's death and Emmott knew that the family would not have survived much longer without the income and support of a man in the house.

Three days later, after spending time playing with Josiah

Nine

whilst her mother tended her garden, Emmott realised she didn't feel at all well. It was a relief when the child eventually fell asleep, as he usually did of an afternoon. She lifted him from her lap and laid him on the sofa to sleep, and feeling a headache coming on, she sank back into the chair and closed her eyes.

'Emmott, my love, are you unwell? It isn't like you to nod off in the afternoon.'

Emmott slowly opened her eyes and squinted at her mother, her hand going to her brow. 'I don't know, Mama. I have a dreadful headache and although I've been asleep, I feel exhausted.'

'In that case, you can take yourself straight to bed while I make you a warm drink with chamomile. It should ease your aching head and help you to sleep for the rest of the afternoon.'

'I can't leave you to prepare the meal on your own, especially with Josiah to look after.'

'Yes, you can, and I won't hear another word about it. I'll bring the drink up to you and, hopefully, you'll feel well enough to join us for the evening meal.'

Emmott did not rouse that evening and believing it to be for the best, her mother let her sleep on. But during the night, Elizabeth was wakened by Emmott calling out. As she entered her daughter's bedchamber, the stench was enough to confirm Elizabeth's fears. Emmott's breathing was ragged, her face beaded with sweat and her bedding and nightgown covered in vomit and excrement. Her beloved daughter had become the seventh member of her family to have contracted bubonic plague.

Elizabeth swallowed down the wail that threatened to erupt, but could not prevent the tears from streaming down her face as she sank to her knees beside her daughter's bed.

Dear Lord, I beg you not to take Emmott away from me. She is good and kind and means so much to many of us in Eyam. Help her to overcome this plague and live the rest of her life with her beloved Rowland.

Having done this so many times before, Elizabeth stripped Emmott's soiled clothing and bedsheets before washing her down and redressing her in a nightgown, which would be easier to change than any daytime clothes.

Throughout the next two days, the endless round of washing Emmott and changing her clothing and bedding began. Elizabeth also ensured her daughter was given the potions supplied by Humphrey Merrell, and took frequent drinks of water. Though exhausted herself, she rarely left Emmott's room, whilst her new husband, John, took care of Josiah and cooked them all simple meals. Elizabeth would always be indebted to him for his kindness.

In the evening of the twenty-seventh day of April, the first blackening of Emmott's skin occurred, followed soon after by the appearance of buboes on her neck and in her armpits. Elizabeth now knew her daughter's end was near, and that nothing she did could prevent it. Throughout the night she kept her bedside vigil, frequently praying to the Lord that Emmott would find eternal joy and peace in His Paradise.

—

Nine

The following morning, Lydia arrived at the rectory a little later than usual. Catherine was chatting to Joan who was cleaning the sitting room windows while young George amused his little sister by making her toys dance on the rug.

'I'm sorry I'm late, Mrs Mompesson,' Lydia said, her woeful expression and glistening eyes revealing she was greatly upset. 'I… I just met Elizabeth Syddall on her way home from talking to the reverend in the church. I'm sorry to have to tell you that Elizabeth's last remaining daughter, Emmott, died of the plague before dawn this morning. Elizabeth has already washed her and dressed her in a clean set of clothes. She said that Reverend Mompesson will shortly be going to Bagshaw House to say prayers over Emmott's body ready for burial tomorrow.'

Teardrops rolled down Lydia's cheeks. 'Emmott was one of the loveliest young women you could ever wish to meet, betrothed to the handsome Rowland Torre from Stoney Middleton. Elizabeth said the two had been meeting every Saturday in Cucklett Delph over the winter so that Rowland didn't need to come into Eyam while the plague was still here. The poor man is bound to wonder what has happened when Emmott fails to meet him this week, or any other week from now on.'

'Rowland will be in our prayers, as will Elizabeth and so many others who have lost loved ones to the plague,' Catherine said. 'We must have faith that God will not make us suffer for much longer.'

'Yes, I know you're right, but the death of sweet Emmott means that seven of the nine members of the Syddall family have now gone.' Lydia dabbed her eyes and blew her nose, then took a calming breath. 'Elizabeth is inconsolable and will take some time to get over her grief, despite having a new husband to care for her.'

Catherine put a comforting arm around Lydia's shoulders. 'All the more reason why those of us still here should thank God for giving us life in the first place, and enjoy it whilst we can. I don't believe He would want us to do otherwise.'

Lydia sniffed. 'It's just heartbreaking to see so many of our families and friends taken by this evil disease. If the Lord is still punishing us for the pranks of those foolish boys with the cows, His wrath is surely terrible to behold.'

Thankful that William was not present to hear such talk, Catherine could only nod in agreement.

—

By the end of May, when the days had gained a blissful warmth and blossoms and meadow flowers adorned the land, only four more deaths had occurred, two of which were due to natural causes. The spirits of Eyam folk began to rise.

William grieved for the pain and loss these poor villagers had suffered. Mary Hadfield's neighbours, the Thorpe family of nine, was now completely gone, although several of their relatives kept the name alive in Eyam. Along with the rest of the village, he prayed that the months of plague were almost over. But, as he had feared, during the first two weeks of June the heat of summer took hold, and along with it came the anticipated rise in plague deaths.

The 'summer disease' had returned with a vengeance.

'I beg you to take us all away from here,' Catherine pleaded

Nine

as they sat down for one of their chats once the children had gone to bed. It was Sunday and St Helen's had been filled with downcast and tearful villagers for the service that day. 'It is only the fourteenth day of the month and I think we're in agreement that the plague will take more and more of our villagers as the summer progresses. I truly fear for our own children.'

William stared at her, taken aback by her sudden request, especially after what she had said about those 'selfish and irresponsible' rich people leaving the village.

'We could return to Yorkshire... It is too great a risk to stay here. Please let us leave, William, if only for our children's sake.'

He reached out to take his wife's hand. 'You know I could never forsake the people I have sworn to take care of, Catherine, no matter how dire the crisis we face. But it would be a huge relief for me to know that my beloved wife and children were in a safe place.' His brow wrinkled as he thought. 'I shall write to my Uncle John in Sheffield, asking his permission for the three of you to stay at his home until the plague is –'

'No! I refuse to go anywhere without you. Please don't make me do that William. I haven't caught the plague in all the weeks I've been in and out of the homes of plague victims. If you refuse to leave, then I will stay with you. But I agree that our children should be sent to safety.'

'I want you to go with them,' William repeated. 'I would never forgive myself if anything happened to you because I allowed you to stay.'

'And I would never forgive you if you made me go.'

William sighed. 'Are you sure you'd be happy staying here without George and Elizabeth, my dear?'

'No, I am not. I'm not sure of anything at present... except that I want all of us to leave Eyam together!'

'You know I can't agree to that.'

Catherine swept her welling tears away with the backs of her hands. 'George and Elizabeth's leaving here will break my heart and I shall miss them terribly. George will think we must hate them both and don't want them with us. Elizabeth is too young to think that way, although she is bound to miss us for some time. But no matter how upset they both feel, they will not be in danger of catching this wicked plague in Sheffield.'

'If you are certain, my dear, I shall write to my uncle with our request and hope he can send his coach to collect them. I'll also ask if he could spare a woman in his employ who is accustomed to dealing with children to accompany them on the journey. I would like to see them leave for Sheffield before the end of the month.'

'Why can't we all go to Uncle John's?'

William heaved an irritated sigh. 'You know the answer to that, and constantly repeating the question will *not* make me change my mind. You have already agreed that our children will be safer in Sheffield, and I would feel a great deal happier if you agreed to go with them.'

Catherine's tears rolled down her cheeks as she seemed to accept that William would never be persuaded to abandon his responsibilities to the people of Eyam.

'Yes, I did agree to sending the children away and will abide by that decision. It will be a great worry lifted from my shoulders. But my duty lies here, with you, and I will not forsake it. How would I know you were safe if I was in

Nine

Sheffield? You could catch the plague and I wouldn't be here to take care of you.'

'You mustn't think that way, Catherine. Everyone in Eyam is at risk of catching the plague and God will take whomsoever He wills. I pray daily to be permitted to live long enough to guide our parishioners through this awful time.'

Catherine paused, seeming to think about that before nodding. 'Yes, George and Elizabeth must go to your Uncle John's, but I beg you to let me stay here with you.'

'I will agree to that, although it is against my better judgement.' He smiled at her and changed the subject. 'Now, I'd like to discuss the very situation that has prompted us to decide to send our children away.'

William was silent for some moments before taking a breath and admitting, 'I'm not sure how to tackle the situation in the village for the best. I've thought of a few things we could do to help matters, but whether or not people would accept them is a different matter. Would you care to hear my thoughts on this before we take to our bed?'

'I am always happy to hear them, as you well know.'

'Very well. Perhaps you alone know how hard I have worked to build up the villagers' trust in me.' Catherine nodded. 'Yet even now, after almost two years, most of them will still not join in with the services I hold, despite the church being packed to the door every Sunday. Oh, they listen to my sermons well enough, but they still won't say the prayers or sing the hymns from the Book of Common Prayer.'

'Yes, I've observed all that every week. It is my belief that your parishioners do not flock into church every Sunday to hear your services. They were led to detest the Anglican Church and its new prayer book by that rabid Puritan, Reverend Stanley. They come to church because they fear God's wrath if they do not.'

William's eyebrows rose but he did not chide her for voicing such an opinion. 'Admittedly, the village being stricken by plague so soon after our arrival hasn't helped, but I do feel that it isn't me, personally, they cannot accept. It is just my Anglican beliefs.'

'Most of the villagers really like you as a man, William, as they do our family in general. They are just extremely devout Puritans, and a faith so deeply ingrained cannot be dismissed or overturned in a mere two years.'

'That's the way I see it, too. It will probably take a few generations before the people of Eyam accept the Church of England, no matter what I – or any other Anglican clerics – do or say. Persuading them all to do what is best for the village may well be impossible.'

Catherine frowned. 'Where, exactly, is all this leading?'

'I'm trying to say that in the interests of the people of Eyam, whilst the plague is upon us, I ought to impose certain sanctions.'

'Have you any in mind?'

William rested his head on the high-backed sofa and momentarily stared at the ceiling. 'I've thought of two,' he said, fixing her with his dark-eyed gaze, 'both of which will be aimed at preventing the plague from spreading freely through the village. I also have a third sanction in mind, but for a different purpose. It will doubtless be the most difficult for the

Nine

villagers to accept.'

He paused, and Catherine knew he would be collecting his thoughts.

'The main thing to realise,' he continued, 'is that any sanctions I issue would be based on the fact that I don't believe plague is caused by a miasma in the air, emanating from heaps of rotting waste in our streets, as they believed in London. They had a huge clean-up in the city at the start of the plague, and I'll grant you, doing so would make any city or town a cleaner and more attractive place to live in. Yet it did nothing to stop the disease from spreading. Nor did keeping braziers constantly glowing in the streets, or killing all the cats and dogs.

'No, my dear, I believe that plague is more likely to be passed on between people and, as I said, I want to focus on ways we can stop it spreading unrestrainedly in Eyam throughout the summer.'

Catherine thought about that. 'I think you are right about plague being passed from person to person. Most people in Eyam realise it takes just one person in a family to catch the disease for most, if not all, of that family to succumb to it. We only have to think about the poor Thorpes and Syddalls.'

William nodded. 'Unfortunately, there is nothing we can do to prevent that happening, which is why we must find ways of lessening the number of people being stricken in the first place. My main worry, of course, is that the villagers could outrightly refuse to obey any sanctions issued by me.'

'You may be right, especially as they still don't accept your religious teachings. We've even had to forego our celebrations of Christmas and Easter because the Puritans don't accept the

Anglican dating of them.'

William heaved an irritated sigh. 'I realise that, my dear, but I'd rather we didn't pursue that issue tonight. Combating the plague must be our priority and I really believe that sanctions are necessary in order to do that. But I need time to work a few things out. And, in order to do so, I need the advice and support of Reverend Stanley, who knows this village and its people better than I.'

Catherine could not help shuddering on hearing the former rector's name, but decided to say nothing. William had already made up his mind regarding his intentions.

'Tonight, my dear, I shall write the letter to John Bielby so it can be on its way tomorrow. And in the morning, I intend to walk over to the house of that "rabid Puritan", as you aptly named Reverend Stanley, and put my ideas for sanctions to him. I just hope he doesn't slam the door in my face when I arrive and will be prepared to hear me out.'

Ten

Reverend Stanley's cottage was located almost a mile from the centre of Eyam and less than a quarter of a mile from Eyam's boundary. Although William hadn't known its precise location, a brief word with Lydia had been enough to help him find it with ease. Set some fifty yards back from the Lydgate Road, it nestled amidst a large copse of oak and silver birch, dotted with a few ash. William's first impression was that Stanley had chosen a perfect place in which to conceal his continuing presence in Eyam.

He followed the winding path through the pretty, flower and shrub-filled garden, admiring the array of colours and savouring the heady scents of the many-hued roses, the blood-red poppies and snow-white lily-of-the-valley. Birds tweeted and trilled from the leafy branches of nearby trees while butterflies flitted and bees buzzed amongst the lovely blooms. An abundance of cream and yellow honeysuckle flowers embraced a wooden trellis around the oak door of the little whitewashed cottage. Thinking how out of keeping so much beauty seemed against the suffering of the villagers, William steeled himself to knock.

The door opened a fraction and one side of an ageing face appeared. 'Well, you're the *last* person I expected to see,' a voice sneered, leaving William wondering if this would be as far as a conversation with the former rector would get. But Stanley evidently soon recovered from his shock and deigned to show himself in entirety.

For a few moments, he continued to glower at William as though deciding whether or not to invite him in. Good manners seemingly prevailed and he heaved back the door, stepping aside to allow William to enter.

To William, Stanley appeared little different to the way he'd looked on the day they had encountered each other in St. Helen's eight months ago. On closer inspection, he realised that the hair on Stanley's now hatless head was even greyer, wispier and more dishevelled than it had been then, and the creases on his thin face were more deeply etched. Today, as dictated by the hot weather, Stanley wore a loose-fitting white shirt with a large collar and cuffs, tucked into knee-length breeches of a deep shade of brown. Around his waist was a brown leather belt with a silver buckle.

'Thank you,' William said as the ageing cleric gestured to a comfortable chair, inviting him to sit in the simply furnished but wonderfully bright and sunlit room. 'I trust you are keeping well?' Stanley gave a single, regal nod that made William smile. 'As you probably realise, I would not be disturbing your retirement unless I felt it vital to do so.'

'No, I don't believe you would, and had already come to the conclusion that you wish my advice, or assistance, on a matter pertaining to my… to our… village.'

William shuffled, wishing Stanley would return his smiles once in a while. But then again, perhaps the man's solitary existence would give him little reason to smile. 'Your deduction is an astute one, and although I've only seen you once in the village since my arrival in Eyam, the villagers often speak of the great respect they have for you. You will also be glad to

Ten

know how steadfastly they cling to their Puritan principles.'

'I did warn you they would not willingly accept the Church of England's views, did I not, Reverend Mompesson? However, I must confess that Daniel Lowe – the young man responsible for keeping my garden so well stocked and tended – has spoken on several occasions of the high regard in which the people hold you and your family.'

'Thank you, that is good to know.' William, nodded, unsurprised at the continued formality with which the old man conversed. He had not expected otherwise. 'I have always known it would take more than my lifetime for them to fully accept the prayers, sacraments and rites of the Church of England set out in the Anglican Prayer Book.'

Stanley shrugged. 'Most of us tend to cling to the beliefs and practises with which we grew up.'

'We do, indeed,' William admitted. 'But although I was raised to follow the teachings of the Church of England, I firmly believe that whichever Christian Church and style of service we follow, our basic belief in Christ is just the same. We are all Christians, and as such, we are taught to love others, no matter what their nationality, beliefs or customs. Hasn't there been enough persecution and hatred between us since the last King Henry turned his back on Rome? And the enormous clashes between King and Parliament that resulted in the Civil War served to multiply the conflicts between the Catholics and Anglicans who supported King Charles and the Puritans who supported Parliament. But surely, now the war is over, we should all be kind to one another?'

'Your views are a little naïve if you think there will be any peace for Puritans whilst the son of the beheaded Charles I is on the throne.' Stanley scowled. 'You must know that people of my faith have been leaving England for countries in which they would not be persecuted for the past four decades. And you expect us to give up our dearly held beliefs just like that.' Stanley clicked his fingers to illustrate his point. 'The fact that members of the Church you love so much are intent on converting all Puritans to their beliefs, speaks for itself.'

'I didn't come here to argue over our respective faiths, Reverend Stanley. I was hoping we could put our differences aside and work together as people who care about the people of Eyam and, indeed, about God's people everywhere.'

Stanley tilted his head and continued to stare at him as though weighing him up, but William surged ahead as though he hadn't noticed. 'I am in need of your advice on how to go about putting certain sanctions into place in order to prevent further, needless, spread of plague. After a welcomed drop in deaths from plague over the winter and spring, June has seen a sudden increase, which I fear will greatly escalate over the next few months.'

'You have thought of ways of preventing that happening?'

William shook his head. 'Nothing we do will stop the number of plague victims increasing with the heat of summer. But a few changes in the way things are done in Eyam could limit the ways in which plague is passed amongst us. The idea of a miasma in the air being the means it is carried is highly unlikely. Do you agree, Reverend Stanley?'

'Yes, I do… although, if that is so, I couldn't say how plague was brought to Eyam in the first place.'

William shrugged. 'There are some things to which we have no answers, but I am almost certain that people catch the plague by being in close proximity to someone who already has the disease. As my wife put it, we only have to think of the way in which plague has swept through entire families in a matter of days. And yet…'

He paused as his next point hovered in his thoughts. 'There are some plague-stricken families in Eyam in which some of their members remain free of the disease. Take Mary Hadfield and her husband, Alexander, for instance. Although the young journeyman, George Viccars, and Mary's two sons died of plague last autumn, as of today, neither Mary nor Alexander have succumbed to the disease. Perhaps even more surprising is the fact that Mary nursed all three of them until the end. The Hadfield's immediate neighbour, Jane Hawksworth, has similarly buried her husband and two young children, yet she remains free of the plague.'

Stanley nodded. 'As you said, Reverend Mompesson, there are some things to which we have no answers. We must simply trust that they are the Lord's will.'

He stood and walked over to gaze through the window at his lovely garden. 'A passing traveller coming from Derby a month ago mentioned that the residents of London were certain that some people contract a type of plague that is more deadly and displays different symptoms to the disease we generally refer to as bubonic.' William had not heard of this and his ears pricked up. 'Sufferers develop an ailment of the lungs, somewhat akin to pneumonia, which, in addition to the weakness, fevers, and headaches of bubonic plague, causes them severe chest pain and shortness of breath. They also sneeze and cough a great deal, often coughing up blood. You will surely see, Reverend Mompesson, how those latter two symptoms could be dangerous to anyone standing in proximity to such stricken plague victims.'

Stanley returned to his seat. 'So, do either of the sanctions you wish to impose take into account the idea of keeping away from other people?'

William nodded. 'They do just that, as a matter of fact, although I intend to hold a meeting for all villagers – at which I sincerely hope you will be present – during which everyone will have the opportunity to air their views, or question any of the sanctions put to them. I am very aware that any measures suggested will simply not work without their full cooperation.'

'I agree, so what proposals do you have in mind?'

'Firstly, I intend to hold all church services for the near future out in the open air, away from the closely packed pews within the confines of the church. Families will be expected to stand together, some distance from others, whilst the church itself would remain locked.'

Stanley's face indicated his concern regarding this proposal. 'The idea in itself is admirable in all but one thing. People of my faith are taught that to miss a single week of praying and confessing our sins in the House of the Lord will incur His wrath so greatly that we risk our souls being accepted into Heaven.'

'Many Anglicans believe the same, Reverend Stanley, but I'm sure there must be times in life when God will accept our reasons for worshipping in a place that is not a church. After all, we are not proposing that the villagers actually forego communal services. Did not the Israelites miss many services in the House of God when travelling to the promised land of Canaan? And did not Our Saviour teach many of His sermons out of doors?'

William held out his upturned hands as his thoughts poured forth. 'In my heart, I believe that God will know we are doing our utmost to save people's lives by overcoming this plague. Surely, He gave us all free will to act as we see fit?'

Stanley remained quiet for some moments as he considered William's words. Eventually, he said. 'Yes, you have a valid point, one I shall ponder on tonight. Now, have you any specific location in mind for holding your outdoor services?' William shook his head. 'Then I suggest you use Cucklett Delph.'

'I have heard that name mentioned a time or two, but despite living in Eyam for almost two years, I confess to having no idea of its location.'

'It is a delightful place, especially in summer. A little stream, known as the Jumber Brook, runs down from the moors to the north to flow through the middle of it. The stream appears to have cut its way through the limestone to burst out into the flatter area that has gradually widened over the years to resemble an old Greek or Roman amphitheatre.'

William nodded, appreciating the image thus far described, and Stanley continued, 'As far as your sermons are concerned, the best thing about Cucklett Delph is that part-way up the hillside to one side of this "amphitheatre" is an outcrop of bare limestone into which a shallow cave has been carved over the years. The flat platform left in front of this cave resembles a small stage, which would serve as an excellent pulpit. All your congregation would be able to see you up there, and your voice would easily be heard. Anything you say would be contained by the grassy hills on three of the delph's sides, whilst a fourth side, where the brook continues on its way, is wooded. And, of course, all the villagers will know where Cucklett Delph is.'

'It sounds perfect; thank you for suggesting it, Reverend Stanley. If you could give me directions to it, I'll take a walk out there as soon as I can.'

'I'm sure Lydia will do that, if you ask her. Now, what other sanctions had you in mind?'

William thought for a moment before replying. 'My second sanction is an extension of the first, albeit with its own particulars…'

They continued to discuss the second sanction, quickly reaching agreement on its importance and how it would be implemented. 'That all sounds straightforward enough,' Stanley said, pushing himself up from his comfortable chair. 'But there is another sanction I'd like to see imposed, which you may or may not have thought of. It could, however, prove to be the most difficult of the three to enforce, as well as being one for which we would most certainly require the consent of the majority of villagers. I would like to suggest it if I may.'

William smiled, pleased that Stanley was as enthusiastic as he was regarding imposing restrictions. 'By all means do, although it could well be similar to what I had in mind for my third sanction.'

Stanley's nod was tempered by a small frown that caused his wispy eyebrows to meet in the middle. 'Before I continue,

Ten

might I suggest we stroll around my herb garden to the rear of my cottage in order to enjoy a little fresh air as we speak?'

'If your rear garden is as lovely as your front one, I would be happy to stroll between the colourful and aromatic plants.'

'Good. Then we can return indoors and enjoy a cold drink whilst we devise our plan of action for this third sanction. That is, of course, dependent upon us being in full agreement regarding its implementation in the first place.'

They headed out to the rear of the cottage and William was greeted to another display of glorious hues and fragrances. After wandering between the many beds of herbs for a while, they sat on a wooden bench in order to talk.

Stanley twisted round to face William. 'Before you mentioned your idea of imposing sanctions on our villagers you said something that directly applies to what I am about to suggest. If I recall correctly, you pointed out that both you and I are men who care about the people of Eyam and, indeed, about God's people everywhere.'

'I did, and I truly believe it.'

'Then, let me reiterate a few facts that you will, doubtless, already know. Firstly, the plague has been raging in the city of London since the summer of last year. We know it was taken to other major towns, and likely a few villages, by some of the richer folk who fled there from London, as well as tradespeople and suchlike.'

Stanley paused, just long enough to gather his thoughts. 'Secondly, neither of us knows how the disease came to Eyam, but since we both discard the idea of it being carried by a miasma in the air, we must assume it was brought here by some person or persons. And given the areas in which plague has been prevalent, we can also surmise that it was brought to Eyam either from London, or one of the towns infected later on.'

'Most certainly, and I have said exactly the same to Catherine. Although, we still can't be certain that the disease was not sent by God as punishment for our sins, or even for the sins of a mere few.'

'No, we can't rule out that possibility, Reverend Mompesson. But now that plague is here, and set to rage through Eyam over the summer, for the people's sake we must deal with it as effectively as possible. 'Your first two sanctions should help to limit plague deaths *within* the village. Some people probably won't like them, but I'm sure that most will see the sense of them.'

Stanley was silent for some moments before he continued, his expression pensive. 'I confess, your earlier words jolted my thoughts, and I realised the wider implications of the plague that has taken hold of Eyam.'

'Are you saying we should find some way of ensuring the plague does not leave our village?' Stanley nodded. 'Then I must tell you, I have thought long and hard as to how that could be achieved. Unfortunately, the Bradshaws and other wealthy employers in Eyam who had the authority to insist that no one must leave the village, have already fled themselves. "Selfish and irresponsible" is how my wife described their actions.'

'Indeed, I quite agree. And it leaves you, Reverend Mompesson, as the one with the authority to take control. You are, after all, rector of this parish.'

'I have already had this conversation with my wife. I told

her that my authority is paltry compared to that of the titled and wealthy. But I confess to realising that in their absence, I am the one who must decide how things are done. I suppose, in part, I came to you as former rector, to give me some guidance on just how to go about taking control without the villagers refusing to do my bidding.'

'Make no mistake in believing that they will jump to any orders of mine. Besides, since you are the person in charge of their welfare, any orders you issue must be seen as coming from you.' Stanley heaved a sigh. 'It's all about trust. The villagers need to trust you to say and do the right thing, and make choices and decisions with their interests at heart.'

'I know that, but as long as I preach the Anglican faith, gaining their complete trust is not likely to be easy to achieve.'

Stanley gave an indignant grunt. 'So, you show your true colours at last! You have come to me in the hope that I will agree to soften the villagers up a little before you give the order that no one must leave the village.'

Stunned by the outburst, William inhaled deeply, allowing the aromatic scent of lemon balm that drifted on the breeze to calm his rising temper before he spoke. 'That remark is unworthy of you, Reverend Stanley. If you knew me better, you would realise how far from the truth your accusation is.' He sighed. 'I need your assistance and guidance in deciding the most needful sanctions, and how they may be implemented and managed. I do not ask you to persuade the villagers to accept them, although I am certain your very presence beside me at the meeting would be enough to let them see that you at least believe what I ask of them is the right thing to do.'

Stanley momentarily glared at him then slowly nodded, although William noted that no apology was forthcoming.

'So, Reverend Mompesson, we are agreed on the need to seal off our village: no one can leave and no one can enter.'

'We are. Quarantine is the only way to prevent the plague from spreading further afield. But, for as long as it is enforced, Eyam must continue to function efficiently. Which means that you and I must decide just how the problems of doing that can be successfully overcome or managed.'

Stanley nodded. 'I can think of several issues related to this sanction, so I suggest we leave our discussion at this point. Then tomorrow, when we have both had time to think things through, if agreeable to you, I will visit you at the rectory where we could discuss each other's ideas. I'll make sure I walk along Church Street so that as many villagers as possible see me. I may even stop and chat with a few of them, so they all know I am calling on my fellow clergyman. They will, of course, believe I am just visiting Eyam.'

'That's an excellent idea. Letting people know we're on affable terms will be extremely beneficial when I present them with my intentions.'

'Indeed, but now we need to return indoors for a cold drink. I have cider or ale, if you'd care to join me.'

The two reverends enjoyed their mugs of ale and eventually shook hands and made their way to the front door. 'Ideas will be swimming around in my head as I walk, Reverend Stanley. But I shall commit them to paper before we meet in the rectory tomorrow. I thank you for your hospitality and will look forward to hearing your thoughts on quarantining the village.'

Ten

As he stepped into Stanley's pretty front garden, William said a silent prayer, thanking God for enabling his meeting with Stanley to take place without too many harsh words or major disagreements.

Eleven

The following morning at precisely nine o' clock, Reverend Stanley knocked on the rectory door. It was answered by Joan, who grinned in delight at the sight of him.

'Would you kindly inform Reverend Mompesson of my arrival, my dear.'

'Step inside, Reverend, and I'll tell him you're here.'

'I won't, thank you, Joan. I would rather Reverend Mompesson personally invited me to do so.'

'Very well, sir, I'll tell him what you said.'

The young woman hurried across to the study, while Reverend Stanley stepped back from the door to await William's appearance.

'Good morning, Reverend,' William said, shaking Stanley's hand as his attention was drawn to the rectory gates, where almost a score of the villagers had gathered. 'You appear to have attracted a following.'

'Indeed. Amongst them are a few I have already spoken with. I deliberately mentioned I was on my way to see you in the hope that they would follow and witness our genial greeting.'

'Well, it seems to have worked,' William said as the two men headed indoors to the rectory's spacious library and study.

Stanley sighed, gesturing at two of the walls where floor to ceiling shelving was crammed full of books on a vast array of subjects. 'You know, Reverend Mompesson, the library was always my favourite room in this house. I felt so at peace in here, amidst all these books. It was always light and airy in here, too, no matter what the season. I could sit at that wonderful oak desk and gaze at the garden through the open glass doors, listening to the birdsong and admiring the regal old trees. But now I do the same through the windows of my cosy little cottage and feel equally at peace.'

'I am glad to know that,' William replied, inviting the former rector to sit on one of the two armchairs and seating himself in the other. 'I imagine that life after retirement could seem without purpose to many people. As for this room, it is, indeed, lovely and bright, as well as being conducive to work. Catherine has used several of these excellent tomes while teaching our son, George, to read. And those with colourful illustrations of animals, plants, landscapes and such like, have proved invaluable in teaching both of our children about the natural things on God's earth.'

William paused as he thought about what he would say next. 'I must tell you, Reverend Stanley, I thought it prudent to send our children away to safety until the plague is over. I have recently written to my uncle in Sheffield, asking if he would agree to taking them into his home until it is safe for them to return to Eyam. I should receive a reply from him within the week and, hopefully, a coach to transport George and Elizabeth will arrive a day or so after that.'

Thomas glared at him. 'That just reeks of hypocrisy! Only yesterday you quoted your wife's thoughts on the wealthy folk abandoning Eyam, and now you say that you intend to make that very same provision for your children. You *cannot* have one rule for the people of Eyam and another for your own family.'

Determined not to lose his temper, William took a deep breath and exhaled slowly. 'I don't believe it *is* hypocritical, since I intend to offer the same course of action to all parents in Eyam. At our meeting I will suggest that before the quarantine is in place, families in plague-free homes will be permitted to send their children to places of safety, should they so wish. This will, of course, only be of use to those who have family or friends living elsewhere who are willing and able to support them. It is also likely that many children from such fortunate homes have already been sent away.'

William ignored Stanley's sour expression and continued, 'As far as I can see, the only problem in implementing this rests upon us being able to trust that the children leaving Eyam are not from plague-stricken homes. After all, children are not exempt from being afflicted by the disease, or of carrying the seeds of it elsewhere. We must pray that no one in Eyam would wish to be responsible for causing harm to their relatives or friends.'

'I still think your motives in this are hypocritical, Reverend Mompesson, and as such, I cannot endorse them. You will be granting the option to villagers simply to justify your own intentions. But, if you are intent upon proceeding with it, you must make it clear to them that children who remain in Eyam during the quarantine must adhere to the rules we set out.'

'Your views on this are duly noted,' William replied. 'But I will not be changing my mind, and I refuse to see the option as being hypocritical. It is simply another means by which we can help to prevent a few innocent lives from being lost.'

Stanley scowled but said no more on that particular point.

Eleven

'Shall we sit at the desk and discuss each other's notes? I have a few points to mention as, I'm sure, have you.'

'By all means,' William replied, striving to keep the mood affable as he carried a second wooden chair across to the desk. 'I do have a few points to mention, and it wouldn't surprise me to find that we have overlapped on at least a couple of them. So, if you would mention the first on your list, we can take things from there.'

'Very well, although my first point is probably a mere triviality,' Stanley said as they sat opposite each other at the desk, 'but I believe we should agree on every *other* aspect of the quarantine before we present them to the villagers.' William nodded. 'So, before we discuss how the difficulties created by being quarantined could be overcome, we need to think of a means of denoting the parish boundary; some kind of markers to remind people of the village limits, and outsiders to know the line beyond which they many not enter.'

'Yes, I see the logic in that.'

'Then I propose we enlist the help of villagers from different sides of Eyam to collect a number of large stones or small boulders, each of a size to be easily lifted and carried but large enough to be seen from a short distance when in place on the ground. These would be laid along the parish boundary, which – with a couple of exceptions – is almost a mile from the centre of Eyam.'

'Stones would make a perfect boundary,' William agreed, 'and I doubt anyone will have difficulty in finding enough of them in this area.'

They spent some time discussing suitable distances to lay

the stones before Stanley added, 'To my knowledge, there are just two areas where the parish boundary exceeds a mile from Eyam's centre. On the hillside to the east of the village we have the Talbot and Hancock homes to include and to the west, we have the Shepherds Flat area where the Mortens and Kempes live.

'You and I, Reverend Mompesson, will doubtless be needed to ensure that those placing the stones know the route to follow. If you will check the boundary is followed along our west and northern sides, I could take care of the east and south. We will probably both need to refer to a map in order to be certain of the boundary's direction in some sections.'

There seemed nothing more to be added to that point and Stanley moved on. 'Now, might I ask if your notes address the biggest of the problems a quarantine would cause?'

'If you refer to the difficulties of maintaining regular food supplies, then yes, they do.'

'I rather thought they might. As you will know, Reverend Mompesson, although a few farmers around the village provide some of the foods we need, Eyam is by no means self-sufficient. Many of the women travel regularly to Tideswell and Bakewell markets to buy foods and household goods not available here. Small industries in the village – the cobbler, the tailor, and even the blacksmith, for example – rely on any number of goods from other villages and towns to keep them running. Even the inn relies on barrels of ale from brewers in Sheffield. The quarantine would, of course, bring a temporary halt to all that.

'I don't doubt that some people from neighbouring villages will be willing to leave foodstuffs along our boundary, especially those with relatives in Eyam,' Stanley nodded as his thoughts poured forth. 'But most will only do so if they are paid. Many of them are poor and cannot be expected to give food away, or other items come to that. Regarding which, I suspect that people from other villages wouldn't want to be handling coins from a plague village.'

'They would not, which is why I made note of a way in which that problem could be overcome.'

Stanley's eyebrows rose in anticipation and William explained, 'We all know that water can cleanse, so we must ensure that collection points are at, or close to, places along our boundary where there is water… preferably running water. Shallow streams like the Jumber Brook, at points where they enter or leave Eyam, are perfect. According to Lydia, Jumber Brook enters Eyam along our north-west boundary, then continues south through Cucklett Delph to leave Eyam along our south-westerly edge.'

'Wells close to our boundary would also be ideal,' Stanley said. 'One such well is located at the north-east of the village, just where the top road curves and heads north across Eyam Moor. It is fed by the Hollow Brook at a point where it flows underground.'

'I know the well. I believe it's also used as a stopping place for travellers to water their horses.'

'It is, but as I was saying, Hollow Brook surfaces again a short distance south of the well, only to flow for perhaps half a mile or so before disappearing again beneath the limestone. Unfortunately, that leaves the south-easterly section of our boundary lacking in both springs and wells.'

William nodded. 'A problem to which I have given a great deal of thought. We need to find a large boulder, approximately two to three feet wide and at least a foot high – and a means of transporting it. I am hopeful that someone in Eyam can loan me a pony and cart in order to do that. I will also need one or two volunteers to help me lift it both into and out of the cart.'

'And what do you mean to do with this boulder? It's hardly a source of water, is it?'

William smiled, despite Stanley's continuing sour mood. 'No, it isn't. I plan to gouge a few holes into the top of it, which can then be filled with water – or better still, vinegar, an excellent substance for purifying things. Our villagers will be able to drop their coins into it when paying for goods from, say, Stoney Middleton.'

'And how will you make these holes?'

'With something like an awl, or even a simple hammer and chisel. I hope to enlist a couple of the villagers to help me in this.'

'This holey rock is doubtless a clever idea, Reverend Mompesson, but it will greatly rely on the honesty of Eyam folk, as well as those bringing the foods.'

'That would apply equally to the leaving of coins in wells and at the shallow sides of streams. But since we have little choice in this, we must have faith in our villagers' integrity.'

'Then we must impress that upon them at the meeting. So, have you any other thoughts on how, or from where, foods and suchlike could be obtained?'

'I do have one more idea but I won't be divulging it unless the villagers agree to the quarantine in the first place.'

Stanley grimaced. 'And that alone is likely to task all our powers of reasoning and persuasion. There may well be several families already planning to leave Eyam before plague deaths soar with the heat of July.'

Further discussion was halted by the knock on the study door.

'That will be Lydia with our cocoa.' William headed across the room to open the door, enabling the smiling cook to enter.

'You're a welcome sight, Lydia. I'm sure Reverend Stanley will recall how wonderful your baking, is.'

Stanley grinned. 'I most certainly do. Mrs Chapman has always been the best cook in this village.'

Lydia smiled at him as she carried the tray over to the desk. On it sat not only a pot of cocoa and two cups and saucers, but a platter of delicious looking pastries and cakes. 'Well, Reverend, I saw you arriving this morning and thought you looked a little peaky… and rather too thin, if you don't mind me saying so.'

'Did you, indeed? I thought I looked just as thin in my younger days, but evidently, I did not'.'

'You certainly didn't, so I thought I'd tempt you with a few of the sweet things you used to love when you lived in this house. I can tell you that Reverend and Mrs Mompesson also love them, not to mention young George and Elizabeth. Now I'll leave you both to enjoy them and get back to my work.'

The two reverends sat to enjoy a short break in their planning, discussing some of Lydia's wonderful dishes whilst devouring a pastry or two. Eventually, Stanley said, 'Before our short break, you mentioned another possible means of acquiring foods during the quarantine. Do you wish to discuss it with me now, or not?'

William's brow furrowed in thought. 'It would probably be best to leave it until we have a little more certainty over events yet to unfurl… notably my hopes for this further food source and the people's acceptance of the quarantine.'

Stanley nodded. 'If the quarantine is rejected, we will have no control whatsoever over how far from Eyam the disease spreads. Although, as you mentioned, the villages and towns close to Eyam have employed guards in order to stop people from Eyam getting in.'

'Indeed, they have. Sheffield erected a barrier across its main entrance months ago, but I daresay there'll be some Eyam folk who will find ways of sneaking in. Guards can't be everywhere on the perimeters of towns.

'All I can do now, Reverend Stanley, is to write out a few notices about a meeting the day after tomorrow and pin them in prominent around the village. I will stress that attendance will be in their own interests as there will be a vote on one issue, the result of which will affect the immediate future of *all* Eyam citizens. We will meet at Cucklett Delph at eight o'clock in the evening, which will allow those who work during the day to go home for a meal first.'

'Then I will see you there. It will be good to meet with so many people I haven't seen for some time.'

William stood and held out his hand to the former rector. 'Your help in this matter has been greatly appreciated, even if we disagree over one aspect related to it. I'm sure there will be some villagers who won't be happy with any of the sanctions, but persuading them to agree to a quarantine will be the most difficult task we face at the meeting.'

'Hopefully, my attendance will impress upon them that I wholeheartedly support your plans. If I can think of a good argument or two with which to bolster those plans, I will, of course, use them.'

William smiled at the former rector's change of heart regarding his role at the meeting. 'Thank you, that is good to know.'

At nine thirty the following morning, William drew rein outside the stables of the stately Chatsworth House, a little under six miles to the south-east of Eyam. It was currently the home of Sir William Cavendish, the third Earl of Devonshire, with whom William hoped to gain audience, despite his unexpected arrival.

The ride had not been a pleasant one as he fought to quell the niggling fear that his mission might fail. After all, he had no reason to think that a mighty earl would believe the plague to be any more his concern than had the gentry and wealthy land or mine owners of Eyam. Yet he clung to the thought that, as Lord Lieutenant of Derbyshire, Sir William would deem it his duty to do anything in his power to lessen the suffering of one of the many villages under his control.

Leaving his hired horse in the care of the grooms, William headed to the main entrance of the house. There he stood before the great oak doors and tugged on the length of thick rope that hung beside them. A large brass bell above him responded with a single, loud chime and William stepped back to await a response.

Within moments the door was opened by a smartly dressed young man with his dark hair tied neatly back. 'Good morning, sir. Have you an appointment with his lordship? I saw no one on my list scheduled for interview this morning.'

'I'm afraid I don't. I came here hoping the earl would be willing to spare a few minutes to see me. My name is Reverend William Mompesson from the parish of Eyam.'

'I see…' The young man's face revealed he knew exactly what was happening in Eyam. 'If you'd care to step inside and take a seat for a few moments, Reverend, I'll check if Sir William can see you. I believe the family has finished breakfasting and his lordship has retired to the library. My name is Anthony, by the way. I am the underbutler here.'

As he waited, William glanced around the hall, thinking that the house, built on the orders of Bess of Hardwick during Queen Elizabeth's reign over a hundred years ago, was in great need of restoration. Five minutes later, Anthony showed him into a room off the hall which, from the great range of bookshelves, William knew could only be the library.

The earl held out his hand in welcome as Anthony intoned William's name, while William rapidly assessed Sir William's appearance. He was a dark-headed man of late middle age, with a wiry build and an oval face from which sharp brown eyes seemed to be considering William's appearance and countenance in return. The earl's clothing was of the highest quality, both waistcoat and breeches having a silken appearance. Yet he did not exhibit that pompous manner that William had seen in many titled and wealthy men.

Eleven

'I don't believe we've met, Reverend Mompesson, so whatever business you have come to discuss, this is a perfect opportunity for us to become acquainted. Your appointment to the parish of Eyam was made by Sir George Savile, whom you probably realise is deputy to my position of Lord Lieutenant of Derbyshire.

'Please, take a seat,' he added, directing William to an armchair at one side of a wide marble fireplace and lowering himself into an identical chair at the opposite side. 'You were appointed as rector in Eyam two years ago, I believe?'

'I was, Sir William, and it is with regard to the welfare of the village I have come here today.'

The earl nodded, a frown on his face. 'I am told that Eyam is held in the grip of plague to which, I hope, your own family has not succumbed.'

'My wife and children have, as yet, remained unaffected, as have I, thank you Sir William. But it is with a request regarding the continuing wellbeing of our villagers that I am here to see you today.'

'A request to me, you say. I'm not sure how I can help in that respect, although I sincerely hope the plague is being securely contained within your village. If it spreads from Eyam, it could travel in any direction, even towards Chatsworth.' He shuffled a little in his seat. 'I am, of course, concerned for the whole of Derbyshire.'

William nodded, realising where the earl's priorities lay. 'As you probably know Sir William, bubonic plague arrived in Eyam in the autumn of last year, although from where, none of us know. It greatly abated over the winter months, as is usual with such diseases, but did not disappear entirely. With the onset of the warmer weather, plague deaths are rising again and I fear the disease will inflict its fury upon us during July and August and probably linger throughout the autumn.'

'My heart goes out to the good folk of Eyam, but I still cannot see how I can help you.'

'Then I'll explain, if I may.' The earl nodded and William said, 'I have devised a plan of action which will be in place from early July and throughout the rest of the summer and autumn. I believe it will ensure the plague spreads no further than our village.'

'It sounds an excellent idea, Reverend, but how can you be so sure it will work?'

William explained about the three sanctions, with particular emphasis on the quarantine. Unfortunately, he was also obliged to omit Thomas Stanley's role in co-devising any of them. Since Thomas had been ousted as rector of Eyam by members of the Church of England – including the Earl of Devonshire, a steadfast Royalist – the staunchly Puritan former rector's interference in any decisions pertaining to its parishioners would be seriously frowned upon. Especially if it became known that Stanley was still residing in Eyam.

'So, you see, Sir William, I believe that, as good Christians, quarantine is the only path that the people of Eyam can take. My main problem now rests upon maintaining regular food supplies from nearby villages, and I hoped you could help in this respect. I need to be certain that foods will be made available for the villagers to purchase before I even suggest quarantining ourselves.'

Eleven

The earl gave a thoughtful nod and William explained the various methods he had devised by which payments for goods could be made by villagers from all sides of Eyam.

'It sounds to me that a great deal of thought has gone into planning of all of this.'

'It was the only thing I could do in the circumstances, Sir William. Like you, I truly believe that if we allow things to continue the way they are, the plague will spread rapidly throughout the rest of Derbyshire, and even further afield.'

For some moments, the earl remained silent, his elbows resting on the chair arms and his chin propped on steepled fingers as he thought. Eventually he said, 'I will supply Eyam with a selection of foodstuffs on a weekly basis to the boundary stone at your south-east. I will also ensure that villagers are sent a regular supply of firewood for their homes. Requests for any items not anticipated by us, such as particular medicines or household goods, or even certain foodstuffs, must be requested by notes left at the stone. Payments for such extras must be left prior to receipt of them. Does that sound reasonable, Reverend?'

William was overcome with relief, despite believing the earl's positive response to be driven by his desire to keep the plague well away from Chatsworth. But he was completely taken aback when Sir William added, 'And please let it be known that I will not expect payment for the regular deliveries of foods or firewood. Those I give freely to the people of Eyam from my own supplies. If you write to inform me as to when you wish the first foods to be delivered, they will arrive on that day, and every following week throughout your quarantine.

The firewood will be delivered fortnightly and on a different day of the week.'

William struggled to find words in response to the earl's generosity, other than to mumble his sincere gratitude.

'I hope my deliveries will add to other anticipated supplies of foods to ensure that the good people of Eyam do not starve for participating in this most Christian of gestures.

'Now, Reverend, if you will excuse me, I believe my wife has invited guests for luncheon and is expecting me to be on hand to welcome them. I will pray daily for you all until this dreadful disease leaves your village.'

Twelve

Eyam: Wednesday June 23 1666

Richard Talbot ensured his precious tools were securely stored away and left his stone-built smithy, locking the doors behind him. He sighed at the thought that no more business would be coming his way until Eyam was rid of this cursed disease. News of the 'plague village' had evidently travelled far and no outsiders ventured near. With no coin coming in, he and his family were looking at a few hard months. Not that food was a particular problem. The family had kept the sizeable vegetable garden going, along with a dozen laying hens, a few goats and a small drove of pigs. A couple of the pigs could be slaughtered for meat if necessary, and a few of the hens.

Reverend Mompesson had called a meeting for tomorrow night and Richard wondered what that could be about, especially as he'd heard that Reverend Stanley would also be there. Notices around the village had clearly stated that children could accompany their parents, though Richard decided that his large family might be just a few too many. Perhaps he and his wife, Katherine, could go, along with their two eldest daughters, Bridget and Mary. The young'uns would be happier staying with their grandma, anyway. His mother, old Bridgett Talbot, loved having the youngsters to herself and could keep the rascals quiet for hours with her old and fanciful stories.

Richard loved his children and smiled as he thought of them. The young ones spent most of their days running wild with John and Elizabeth Hancock's kids, who lived almost half a mile away along the hillside. But why not? They were only having fun and, when all's said and done, they'll only be young once. It could be lonely out here, on the very edge of Eyam, with no one but the Hancocks close enough for the kids to play with. Although, with plague in the crowded village at the bottom of the rise, perhaps that was just as well.

But, he supposed, they should go to this meeting in the delph. It must be important or Reverend Mompesson wouldn't have bothered writing out all those notes to pin around the place.

Having made that decision, Richard headed indoors to discuss things with his wife and mother.

Thursday, June 24 1666

Accompanied by Catherine and their two young children, William arrived at Cucklett Delph half an hour earlier than the planned eight o'clock start for the meeting. Having had neither time nor opportunity to do so before now, he wanted to browse around before the villagers appeared. The warmth of the lowering midsummer sun caressed his cheeks, whilst scents of newly scythed hay drifted on the breeze to mingle with those of the delph's sweet meadow flowers. William inhaled deeply, as though the heady bouquet would allay his niggling fears that folk would spurn the sanctions he was about to impose.

'Good evening, Reverend Mompesson ... Mrs Mompesson.' Reverend Stanley gave a tight smile as he emerged from amidst the trees, the lush greens of the undergrowth having effectively camouflaged him in his dark green doublet and breeches. 'It seems we had the same idea in arriving early.'

William nodded. 'It's such a lovely evening, so we decided to familiarise ourselves with the delph before the villagers arrived. We had intended to do so yesterday, but another pressing matter kept me busy. And you…?'

'I, too, wished to enjoy this glorious evening but also to remind myself how much my dear wife, Constance, loved it here. From what I can see, it has changed little since I last visited three years ago, although the trees appear somewhat taller than I recall. I take it you followed Lydia's directions in order to find it?'

'We did and, as always, her instructions were faultless.'

'Now, Reverend Mompesson, shall you and I take a look at your new pulpit before anyone arrives? It's a gentle climb and we can address the villagers from up there tonight.'

William glanced at Catherine, eyebrows raised, but she had evidently anticipated his question. 'We will be perfectly happy having a wander whilst you and Reverend Stanley speak. I imagine there will be lots of interesting things to look at in the woodland and this delightfully babbling brook merits closer inspection.'

'Thank you, my dear, but as soon as all the villagers have arrived, the three of you must accompany Reverend Stanley and I to the little cave up there, so they can all see that you support our proposals.'

Catherine agreed and she and the children wandered over

to the woods as the two reverends, garbed in their everyday, clerical attire, climbed the slope to stand on the platform in front of the shallow cave. 'This will be perfect for delivering my sermons,' William said, gazing down at the delph's grassy floor with its carpet of colourful flowers. 'Thank you for suggesting it.'

His arm swept round to encompass the grass-covered hillsides and the dense, green woodland. 'I can understand what you mean about sound being trapped between the hills and the trees… But I won't test that out just now as I can see our first villagers arriving.'

Stanley's light touch on his arm stayed him. 'Before we descend, I want you to know that I will support you wherever possible as you address the villagers. I have thought of a few arguments I could use and I want them all to know that I fully agree with your plans. I don't wish to be just a silent presence up here.'

'My heartfelt thanks,' William said. 'Your vocal support will mean a great deal to people.'

'I can only hope it will.' Stanley gestured at the downward path. 'Shall we…'

William sensed a definite air of anxiety as he and Stanley greeted each group on their arrival, despite their assurances that the meeting was not in order to deliver reprimands. He also realised that his sanctions would make them even more concerned.

When it seemed that no one else would arrive, he and Stanley, accompanied by Catherine and the children, climbed up the slope to what William now considered his pulpit. He stared down at the sea of wide brimmed hats, interspersed with white coifs, reminded, yet again, of the villagers' Puritan faith. He thanked God that Stanley was with him.

'Reverend Stanley and I sincerely thank you all for attending this evening,' William's voice rang out, 'especially those amongst you who have been obliged to bring young children along. And, of course, those who have had little time to eat and relax after a hard day's work. We also thank all our womenfolk who have spent the day cooking and cleaning, and caring for young ones. I assure you all that what I have to say is of sufficient importance to ask you to forego your evening rest. I also ask that those amongst you with neighbours unable to attend tonight, inform them of what was presented.'

The murmured buzz abated as William held up his hands. 'Last winter, we were all relieved to see a huge drop in the number of deaths from plague and we prayed that this deadly disease would not return with the warmth of spring. And yet, with the onset of June, numbers have begun to rise again.

'Today, the twenty-fourth day of the month, we buried Anne Skidmore, the sixteenth person to die of plague since the end of May. Anne's family and friends will mourn her passing for some time and as we head towards July, we must all be wondering how many more families will be left bereaved.' He paused, just long enough to allow that thought to sink in. 'I can say with some certainty that as we move further into summer and the heat increases, the plague will really take hold…

'And the death rate will soar.'

All was quiet until a small child whimpered, setting off one or two others. When silence resumed, William moved on. 'I firmly believe that as a village – a community of closely knit people – we must work together in an attempt to stop the plague from spreading rapidly amongst us, from person to person.'

Murmurs of confusion followed William's last words and Stanley stepped forward, holding up his hands for quiet. 'Although Reverend Mompesson and I cannot state for certain that plague is not carried by a miasma in the air, we do believe that it is more likely to be spread by healthy people coming close to someone who either already has the disease or is harbouring the seeds of it before the later symptoms become apparent.' He gestured at Catherine. 'As Mrs Mompesson aptly put it, "Most people in Eyam realise it takes just one person in a family to catch the disease for most, if not all, of that family to succumb to it".

'It is with such thoughts in mind that I pass you again to Reverend Mompesson, who will explain the two sanctions he intends to impose in order to avoid plague being spread rapidly amongst us during the summer.'

William nodded his thanks to Stanley and stepped forward. 'My first sanction is this: as from this evening, the Church of Saint Helen will be locked, which–'

Words of disbelief and outrage followed, forcing William to wait for the noise to subside before he continued, 'Locking the church will mean that no one will be able to enter at any time of day or night to pray, as we have been accustomed to for many years. It also means that no more Sunday services will be held in the church, a place where we are packed very closely together, making it easy for plague to take us.'

Twelve

'Where *will* services be held, then? Or are we expected to just stop our weekly worship, something that could cause our souls to be barred from Heaven when we die? And what about christenings, weddings and funerals? Would they have to wait until the plague has gone, too?'

'If you had given Reverend Mompesson time to explain, Francis, you would have had no need to ask that question,' Stanley answered in William's stead.

'Beg pardon, Reverend Stanley, and yours, Reverend Mompesson.' Francis Wilson hung his head. 'I won't interrupt again.'

'That is good to know,' William said, refocussing on everyone present. 'During the weeks of summer and autumn when our church is locked, Sunday worship, christenings and weddings will be held here, in Cucklett Delph, surrounded by the beauties of God's creation. Funerals are a different matter, and I will explain about them in a moment. Naturally, should there be heavy rain, services will be postponed and arranged for the first dry day. But for any type of service, I am sure we could all abide a spot of gentle, summer rain.

'So that is my first sanction,' William continued. 'The second is, in part, related to the first. With the church being locked, there will be no further funeral services in St Helen's, or burials in our cemetery.'

Again, the inevitable buzz of confusion and anxiety exuded from the gathering and William held up a hand for quiet. 'We presently have no sexton in Eyam, so what I am about to say is partly due to that. Until a new sexton is appointed, the responsibility for burying the dead will rest with the family concerned, who *must* adhere to the following rules…

A Boundary of Stones

'Firstly, anyone dying from plague must be buried as soon as possible, a requirement that has been in place since the plague struck Eyam last year. Secondly, the burial must be either on your own land, whether that be a garden, a small area owned by you in the village, or on common land, such as a small copse or stretch of open countryside that lies within Eyam's boundary. Naturally, no burials will be permitted on the village green.'

No questions were forthcoming so William pushed on, 'No coffins will be available for purchase during the plague, so the deceased must be transported to the grave in a shroud. If anyone is uncertain of how to do this, please see me at the rectory for advice. No headstones will be available either, so you may wish to mark the grave with a wooden cross or a lump of stone with the name of the deceased scratched or engraved into it.

'And please remember that in the event of the last survivor in a household being elderly or infirm, family members living elsewhere in Eyam will be responsible for the burial. Failing that, close friends or neighbours will be asked to lend assistance. Please bear in mind that all deaths must be reported to me for recording in the parish register.

'Now, are there any questions about either of these two sanctions before I move on to the third?'

Pleased to see that no hands were raised, William silently prayed that the final sanction would not cause total uproar. He took a breath, 'Those two sanctions are of utmost importance to the continuing good health of people within our own village, and were devised with that in mind. As such, I presented them to you in my capacity as rector of this parish and none of you has any option other than to accept them…'

Twelve

William let that thought hang, before adding, 'But Reverend Stanley and I believe that the third sanction is of such importance and possible consequence to us all that you will each be asked to vote on whether or not to accept it. I can only say that it draws on your love, kindness and consideration for people living *beyond* our village.'

William paused for a moment, allowing his words to sink in. 'We are well aware of what we are asking of you all in this, but we present our plan in the hope that, as good, Christian people, you will agree to it. Should those who oppose it be outvoted by the majority, they will have no other choice than to conform to the strictures laid down. If the plan is rejected by the majority, then so be it; we pursue it no further. Either way, as from tomorrow, the second sanctions will be in place with the first.'

William gestured at Stanley by his side. 'Reverend Stanley and I have put a great deal of thought into devising this sanction. We truly believe it to be the only path that God would want us to take.'

A sense of unease emanated from those below as they shuffled and clung to their loved ones, and William drew breath, 'There is no easy way of revealing our intentions for this sanction, other than to state the key point straight away and fill in the details later. So here it is: the third sanction involves us all agreeing to place our village under quarantine until the plague is over.'

This time the clamour of response was loud, with gasps of great trepidation amongst it. Babes in arms wailed and young children, alarmed by the unrest of the crowd, held up their arms, pleading to be lifted up, in need of assurance that all was well.

At length the noise subsided and William continued, 'Quarantining ourselves from the rest of the country would mean that the plague could not be passed on to families and friends in neighbouring villages. After all, the disease reached Eyam from some stricken village, town or city. And because many travellers and merchants pass through here, perhaps stopping for a meal or drink at The Miners Arms, or simply needing to stretch their legs, we have no idea how, or from where, the plague reached us…

'In short, agreeing to a quarantine would mean that none of us could cross a boundary line that we would mark around the village, and no outsiders would be permitted across that line to enter. If we agree to uphold this course of action, I will explain how the boundary will be marked.

'What about those of us who work beyond our boundary, in the lead mines or at the quarry?' a belligerent male voice called out. 'You can't mean we wouldn't be able to go to work!'

'Yes, I do mean that, Michael. Quarantining ourselves would be pointless if Eyam's miners and quarrymen were permitted to work alongside people from other villages. The same applies to anyone who works on one of the farms, or owns farmland beyond our boundary. Quarantine means that *no one at all* can cross our boundary line either to enter or leave Eyam.'

Michael Kempe said no more and William continued, 'If we vote in favour of a quarantine, I will explain how some of the problems caused by it can be overcome. If the proposal is rejected, further explanation would be unnecessary. As for myself, I truly believe that God would want us to quarantine our village.

'Now, I can see that Reverend Stanley wishes to address you all.'

Stanley stepped forward and held out his arms to encompass those gathered. 'Good people of Eyam... Most of you have known me for some years. I have lived amongst you and you have listened to my sermons, been baptised and married by me, and many of your long-deceased relatives were buried by me in our church's cemetery. Now I am too old to perform such duties well, and I have left you in the capable hands of Reverend Mompesson. Although he may not be of the same religious persuasion as most of us, he is a devoted Christian, with an equally Christian wife who has cared for many of you during this heartbreaking time.' He gestured at Catherine, who raised a hand in acknowledgement of them all.

'Believe me when I tell you that Reverend and Mrs Mompesson have your interests at heart as much as do I. And we cannot stress strongly enough that quarantining the village is vital if we are to stop the plague spreading from here to nearby villages such as Stoney Middleton, Foolow, Tideswell and Bakewell – or as far as towns like Buxton, Chesterfield or Sheffield. And from there it would continue to spread to the east, the west, or even to the very north of England. Surely, as devout followers of Christ, isn't it our duty to ensure that this fatal disease does not cause devastation throughout the entire land?'

Stanley paused to gather his thoughts, while all those below remained silent. Then a hand went up from a man that

William knew to have a wife and several children, and lived on the eastern edge of the village where he pursued his life as a blacksmith.

'Ah, Richard,' Stanley said, acknowledging this man with a smile. 'Have you a pressing question to ask at this stage?'

'I do have something to say, Reverend, but it isn't a question. It's more of a statement.' Stanley urged him to continue. 'It seems to me that you're asking Eyam folk to die for the sake of people outside our village… people we don't even *know*.'

Chaos erupted as villagers yelled in agreement with Richard Talbot, voicing their objections to the unfairness of doing such a thing, and the fact that they had children to think about.

For some time, Stanley allowed them to vent their anger, then he held up his hands for order. 'It is, indeed, a great sacrifice we ask of you all, as well as ourselves. But I stress again that we are all devout Christians here, which means we are all followers of Christ and honour his teachings. And his actions. Did not Jesus suffer death on the Cross to ensure the redemption of the world for all time? In other words, Christ sacrificed his own life to save us all.'

Not a sound could be heard as villagers thought about Stanley's words. Then he added, 'Yes, that is, indeed, what Reverend Mompesson and I are asking us all to do: to offer our own lives in a similar sacrifice. Christ said, "Greater love hath no man than this, that he lay down his life for his neighbours". He also told us the wonderful parable we know as "The Good Samaritan", a man who, without hesitation, helped a neighbour at a time of need. A man, I must add, from a different land.

'Our own neighbours are in need of being saved from a

disease that could kill hundreds, if not thousands of them. I truly believe it is within our power to stop the further spread of bubonic plague here, in our peaceful little village with its courageous people.'

The silence seemed oddly out of place as villagers considered their former reverend's words. Then a woman called out, 'But if we can't leave the village and no one can come in, how will we feed ourselves and our families? Some of us have vegetable gardens and keep a few hens or a couple of goats, but not all of us. Farms around the village might provide milk and other produce, but how would they sell them to us if they can't come to the Friday market?'

At that point, Michael Kempe again added his voice to the argument, 'And if folk with jobs outside of Eyam can't work, only those who have savings will be able to pay for food, wherever it comes from.'

'Two good points,' William said, 'To which Reverend Stanley and I have given a great deal of thought. Firstly, Margaret, you are right to question our overall food supply, since that will undoubtedly be our biggest problem during the quarantine. Local farmers have agreed to leave milk and other fresh produce along our boundary, and the people of Foolow and Stoney Middleton will leave us any foods they can spare. I must stress that anyone requesting goods from those villages and farms will be expected to do so by leaving a note, and all goods must be paid for in advance. If those items are not available, your money will be returned with words to that effect written across your note.'

He gestured at Michael Kempe.' I do have a solution to

your concern, Michael, but I will only need to discuss it if the quarantine is accepted.'

He paused, giving them time to think about that before continuing, 'Something to which I gave a great deal of thought was exactly how payments could be made so that our neighbours are not afraid of catching the seeds of plague from our coins. I decided upon one or two ways, which I will explain to you now.'

William proceeded to describe how the exchange of foods and coins would be made at places with running water or shallow wells. 'As for those of you who live close to the south-east of Eyam where streams and wells are absent, over the next few days, I intend to create something that can be used instead. We need to find a sizable boulder, which will be placed along our south-east boundary: the reason I'm calling it the Boundary Stone. Once in place, several holes will be bored into the top of it. A boulder of that size shouldn't be hard to find, so close to the Stoney Middleton quarry –'

A buzz of confusion momentarily halted William's words, prompting him to describe the purpose of the holes, and the vinegar with which they would be filled. 'I also realise I need to hire a pony and cart to transport the boulder to the place where it would be worked on and subsequently used.'

'You're welcome to use mine, Reverend,' Joe Wilkins called out. 'I'm only too happy to help.'

'Thank you, Joe, I appreciate that.' William raised his hand to the jovial landlord of The Miners Arms. 'I also need two strong men to lift the boulder into the cart and out again at its allotted place. In addition, I need the help of one or two men who possess awls, or just hammers and chisels, to gouge out the holes. Any volunteers to assist me in either of these tasks would earn our utmost thanks and possibly some of Mrs Chapman's superb honey cake and currant buns.'

Stanley stepped forward to William's side. 'Your rector's plan is an excellent one and I know how long he has spent thinking about how best to bring food into Eyam. Indeed, he has secured another source of supplies for us all and, as he has said, he will gladly divulge that to you if the quarantine is accepted.

'But now, I believe Reverend Mompesson has one more thing to say before we all vote upon whether or not, as individuals, we are prepared to quarantine our village. I love each and every one of you, and trust in your charity and belief in Our Saviour, Jesus Christ, to do the right thing. Reverend Mompesson…'

'Reverend Stanley's trust in you all mirrors my own. We both believe that quarantining Eyam is a way of showing our fellow countrymen that we truly care for their futures, as well as our own. And remember, the first two sanctions should help to lessen the number of deaths from plague *within* our own village.

'One thing I will say before we vote, is that any children in the village may be sent away to stay with family or friends outside of Eyam for the duration of the plague, if you so wish. This is on the condition that the children are free of the plague themselves and do not come from a plague-stricken home.'

William gestured at George and Elizabeth. 'My wife and I intend to send our own children away and I felt that anyone else in the village worried for their children's safety should be given the opportunity to do the same.' He paused, as another thought crossed his mind. 'Your success in doing this will depend on the village to which you take your children. The main roads into several villages nearby are barricaded and the guards may well refuse entry to anyone from Eyam, including children. If you should be turned away, I can only advise that you accept it in good grace. Arguing with the guards, or even attempting to cajole them, will not make them disobey their orders.'

He glanced round at the listeners. 'As Reverend Stanley mentioned, if the proposed quarantine is rejected, nothing further will be said about it and we will all go home to face the summer months together.

'Now, I need a volunteer to stand beside us on this ledge to preside over the voting and count the number of raised hands…'

'I'll do it, Reverend,' Richard Talbot called out.

'You have our thanks, Richard. Please take your place beside us. And while Richard makes his way up here, I must remind you all that anyone who is sixteen years and over will be expected to vote on whether or not Eyam should be quarantined. May God give you guidance in your response.'

William stood back with his family and Reverend Stanley as the blacksmith conducted the voting. 'First, I ask all those against the proposed quarantine to raise their hands….'

William held his breath as the villagers hesitated to act. Then a few tentative, raised hands began to show and were quickly counted.

Twelve

'Sixty-two against,' Richard reported. 'Now, all those in favour of the proposed quarantine please raise your hands...'

Reverend Stanley, William, Catherine and Richard Talbot promptly raised their hands but at first, only a few were raised below. Then, almost as one, the rest followed – and William released his withheld breath.

'I see no need to count hands this time, Richard,' Stanley said, focusing on the villagers below him. 'There must be almost five hundred of them, and Reverend Mompesson and I could not be prouder of you all for your response.

'We have a harsh summer ahead, my friends, but in my heart, I know that the Lord guided your thoughts in this direction. I can only stress that those who voted against this course of action must adhere to it with the rest of us. We all know that some of us will die... But that would still be the case if we were not quarantined. I am certain that following Reverend Mompesson's sanctions regarding avoiding contact with anyone outside your own family will keep the number of plague victims within Eyam as low as possible. Now, Reverend Mompesson will mention a few issues left unanswered before we voted.'

William nodded. 'Thank you, Reverend Stanley. Regarding food supply for the village, yesterday I rode out to Chatsworth House to speak with the Earl of Devonshire–'

Murmurs of awe rippled through the villagers, to whom visiting an earl must have seemed tantamount to visiting the king. 'I found Sir William to be an understanding and gracious man, and he has pledged his support of our proposed quarantine, promising to have foodstuffs delivered to our Boundary

Stone once a week and firewood every two weeks.'

'Did he say how much he'd charge us for it all, Reverend? Rich folk don't give owt away for nowt. That's how they got rich in the first place.'

Laughter sounded for the first time that evening. 'Believe it or not, Edward, Sir William will be charging us absolutely nothing for the food, or the firewood.' An appreciative hum carried round the delph. 'Myself and two others will collect each delivery and take it to the rectory to be divided up for collection. That way, I will know that everyone is benefitting from the earl's generosity.'

William gestured at Michael Kempe. 'As I said earlier, Michael, being unable to earn coin for food and fuel may not be as big a problem as you imagined.' Michael raised his hand and nodded in appreciation. 'Additionally,' William continued, addressing them all, 'requests for goods not included in the earl's regular deliveries can be made by leaving a note at the Boundary Stone. Sir William will be happy to seek out sources of those, but we must be aware that he may not be successful in finding them. Also remember that extra items will *not* be free and must be paid for in advance, whether they be medical supplies, spinning whorls, needles, or even particular foods not included in the free deliveries. If requested goods are not available, your coin will be returned to the Boundary Stone along with your request note.'

A few older children had begun to chase each other around, while younger ones wailed, overcome by tiredness. Parents struggled to keep them all quiet and still. 'We realise that this has been a long meeting,' William eventually managed to say, 'and we have given you a lot to think about. But I beg you to bear with us just a few more moments.

'Both your former rector and I feel that something must be said regarding the proposed exchange of foods and coin. We cannot stress strongly enough the need for total honesty from everyone if this system is to work. Anyone caught stealing coins from the collection points, or taking someone else's delivered goods, will not only be banned from partaking in the exchange, they will also spend a full forty-eight hours in the village stocks. Rain or shine. We sincerely hope we are given no cause to resort to this measure; we would be greatly saddened by having to label anyone as "thief".

'Now, before we all make for home, I need volunteers to assist with the collection, shaping, and delivery of the Boundary Stone to its designated place. So firstly, anyone willing to help me to find and transport a suitable stone, please remain for a short while after everyone has gone.

'Secondly, anyone willing to help me in gouging holes in the tops of the stone please stay behind to see me. Finally, I ask those of you who live close to the perimeter of our village to organise yourselves into groups in order to collect smaller boulders to use as boundary markers. I stress that you must manage this yourselves, although once you start to lay the stones, Reverend Stanley and I will be on hand to check the boundary is being followed. Ideally, the stones should be laid three or four yards apart, and be large enough to be easily seen. Across all roads and paths into Eyam the stones need to be no further than one foot apart.'

William gestured to the former rector. 'Reverend Stanley

and I sincerely thank you for coming this evening. We must aim to complete all work by the evening of Wednesday, the last day of June, before the quarantine starts the following day.

'We have a busy six days ahead of us.'

Thirteen

Eyam Monday, June 28 1666

In the days following the meeting Eyam was a hive of activity as villagers readied themselves for the quarantine. Some spent time preparing and taking their children to relatives or friends away from the village, while others collected stones and laid them along Eyam's boundary. Some helped William to find, lift and transport a large boulder and gouge holes into it ready to be filled with vinegar.

In the rectory, in addition to her usual kitchen chores, Lydia baked honey cakes and buns for sending out to the men helping William with the boulder, whilst Catherine began packing a small travel trunk with her children's clothes and a few beloved toys. Tomorrow, the coach from Uncle John would arrive, and she would not see her children again for months. Her heart ached at the thought, but she refused to allow William to see her tears. If he did, he would give her no other choice than to go to Sheffield with them.

'Can I have a word with you, Mrs Mompesson?' Joan asked as she swept the hall floor.

Laden with a heap of freshly laundered children's clothes and her foot on the bottom stair, Catherine halted in her tracks. 'Will it wait until I've finished packing?'

'I'd rather tell you while it's on my mind, mistress. It won't take long to explain.'

Catherine placed her load on a chair. 'Come, let us go to

the sitting room where we can speak in comfort.

'Now Joan, what is it that is of such importance to you?'

'I believe I am with child, Mrs Mompesson, and at the worst of times. It won't be born until next year – probably January – but if I catch the plague, then both me and the babe will die. And what if Robert dies but not me and I am left to fend for myself? Without Robert's wage and with no paid work of my own, I'll have no coin to buy food, or wood for the fire. I know we'll have the free food and wood from the earl while the quarantine lasts, but once it's over I'll have nothing.

'I know I shouldn't think about such things, and I pray that both Robert and I survive this disease. But such thoughts refuse to leave me and even fill my dreams at night.'

The young cleaner sobbed, and Catherine was grieved to see it. She also understood how such negative thoughts can destroy every trace of a person's happiness.

'I think the first thing we should do is to get down on our knees and pray to God to keep your family safe. I know my husband would say we should pray for the safety of entire village, but I do that every day, anyway. I'm sure God is benevolent and understanding, and will not mind a prayer of a more specific and personal nature as well.

'Shall I say the words for us, Joan, and you can listen and thank God at the end?'

Joan nodded her bowed head and knelt on the rug beside Catherine as she prayed:

O Lord our Father, Creator of all Things
Hear the prayer of this lowly woman.
In your infinite wisdom and love, I beseech thee

Thirteen

Look upon my dear friend Joan.
Watch over her and the child she carries
And the husband who provides for their needs.
Love them and bless them and keep them safe
Until the deadly plague recedes.
Amen

'Amen', Joan repeated, before they rose to their feet. 'Thank you, Mrs Mompesson. I'm sorry to have burdened you with my problems. I just thought you should know that I'll have no other choice than to leave your employment as soon as I grow too big to be doing a great deal of cleaning. I hope to stay as long as I can.'

'Joan, you have no need to fear that we will turn you out should Robert die of the plague. Heaven forbid that that *should* happen, but if the need arises, knowing you will always have food and a bedchamber here, with us, may give you some peace of mind.'

'Oh, mistress, you are so kind, I don't know what to say.'

'Then, just say," Thank you" and be done with it.' Catherine smiled. 'It will be quiet here with George and Elizabeth in Sheffield, and there'll be much less clutter for you to clear away, so you could get plenty of rest when you need it.' She pointed to the front door. 'Now, nowhere else in the house needs cleaning so you can go home and put your feet up. And don't worry about losing some of your wages; we will gladly pay you for a full day's work. I just need to finish packing…'

Catherine squeezed her eyes shut, determined to hold her tears at bay. 'The carriage from Mr Bielby will be here some time tomorrow and I don't know how I'll cope without my little ones. But I shall try to be strong and remember it's for the best. At least they'll be safe from the plague in Sheffield. Now, I'm sure I'll see you again in the morning, so put the broom away and be off with you.'

Joan threw her arms around Catherine. 'Reverend Mompesson must be blessed to have such a lovely wife as you. I will add a few extra words for you and your family in my prayers tonight.'

—

By half past five the following afternoon, William and Catherine were beginning to wonder what had happened to the coach they were expecting from Uncle John. They had expected it to arrive around noon and William had forgone an afternoon of overseeing the layout and route of the boundary stones in order to meet the lady who was to take care of the children.

'Perhaps it's late because a wheel came off… or the coach was set upon by thieves, or even cutthroats.' Catherine's face reflected her concern, although the childlike manner in which she expressed it made William smile.

'I don't think we need to consider such drastic events just yet, my dear. A wheel coming off would be rectified easily enough, but if you dwell on your other possibilities, you will only succeed in distressing yourself. We must believe there is some simple reason for the coach's late arrival.'

Fifteen minutes later, Joan came to inform them that their gardener, Joseph Taylor, was at the front door.

'A tiddler of a coach has stopped outside the rectory gates,

Thirteen

Reverend,' Joseph said, standing aside so William could see for himself. 'And the driver's gawping this way.'

William grinned at the gardener's choice of words as his gaze followed the direction of the pointing finger. 'Thank you, Joseph. We were expecting a small coach to arrive today, although it's later arriving than we would have hoped.'

William headed to the gates, raising his hand to acknowledge the driver before assisting a middle-aged lady with a kindly face to alight from the coach's plush interior.

'Good day, Mrs Barton. I trust your journey from Sheffield was not overly tiring? I am Reverend Mompesson, by the way, nephew of Mr Bielby.'

Mrs Barton took William's hand as she stepped from the coach. 'It is not a long journey, thank you, Reverend, and the coach is extremely comfortable. Unfortunately, we left Sheffield later than planned because Mrs Bielby had previously arranged to visit her sister in Doncaster today, and was a little later than usual getting back.'

William smiled. 'No matter; these things happen. I'm just grateful to my uncle for agreeing to take the children and arranging for your good self to accompany them. You have travelled directly from Sheffield?' Agnes Barton confirmed that to be correct. 'And now you intend to turn around and travel back again?'

'We do, Reverend, so we cannot dally for long in Eyam. But, if I may be so bold, a refreshing drink would be very much appreciated before we set off again.'

'Considering the late hour at which you would arrive back in Sheffield should you travel back this evening, might I suggest you spend tonight here, in the rectory? We always keep two or three bedchambers ready for unexpected guests. I'm certain Catherine would love your company for the evening. Besides, the children have not yet had their evening meal and there is still their baggage to load onto the coach.'

Agnes glanced at the coachman, whose wide grin told William what his reply would be. 'That's very kind of you, Reverend,' Jonathan Ashe said, tipping his cap.' I'd much prefer to travel with little'uns earlier in the day. They can get a bit cranky when they're tired.'

'And you, Mrs Barton?'

'I would be more than happy to accept your kind offer, Reverend – on the assurance that no one in your household is suffering from the plague. Mr Bielby explained why your children are being sent to him in Sheffield.'

William held back the sharper rebuke stinging his tongue, and gave a benign smile. 'Had that been the case, I would not have been sending our children to stay with my uncle, nor would I have invited you to stay overnight. Rest assured you will not be contaminated with plague whilst staying under our roof.'

Agnes Barton's face reddened. 'Then please accept my apology for asking, Reverend. One hears so many tales about the effects of plague and we know what a truly horrendous affliction it is. I would be honoured to accept a room and a meal in your home, and I look forward to meeting Mrs Mompesson. Mr Bielby tells me she is a delightful and eloquent lady, and a wonderful conversationalist.'

'My wife is, indeed, everything my uncle said, and she and

our children are my greatest delights in life. Catherine is also an extremely sensitive and caring person, and could entertain you all evening with her chatter.'

They all grinned at that, then William instructed Jonathan to drive the coach through the wide gateway and alongside the rectory gardens, continuing round to the rear of the house. 'It will be quite safe there overnight. Unfortunately, we have no provision for horses, so you will need to walk them along to The Miners Arms for feed and stabling overnight.'

William pointed along the road in the direction from which the coach had entered Eyam. 'You will see the inn a short distance from here, set back from the road on your left. The innkeeper, Joe Wilkins, is used to travellers leaving their horses with him for overnight feed and stabling. Tell him I'll send payment with you when you collect them in the morning.'

'I spotted the inn as we passed, thank you, Reverend, so as soon as I've unhitched the coach, I'll be off to see Mr Wilkins.'

'Good,' William said. 'Then tomorrow, once you've both had breakfast and the coach is loaded, you can all set off for Sheffield.'

The evening meal, prepared and cooked by Lydia, was a delicious chicken and ham pie, and conversation flowed pleasantly as they enjoyed it. Yet, whenever talk revolved around the journey back to Sheffield, or of Sheffield itself, William could see that Catherine was struggling to hold back her tears.

Elizabeth was still a little too young to sit with the adults at mealtimes, so Catherine had given the child her meal earlier, as was the usual procedure in the evenings. The little girl now played on the floor in a corner of the room, surrounded by a clutter of toys. But George, a spirited and inquisitive six-year-old, delighted in having visitors to chat to whist he ate. He showered Jonathan with questions about driving a coach, and what they might see on the route they would take tomorrow.

William allowed his son to chatter, pleased that he hadn't noticed his mother's distress. He also wondered if the boy fully understood that he would not be returning to Eyam until the summer and autumn months were over.

But Agnes *had* noticed Catherine's state of misery and, sitting at her side, the kindly lady patted her hand. 'We'll take good care of them, Mrs Mompesson, you can be sure of that. Mr and Mrs Bielby wouldn't have it any other way. And nor would I.'

Catherine gave the smallest of nods. 'Thank you, Agnes. I know you'll look after my little ones, but that won't stop me from missing them. For everyone's sake, I will put on a brave face tomorrow and make sure the children leave here in a happy mood.'

Alone in their bed that night, Catherine's quiet sobs kept Willaim awake for hours. Yet she refused to be consoled by his pacifying words or comforting embrace. He prayed that the passing weeks would enable his wife to accept that when the plague was over, their children would still be alive and well… unlike many who stayed in the village.

When morning came, it was thought prudent to strap the baggage to the coach roof while George and Elizabeth were still at breakfast. In order to do so, William and Jonathan had breakfasted earlier. The children were used to their father's absence for this meal, so George made little fuss when told that Jonathan had also taken his meal early in order to give

Thirteen

him time to collect the two horses.

'Do you think Jonathan will let me sit up there and help him to drive, Mama?' the boy asked as they stood beside the coach ready to clamber aboard.

'Absolutely not, you are far too young, George. Besides, Jonathan needs to concentrate on the road, which he wouldn't be able to do with you chattering away beside him, would he?'

'No, I suppose not... But what if I promise to keep quiet?'

'The answer is still no, so please don't ask again. Imagine what would happen if you fell off.'

George opened his mouth to try a different tactic, but clamped it tightly shut when his father's finger loomed before his nose.

'Now, I want you both to be good, and don't do anything to make Uncle John cross,' William said. 'You will love his big house and the large gardens surrounding it.'

George beamed at the image his father had created, but Catherine added, 'You must promise me that you will never go wandering outside the gardens unless Mrs Barton or another grown up is with you. Sheffield is a big town with lots of streets, and you could easily get lost. It's also a busy place, with a big iron works that makes lots of knives and forks for people to use. The iron works is a dangerous place for anyone other than the people who work there.'

'Don't they make spoons there as well? Someone must make them because there are plenty about.'

William ruffled George's dark hair. 'Yes, they make spoons as well. The people who make all those things are called cutlers, but the iron works makes lots of other things as well. Uncle

John will know more about it than I do, so perhaps you can ask him what else is made there. But now, your mama is waiting for you to promise not to leave the gardens on your own.'

George shrugged and mumbled his promise, but whatever else might have been said was curtailed by Jonathan's call from the driver's seat, 'We're ready for off as soon as the young'uns are aboard, Reverend.'

'Many thanks,' William replied and turned to Mrs Barton. 'We know they'll be in good hands with you as their nanny, Agnes. My wife and I thank you for accepting the task and look forward to seeing you again when we come to collect the children once the plague in Eyam is over.'

'Thank you for your kind words, Reverend, and for your hospitality. I can assure you that your children will be well cared for over the next few months. Let us hope their tears on leaving you both today won't last for too long.'

With that, Agnes boarded the coach, followed by young George, and William lifted little Elizabeth inside to join them.

'You can wave to your mama and papa though the back window,' Mrs Barton said as William closed the coach door.

George waved frantically through the window as the coach moved steadily along the path towards the road. 'See you soon!'

Catherine gave a fleeting wave before bursting into tears. 'I can't do this! We should be leaving with them!' As the coach rounded the side of the house, she fled indoors, her tears flowing like raindrops.

Nursing his own aching heart, William swept a few errant teardrops from his manly cheeks and followed his wife back into the rectory.

Fourteen

July - August 1666

At ten o'clock on Sunday, the fourth day of July, William arrived at Cucklett Delph to hold his first service in the open air. It was a glorious summer's morn and the warm sun beamed down from a cerulean sky, striving to erase the sense of woe that seemed etched into people's faces.

From his elevated pulpit, William gazed down at the large gathering and held his arms out wide. 'Good people of Eyam, I thank you all for attending our first service in Cucklett Delph. Let us first take a moment to look around us, allowing the beauty we behold to delight our senses. Savour the caress of the warm breeze and inhale the sweet scents of meadow flowers it carries. See how it sways the tall summer grasses as you listen to the tinkling voice of the glistening brook as it joins its song to that of the birds singing amidst the verdant canopy of woodland…

'Let us now say our own silent prayer of thanks to the Lord that even in the midst of plague, the beauties of the Earth are a constant reminder of His abiding love.'

William continued with his sermon, which today included the parable of The Good Samaritan. Once again, he hoped the story would help them justify to themselves their reasons for agreeing to the quarantine. The villagers listened attentively, but when it came to saying the prayers from the Anglican Prayer Book, their reaction was no different to how it had been in the church. When asked to repeat each line of the prayers as William recited them – the only thing he could do in the absence of the prayer books – not a voice could be heard. Though admitting to himself he had no real reason to believe things would be different out here, he had clung to the hope that people had begun to trust and respect him enough to pray with him by now.

William chose not to remark on their silence and took the opportunity to deliver a general update on events. 'From the way families have grouped themselves with at least six feet between them, I am pleased to see that no one needs reminding that the quarantine started on Thursday. I am also happy to announce that during the past few days we've had offers of help from two more villages. The people of Bubnell, lying a little over six miles to the south-east of Eyam, just three miles from Chatsworth House, have kindly offered to send us supplies of freshly baked bread on a weekly basis. Each delivery will be collected from the Boundary Stone by me every Monday at noon, for which Joe Wilkins has again agreed to loan me his horse and cart.

'You have my thanks again, 'Joe,' William called out, gesturing to the innkeeper standing with his wife and three young children. 'One person from each family must collect their share from the rectory either later that afternoon or early in the evening. Deliveries from Bubnell will start this coming week. Each family will be given enough bread to last up to two days, the amount given dependent upon how many people are in that household. It will mean, of course, that families will need to continue baking their own bread for the rest of the week.

Fourteen

'Which brings us to the question of supplies of flour. Yesterday, I spoke with the Torres, the family of millers in Stoney Middleton, who assured me that, as yet, they have no shortage of either wheat or rye flour. And this year's grain harvest has yet to begin.'

William allowed the congregation a moment to digest that information before continuing, 'Please remember, you will be expected to pay for flour, although the Torres have kindly offered to reduce the price per bag by half for Eyam folk during the plague. Orders must state not only how many bags are wanted in total, but how many of them should be wheat flour and how many of rye. All orders must be left at the boundary stone at our south-east corner and deliveries will be there the following week.'

A low buzz passed through the listeners as they shared that piece of news.

'My final notice concerns a village that some of you may never have heard of, since it is almost twelve miles to the north-east of Eyam.' The chatting stopped and people again gazed up at him. 'Fulwood is on the edge of Sheffield, so close as to be almost a part of the town. The people of that village have offered to leave us foods and other supplies, as requested. Please leave notes requesting goods from Fulwood, and payments for them, at the well at the north-east corner of Eyam. The items requested will be left there for collection.

'And finally, my friends, remember that none of us must leave Eyam until the number of plague deaths plummets with the onset of winter. But I urge that you continue to live as you have always done, wherever possible. Neighbourly chats are a good means of keeping loneliness at bay, as long as the specified distance between you is maintained. As for paid labour,' he added, holding out his upturned hands, 'unfortunately – though of necessity – work at the lead mines, quarries and farmland beyond our boundary, has ceased. All work within the village can continue for as long as supplies needed for that business to operate can be obtained… as in the case of our fine inn and lodging house, The Miners Arms. But please remember the importance of keeping a distance between you, whether you are pursuing a paid occupation, enjoying a drink at the inn, or simply chatting in the street or at a neighbour's door. I must also remind you that for the time being, all burials must be undertaken by the families concerned.

'Until we meet here again next week, I ask each of you to pray to God to look kindly on our village during this most difficult of times.'

A little after seven o'clock in the evening, two days later, Catherine was clearing away the dishes after their meal when there was a knock on the rectory door. Wondering who could be calling at this time of day, William was surprised to see one of the villagers he'd had neither chance nor cause to speak to until now, standing several feet back from the doorstep. He was a veritable giant of a man with coarse features and long, unkempt brown hair topped by a floppy, wide-brimmed brown hat. William knew his name to be Marshall Howe and that he lived in the Townhead, not far from Humphrey Merrell. The man had worked at the lead mines and had the reputation of having a rough, unfriendly manner.

Fourteen

'Good evening, Rector, I wondered if I might 'ave a word with you. It won't take long but what I intend to ask could be of use to the village.'

'Then I'll be pleased to hear it, Mr Howe.'

The burly man nodded, 'I just wanted to offer me services to folk in the village who can't, or don't want to bury their own dead. I've seen a few old'uns, and womenfolk, struggling to dig graves, and a few 'aving problems pulling the corpses around in them shrouds.'

Taken aback by this request, William had no immediate yes or no for an answer. 'It sounds like a good idea,' he said, slowly, 'if you are willing to take the risk of catching the plague yourself. Our previous sexton was taken by the disease earlier this year.'

Howe shook his head, his chest seeming to puff out with pride. 'No worries on that score, Rector. I've already 'ad it once and recovered. They do say that plague can't strike a person twice. I was just strong enough to fight the bloo… er… the cursed disease off.'

William frowned as he thought. 'I'm not sure it works that way, but if you're willing to risk catching it again, I suppose I have no reason to object. You do realise that, as sexton, you'd be expected to perform the whole ceremony of digging the grave, collecting and transporting the corpse to the grave and filling it in after the burial?'

'Course I do, Rector. I've a nice, big push cart that'll come in 'andy for that.'

Although uncertain of the man's motive for requesting this work, William nodded. 'If you're expecting payment for performing this role, I'm afraid I can only offer a small wage. Unfortunately, the stipend I receive will not stretch to more. Nor will the villagers have spare coin with which to pay you. Most of them have no income at present and any savings they might have must be kept for the payment for food and other necessary goods from outsiders.'

'Ha, don't I know it! Being unable to work at the mines 'as beggared my life up good and proper; I've a wife and child to provide for. Village folk can always pay me with bits and pieces from around the 'ouse that they can manage without.'

'Then I'll leave that to you to organise. Would you like me to write out a few notices to let people know of your new role, or can you do that yourself?'

Howe looked a little sheepish. 'I never took to book learning, Rector, and never learnt to write, so I'll accept your kind offer. Would you let folk know that I'm willing to start right away?'

'Yes, I'll do that. Come back to the rectory in the morning when I've looked at my books and decided on a weekly sum to offer for your services. I'll write out half a dozen notices tonight, so you can collect them and pin them wherever you wish around the village when you leave.'

'Thank you, Rector.' Howe turned away with a grin on his face.'

—

Margaret Ashe scowled as she considered her plight. Having been a widow since the death of her husband last August,

Fourteen

she'd become accustomed to pleasing herself what she did and when she did it. But she was lonely living alone, up here in Orchard Bank, a small area of the Townhead. She had no one to talk to all day, especially as she didn't get on with her neighbours. Although she and Tom had been wed for almost fifteen years, they'd never had children. After his death, she'd taken to visiting her sister and two brothers in Tideswell once a week to ease the boredom. The larger village was only five miles away and it had been Margaret's weekly treat, especially when she visited on market day. She could pick up a few bits and pieces while she was there.

All that had come to an end when that pompous Anglican rector slapped a quarantine on Eyam. Margaret was one of the villagers who had voted against it, but it made no difference. Most of them had been talked into voting in favour of it by Reverend Stanley. Now she was stuck in this plague-ridden village for the entire week. Every week.

Disgruntled, she clomped around her cottage wondering what she could do to relieve her boredom. Then an idea came to her. Tomorrow, she would leave home before sunrise, when few folk were about, and take herself off to Tideswell. It was market day and she could do with a couple of things she couldn't get in Eyam. A nice bit of fish, for a start and, perhaps, a couple of pairs of stockings. No one would know who she was, or where she'd come from, so she had no worries about being recognised.

The sun was peeping over the horizon as Margaret neared Tideswell the following morning, though she knew that most market traders would have already set up their stalls for business. She decided to go straight to the market and buy the things she wanted before visiting Anne this morning and Peter and John once they got home from work late this afternoon. The July days were long and it would still be light when she walked home.

Unfortunately, Margaret hadn't considered there might be a barrier across the main road into Tideswell, with a couple of brawny guards patrolling it. She scowled, stopping in her tracks some thirty yards away, watching them laughing and slapping each other's backs, seemingly engrossed in some amusing conversation. She glanced about, looking for a way she could get past, unseen, and noticed a row of bushes, thick with summer foliage, along the edge of the road to her right. With her eyes fixed on the guards, Margaret sidled towards them, hoping to get behind the bushes while the guards weren't looking…

'Oi, you there… what the hell d'yer think yer doing? We ain't standing here fer the good of our health. Get over here. Now!'

There was nothing Margaret could do but to obey. 'I'm sorry,' she said as sweetly as she could. 'I thought the barrier was only for carts and wagons.'

They both glared at her and the older of the two said, 'What's yer name and where yer from?'

'Edith Lowe, and I live in Orchard Bank.'

'Orchard Bank…? Never heard of it. Have you, Sam?'

The younger man frowned as he thought, then shook his head. 'Nah. Can't say I have.' He scrutinised Margaret from head to foot. 'Where, exactly, is this Orchard Bank?'

'Oh, it's a lovely little place with only a dozen houses.' She

Fourteen

pointed to the south. 'It's seven miles that way, in the Land of the Living. But we don't have a market, so I decided to pick up a few provisions here.'

'The Land of the Living…? I've never heard of that place, either. Have you Pa?'

'No, I haven't', probably 'cos it's so small. So we'll just have to let her through.' He looked pointedly at Margaret 'If yer'd come from anywhere near the plague village of Eyam, yer'd be heading right back there.'

The two inched away from a gap between the makeshift barrier of barrels and Margaret stepped through, heading for the village centre, chuckling to herself at how easily she'd fooled the stupid guards.

Tideswell market was already buzzing with trade. Women scuttled between the many stalls to purchase a much wider variety of goods than those on offer at Eyam's little farmers' market. Here there were stalls selling everything from shoes and stockings, leather gloves, bales of cloth, needles, wools and embroidery silks to soap, and a variety of different foods, including cheese, sausages, fish and freshly baked breads. Margaret felt at ease amongst the crowds, deeming it unlikely that anyone would know she came from Eyam, unless any of Anne's friends had spotted them together at some time or other.

She was handing over the coin for her new stockings when a woman's voice rang out, shrill above the clamour of the crowds:

'A woman from Eyam!'

Terrified shoppers scrambled to distance themselves from Margaret, to reveal a woman with her arm outstretched, her finger pointing.

'She's from the plague village! Get her out of Tideswell!'

'Let's give her a send-off she won't forget!' another woman yelled.

With that, a variety of rotten vegetables struck Margaret's head and body, in addition to clods of earth from the verges around the market square. With tears welling and heart thudding, she fled along the Eyam road with a horde of outraged villagers on her heels. Avoiding the barrier of barrels and the two surprised guards by again darting behind the roadside shrubs, she kept running until certain that no one was still chasing her.

Eventually, she sank to the grass edging the road, tears warm on her cheeks as she wiped the residues of rubbish and rotting foods from her clothes. The only thing she could think of was that at least she'd bought her new stockings. But as she walked on, it struck her that she'd be hard pushed to get back to her home without being seen by her gossiping neighbours.

—

Catherine squinted in the sunlight as she and William strolled around the rectory garden on an overly warm Sunday afternoon. Around them, insects fluttered and buzzed amongst the bright, midsummer blooms of bushes and plants, while damselflies with iridescent wings hovered over the little pond.

'The bread from Bubnell is a blessing, as well as being delicious,' she said, bending to inhale the fragrance of colourful wallflowers alongside the path. 'After two weeks of quarantine the supplies from our neighbours still seem to be plentiful, and,

Fourteen

as far as I know, the methods you devised for the payment of goods have not been abused.'

'Yes, it all seems to be working well, my dear.'

'The biggest blessings of all are the free food and timber supplies from the earl and I'm so proud of you for even thinking of approaching such a great man. His deliveries are generous and much appreciated gifts, especially to those whose incomes have ceased altogether…

'But I grieve for the deaths of so many, William. Our villagers are finding it harder and harder to put on a brave face. I believe we have lost thirty poor souls since the beginning of July and it is only the eighteenth of the month. How many more will die before this evil disease leaves us?'

William was momentarily silent as the truth of Catherine's words sank in, not for the first time berating himself for allowing her to stay in Eyam. But he kept his thoughts to himself for fear of causing her distress over their absent children to surge anew. He opened his mouth to agree with the tragedy of it all, but Catherine's question put paid to that.

'Did you know that a few of the villagers have disregarded the quarantine and fled from Eyam?'

'I'd heard of Andrew Merrell's flight to the moors, but that was before the quarantine was imposed. I do know that his father, Humphrey, isn't too happy about it, though. If you know of more recent departures, I have no idea who they are. Like Andrew, they may camp on the moors, or try their luck at gaining entrance to other villages. But that won't be easy with patrolling guards and the barricades that some towns have set up.'

'Speaking of which, William, have you heard what happened to one of our village women who actually managed to gain entry into Tideswell earlier this week?'

William shook his head and Catherine chatted on, 'It seems a foolish thing to do, especially in a village as close to Eyam as Tideswell. But I imagine that some people are foolish enough to break the rules, even when there's a possibility of being recog–'

'Are you going to tell me about this woman, or not?'

'Patience, husband,' Catherine chided with a smile on her face. 'It seems that a woman who lives in Orchard Bank in the Townhead, managed to get past the barrier into Tideswell last Monday. She – I think Lydia called her Margaret – cleverly fooled the two guards…'

They sat together on a wooden bench while Catherine finished the tale, shaking her head at the absurdity of it all. 'I believe Margaret only wanted to buy a few goods at the market and visit some of her family. But the actions of the Tideswell villagers show how scared people are of catching the plague, which is quite understandable. The incident will also make Margaret think twice about breaking the quarantine in future.'

'What a sorry tale, although, as you, my dear, I hope it taught Margaret a lesson. Is she now back in Orchard Bank?'

'She is, but according to Lydia, her neighbours aren't too happy with her for such selfish actions and say they're having nothing to do with her from now on. Serves her right, I say. But I suppose that's very unchristian of me, especially as Margaret lives alone and has no family in the village. Lydia said she had been planning to move to Tideswell to be close to her sister and brothers before the plague came to Eyam.'

Fourteen

'You know, Catherine, I decided it would not be necessary to implement punishments for breaking the quarantine, simply because those who fled earlier have not returned. In Margaret's case, I think being shunned by her neighbours is probably punishment enough.'

William paused as he thought. 'Although, should Margaret die of plague, living alone and having no family in Eyam could be a problem. Thanks to her recent actions, none of her displeased neighbours would know of her death. Even if they did, I suspect that none would be willing to bury her. Which means we'll have to make a point of noticing whether she comes to collect her free food deliveries every week. If she doesn't arrive, I'll head to the Towhead to check she's alive and well.'

'Which lays yet another responsibility on your shoulders.' Catherine shook her head. 'You really must allow yourself time to rest or you will become too exhausted to do anything at all.'

'I will try, my dear, and hope that Margaret remains free of plague.'

Little was said for some moments as they enjoyed the beauty of the garden and the warmth of the sun on their faces. Catherine was the first to break the silence. 'You obviously know that five members of the Talbot family have died since the fifth of July.'

'Yes, their deaths and burials were reported to me.'

'And the Talbots live a long way from the middle of Eyam,' Catherine added. 'Joan mentioned on Friday that people in the village are wondering how the Talbots could have caught the plague when they live half a mile from their nearest neighbours, the Hancocks. Especially since Richard put notices along the

A Boundary of Stones

top road and near the well saying his smithy will be closed until December.'

William nodded, keeping his thoughts to himself on the Talbot's sad news. The last thing he wanted was Catherine repeating what he believed to anyone in the village. He realised the Talbots lived an almost secluded life out there on the hillside, so the likelihood of being infected by any of Eyam's villagers was slight – except for on one particular occasion.

The first deaths in the Talbot family had been those of Bridget and Mary, Richard and Katherine's eldest daughters. Both of those young women had attended the meeting in Cucklett Delph with their parents on the twenty-fourth of June, just eleven days before the two sisters' deaths. Eleven days would have allowed time for the plague seeds to take root and the symptoms of the disease to become manifest.

William could have wept when he faced the awful truth that it could have been *his* fault that the plague was carried to the Talbot's home. Why, oh why, had neither he nor Reverend Stanley thought to insist that families must stand six feet apart at the meeting? They had both suspected that the seeds of plague could be passed on to others by people in whom the symptoms had not yet become evident.

And yet, William admitted to himself, the organisation of the meeting was nothing to do with Reverend Stanley. It had been *his* responsibility alone. He had just been too engrossed in what the sanctions should entail, and how they'd be presented, to even consider how they should stand in Cucklett Delph on that evening.

Such an oversight was unforgiveable, and he would bear

Fourteen

the guilt of it for the rest of his life. And yet, a small voice in his head asked, if not for his sanction of closing the church for Sunday worship during the plague, how many more people, crushed together like seeds in a pod, would be infected over the coming weeks?

But at this moment, that thought could not persuade William to forgive himself.

—

Sunday July 25 1666

The death toll in the village continued to gain its anticipated momentum and the air of grief ravaged William's conscience relentlessly. He constantly questioned his right to have inflicted a quarantine on Eyam, denying people the chance of saving themselves by leaving the village. What right had *he* to demand so great a sacrifice of them all?

Then his better instincts would prevail and he reminded himself that the majority of people in Eyam had agreed to the quarantine *of their own free will*. And their reason for doing so would again loom before him: they were prepared to lay down their lives in order to save the lives of countless others.

Thoughts of Christ sacrificing his own life to save mankind washed over William like a gloriously soothing balm, reminding him there was no greater way for Eyam's suffering people to show their love for their neighbours. He beseeched God daily for the strength to cling to that knowledge when reports of ever-increasing numbers of deaths reached him. Since the first day of July, thirty-eight villagers had died.

And on a more personal level for William and Catherine, Lydia had been too ill to come into work for the last four days.

Today was Sunday, the twenty-fifth of July, and they were taking an early evening stroll up the gentle hill at the rear of the church. But the tranquillity of the evening was marred by Catherine's constant fretting about Lydia.

'Oh, William, I can't imagine what Lydia's family will do if she dies. They will be truly heartbroken. I have prayed for them every night since Lydia's husband told us how ill she was. Lydia and Joan are my closest friends in the village and I don't know how I'd bear it if I lost either of them, so how much worse would their loss be to their families?'

'Losing loved ones is never easy, Catherine. But Joan isn't ill, so you have no need to fret about her, particularly as you are making yourself ill by doing so. As for Lydia, I do know how you feel because I share your distress. Lydia has become almost a part of our family. She has done her utmost to help us settle into the village and I am greatly indebted to her for that. Not only has she helped you to become acquainted with many of the villagers, she has given me an understanding of Puritan beliefs and way of life. Most of all, we've both become used to enjoying Lydia's friendship and her cheerful presence in the rectory.'

William was silent for some moments as he fought to overcome his own emotions at the thought of losing a dear friend. He dreaded hearing that Lydia had died as much as did Catherine, and once again he questioned whether quarantining the village had been the right thing to do.

Fourteen

His thoughts were curtailed by Catherine's voice. 'I can't begin to imagine the grief old Bridgett Talbot is suffering. She has now lost her son, Richard, her daughter-in-law, Katherine, and five of her grandchildren. Katherine only gave birth to another child two months ago, a daughter whom they also named Katherine. The infant is just so young to be left without a mother.'

'The Talbot's story is extremely sad, my dear, and I note what you have said about the grandmother's plight. But other large families in the village have similar stories. We only have to think of the Syddalls and Thorpes. Sadly, there is nothing more any of us can do about it, other than to pray.'

The following morning, Joan arrived at the rectory in floods of tears. 'Whatever's the matter?' Catherine asked, wrapping her arms around the distraught young woman. 'Your husband hasn't –'

'No, Mistress, Robert is well enough.' Joan dabbed the tears from her eyes and blew her nose. It's Lydia… and her daughter. N-nothing will be the same without Lydia. Sh-e's always b-been a part of my life, and Anne was but a young girl… Poor Samuel's in a state, and he has to b-bury his wife and only child today.'

Catherine's tears gushed to match those of Joan and the two women clung to each other, sobbing at the loss of a dear friend.

'Is it Lydia?' William asked, coming through the study door.

Catherine sniffed back a sob. 'Both Lydia and her daughter died in the night. Oh William, I prayed so hard that Lydia would survive, but it seems that no amount of praying can save anyone from this wicked disease.'

'God will have heard your prayers, Catherine, and we must never question His reasons for allowing diseases like plague and typhus to take the lives of so many. Perhaps such diseases *are* sent as punishment for sins committed in our village.' He sighed. 'Remember that memories of our loved ones lost to the plague will be forever locked in our hearts, and we will be reunited with them when our own time comes to enter God's Paradise.'

Catherine nodded. 'I shall think of that whenever grief at the loss of a beloved friend threatens to overwhelm me.'

'As will I, thank you, Reverend.' Joan took a deep breath as she fought to steady her voice. 'So many in Eyam will mourn for Lydia. She was a dear friend to most of us and her kindness will not readily be forgotten. But now, I must make a start on my work.'

William shook his head. 'You must both allow yourselves time to grieve, so you, Joan, will take two or three days away from work.' He held up his hand as the young woman opened her mouth to protest. 'I will ensure you are paid for however long you decide you need, so you have no reason to worry about a drop in your weekly wage.'

'Bless you for your kindness, Reverend. It will give me time to visit Samuel and see if he needs help with the collection of his provisions.'

William sighed. 'Please give him our heartfelt condolences, and tell him I will call on him early this evening. But, Joan, do remember not to enter the house and to stand well away from the door.'

Fourteen

Saturday, July 30 1666

'I'm off out,' Marshall Howe snapped, placing his floppy hat on his head and glaring at his eight-year-old son. 'And when I get back, I want to see that brass bowl over there so shiny I can see me face in it. And don't you dare break any of them pot bowls and vases, or yer'll feel the sting of my belt. D'ya hear that, William?'

The boy glanced up from the heap of clothes he was folding. 'Yes, Pa… Where're you going?'

'That's none of yer business, and I've told yer afore not to ask. All you need t' know is that I've got another grave t' dig like I did yesterday.'

'Will Ma be getting out of bed today so we can have summat different t' eat than just bread?'

The brawny lead-miner shrugged. 'She might, or she might not, dependin' on whether she feels like it. Yer'll 'ave t' wait an' see. And while I'm out, yer'd best make sure you let no one in. I don't want anyone pokin' their noses in places they're not wanted, no matter who they say they are. Is that clear?'

'Yes Pa. Pa… why do mam's eyes keep going all black and her face all swelled up? She 'a'n't got the plague, has she?'

'No, she 'asn't, so stop askin' daft questions. If she gets the plague, she'll be sick all over the place and get the runs. As far as I know, she 'a'n't got either of them things.'

'But she does cry a lot when she's abed. And she sometimes groans. I can hear her from down 'ere, sometimes.'

'Take no notice, she's only wanting someone to run around after 'er while she lounges about in bed. If she thinks I'm going t' wait on her, she can think again. No one's makin' her stay in bed.'

'But Pa –'

'You just get on with the jobs I've given yer, and yer'll have t' make do wi' bread t' eat till I get back. And yer'd best not let anyone through that door except me.'

—

Catherine slumped at the kitchen table, leafing through Lydia's many books of receipts in an effort to decide what to cook for the evening meal for William and herself. In truth, she found the activity neither tedious nor unpleasant, but her progress was hampered by the tears that constantly clouded her eyes. Once again, she pulled a kerchief from her apron pocket, the third she'd soaked that day, and it was barely noon.

It was now over a week since Lydia's death, and August was underway, yet barely an hour went by without her kindly face filling Catherine's mind. Alone in the kitchen, she felt Lydia's presence so keenly – as though she were standing beside her, directing her in everything she attempted to cook.

The oneness Catherine felt with her dear, departed friend gradually became a salve to her grieving, enabling her to dwell upon memories of happy times they had shared. Lydia had been the first person in Eyam to befriend her, and she knew her visits to the market would never be the same again. Catherine would mourn for the wonderful, kind-hearted Lydia, one of the most loved and respected women in Eyam, for a very long time.

Catherine soon took to cooking for herself and, fortunately, a leather-bound book of receipts of Lydia's favourite dishes she had found in one of the kitchen's many cupboards had become her most used manual. Despite never having cooked a single meal since she and William had moved to Eyam, nor even used the rectory's spacious kitchen, without the children here to take up most of her day, Catherine had time to spend familiarising herself with both the kitchen and Lydia's receipts.

'This is an extremely tasty beef stew, my dear,' William complimented one evening in early August. 'And there will be plenty left for us to enjoy tomorrow.'

Catherine nodded. 'I'm doing my best to make our food allowance last the week. Oh, I've been meaning to ask… did you know that Lydia had a wonderful selection of herbs growing in a small bed in the rear garden? She also kept numerous jars of spices in the pantry, which I've started to explore.'

'I knew about both, my dear. Lydia told me she'd had the herb garden for years – tended it herself, too. And she stocked up on spices on her monthly trips to Bakewell market. She certainly made good use of them in her cooking, as you also seem to be doing, going by this delicious stew. You'll be as adept in the kitchen as Lydia was in time. It just takes a little practise and, no doubt, a lot of patience.

'As to our food allowance,' William went on, 'I can only hope that other families in the village are managing as well as we are. I always make sure that the larger families have a greater portion of the bread from Bubnell, as well as the meats, eggs, cheeses and butter from the earl. Villagers who don't keep their own goats for milk, are relying on surrounding farmers or people from nearby villages for that. So far, things seem to be working out quite well.'

Catherine was quiet for some moments and William asked, 'Is something bothering you, my love?'

'I was just thinking of all the people we have lost since the beginning of July. Some of them were dear to us, like Lydia, but everyone who dies is dear to somebody.'

'July was the saddest month for our village so far; fifty-six dead in a single month is hard to think about. Sadly, Catherine, this hot weather seems set to last and I can foresee August numbers being even higher. We are only three days into the month and already another fourteen people have died – seven of them today. Including Alexander Hadfield.'

Catherine sighed. 'I intend to visit Mary tomorrow. She has lost everything in her life, not only her first husband, but both of her sons and now her second husband. The poor woman has also lost so many relatives in the village that she has barely anyone left to turn to.'

'I'm sure Mary needs a friend at this time, and you are perfect for that role, my dear. Please give her my heartfelt condolences and tell her I will call on her soon.'

Fifteen

Riley Farm, Eyam: August 3 1666

Inside a farmer's cottage on the hillside to the east of Eyam, John and Elizabeth Hancock sat on the sofa together in silence after ensuring their four remaining children were asleep in their beds upstairs. No work had been done on the farm for the last few days, other than milking the goats and collecting the eggs. And today, the burial of two of their six children, eleven-year-old John Junior, and nine-year-old Lizzie, had been the priority. Of necessity, it had been Elizabeth upon whom that task had fallen. Since yesterday, John, too, had been feeling unwell, along with two more of their children.

He suddenly clenched his fists and broke the silence by starting to rant. 'What I want to know is how this stinkin' plague got to us out here. We live a fair distance from the rest of the village, we've had no visitors for days and haven't even been into Eyam for Sunday worship for the past two weeks!'

John slammed his hand on the chair arm in his rage. 'I bet those bloody Talbot kids gave it to us! John and Lizzie were always runnin' wild across the hills with 'em. Young Will and Ollie often tagged along with em an' all. And how often have our kids been in the Talbot's cottage – or the Talbot kids in ours, come to that?'

Elizabeth recoiled at the vehemence of his words. 'Please stop shouting, John; you're frightening me. You've got a sweat up already with your yelling and slapping, and it won't bring

John and Lizzie back, will it? You also need to respect the fact that most members of the poor Talbot family are now dead. There's only old Bridgett and her little three-month-old grandchild left. Bridgett's getting on in years and will be struggling to care for the babe, especially if she keeps her awake all night.'

Elizabeth's tears welled again and she quietly sobbed. 'I'm sorry, love,' John said, reaching for her hand. 'It's just that you and the kids mean the world to me, and we've tried so hard to keep ourselves safe from the cursed disease. P'raps we should've kept our doors locked to the Talbot children.'

'That's easy to say, now,' Elizabeth whispered. 'Neither of us guessed any of the Talbots were ill. They always looked so well and full of life. Which is more than I can say for you, or William and Oliver, tonight. Both boys were still complaining of headaches and feeling sick when they went to bed.'

'Being so upset today is enough to give anyone a headache. I feel like someone's been using my head as a punch bag, and I can't keep a thing in me belly. I just hope a good night's sleep will clear 'em both.'

'You should never have left your bed today. I'm strong and fit enough to dig graves and –' Elizabeth suddenly realised what she'd just said, and more tears brimmed. 'I shall pray that you and our little boys will be well by tomorrow and that no one else in our family dies. I'll sleep on the sofa down here tonight so I don't disturb you when I need to tend to Will and Ollie. If you need me to fetch you anything in the night, you'll have to call out.'

Wakened a little before sunrise the following morning by five-year-old Oliver calling for her, Elizabeth headed up to the

Fifteen

room the boy now shared with only William since the death of their older brother, John Junior. She swept the child's curly brown locks away from his sweaty face. 'What on earth's the matter, Ollie? You feel very hot, but you're shivering. Did the night terrors come again?'

Oliver shook his head and tears rolled down his cheeks. 'I feel really sick and my tummy hurts. And I think I've pooed the bed.'

'Are you strong enough to get out of it to let me have a look?'

'I don't know, Mam, my legs have gone all wobbly.'

Elizabeth lifted the little boy from the bed and sat him on the floor. To her dismay, Oliver's nightshirt and lower sheet were covered in reeking, runny excrement.'

William peeped out from beneath his blankets. 'Mam… I've been sick on the floor three times in the night and I think I've just messed my bed. It feels all wet and slimy. And my belly really, really hurts.'

'Just lie still for a few moments, Will. I'll get you all nice and clean as soon as I've got Ollie cleaned up. Just remember, you're a big boy of seven and know how to be patient.'

Not wanting her little ones to see just how bad she knew their illness to be, Elizabeth blinked back her tears and set to, washing them down and changing their nightshirts and bedding. Once they were clean and comfortable, she kissed them both before scooping up the soiled items and heading downstairs to place them in a tub of water outside the back door.

Dawn was breaking as Elizabeth returned to the silent living room where she fell to her knees in desperate prayer:

Dear Lord, I beseech you not to take my two little boys from us. They have the early symptoms of plague and with your help, they could recover from this hateful disease. They are innocent babes and deserve a longer life than a mere few years.

Elizabeth pushed herself to her feet, determined to stay strong and keep her tears at bay for the sake of her ailing children. And the only way she could do that was by keeping busy. She would start by milking the goats before the rest of the family stirred.

Rays of the rising August sun warmed Elizabeth's cheeks as she returned from the goat pens across the yard with a pail of milk. Not daring to dwell on what the new day might bring, she headed upstairs, convincing herself that her beloved husband would be awake and well after a good night's sleep.

Surprised to find John still asleep, she pulled the bedclothes back from his face, heaving a sigh of relief at seeing him still drawing breath. She stroked his cheek but when he failed to rouse, she panicked and pulled the blankets further down… and recoiled at the reek that assaulted her nostrils. The bedsheets, along with John's nightshirt and legs were covered in the stinking product of diseased bowels.

By the time Elizabeth had removed her husband's soiled nightshirt and bedding, washed him down and replaced the filthy items with fresh ones, their two eldest daughters, Alice and Anne, were up and about.

'Where is everyone?' Alice asked, her eyes fixed on the rolled-up sheets in her mother's arms as she came downstairs. 'The boys are usually gulping their breakfasts down by now and Pa's ready to head outside with me and Anne to see to the

Fifteen

chickens and goats.'

'Will and Ollie are still feeling poorly, probably after all the upset we had yesterday, and your pa's not feeling too well, either,' Elizabeth said, too overcome by her own grief at that moment to have dealt with floods of tears from her eldest daughters. 'I'm sure your pa would appreciate you two feeding the hens and collecting the eggs. I've already fed and milked the goats.'

Alice and Anne headed off to do their chores, returning as Elizabeth was about to climb the stairs, laden with clean clothing and bedsheets.

Elizabeth attempted a smile. 'Thank you, girls. Neither your father, nor your brothers will be leaving their beds today. They're all feeling too unwell.'

The two girls stared at her and Elizabeth placed the sheets on the chair and wrapped an arm around each of them, holding them close.

'They'll be better by tomorrow, won't they Mam? They aren't going to die like John and Lizzie?'

'I don't know, Anne. All we can do now is to pray to the Lord to watch over them.'

—

Eyam village: August 5 1666

William knocked on Mary Hadfield's door before stepping back to await a response.

Within moments, the door swung back and Mary gave a

wan smile. 'Good morning, Reverend. Mrs Mompesson mentioned you would be round to see me soon.' She pushed errant strands of light brown hair back beneath her coif, reminding William of Catherine's habit of doing the same. 'As you see, I have not yet succumbed to the plague and there is no one left in my home but me.'

Tears brimmed in Mary's eyes and she knuckled them away, clearly embarrassed at displaying her grief. 'I'm sorry, Reverend. I thought I'd cried my last tears when my brother and I buried Alexander in the small stretch of meadow beyond our cottage two days ago. My first husband bought the field a few months after we were wed but he died before he got round to buying the goats he'd intended to keep on it.'

William nodded and raised his eyebrows, hoping his expression of interest would encourage Mary to continue.

'It had never been used for anything until it became my family's graveyard,' she added with a little smile that failed to disguise the sobs still threatening to escape. 'There is still plenty of space out there for my brother and I, should we die before the plague leaves our village.'

'Having survived this far, Mary, I sincerely hope you outlive the plague.'

'It's a lonely life on my own all day, Reverend. I find myself thinking I ought to start preparing a meal, or doing the washing, or even reading a story to little Edward. Then I remember, there's only me to cook for and my small amount of washing to do. And my two, dear sons are gone.'

'If you'd be kind enough to accompany me to the rectory, Mary, I have a proposition to put to you that you may or may

Fifteen

not like. Naturally, I'm hoping it will be the former. Catherine is there, although she has no idea of any such proposition, but I'm certain she'd be delighted if you agreed to it.'

'Well, Reverend,' Mary replied, unable to prevent an amused smile brightening her face, 'I think I must agree to your request, if only to make sense of the nonsense you've just spouted.'

Catherine was in the kitchen when William walked in with Mary. William smiled at his wife, who seemed to be poring over books of receipts on the long oak table, surrounded by heaps of ingredients. But he didn't miss her glistening eyes or the rapid return of the kerchief to her apron pocket as she spotted them in the doorway. Anguish over Lydia's death was slow in releasing Catherine from its grasp.

'What a pleasant surprise,' Catherine said, bravely adopting a cheerful face. 'Please try to ignore the mess. I'm attempting to decide what to cook for our evening meal, although I am not yet familiar with many of these herbs and spices. I'm certain William would not want to suffer griping pains from some ingredient I used too much of.'

She sighed and held out her upturned hands. 'I've managed to present a few acceptable stews but, I confess, I have always been happy to let more confident cooks than I rule the kitchen. People like Lydia…'

Catherine's face crumpled on uttering her departed friend's name and William patted her hand, assuring her he understood her lingering grief.

'Oh, my goodness,' she suddenly yelped, removing her apron and brushing away the flour that had found its way to her dress beneath. 'You must think me completely devoid of manners, Mary. Please go through to the sitting room and I'll fetch you both a cup of cocoa.'

'Shall we all just sit here for a moment first, while I have my say to you both?' William gestured at the table. 'It won't take long and we could enjoy our cocoa in the sitting room afterwards.'

Once they were seated, William started, 'Before you say anything, Catherine, I have a proposition to put to Mary that I am certain will be beneficial to the three of us.' The two women glanced at each other and Catherine shrugged.

'Since you are on your own now Mary, and are, understandably, feeling lonely, I was wondering if you would consider becoming our cook now that Lydia has passed away. Although Lydia continues to be greatly missed for the lovely person she was, I am only too aware of my wife's inexperience in the kitchen.'

Mary and Catherine shared a glance, equally surprised at this suggestion.

'What do you say, Mary?' William asked. 'Or, perhaps before you say anything, I should probably add a couple of things in relation to what the position entails.'

'I would be happy to hear a few details, Reverend.' Mary grinned. 'It will give me time to recover from my surprise.'

'Then first of all, before I expand on particulars, I'll say a little about the work Lydia did for us. You may wish to ask questions regarding some aspects of it, or simply say that it is not for you. So, in a nutshell, here it is. First and foremost, it involves you becoming nothing more than our cook, so no cleaning will be expected of you anywhere in the house but the kitchen.'

'I am interested already, Reverend. If you had required a cleaner, I would probably have declined. I already have enough cleaning to do at home. Dust settles everywhere, even with only one person living in the house.'

'A promising start, then. Now I shall endeavour to tempt you a little more. You would be most welcome to stay here and share the meals you cook for us, although you would need to add a small portion of your food ration to ours to do so on a regular basis. Catherine and I have the same food allowance as every other two-person family in the village, and cooking for three would obviously take a little more.'

'That is an extremely kind and neighbourly invitation, Reverend Mompesson, and one with which you have succeeded in tempting me further.'

'Excellent,' William replied. 'Then I shall add a little more. You would also be most welcome to stay in the rectory, overnight, should you wish, especially until your loneliness abates. There will always be a bedchamber upstairs for whenever you wish to use it. It would give Catherine great pleasure to have another woman to talk to of an evening, especially when I have paperwork to deal with.'

Mary nodded so William continued, 'In addition to preparing and cooking our evening meal, you will be asked to provide a simple daily luncheon and make cocoa for the three of us and any guests we might have, at mid-morning and mid-afternoon on weekdays. We would also be extremely pleased if you would bake a few pastries and buns now and then, should our rations stretch to it.'

Mary laughed at that and William added, 'You will be paid the same wage that Lydia received. Over the weekend, Catherine should be able to manage the cooking, if you would prefer to have those days to catch up on your own housework.'

Catherine could hold back her enthusiasm no longer. 'Oh Mary, it would be wonderful to have you here… But I will understand if you would rather be in your own home.'

'I would be honoured to be your cook. I love cooking, and have no one but myself to cater for now. And if I did choose to have weekends at home, I'd be sure to leave you a stew, of perhaps some soup, to help with your meal preparations, Mrs. Mompesson. But I'm not sure about staying here overnight, at least, not every night.'

'Staying overnight is not an essential part of the role,' William explained, 'but the option to do so is there, if you wish to use it. It would not affect the wage you receive if you did stay overnight. Either way, you are welcome to share with us whatever evening meal you make. It would relieve you of the need to cook for yourself once you get home.'

'It all sounds perfect,' Mary replied, 'and yes, Mrs Mompesson, it would be lovely to have you to chat with of an evening. I take it that your cleaner, Joan, goes home earlier?'

'Oh dear,' Catherine said, her hand pressed to her forehead. 'I forgot to tell you… Joan called in earlier to say she wouldn't be coming back to work for at least another few days. Her husband has been very unwell and now has several symptoms of plague. Joan fears he won't live for much longer. Understandably, she is extremely distressed and only stayed

Fifteen

long enough to deliver her message.

'It is all so very sad. The poor woman's expecting their baby early next year and, as you know, William, she hasn't been into work for a few days now. I thought she must be feeling poorly due to being with child but she has stayed at home to care for Robert.'

'Robert will be in our prayers, my dear, and our hearts go out to Joan, who may well catch the plague from him. We'll just have to wait and see what happens.'

'Oh, William,' Catherine said, close to tears at the thought, 'by the time this evil plague leaves Eyam, there'll be hardly a soul left here alive.'

—

On the sixth day of August, Joan French buried her husband in the small garden to the rear of their cottage. Although adamant never to ask the despicable Marshall Howe to do it for her, digging the grave seemed to take hours. And although she followed William's advice on how to use the shroud to pull the body down the stairs, she found it very difficult. The corpse of her beloved Robert slid down the last few wooden steps of its own accord, causing Joan to tumble with it.

Naturally distressed and praying she would not lose the child she carried, Joan rearranged Robert's body on the shroud and dragged it to the waiting grave. Bruised and weary, she sat beside the open grave in silent prayer for the next half hour before lifting the shovel to begin the work of filling it in.

The following day, Joan made a brief visit to the rectory,

where she remained several feet from the doorstep to report Robert's death and burial to Reverend Mompesson.

'You have our sincere condolences, Joan,' William said as the young woman fought back her tears.

'Thank you, Reverend. Would you tell Mrs Mompesson, I shall be ready to return to work in a day or two? I have no symptoms of plague.'

William shook his head. 'I must ask you to stay at home for another five days and return to work on the thirteenth of August. That way we can feel a little more confident that you are not harbouring the seeds of plague and are able to mix with people again.'

'I understand, Reverend, and will see you all again on the thirteenth.'

Riley Farm: August 7 – 10

It was mid-morning on the seventh day of August when little five-year-old Oliver became the third member of the Hancock family to die. By the time Elizabeth had controlled her flooding tears enough to start preparing him for burial, his older brother, William, had taken his final breath. Then, barely an hour before noon, their father, John, closed his eyes for the very last time.

Drowning in her grief, Elizabeth washed each of them down, baulking at the dark patches of bruising and the ugly, weeping buboes that had appeared the previous day, just like the ones she'd seen on Lizzie and John Junior. Wrapping each

Fifteen

in a sheet, she left them on their beds to await burial.

By late afternoon, Elizabeth had dug three graves next to those of Lizzie and John Junior in their meadow adjacent to the house, and one by one, she hauled her husband and their two youngest sons down the stairs and out to the waiting graves. She had hoped for help in doing this from her older daughters but, soon after midday, both Alice and Anne had taken to their beds. Frequent vomiting had emptied the meagre contents of their stomachs, but they continued to retch and soon they lost control of their bowels. Gripped by such weakness, they could not leave their beds when the bouts of diarrhoea took them.

Elizabeth struggled to maintain the constant cleaning of Alice and Anne whilst ensuring the three burials were completed that day. By the time she was shovelling the earth back into the graves to cover the bodies of her husband and their two young sons, it was by the light of a single oil lamp and the beams of a waning gibbous moon.

Not yet ready to sleep in the wide bed in which she had slept with her husband for the past nineteen years, Elizabeth spent another night on the sofa in their only downstairs room. By the time she roused after a mere few hours of sleep, the murky, grey light of the predawn was squeezing through the shutters. Still wrapped in a happy dream of her childhood friends in Eyam, she contemplated going down to the village to spend some time with them all. Perhaps they could take a stroll down to Cucklett Delph together –

Then the painful truth of reality slammed into her.

'John was dead! Her wonderful husband was dead. And so were four of their precious children. Only the two eldest girls were left and Elizabeth was certain they would be taken from her soon. She thanked the Lord that their eldest child, eighteen-year-old Matthew, was safe. Apprenticed to a cutler in Sheffield for the past three years, their son was fourteen miles away from this plague-riddled village.

Fifteen-year-old Alice, and Anne, a year younger, were the only ones in her family left here in Eyam. John had been so proud of them. 'Pretty as pictures, the two of 'em,' he'd boasted. 'It won't be long afore we have village lads queueing at our door asking for their hands.'

That was before the cursed plague had struck.

Elizabeth dreaded climbing those stairs. How could she go on living if plague had taken Alice and Anne? *'Dear Lord,'* she pleaded, *'if you must take my daughters, I beg you to take me, too.'*

The following day, the first signs of bruising appeared on the girls' bodies and during the night, the repulsive buboes appeared.

Elizabeth wept bitter tears as she washed and redressed them, noting that Alice and Anne were covered in flea bites, like the rest of the family. She could attribute no particular significance to that, other than the fact that there had been an abundance of rats again this summer. It seemed likely to her that the fleas were harboured in the creatures' fur. In the still of night, the constant gnawing and scratching of rats tunnelling their way through the edgings of walls and floorboards was enough to set her nerves on edge, especially outside in the barns and storage sheds. Even the keen eyesight and razor-sharp claws of three vigilant farm cats were futile against such hordes.

Consumed with dread at the prospect of losing her daugh-

Fifteen

ters, Elizabeth thought no more about the rats. They would still be here long after the Hancock family was gone.

As the sun rose on the tenth day of August, shedding golden light across the green-swathed hillside, Elizabeth dragged the bodies of Alice and Anne out to the waiting graves, screaming at God for dealing her family the cruelest of blows. Toiling to return the loosened earth to the graves, she was consumed with hatred for the god who had taken her family – seven innocent lives – within a mere eight days.

Never again would she pray to that god, inside a church or out. She would stay at the farm for the next few days and once certain that God had ignored her plea to take her with her daughters, she would pack her few belongings, set the hens and goats free to roam, then head off to Sheffield. One way or another, she'd get inside that barricaded city and live with Matthew for a while. Once she'd found some paid work, she would rent a small place of her own. And her life would begin again.

'To hell with it all!' she yelled, anger and bravado taking the place of teardrops and sobs. 'And to hell with you, false god! You care naught for the people who trusted you to keep them safe!'

Alone and unable to sleep, Elizabeth spent that night sitting beside the graves of her beloved family, singing them to everlasting sleep with sweet lullabies.

—

The following day, old Bridgett Talbot arrived at Elizabeth's door carrying her three-month-old grandchild, Katherine.

Despite having been in the middle of a fitful nap after a night devoid of sleep, Elizabeth hadn't the heart to turn an old friend away. Besides, she knew that in her fragile and arthritic state, Bridgett would not have struggled here, almost a half-mile from Talbot's smithy, if what she had to say was of no consequence.

Elizabeth insisted the old lady should sit on the sofa to rest and lay the child down beside her. There would be time for chatting once the panting had stopped.

'I need to ask a great favour of you, my friend,' Bridgett started, once she had caught her breath and Elizabeth was seated in a chair opposite. 'I ask you… no, I *implore* you… to take this babe and rear her as your own. I realise that you and John already have a large family, but I know what wonderful parents you are. There is no one else I would trust to take care of my precious grandchild.'

Too stunned to speak, Elizabeth's head whirled at the possibilities, and the difficulties, of agreeing to Bridgett's request. It was apparent that Bridgett had no knowledge of the deaths of Elizabeth's family, and how truly wretched and heartbroken she was. But she glanced at the tiny infant in her motherless state and her heart melted.

Bridgett's weary voice cut across Elizabeth's thoughts. 'As you may know, I have lost everyone in my family but for this small, innocent babe.' She shook her stone-grey head, squeezing her tired eyes shut to halt the flow of welling tears. 'I am old, and can barely bend to lift the child from her crib. And the constant warming of goat's milk for her feeds keeps me on my arthritic legs for far too long, especially during the night. Things I coped with in my younger days now only serve to

Fifteen

make my many ailments seem more painful.'

Elizabeth's heart went out to this proud old lady, who had spent all her adult life caring for her family. 'Yes, it must be very hard on you, Bridgett; I said as much to John only a few days ago. A child's earliest weeks are a drain, even on young, strong parents. But I'm not sure that taking a babe into our home at this time of plague would be wise. Much as I admire and love you, you ask a great deal of us and –'

'I fear I have little time left on God's earth, Elizabeth. I am old and with the heartache I carry, I am ready to meet my Maker. Our physician told me a year since that my heart was weak and any great strain on my body could be the death of me. And the babe grows heavier by the day. I fear that if I die, her death will soon follow. And little Katherine deserves a chance at life. Who would know if I took a tumble and died with her in my arms, or I caught the plague and collapsed?'

Elizabeth had no answers to Bridgett's questions, though her pity for the old lady welled. Nor could she bring herself to confess that her own husband and children were dead, or that she was leaving here tomorrow.

Yet the more Elizabeth gazed at the babe, the more her maternal instincts dictated her judgement. Yes, she could rear another child, an infant who had not been close to anyone infected with plague. She doubted it would ease the pain of her own sorrows, but Bridgett was right: little Katherine did deserve a chance at life.

'I will take the child, Bridgett,' she said quickly, before she had chance to change her mind. 'I can see you are in no state to care for her. Just go home and look after yourself, knowing that I will be taking good care of your grandchild. Katherine and I will call on you in a few days, just to see how you are.'

Tears of relief and gratitude rolled down old Bridgett's face as she thanked and hugged Elizabeth before leaving the cottage. There was nothing more to be said and Elizabeth held the babe in her arms as she watched the old lady hobbling along the narrow lane across the hillside, on her way home.

Sixteen

Friday, August 13 1666

Catherine was happy to see Joan back at work, although she could see just how much her husband's death had taken its toll. The rosy bloom of Joan's cheeks had been replaced by a sallow hue, and her sunny smile was gone. Catherine's love and pity reached out to her as she welcomed her back to work with a hug.

'You really mustn't overtire yourself, Joan,' she said. 'You have your unborn child to think of and I told you a short time ago that there is little cleaning to be done now that our children are in Sheffield. Just the flick of a duster here and there will be enough for now. And remember that my offer of a room and your meals here, with us, is still open. I sincerely hope you accept it, even if only until the sharp pains of your grief have dulled.'

'I will gladly consider your kind offer, Mrs Mompesson. But for a week or two I need to feel close to Robert and able to talk to him so he doesn't feel lonely and forgotten in his grave. I hope you understand, Mistress. Perhaps after that I'll be happy to stay in your lovely home until the plague is over and George and Elizabeth are here again.'

'I do understand, Joan. It took me some time to get used to the idea of our children being away from us. They've been gone for over six weeks now, and I think of them constantly, wondering what they're doing and if they are happy.'

'People say there's nothing as strong as a mother's love, Mistress. I'm already feeling it and our babe isn't even born yet.'

'As did I, on both occasions. Well then, on that positive note, let us go to the kitchen and pester Mary for a cup of her delicious cocoa.'

For the next two days, Joan came into work, although on the second day, the fifteenth of the month, she asked to finish early due to a throbbing headache.

'Of course you can,' Catherine said, guiding her friend to the door. 'Be sure to go straight to bed in a cool, darkened room and close your eyes. Hopefully you will soon nod off and waken with your headache gone.'

'I do hope so, Mistress. I've never had a headache as bad as this one before.'

'Hmmm. Mary tells me that willow bark is one of the best cures for headaches but, unfortunately, we have none to offer you because neither William nor I have ever needed it. Have you any at home?'

Joan shook her head. 'I've always made a drink from chamomile for my headaches because we have some growing in our garden.'

'That is probably just as effective, so remember to make a potion before you go to bed.'

'I will, thank you, Mistress. I'll see you in the morning, if this headache is gone by then. If I am not here by nine o'clock, you will know that I am feeling no better and need another day to recover.'

—

Sixteen

Riley Farm and Talbot's Smithy: Sunday August 14, 1666

After struggling to feed little Katherine on warm goat's milk from a spoon for a few days, Elizabeth Hancock decided to walk over to the Talbot's house to ask Bridgett if she had some kind of feeding vessel. By the time she got there, the child was fast asleep.

Elizabeth knocked on the door but after some moments with no response, she tried the latch on the shiny brass door handle. Surprisingly, the door was unlocked. Swallowing down the feeling that something was wrong, she pushed the door open and stepped inside.

The putrid stench was the first thing that hit her; a smell she had come to know well over the past two weeks. It was the overpowering reek of vomit and uncontrollable bowels. And something else. It was as though a body was rotting away, inside and out.

Plague lurked in this house.

And to Elizabeth's knowledge, only Bridgett was here.

She lay the sleeping babe in an armchair and, with great trepidation, climbed the stairs. Despite expecting to find the old lady dead, the sight that met Elizabeth's eyes made her stomach heave. Acrid bile rose to her throat and she was forced to swallow it down before she emptied the meagre contents of her own stomach. There, on the floor, beside the bed she had slept in alone since her husband died a decade ago, Bridgett lay on her front, her face in a patch of dried vomit on the wooden floorboards. Whether the old lady had been trying to reach her bed or walk away from it, Elizabeth could not tell. But either way, Bridgett must have slipped on the combination of vomit, urine and faeces that covered the wooden floorboards near the bed.

And there had not been a soul in the house to help her.

Elizabeth's pity and anger welled. How could a supposedly loving god allow such a kind and caring person as Bridgett to end her life in this way? The old lady's nightgown and lower legs were covered in faeces, as Elizabeth had seen so many times with her own family. Intent on washing Bridgett clean and burying her with the rest of the Talbot family, she hurried downstairs for a bucket of water and a bundle of cloths.

By the time Bridgett was washed, dressed in a clean nightgown and wrapped in a bedsheet, Katherine was in full voice, which meant that the burial must wait until tomorrow. Having no intention of leaving Bridgett in this stinking room overnight, Elizabeth dragged her body down the stairs to the living room.

Ensuring the door was pulled firmly shut so no wild animals could get in, Elizabeth headed home, absently thinking that all she had come for was an easier method of feeding the babe her milk. That seemed such a trivial and pointless worry, now. Within the next few weeks, the child would be able to manage a variety of mashed vegetables and finely chopped meats. Until that time, Elizabeth would persevere with the bread soaked in warm goat's milk.

On returning to the Talbot's cottage the following morning, Elizabeth's first task was to find a suitable shovel. Reasoning with herself that there must be at least one around the place

Sixteen

somewhere, or the rest of the Talbots could not have been buried, she headed towards a row of outbuildings. In the second shed she tried, she found an array of tools, including garden forks, spades, shovels and rakes. She selected a suitable long-handled shovel.

Elizabeth laid the child on a folded blanket close to the Talbot graves, hoping she'd be content for a while after the milk and bread she'd had before they left the Hancock house, and commenced digging.

Tears fell anew as Elizabeth thought of the seven graves she'd already dug for her own beloved family. But, she told herself, though she may shed a bucketful of tears, nothing she could do would bring her loved ones back. She must simply accept that they were gone and think about the future for Katherine and herself.

As her thoughts turned to her new daughter, Elizabeth promised to love her as much as she had loved her own little ones, and to raise her to be a kind, thoughtful and loving person. In a couple of days, she would walk down into Eyam to see Reverend Mompesson. He would want to know the names of all plague victims and where they were buried. He also needed to know that she, Elizabeth Hancock, was now the guardian of three-month-old Katherine Talbot.

Refusing to pray to the god who had taken everything else from her, all she could do now was hope with all her heart that the plague would leave this innocent child alone.

With old Bridgett's burial completed, Elizabeth set about releasing the Talbot's goats and pigs from their pens and the hens from their coop. As she walked along the narrow road home, it occurred to her that now she'd decided to stay in Eyam, it was fortunate that she hadn't already released her own livestock.

—

Tuesday, August 17 1666

Catherine sat in the rectory's comfortable sitting room with her husband, unable to enjoy the morning cocoa due to her deep concern for Joan. Oblivious to her disquiet, William was devouring a warm blackberry tart, made by Mary with some plump blackberries she'd collected that morning along the footpath beside the church that led up the hill to the top road and the well.

'I can't help wondering how Joan is feeling now,' Catherine said as her husband licked the crumbs from his lips. 'She did say she'd be back at work yesterday if her headache had gone by then. Two days seems a long time for a mere headache to last and, I confess, I can't help fearing the worst. You know as well as I do that a severe headache can be one of the earliest signs of plague.'

'I understand your concern, Catherine, though I'm afraid to say, I hadn't realised Joan had been absent from work again. I've been so busy over the last few days collecting and recording foods from the earl and the bread from Bubnell to notice. I also had a very distressed widow named Lydia Kempe from the Shepherds Flat area visit me yesterday. She wanted to report the deaths and burials of all four of her children. I can only

Sixteen

hope she won't be stricken next.'

'Isn't Shepherds Flat the area outside the village, between Eyam and Foolow?'

'It is, although it's within our parish boundary. I believe there are only the two families living out there at present, the Kempes and the Mortens. Both are farming families, and close neighbours whose children play together. The Mortens of Shepherds Flat are just one small branch of the family that lives in Eyam. Two Mortens from the village have died since the end of July but, as yet, I have no record of the deaths of any Mortens at Shepherds Flat.'

'But you believe that now the Kempes have been stricken, that could be a possibility, or even a probability?'

'I'm afraid my answer is yes, I do.' William sighed. 'Now that the plague has stricken one of those families, it will continue until most, if not all, members of both families are dead. The fourth and last child in the Kempe family died two days ago. Their poor mother, Lydia, is already a widow and now she's on her own.'

There seemed nothing more to say about the Kempes and Mortens and Catherine said, 'I'll visit Joan this afternoon and find out how she is. I know she's already finding it hard being in the house on her own since Robert's death, without being poorly as well. But she did say her neighbours are kindly people who make sure she doesn't feel completely alone, so I am glad about that.'

William smiled at his wife, whose concern for others was one of her most endearing qualities. 'I sincerely hope you find Joan to be well, my dear. She is such a pleasant young lady.'

As it turned out, Catherine had no need to visit Joan. One of the Frenchs' next door neighbours, an old man by the name of Henry Fryth, came to the rectory early that afternoon. The rap on the door was answered by Mary, who hurried to the sitting room to find Catherine.

'I'm afraid Henry won't tell me what it's about, Mrs Mompesson. He insists he needs to see you, and that is that. I must warn you, though, he's upset about something, so you'd best be prepared for bad news.'

'You say he is one of Joan's neighbours?'

Mary nodded. 'Henry has lived in that house for as long as I can remember. He and his wife, Elizabeth, are a lovely old couple, and they have a large family… at least, they did have, before the plague took several of them.'

Catherine's heart pounded in her chest. 'Then would you tell Mr Fryth, I'll be there directly, Mary?

'I hope he isn't here to tell us that Joan has the plague,' she said, once Mary had left the room. 'I've been dreading hearing that since her husband became ill. Losing another dear friend to this… this… *vile* disease will not an easy thing to bear, and I cannot help being upset at the thought of it.'

William patted her hand. 'Perhaps you should hear what Mr Fryth has to say before you assume the worst, Catherine. I am fond of Joan, too, and will pray that the news is good. But if it is not and Joan has passed, remember that it always helps with the grieving to think of death as being the end of a person's suffering. And if they led good and honest lives, we must rejoice that they will be taken to enjoy everlasting peace in Heaven with the Lord.'

Sixteen

Catherine nodded and hurried to greet her visitor.

'Hello, Mr Fryth,' she said as cheerily as she could at the rectory door. 'Mrs Hadfield says you have some news for me.'

Henry took off his wide-brimmed hat as good manners dictated, whilst what he had left of his wispy grey hair seemed to stand to attention. 'That I do, Mistress, although I'm afraid to say there's nothing at all good about it.'

'It's about Joan, isn't it?'

Henry nodded, his lined face reflecting his own sorrow, and Catherine took a deep and calming breath. 'You are here to tell us she is abed with the plague.'

'No, Mistress, I am not. I'm sorry to tell you that Joan died of plague in the night.'

Catherine covered her mouth with her hand in an effort to prevent the wail welling in her throat from emerging. But there was nothing she could do to stop the teardrops brimming.

'There was no answer when my wife knocked on Joan's door this morning,' Henry continued. 'We wanted to ask if she'd like us to collect her rations from the earl this afternoon. She wasn't feeling at all well yesterday, you see, complaining of still having a headache and having griping pains in her belly. So when she still didn't answer the door by noon, we feared the worst. I'm afraid I had to kick the rear door in to get inside.'

Catherine's tears flowed, and the old man stood there in silence for some moments, twiddling his hat, until she blew her nose and composed herself.

'My wife has washed Joan, dressed her in a clean nightgown and wrapped her in a bedsheet in readiness for burial. I pulled her body downstairs, but we thought we ought to report Joan's death before we buried her this afternoon.'

'Thank you for your thoughtfulness, Mr Fryth. Not everyone remembers to do that.'

'Aye well, I suppose most people are too upset to think about it. But as I was saying, we hope to bury Joan beside her husband at around four o'clock, as soon as our son, Francis, can come round to dig the grave for us. Joan was a kind and generous person, and to think she died while she was with child, makes her death seem all the more tragic. We'll all miss her and Robert, and will be saying prayers for them both today.'

'I'm glad to know that Joan had such kind neighbours as you and your wife, Mr Fryth. It helps me to know she didn't lie there alone for too long. Joan was not only our cleaner, but my dear friend, and I shall miss her terribly. I know you will bury her with the respect she deserves, and please give my thanks to your son for digging her grave. I imagine you didn't wish to make use of Marshall Howe for the task.'

Henry harrumphed. 'I wouldn't want that man digging the grave of anyone I knew, Mistress. If truth be told, he's one of the nastiest people I've ever met. More than a few folk in Eyam could tell you what an evil piece of work he is. I've heard say he'd beat his own mother if she didn't give him the coin he wanted when he was a lad. He's a born bully, that one, and we all feel sorry for his poor wife and son.'

'Joan told me about people's fears for Marshall Howe's family, Mr Fryth, and I believe William intends to pay them a visit as soon as he has a spare moment. I don't believe I've seen any of them in church, but we do have their address.'

'I've a feeling Mrs Howe wouldn't open the door if she saw

Sixteen

the rector through the window. She might feel comfortable speaking to you, Mrs Mompesson, but I doubt the rector would be happy with you entering the house alone, in case that wicked bully returned while you were there. But I'll leave that to you to decide, and be on my way.'

'Thank you for coming,' Catherine said as Henry nodded and replaced his hat before turning to walk slowly away. She closed the door with tear-filled eyes and a heavy heart, trying hard to rejoice that Joan was now in Heaven with the Lord.

After a particularly peaceful start, sampling Mary's delectable blackberry tarts, the day had become busy and stressful for William. The sad news of Joan French's death rendered Catherine distraught and tearful, and in great need of comforting. On top of which, he'd had the foods from the earl to collect and distribute, and a visit from Elizabeth Hancock from Riley Farm. The poor woman had come to report the deaths and burials of seven members of her own family and another of the Talbot's. She also needed to inform him of her adoption of the babe, Katherine Talbot. All of which needed adding to the parish register.

So now, William was in no mood for spending another couple of hours poring over his books. Mary had gone home after washing the dishes from the evening meal, and William decided that an hour or so in the fresh evening air was needed.

'Would you care to take a walk we me, Catherine?' he asked his wife, whose red eyes still glistened with unshed tears.

'It's a beautiful evening and I think we both need a little time outdoors in order to come to terms with recent events, and simply enjoy the scenery.'

'Yes, that would be nice,' Catherine replied, the dull monotone of her voice at variance with the enthusiasm relayed in her words. 'Are you sure you won't be sorry tomorrow when you realise how much paperwork you need to catch up on?'

'Quite sure, my dear. Now, shall we walk out to Cucklett Delph or along the footpath up the hill behind our church, where Mary picked those wonderful blackberries to make her tarts this morning?'

'The little footpath, I think. It's a lovely walk at any time of year and our children loved it up there.'

On that thought, Catherine's tears could no longer be contained by her eyelids and trickled down her cheeks. William stood, pretending not to notice. 'Then we should go right away. I'll fetch your shawl, my dear, just in case it grows chilly as the sun starts to set.'

The green of the hillside and the fresh evening air soon helped Catherine's spirits to rise. Trees and shrubs lined the boundaries between the fields, many with berries or fruits at varying stages of maturity. Stiles along the way needed to be climbed over or squeezed through, their purpose to ensure that grazing sheep and goats remained in their designated fields.

'It is idyllic, is it not, William?' Catherine said, gazing down at the village from part-way up the hill and taking deep breaths of the evening air. 'But I cannot imagine why the air should smell so sickly sweet when so many delightfully scented meadow flowers are in bloom. I confess, it is not a pleasant scent at all and is remarkably cloying to my nostrils. Yet I can't determine the source of this smell. Do you smell it, too?'

'I detect many scents in the air, my dear, so I couldn't say whether or not any are overly sweet,' William replied, trying with all his might to conceal how Catherine's words had sliced into his heart, destroying all hope of a future together. Sensing a sickly, sweet smell in the air was one of the early symptoms of plague.

'Shall we collect a few more blackberries for Mary before we walk back?' William forced a smile as he pulled a large, white kerchief from the pocket of his breeches. 'I'm afraid I didn't think to bring a bowl.'

Catherine smiled. 'If you're certain you don't mind using a blackberry-stained kerchief in future, we could probably collect enough berries for a few more tarts.'

Seventeen

Wednesday August 18 1666

The day after Joan passed away, Marshall Howe was digging a grave in the rear garden of the home of Geoffrey Unwin, an old man who was nearing his end. Having had so many corpses to bury during August, Howe had had barely a moment to himself. Not that it bothered him in the least. On the contrary, he was rubbing his hands at the thought of all the household goods that had come his way.

In order to manage so many burials – often three or four a day – Howe had taken to digging most of the graves in advance. Yet, despite knowing full well that his actions caused distress to the dying person's loved ones, who could often see him working through a window, Howe merely grunted. Their sentimental drivel would not delay his route to their prized possessions.

Leaving his shovel beside the newly dug grave, Howe headed to the rear door of Unwin's house to speak to the dying man's daughter. On the death of her mother some years since, Edyth had become her father's housekeeper and nurse, and since he'd been stricken with plague she had rarely left his side.

From what Edyth had told Howe that morning, it seemed likely that the old man may well hang on to life for another few days. His wrinkled body had not yet developed the patches of bruising and there were no traces of buboes. Yet he continued to suffer from exhaustion and great weakness of body, no doubt worsened by the vomiting and diarrhoea. Her father was seldom awake, adding to the certainty in Edyth's mind that he had the plague. All she could do now was to ensure he was kept clean and dry and received frequent drinks of water.

Still, Howe thought with a shrug, the grave was dug, ready to be occupied by the old man. All he could do now was wait.

Howe's rap on the door was answered by an extremely tearful Edyth. 'Oh, Mr Howe, my father passed away about twenty minutes ago. If you give me an hour or so to clean him up, change his clothes and say goodbye to him, you can take him out for burial. I know you have the grave prepared because I saw you digging it through the window.'

'Right you are Miss Unwin,' Howe replied, surprised but pleased by the young woman's assertion. 'I'll pop back 'ome for a while then come back to do the burial. We can decide what yer'll give me as payment once your pa is buried. Have you got somethin' t' use as a shroud?'

'We have plenty of old bedsheets although, as you know, my father is… I mean was… a big man, and much too heavy for me to pull downstairs. I think I'll manage to wrap him in the shroud but I'll rely on you to take him out to the grave.'

Edyth's tears welled, seemingly at the images her own words had evoked. Not being a man to respond to emotion Howe stepped back, mumbling he'd be back in a couple of hours and left her to her chores.

At three o'clock in the afternoon Howe dragged Unwin's body down the steep stairs, taking little care to prevent the body from bumping hard on each step. The doorstep out to the rear garden caused a further loud bump, as did the uneven terrain of the garden itself. Edyth followed behind, her constant sniffling and snuffling setting Howe's nerves on edge.

Beside the waiting grave, Edyth said her own silent prayer over the corpse of her beloved father. Howe heaved a frustrated sigh, wanting to get inside the house and grab some of the old man's possessions. Geoffrey Unwin had the reputation of being a collector of fine pottery.

Eventually, Edyth stepped back to enable Howe to move the body into the grave. But as he bent down to do so, Mr Unwin called out, 'Water! I need a drink of water.'

Startled and terrified, believing he'd heard a voice from the dead, Howe lost his footing and slipped partway into the grave himself. He clambered out and fled, the goods he'd so looked forward to collecting from Unwin's house, completely forgotten.

—

Eyam and Bubnell: Wednesday, August 18 1666

Whilst Marshall Howe was digging Unwin's grave, a carter drew rein at Eyam's boundary stone, his wagon laden with firewood from the Earl of Devonshire. It was already mid-morning and Jacob was determined to be home in Bubnell by one o'clock. His wife had been making a mutton pie for their dinner when he left and he was intent on enjoying it while it was hot. He licked his lips at the thought, his stomach gurgling unashamedly.

It had been raining when he'd left Chatsworth, a drenching drizzle that had soaked him right through. Although it had stopped before he reached Eyam, Jacob feared that if he didn't get home to change his wet clothes soon, he'd catch more than a chill – another reason to get the wood unloaded and be on his way home, fast. But to do that, he needed help. Unfortunately, not a soul was about.

Jacob scratched his whiskery chin as he thought. He couldn't possibly catch the plague from spending just a few minutes in the village, could he? Surely, the earl was being a mite overcautious with his warnings about not crossing Eyam's boundary and would understand the need to find help to get the wood unloaded quickly, before it rained again.

He shifted the stones from across the lane, climbed into his cart and headed to the village, hoping to enlist the help of a handful of men. He'd warn them that if no one volunteered, he'd drive the whole load away again. Yes, that'd make them all rush to help him.

But not one of the villagers offered their aid, all mumbling that Jacob had broken the quarantine rules and scurrying away. Then that sour-faced rector appeared, slinging insulting remarks at him.

'Turn that animal around and be gone from here,' the rector growled. 'Eyam is a quarantined village, and for very good reason. Have you no common sense, man, or do you wish to inflict bubonic plague upon yourself, as well as thousands of others? You give me no other choice than to report your recklessness and stupidity to the earl.'

Then he just stormed off, leaving Jacob with no other option than to turn around and unload the timber himself by the boundary stone. By the time he'd finished, it was almost dinner time. He just hoped Mabel had kept the pie warm in the oven for him. She knew how much he hated cold mutton pie.

Once home in Bubnell, Jacob changed his wet clothes and ate his cold pie, grumbling with every mouthful. By the time he'd left the table, Mabel had had enough.

'Think yerself lucky I made a pie at all. If it hadn't been for Maggie next door giving me that bit o' mutton, yer wouldn't be havin' meat for yer dinner, let alone a pie. And if yer'd just got on with your job and not gone grovellin' round that village for help, yer'd have been home an hour earlier. Yer've always been a lazy oaf, which is why I never have coin to buy meat meself.'

Mabel's temper was now up and she continued to rant. 'Then yer had to go blabbin' yer mouth off to the neighbours about goin' into a plague village! Have you lost yer senses, Jacob? If the earl gets wind of yer capers, yer'll be in for an ear bashin', you mark my words. What's worse, yer'll probably get no more custom from 'is lordship and, God knows, yer get little enough work as it is.'

Jacob hung his head. He'd never thought of that. The earl employed a few men from Bubnell, two of them being carters, like him. He knew very well that he'd only been asked to take the timber to Eyam because both of them already had jobs for the day. Now he thought about it, neither of those men liked Jacob, for some reason, and he wouldn't put it past either to go tellin' tales to the earl.

But even if they didn't, that bad-tempered rector from Eyam probably would.

—

Seventeen

Jacob didn't have long to wait to face the consequences of his thoughtlessness. The following day he was summoned to Chatsworth. He didn't feel too well, and convinced himself he'd caught a chill after being cold and wet for so long yesterday. But there was little point in mentioning that to his hard-hearted wife. She'd only say it served him right for prolonging the job. And, since he was renting one of the earl's cottages, chill or no chill, he'd have to do his lordship's bidding. On top of which, Jacob refused to believe he could be facing chastisement and set his sights on being offered further employment.

Once again, he was sadly disappointed. Ordered to stand some feet away from the men seated behind a trestle table set up in the stable yard, Jacob's knees began to quiver. Although he'd never set eyes on Sir William before today, he knew without asking that the man wearing a silken waistcoat was the celebrated Earl of Devonshire. He could also see that he was exceedingly angry.

'State you name and place of residence,' a grey-headed man at the end of the table demanded. Armed with an ink pot and quill, with a large wad of paper before him, this clerk, or secretary, was stern and brusque. 'Come along man, his lordship hasn't got all day to wait for the likes of you to respond.'

'Jacob Willows, sir. I live at Beech Tree Cottage in Bubnell. It's called that because –'

'Just answer the questions you are asked. Sir William will question you now, so remember what I said.'

'I will, sir,' Jacob replied as he focused on the earl in his fancy clothes. His hopes of further employment promptly died as the earl continued to glower at him. Discomfited, Jacob

243

stared down at his feet.

'Look at me, man! Are you totally stupid or just plain rude?'

'Neither, I hope, your lordship. I'm a good carter, and strong enough to lift goods on and off my wagon.'

'Well, let me remind you of one thing you're hopeless at doing. Obeying orders!' Jacob's heart pounded as it dawned on him that there would be no offers of employment from the earl today… or any other day.

'I take it you recall your delivery of firewood to Eyam yesterday?'

Trembling in his shoes, Jacob nodded.

'Has the cat got your tongue, man?' the clerk bellowed. 'His lordship asked a question and expects to be answered in kind!'

'I do recall that delivery, Sir William. It rained yesterday morning.'

'Neither sunshine nor rain have anything to do with this issue, Mr Willows. Tell me, did you adhere to the rules of Eyam's quarantine when delivering the firewood – firewood from my own supplies that I sent to that suffering village?'

'Er… well… not exactly, your lordship.'

The earl heaved a loud sigh. 'Come man, you either did or did not obey the rules. In simple terms, did you cross over the boundary stones and enter the village of Eyam?'

Jacob again stared down at his feet, realising he couldn't lie; enough people in Eyam had seen him, including that miserable rector. 'I did enter the village, but only for a few minutes. I needed to find people willing to help me unload the firewood.'

The earl rubbed his brow. 'Every other carter I've hired for this particular delivery has managed to unload the wood all

Seventeen

by himself. Are you saying you are too feeble to manage that?'

'No, your lordship, I am not. But it'd been raining.'

Jacob stood there, agog, as the men roared with laughter. 'And you don't like the rain?'

'It wasn't just that, your lordship. I was very wet from the journey and I wanted the unloading done… well, quick like… before it rained again.' He suddenly sneezed and pulled the rag from his pocket to wipe his runny nose.

Sir William glanced at his clerk before glaring again at Jacob. 'This is becoming tiresome, and if you don't fully explain yourself without continuous prompts, I will ensure that no one ever employs you again! Now, continue with the complete answer regarding why you entered Eyam, starting with your need to unload the wood quickly.'

'Well, as I said, it had been raining and I wanted to get the wood unloaded quickly so I could go home. And I've already caught a chill from being wet for so long.' Stern faces scowled at him for veering from his explanation, so he rapidly resumed. 'My wife, Mabel, was making a mutton pie when I left Bubnell that morning, too, and I wanted to get back home for me dinner before the pie got cold. I don't like cold mutton pie, you see, your lordship, so I thought that if some of Eyam's villagers helped me to unload the wood, the job would get done quicker.

'That's it, Sir William,' he added when the men glanced at each other, shaking their heads.

When the scowling earl eventually spoke, his voice rumbled in his throat, deep and ominous, like that of a goaded chained bear. 'Believe me, Mr Willows, if it wasn't for the fact that you have a wife dependent upon your earnings, you would not be receiving payment for such a slipshod delivery to Eyam.'

Sir William paused, and feeling badly done to, Jacob drew breath to remind them all that the wood *had* been delivered. But before his protest could be uttered, his lordship continued, 'The poor people of that afflicted village have chosen to quarantine themselves in order to prevent the plague from spreading elsewhere. They were thinking only of others, whereas *you* obviously cannot think further than your belly and your dislike of rain! From the way you're sniffling and sneezing, you could now be harbouring the seeds of plague and spreading it around everywhere you go, including here, and your own village – a village, I might add, whose generosity is keeping Eyam villagers supplied with fresh bread every week.

'Mr Jackson, kindly get in touch with my physician.'

Sir William turned again to address Jacob. 'At noon in three days' time, my physician will be here, where we are today. And so will you. He will examine you for the symptoms of plague. If Doctor Lowe finds you have been infected, you will return to Bubnell and quarantine yourself and your wife in your cottage. I will organise food to be left on your doorstep, which you may retrieve, but two of my guards will prevent you from stepping out of your house.'

Then the earl snapped, 'Get this dolt out of my sight before I have him flogged and put in the stocks.' Two burly guards appeared from the stables, ready to escort Jacob to his cart. 'Mr Jackson,' he added, addressing the clerk, 'make a note never to employ this man again.

'And Mr Willows… don't even *think* of disappearing before

you have seen the physician. If you do, you will he hunted down, dragged back here and thrown into my dungeon. Do I make myself clear?'

'You do, your lordship. I am to see your physician, here, at noon, in three days' time.'

'Good. Now, be gone with you.'

On being requested to examine a man who could be contaminated with plague, the following day, the earl's physician sent his servant to Jacob Willows' house.

'Doctor Lowe sent me to tell you there's been a change of plan,' he told Jacob, standing back from the doorway. 'Instead of going to Chatsworth the day after tomorrow, he wants to see you somewhere out in the open.'

'Well, are you going to tell me where that is, or do I 'ave t' guess?'

The servant bristled. 'No, you do not. You must follow the directions I am about to give you.'

'Get on with it then. I can't stand on the doorstep all day.'

'Listen carefully, and make sure you go to the right place tomorrow.' He pointed along the village street towards the River Derwent. 'When you leave your house, you will walk along this street until you come to the bridge. Do you understand, so far?'

'Course I understand,' Jacob said, irked that the man was treating him as a halfwit.

'Good. Cross the bridge and continue walking along the far bank of the river.'

Jacob couldn't understand why he should be going anywhere near the river, just to see this doctor, but he said nothing. This puffed-up servant would accuse him of being simple if he did.

'Doctor Lowe will see you out there. He intends to ask you some questions which you must answer truthfully in order for him to determine whether or not you are carrying the plague. Is that all understood?'

'It is, and you can tell the doctor that I'll be on that far bank at noon.'

As good as his word, Jacob arrived at the specified place on the bank of the Derwent at noon on the third day after he'd been summoned by the earl. The doctor was already there, waiting on the opposite bank. Garbed in a sombre brown suit, with his greying, brown hair pulled severely back from his sallow face, Doctor Lowe looked an arrogant and humourless man – to whom Jacob took an immediate dislike.

'Good day, Doctor Lowe,' he called across the fifteen-yard breadth of the river, determined to speak before the doctor had chance to remark that Jacob was late. 'Ask me whatever you need to know so we can both get off 'ome.'

The doctor puffed out his chest. 'I intend to, Mr Willows. The earl is relying upon my excellent, medical opinion regarding whether or not you have contracted plague by your foolish actions earlier this week.'

'Get on with it, then,' Jacob yelled. 'Ask away.'

'Very well. I shall list a few indicators of ill health – symptoms as we call them – whilst you listen carefully. If you have felt any of these symptoms since your interview with his lordship, you will be honest enough to say so. Is that clear?'

'Of course it is. I speak English, same as you.'

The doctor harrumphed but made a start. 'Have you had any headaches or sensations of extreme tiredness?' Jacob yelled that he had not. 'Or has your sense of smell become altered, or heightened in any way? For example, can you detect a sweet smell in the air around you?'

'My sense of smell's the same it's always been and I can't smell anything sweet in the air. No headaches or tiredness, either. Next….?'

'Have you felt feverish, or chilly, had a runny nose or been sneezing a great deal?

'No to the first two and the last one, but I did 'ave a runny nose for a day after getting soaked while I was delivering the firewood. That's all cleared up now, though.'

'Have you been vomiting or had any griping pains in your stomach?'

'No and no.'

'Have your bowels become overly loose?'

Jacob hooted. 'No, I 'aven't 'ad the shits!'

'Did you feel dizzy or faint when you got out of bed this morning? Or has your vision become abnormally blurred?'

'No and no,' Jacob replied, feeling the urge to laugh again. But he kept his face straight.

'Have you developed any black patches on your body, notably on your nose, fingers or toes?

'No black patches anywhere, Doctor.'

'Lastly, have you any nasty swellings on your body, particularly in your armpits and groan, or on your neck?'

'No, I 'aven't. And for your information, I know enough

about plague t' know that if I 'ad got black patches and red lumps on me body, I'd be on me deathbed and not standin' here answerin' your daft questions.'

'Very well, Mr Willows,' Doctor Lowe said with a huff. 'I am satisfied that, at this point in time, you are not suffering from the plague.'

'I could 'ave told you that without all the stupid questions. 'I think everyone knows what to look out for with plague. Can I go 'ome now, then?'

'You can, although I was asked to remind you that the earl will be giving you no further employment.'

'I know! I'm not deaf, either,' Jacob retorted as he headed back to the bridge. 'I 'eard what Sir William said. 'So you can write that down on your report of my lack of symptoms if you like.'

Eighteen

Shepherds Flat, Eyam: August 17 – 24 1666

Matthew Morten lashed the rump of his pony and the cart jerked forward at speed. It was almost a mile and a half from Shepherds Flat to the centre of Eyam and he was desperate to find a midwife. His wife's labour had started unexpectedly and birthing pains were becoming rapidly stronger when he left. All he could do was pray that the birth would not be over by the time he returned, or that their three-year-old daughter, Ruth, would waken from her afternoon nap. Margaret was depending on him to be quick.

On top of which, he couldn't leave Sarah alone for long. The poor child was so sick. Tears rolled down Matthew's cheeks as he thought of his lovely little girl. Folk said very few people survived the plague, but surely, the Lord wouldn't take an innocent child of five? Yet Matthew already knew that God *did* take children. Hadn't their nearest neighbour, Lydia Kempe, recently lost all four of her children to the plague?

He drew rein outside Annie Ragge's cottage and leapt from the cart to bang on her door. But it seemed that the woman had spotted Matthew approaching through an upstairs widow, which she opened.

'Come with me now, Mistress, before it's too late,' Matthew yelled. 'Margaret's birthing pains are already strong. If we hurry, we –'

'Be off with you, Matthew Morten. I'll not be coming

with you to Shepherds Flat while people are dying of plague out there. We heard your young Sarah's got it. You'll not get either of the other two midwives to go with you, either. You'll just have to help Margaret yourself.'

With that, Annie pulled the window shut and disappeared.

Matthew soon discovered that not only had Mistress Ragge been right about the other midwives, no one in the village would open their door to him. Panicking now, and praying he could get home in time to help his poor wife, he thrashed the pony into a gallop back to his farm.

'Where's the midwife?' Margaret yelled as he came into the house alone. 'The babe is ready to be birthed!'

'None of them would come to a plague house, but I'm here to help you, love. Just tell me what needs doing.'

All Matthew could do was take the babe's head as it was birthed, then the shoulders and the rest of the tiny body as they emerged, and lay the child on the ready folded sheets. Then, as Margaret instructed, he severed the birthing cord with his razor before wrapping the newborn up.

'Oh, Matthew,' Margaret sobbed, cradling the babe in her arms, 'we have the son we longed for. This should have been such a happy day for us all, but how can it be with Sarah being so ill? Go and see if she's in need of anything, then check to see if Ruth is awake yet.'

Five-year-old Sarah was lying on her back and appeared to be sleeping, just as she'd been before Matthew left the house earlier. The end of her nose had turned black yesterday, as had the tips of her fingers. She also had an ugly red lump on her neck. And now, he was horrified to see that blood was seeping

Eighteen

from the corners of her mouth. He needed no physician to tell him that his perky little chatterbox had not long left on God's earth.

Tears rolled down Matthew's cheeks as he wiped the blood from his daughter's mouth and chin before falling to his knees in silent prayer. The life of his innocent child was now in the hands of her Maker, and Matthew prayed He would take her into His everlasting kingdom.

Hearing his younger daughter calling him, Matthew left Sarah's bedside, sweeping the tears from his cheeks as he headed to the adjacent room to carry three-year-old Ruth downstairs for her afternoon milk.

Sarah's unnatural sleep lingered throughout the night until, just as the first rays of the sunrise flooded the land, she drew her final breath. Having spent the dark hours dealing with the needs of his wife and dying child, Matthew's heart was aching and he was truly exhausted. He would bury Sarah as soon as he was able to leave the rest of his family unattended.

By mid-morning, it became evident that his beloved wife was exhibiting the symptoms of plague. He had initially attributed her exhaustion to the rigors of giving birth, but now he could see that Margaret's feverish and nauseous condition was something else. As far as Matthew knew, vomiting and diarrhoea were not symptoms of bodily fatigue. Twice in the night, he had needed to lay the babe in his crib in order to wash Margaret down and change her clothes. And having been through all that with Sarah, he knew he now faced the possibility of losing his wife as well as his daughter.

Inside, Matthew was screaming at the thought, but he

realised he needed to be strong and take care of her until the very end. He also faced the likelihood that his newly born son might die. The babe was noticeably small and silent for a newborn, whereas both Sarah and Ruth at that age had bawled their little heads off whenever they needed suckling.

'It's probably because I'm so sick, Matthew.' Margaret sobbed, stroking the babe's cheek with her forefinger. 'A whimper's the most I've heard from him all night. Perhaps you'd best lay him in his crib and warm a little goat's milk to feed him from a spoon. My milk hasn't come in yet.'

Matthew did as his wife suggested, managing to get a few drops of milk through his son's lips before laying him back in his crib.

'I haven't heard Ruth yet,' he said, as the thought entered his head. 'I'll go and see if she's ready for some breakfast. Sarah won't be wanting any,' he added, hating himself for keeping the truth from his wife. As far as Margaret knew, Sarah was just too ill to eat, and Matthew would not tell her otherwise unless she regained her own health.

Ruth's eyes opened as he bent over the high-sided wooden bed. Matthew smiled and lifted her into his arms. 'How about you and me going to get some nice oatmeal for breakfast?' he said, knowing she usually loved it with a drop of honey or fresh cream.

But the child shook her head. 'I don't want that today.'

'Well then, shall we both have a boiled egg and some buttered bread?'

'Is Sarah having an egg, too?'

'No, sweetheart, Sarah's already had some oatmeal and has

gone back to bed because she's tired.'

'Is she still poorly?'

'She is, so we need to keep away from her room.'

'Will she be better tomorrow?'

'I hope she will but we must remember to be quiet all day, so Sarah can rest. Not only that, your mama needs us all to be quiet so she can take care of your baby brother and get some sleep herself.'

Ruth nodded, a frown on her little face. 'It's not nice when people are poorly.'

'No, it isn't, and when I get through all my work, you can come and sit on my knee while I read you a story. Would you like that?'

The big smile on Ruth's face was answer enough to that question.

It was mid-afternoon, whilst both his wife and younger daughter slept, before Matthew had time to bury Sarah. He was a strong man and a farmer, used to digging the land. He carried Sarah's shrouded body to an adjacent field, laying her on the grass as he worked quickly to dig the grave before placing his beloved little girl in it and shovelling back the soil. Before returning to the house, he knelt by the grave and said a prayer to God to accept his child into Heaven.

Choking on his sorrow, Matthew dried his eyes and returned to the farmhouse to face a new round of swabbing Margaret down and dressing her in clean nightwear. Then, after placing all soiled items in pails of hot water, he set about warming some goat's milk with which to feed his newborn son.

As he spooned drops of milk into the babe, it occurred to him that the child hadn't even been given a name. 'Robert is a good, strong name,' he said aloud, before he headed upstairs to change the child's wet clout while his wife still dozed. As he entered, Margaret roused and attempted a smile at him carrying their tiny son.

'Is he taking the milk?'

'He is,' Matthew replied, putting on a cheerful face to conceal the grief that was eating him away. 'I wondered if you'd like the name Robert for him, after your pa?'

Margaret was too weak and in too much pain to move a great deal but she smiled and nodded. 'It's a good, old name.'

By the time Matthew had changed the babe's clout, laid him in his crib and persuaded his wife to take a few sips of water, Ruth was shouting him from her bed.

'I'll bring her in here so she can see you for a moment, if you're feeling up to it. She's been asking to see you all day.'

'No, Matthew. Keep her by the door.' She had no need to say why.

The night was another long one for Matthew as he continued his rounds of caring for his ailing wife and feeding little Robert. As the new day dawned, he prayed that Margaret would recover. He knew of one or two in the village who had done so, and refused to abandon hope that his wife would do the same. But as the morning progressed, Margaret grew progressively weaker and the dark patches and red swellings that Matthew had seen on Sarah, blemished her once flawless skin. She rarely wakened and it took Matthew a long time just to pour drops of water through her lips.

Eighteen

Throughout the rest of the day, Margaret seldom roused, which Matthew came to realise was a blessing. On waking, the face of his once pretty wife contorted with the spasms of unbearable pain that racked her body, her heart-rending groans adding to his sense of failure and inability to help.

In the early morning of the twentieth of August, Margaret passed away, by which time Matthew also realised that Ruth was now showing early symptoms of the plague. Complaining of feeling poorly, the ashen-faced child pointed to her head and tummy before lying down in her bed and going back to sleep.

Matthew took the opportunity to bury his beloved wife next to their firstborn child in his meadow. Grief-stricken and blinded by tears, he took some time to dig the grave. Eventually, he placed Margaret's shrouded body at the bottom of the pit and knelt by the graveside, praying to God that his and their two remaining children's deaths be soon.

For two days, little Ruth clung on to life, though she never again rose from her bed. The griping pains in her belly, and the constant retching and diarrhoea, left her drained, even before the appearance of the dark patches and repulsive red buboes. It tore Matthew apart to watch his child succumbing to this cruel disease and, once again, he prayed that God would take her to His kingdom soon.

During periods when Ruth slept that unnatural sleep of the sorely afflicted, Matthew continued to feed his tiny son. Yet, although the babe displayed no outward symptoms of plague, it was evident he was growing continuously thinner and weaker. The few drops of goat's milk he managed to swallow were simply not enough to sustain him. When Ruth died on the twenty-second of August, Matthew knew the babe would soon follow.

Matthew buried his once happy little Ruth beside her mother and sister, the depth of his grief rendering him numb to anything but the overriding desire to die himself. To which end, he prayed: '*Let mine and Robert's deaths come quickly, Lord, that our happy little family may be together again. I have no wish to live without them.*'

But as he sat in the field beside the three graves, he realised that within the next couple of days, he would be needed to dig a fourth grave, one so tiny that digging it would take no time at all.

On the twenty-fourth day of August, Matthew washed the tiny body of Robert for the last time, considering that the week-old babe displayed no noticeable symptoms of plague. He had little flesh on his bones, it was true, but that was because the child simply would not feed. And yet his whimpers had grown in strength over the days, and to Matthew, his cries were unlike any he'd heard from Sarah and Ruth when they were a few days old. His little legs would bend at the knees and thrust against his body, as though dictated by violent spasms of pain. But who was Matthew to say whether such pains were caused by the plague, or the cruel cramps of starvation? In his weakened, undernourished state, Robert would have died soon anyway.

Matthew's grief over his baby son's death was tempered by the fact that he hadn't had chance to get to know him. He was also thankful that Robert had died before him. Had Matthew been the next to die, Robert would have died soon after, and with no one to bury him. He sank to his knees, giving thanks

Eighteen

to God for listening to his prayer.

And now, before the plague rendered his own body incapable, Matthew would bury little Robert, then he would carve the initials of those he'd lost on the barn wall. Tomorrow he must head to Eyam to report the deaths and burials to Reverend Mompesson. And finally, knowing his work was done, he would return home and wait for God to take him to be with the family he loved so much.

The mood of the villagers gathered in Eyam's market hall on the evening of the twenty-fourth of August was not a pleasant one. In the lingering heat of the day, nigh on two hundred of them stood, crushed into the limited space, hot and irritable as they waited for the meeting to begin. Their grumbling rapidly ceased as the man who had called the meeting made his way to the front. In the absence of a raised dais, Thomas Wesley stepped onto a stout wooden bench in order to be seen and heard.

'I'm sure I don't need to explain to anyone why I felt this meeting to be necessary,' the brawny quarryman started, his sombre gaze sweeping the room. 'The quarantine has been in place for less than two months and many of us already regret agreeing to it. The way I see it, we were hoodwinked into accepting it, not only by Reverend Mompesson but by our own Reverend Stanley. They used quotes from the Bible and played on our faith and good will to convince us that the Lord would *want* us to lay down our lives for the benefit of others.'

'That's because we've all been brought up to believe it's the right thing to do. And I, for one, still abide by that belief.' Anne Hall's voice was loud and strong for a woman in her seventh decade and overrode the murmured reaction to Thomas's words. 'If I were asked to agree to a quarantine again, I would do it. Whatever the rest of you decide to do after this meeting, I want it known that I don't agree to any violence or mindless rioting. I'll have no part in causing harm to anyone.'

The hum of varying opinions rippled around the hall and Thomas held up his arm for silence. 'No one will force you to do anything you don't agree with, Anne,' he said, holding his temper in check. 'But please bear in mind that any rioting we may instigate would not be "mindless". It would be aimed at putting an end to a quarantine that is causing dozens of unnecessary deaths and preventing many of us earning a living…

'I'll wager you've no idea how many Eyam folk have died since early July, have you?'

'Not the exact figure, no. But I know it's a lot.'

'Then I'll tell you. Between the first of July when the quarantine started and today, the twenty-fourth of August – less than eight weeks – we've lost a hundred and twenty-three fellow villagers. And we still have another week left of August. There'll doubtless be more deaths throughout September and October, too, until the cold weather sets in.'

Calls of outraged agreement erupted…

'Reverend Mompesson should have let us make our own decisions on whether or not we stayed in this village.'

'Me and my family would've left Eyam before the end of June if we hadn't been quarantined. Because we didn't, my wife and two of our five children are dead.'

'Those of us who had somewhere else to go to should've been allowed to leave. I've lost my wife, my sister and my brother-in-law. Thankfully, we sent our children to my ma's in Bakewell in mid-June.'

A man of late-middle years made his way to the front. 'I'll stand on the bench beside you to have my say, if you've no objections, Tom.'

Thomas shrugged. 'No objections whatsoever, Ben. We all know you as someone who speaks his mind.'

Benjamin Morten nodded his thanks and stepped up to join Thomas. 'I've lost several in my family since plague came to Eyam,' he started, gazing round at the gathering. 'And if our losses continue as they are, there'll be hardly any of us left by the end of October. Even my youngest cousin, Matthew, out at Shepherds Flat, has recently buried his wife and all three of his children, the last of them earlier today. And to think that we Mortens were once proud to be one of the biggest families in this village.'

Murmurs of sympathy filled the hall but Benjamin raised his hands and shook his head. 'Sympathy's all well and good, but it's not sympathy I'm after. We all knew what would happen in Eyam when we agreed to being quarantined. And we certainly weren't *duped* into voting for it. Our two reverends were honest with us. They even told us that a quarantine would mean many deaths in the village. But they also said that many of us would still die, even if we rejected it.

Benjamin held out his arms as he slowly nodded. 'And I'll tell you this, when death comes a-knocking at my door, I'll go to my Maker knowing that by voting for the quarantine, I've helped to stop the plague spreading from Eyam to places all over the country and killing hundreds, maybe thousands, of people.'

He stared down at the many faces. 'I just wanted to let you all know that I believe the quarantine to be the most honourable and Christian thing we could have done.'

In the ensuing silence, Benjamin made to step down, but Thomas held out his arm to stay him. 'I'd greatly appreciate your assistance with the voting, Ben, if that's agreeable to you.'

'I'd be happy to do that, Tom.'

'Thank you,' Thomas said, before addressing the listeners before him. 'In my opinion, we should never have been quarantined in the first place, and the sooner we put a stop to it, the better. I, for one, can't wait for the day when I can work again, and Sunday services can be held in St Helen's.'

He paused, giving them time to consider his words. 'Of course, you will each have your opinions on this, and I want to thank both Anne and Ben for presenting their sides of the argument upon which we are all about to vote. You will be asked to vote either in favour of continuing with the quarantine until the plague is over, or for putting a stop to it, now.'

He gestured at Benjamin by his side. 'Ben and I will both count the raised hands and ensure our numbers tally before we move on. So now, please raise your hand if you believe the quarantine is still the best way for us to deal with this plague and that we should continue as we are.'

He and Benjamin counted the mass of hands and spoke momentarily to be certain their counts agreed. 'Thank you for voting,' Thomas said. 'Now, those of you who think the quarantine was a mistake and would like to see it ended, please raise your hands.'

Again, the votes were counted and compared, Thomas's face revealing the outcome of the vote before the numbers were disclosed. 'I give you this result in the knowledge that the numbers were honestly gained. Those in favour of ending the quarantine numbered seventy-six. Those in favour of the quarantine remaining in place numbered one hundred and eighteen.'

The clamour of voices was loud as the result was discussed, and Thomas gave them a few moments to get it off their chests before holding up his hands for quiet.

'As you see, the result dictates that the quarantine continues. However, we must bear in mind that, for whatever reasons, those of us gathered here tonight represent but a fraction of Eyam's population.' He shook his head at that thought. 'Unfortunately, we could not have forced people to come. But for the benefit of those who were simply unable to attend on this particular evening, I intend to call a second meeting within the next few weeks. Hopefully, attendance at that will be greatly improved.'

'You'd better find a bigger place than this for it, if you do,' Anne Hall called out. 'We're squashed in here like sheep in a market pen as it is.'

'You're absolutely right,' Thomas replied, his brow creased in thought. 'Perhaps we could use one of the larger barns at Bradshaw Hall, seeing as the family isn't likely to be back for some time... Yes, that would be perfect, although by September the nights will be drawing in, so we'll need a few oil lamps with us. Thank you for bringing that issue to mind, Anne.

'But for now, we abide by the result of tonight's vote and continue to obey the rules of the quarantine. On that note, I wish you all a very good night.'

Nineteen

Eyam: August 25 - 27 1666

The rectory was unnaturally quiet. Since Catherine had taken to her bed, William had almost ceased to speak and laughter became a thing of the past. Mary continued to cook his meals, even though most were taken away untouched. Catherine pleaded with him to stay away from her room, lest the plague should strike him, too. But William could never have done that. Although it tore him apart to watch the love of his life growing progressively weaker as her body succumbed to the feverish, destructive forces of plague, he rarely left her bedside.

Already of a weak constitution due to the consumption, Catherine had little strength with which to counter this unholy affliction and before too long she was barely able to move.

Earlier that day, the ugly black patches had appeared on Catherine's fingertips and toes, then at the tip of her nose. And now, as the sun was setting after a glorious August day, three large buboes appeared – one on her neck and two in her armpits. William knew his beautiful, gentle and loving wife would soon be taken from him. And that loss would leave him a broken man.

'Why, oh why, didn't we stay in Yorkshire?' he inwardly wailed.

He ranted at Sir George Savile for finding him a living in this plague-ridden village in the first place. He ranted at Catherine for not going to Sheffield with their children as he had asked. He even raged at God for striking Eyam with this foul and deadly affliction.

But then, his mind cleared and he beseeched God for forgiveness for his unreasonable and selfish outbursts.

Sir George had always sought what was best for William and his career in the Church, and had believed that the drier air of Derbyshire would be of benefit to Catherine's health. How was that gracious man to know that within a year of William's arrival in Eyam, plague would sweep in?

As for Catherine's obstinance, William accepted that it was his own fault for ignoring his better instincts and *allowing* her to stay with him in Eyam. His guilt-ridden mind laid his wife's wretched condition at his own feet.

And God…? It was, indeed, possible that God *was* punishing people for turning their backs on Him and living lives of greed, hypocrisy and sloth. William vowed to stress this point at his next Sunday service in Cucklett Delph… if he lived long enough to hold it. With plague already in the rectory, it was more than likely that he was already harbouring the seeds of the disease, the symptoms of which would show before many more days had passed.

William grieved for the people of Eyam already taken by this wicked plague. Whatever happened now, it would take the village many years to recover from such a terrible ordeal. He thought of the deaths that had occurred in the last few days. Two days ago, the death of the quietly spoken widow, Lydia Kempe, had been reported to him, and this evening, Matthew Morten, also from Shepherds Flat, came to report the deaths and burials of his wife and their three young children. The

Nineteen

poor man's tears had flowed as he'd spoken of his family. And William understood how he'd felt.

Throughout that evening William stayed at Catherine's bedside, frequently dripping water through her parched and cracked lips, washing her down and changing her nightgown. As the hours ticked by, she roused only once. Though her voice was hoarse and broken, she managed to ask William to read the prayers for the visitation of the sick from the Common Book of Prayer to her again. As she valiantly strained with the responses, William realised that this would likely be the last time he'd hear his wife's sweet voice.

How right he'd been. Catherine lapsed into a feverish sleep from which she never awoke. In the final hour of the twenty-fifth day of August, William watched his beloved wife of seven years take her final breath. For some time, he wept for his own and his children's loss, wondering how he could explain to two young children that they would never see their mother again.

He swept the tears from his cheeks, berating himself for his selfish feelings of bereavement when he should be rejoicing that his dearest Catherine, who had devoted her life to the care and well-being of others, would soon be in Heaven with her Maker. He sank to his knees and prayed to God for her immortal soul, entreating Him to take Catherine into His Garden in Paradise.

William prepared his wife's body for burial and at mid-morning the following day, set off for the house of Marshall Howe in the Townhead, whose services he would require for digging Catherine's grave. His knock on the Howes' door was answered by a red-headed young boy of about seven or eight, whose miserable demeanour and bruised arms immediately gave William cause for concern.

'Are your parents at home, child?' he asked the boy from several feet back from the door. He had no intention of carrying the plague into the home of anyone else in Eyam.

'Pa's out, buryin' someone, and Ma's sick.'

'Ah, well then, Master Howe, my name is Reverend Mompesson and I'd like to speak with your ma, if I may. You've probably heard your pa mentioning my name.'

The little boy nodded. 'I think 'e has, cos 'e said your name's William, same as mine. But I don't think 'e'd want you in the 'ouse. Pa says it's only folk who want to have a nosy round at what we've got who ask to do that.'

'I can assure you, that is not why I am here,' William replied, the harsh words muttered by villagers about Marshall Howe and his collection of household goods for his services, coming to mind. 'I'm in need of your pa's help in burying someone, Master Howe, just as you said he is doing this morning. So, would you be kind enough to ask your ma to come to the door so I can ask her where I might find him?'

'Ma's upstairs in bed, right poorly today. Pa said it looks like she's come down wi' the plague.'

'I do hope your pa's wrong about that. Plague isn't a pleasant disease at all.'

'Ma gets ill a lot, so she's in bed a lot. She did summat to her eye last week, 'cos it went all black and puffed up. Her fingers and nose 'ave gone all black today an' all – much blacker than my bruises.'

Nineteen

William nodded, realising that the black eye was most likely inflicted by Marshall Howe's fists, but the black fingers and nose suggested that the brute's diagnosis of his wife having the plague was most likely true. In which case, since plague was already in this house, he could see no reason why he shouldn't enter.

Before he could say as much, the boy held out an arm and pointed to one of his bruises. 'I got this big bruise 'ere when Pa got angry 'cos I knocked over and broke one of his newest vases. He took off 'is belt and walloped me across the arm wi' it. I've been tryin' t' be careful since.'

'That sounds like a good idea,' William said, trying to conceal his fury at a parent who could inflict such a punishment for the accidental breakage of a household ornament. 'Some people lose their tempers a lot easier than others, so you must try not to do anything to make your pa get angry. Will you do that?' The boy nodded. 'Well then, young man, do you think you could go upstairs and ask your ma if she might come down to speak to me for a moment?'

'I'll ask her, but she might be too sick to come down.' Young William sped off upstairs and came down almost straight away. 'Ma looks awake but she's still lyin' down.'

'Then do you think I might go upstairs to talk to her?'

The child momentarily frowned, then he shrugged. 'Yer can, if yer want. She might talk t' yer… but she might not. And if pa comes 'ome for 'is dinner and finds you in the 'ouse, he might rant and yell a lot.'

'Then I'll bear that in mind and try to be quick. Does that sound reasonable to you?'

The boy nodded and moved aside to allow William to enter.

William gazed around the living room, with its many ornaments displayed on the tops of pieces of good quality furniture. A pile of blankets, sheets, table linen and clothing were heaped on the sofa waiting to be folded and put away. William sighed as he climbed the stairs. Villagers' complaints about the man he'd employed as sexton were evidently true. How could he have been so blind to the man's true character?

Joan Howe lay prone in her bed, the reason for which needed no explanation to William. The room stank of faeces and the woman appeared to be in the feverish sleep of the plague-smitten, her red hair encrusted with vomit. And, as young William had said, his mother's fingertips and nose were black.

Joan opened her eyes as William approached and attempted to reach her hand out to him.

'Would you pray for me, Reverend?' she asked, her arm falling back to the bedclothes. 'I don't want to go to Hell.'

'Indeed, I will, Joan. I shall kneel by your bed and ask God to accept you into Heaven, as I did for my own dear wife yesterday.'

As William recited the prayer, he heard the door creak open downstairs, soon to be followed by angry shouting. He continued with the prayer, then said the blessing as Joan drifted off to sleep again. Satisfied the poor woman appeared comforted by his words, William returned to the living room, coming face-to-face with a glowering Marshall Howe, still wearing his floppy, wide-brimmed hat.

'Good day, Mr Howe.' William's benign smile belied his

Nineteen

welling anger. He had no intention of allowing this scowling, thickset bully to intimidate him. 'I have said prayers for your wife's immortal soul, as I am sure you would have wanted me to do. I fear her end will not be long. Before then, I insist you wash the filth from her body and the vomit from her hair. You will also put fresh sheets on her bed and garb her in a clean nightgown. In the name of decency, man, you will need to do all this several more times before she dies. No one should be buried in such a foul state as Joan appears to be in at present.'

Howe nodded, seemingly ashamed of being chastised by a man of the cloth – though the hostile glint in his eyes said otherwise. 'I'll do that, Rector. I didn't realise my wife was in such a mess as you say.'

'Then you obviously didn't bother to look before you left home this morning!'

'I… I 'adn't the time. I needed t' bury Samuel Chapman who died in the night. His only neighbour was an old woman and she couldn't do it.'

'For pity's sake man, your poor wife may not be able to eat or drink, but she needs frequent drops of water through her parched lips. I am returning to the rectory now, but I will return this evening to check that Joan, her clothing and her bedding are clean, and she is as comfortable as possible. I will do the same tomorrow evening.'

'But what about work…?'

'In your absence people must either bury their own dead or ask family or friends to help. At this time, you must put your own family's needs first.'

Howe's glower deepened but William chose to ignore it.

'You will put aside all thoughts of working for others for the next few days, since you will be unable to leave your cottage until your wife has passed. From my own experience with plague, Joan probably has another two days at the most; two days for you to ensure she is given plenty of water and is kept clean. I don't want hear that you left this house for any reason at all. I'm sure your son is capable of collecting any foodstuffs ordered and left at your collection site by the Jumber Brook. Is all that clear?'

'Yes,' the scowling lead-miner grunted.

William breathed deeply, his temper on the boil. 'I shall overlook the bullying, and the threats you have already made to the poor folk who hire you to bury their dead. But as from today, it stops. You may continue to ask, in a reasonable and friendly manner, for household goods as payment. But you will *not* bully anyone into giving you items they do not wish to part with. From what I see in this room, you have little space left for more! If I hear further complaints about you, your role as sexton will immediately cease.'

Before he completely lost his temper with this obnoxious man, William strode to the door. Then he turned, his forefinger thrust towards Howe. 'If I hear of you threatening anyone else in Eyam, I will make sure you never find employment in this area again, including the quarries and lead mines. And believe me, I shall be asking the families and neighbours of those you bury as to your behaviour towards them. Good day, Mr Howe.'

With that, William left, his initial purpose for visiting Marshall Howe forgotten.

Nineteen

The first thing William did on his return to the rectory was to reassure himself that Catherine's body was ready for burial. When he came downstairs, Mary was waiting for him in the hall, her glistening eyes revealing she had been weeping. But she bravely swallowed down a sob.

'I know you've had no breakfast, Reverend, so I wondered if you'd like a bite to eat to put you on until you take your lunch.'

'It's kind of you to think of me, Mary, but I'm afraid I have no appetite for food this morning. I have a grave to dig.'

'You decided not to ask Marshall Howe to do it, then?'

'After speaking to that man and seeing for myself how he treats his wife and child, I can understand why so many villagers refuse to take advantage of his services. A more unpleasant character I have yet to meet and I don't want him anywhere near my beloved Catherine.'

William's eyes again filled up as he spoke and he turned away, embarrassed to be displaying his emotions.

'Oh Reverend, I completely understand. Mr Howe is a thoroughly despicable man and his services are used only by people who have no one else to turn to. As to your grief, it is bound to overwhelm you for a while, so your tears are nothing to be ashamed of. I thought I'd never be happy again when I lost my family. You told me when my little Edward died that time would heal my broken heart, and now I know that to be true. You must take one day at a time and cry your eyes out whenever you feel the need. It does no good at all to put on a brave face the whole time.'

Mary smiled at his earnest expression as he listened to her words. 'I imagine you are like me and will do your weeping in private. That is fine, too. The main thing is to let your grief come out instead of keeping it locked inside. One day you will find you have cried your last tears. That doesn't mean you will have forgotten Catherine; your memories of her will be locked in your heart forever. And you will look back on the happy times you spent with her with a smile on your face.

'There are many in our village who will shed tears for Catherine, Reverend. She was the most gentle and caring person I've ever met and most people in Eyam think the same. I am so sorry she has been taken from you… and from us all. But rest assured, I'll keep the kitchen running for you for as long as you wish. And, if you like, I'll see if I can find a replacement cleaner for Joan.'

'Your kind words mean a great deal to me, Mary, and I will think of them when I am drowning in my sorrows. I would also be most grateful if you find another cleaner. You know the village women so much better than I. Catherine was so happy having you and Joan to talk to.'

'That's settled, then; I already have one particular lady in mind.'

—

The location in the churchyard of Saint Helen's where William chose to bury his beloved wife was a little over twenty feet from the church porch. It was a lovely spot, in the shade of the spreading branches of an old yew tree and close to the Saxon cross that had stood there for centuries. His flooding tears mingled with sweat as he dug, six feet into the earth to prevent the seeds of plague from spreading – just as he'd instructed his parishioners to do. His grief-stricken mind wandered in many directions as he toiled, not least to the guilt he felt for burying his wife in the churchyard. After all, at the end of June, he'd declared the cemetery closed to all burials for the foreseeable future.

Despite having acquired the necessary permission to bury Catherine here from the Church of England bishops – who had agreed to the cemetery's closure barely two months since – he knew he'd have difficulty explaining his privilege to the people of Eyam. He hoped they'd understand that to have buried his wife in the rectory gardens was not an option. The rectory was William's domain only for as long as he was reverend at St Helen's and rector of the parish of Eyam. Once he died, or left the village, the rectory would become home to his successor. So, the church cemetery was offered to him as an alternative by the bishops themselves.

Then he agonised over how to inform his children of their mother's death, knowing it could traumatise them, especially his elder child, George. He decided to write to them later this evening, after he'd returned from Marshall Howe's house. Then, perhaps tomorrow, he would write to inform Sir George of his tragic news. Although William dreaded putting pen to paper to write about Catherine's death at this early stage, he knew there was no way he could avoid it.

He patted the mound of soil covering the earthly body of Catherine Mompesson with the back of his shovel, and with a fresh flood of tears, he vowed that, one day, he would have a tomb built over her grave so that future generations would know how much she had been loved and admired during her twenty-eight years on God's earth.

—

William's visit to the home of Marshall Howe that evening was a brief one. Barely able to keep the tears at bay over Catherine's death, he struggled to be civil to this brute of a man who didn't seem to care whether his wife lived or died. Yet William was relieved to note that although Joan was already close to death, she was at least clean, and a jug of water sat on a table beside her bed.

'I've done as you asked, Rector, and kept Joan clean, but she's been asleep for most o' the day. I did get some water into 'er when she roused, though.'

'I should think so, too,' William snapped. 'You've put this poor woman through enough pain with your fists, and should be ashamed of yourself. Just remember that God will have seen everything you've done… to Joan, to young William, and to the many others you have bullied or physically abused. Be sure to bury her with dignity when she dies, which, I fear, will not be too long now. I nursed my own wife to the very end, and buried her today, so, I am in no mood for hard-hearted, self-centred people like you.'

Howe, stood, head bowed, whilst William ranted, seemingly ashamed of himself. But William wasn't fooled by the man's duplicitous manner. 'I shall call again on you tomorrow evening to see how Joan fares, and before you bury her, you will report her death to me at the rectory. And rest assured, Mr Howe, if I hear so much as a whisper of you threatening and bullying the families of anyone you bury, the entire village will know of it. You would never wish to show your face in Eyam again.'

Later that evening, after Mary had gone home, William lit a couple of oil lamps in the rectory's study and placed them at either end of his wide desk. Then he set out his writing paper, ink pot and a couple of quills. For some time, he sat there, staring down at them, wondering how to begin a letter containing such upsetting news to his two young children. No matter how he described their mother's death, his words would inflict such pain upon them that he could barely think about their heartbroken tears.

Eventually, he picked up his quill and started to write:

My Dearest Children,
This letter brings you the sad news of your dear mother's death, the greatest loss that could befall any child. I have lost a kind and loving wife and you have lost the most caring, generous and understanding mother. We must comfort ourselves in God, and the knowledge that your mother lived a most holy life, caring for others, and is now in Paradise with Him.

I shall endeavour to list some of your mother's excellent qualities in order that you remember her in future years and try to be as good and virtuous as she. That she was a most pious, dutiful and sincere woman cannot be denied and she lived her life according to the doctrines of the Church of England. Her humility and modesty were admired by all, as was her pleasant and cheerful manner. Never would even a maid-servant hear an angry word from her mouth. She abhorred wasteful habits, was ever frugal in her spending and would never turn her back on the poor and needy. Yet she was careful to avoid those who berated and gossiped about others.

I do believe your mother was the kindest wife in all the world and that she loved me ten times better than she loved herself. That she resisted my pleas to flee with you, my dear children, away from this plague-ridden place to the safety of Sheffield, is testament to the fact that she cared more for my safety than she did for her own.

I can assure you, my sweet children, that your mother's love for you was pure and true and she would speak of you both for hours. She suckled you as babes and continued to care for all your needs, ensuring that you embraced life and learning in order that you grow into sensible, caring and knowledgeable people. I must tell you that, even on her deathbed, your dear mother declared her deep love for you both.

As you know, my children, your mother had suffered the symptoms of consumption for some years, and her natural strength was considerably weakened. Yet at her own insistence she visited and offered her aid to many families stricken by plague. Although she could have saved herself by remaining here, in the rectory, she refused to deny those in need of her help. How they loved her for it, and now they mourn her death as they would mourn for a family member of their own.

At the beginning of her sickness, your mother pleaded with me to stay away from her, lest I should also succumb to the disease. I can assure you, my dear children, that I stayed with her to the

Nineteen

end, as I know she would have done for me.

A short time before her sweet soul departed, your mother asked me to pray with her again. When we had done so, I asked her how she felt. Her answer was that she was looking to see when the good hour should come. Then we prayed again from the Common Book of Prayer and your mother strained her sweet voice to make the responses. She died soon afterwards, looking forth to her place in Heaven.

My dear hearts, I could tell you more of your mother's excellent virtues. If I were to sum them up in a few short words, I would say that she was pious and upright in all her conversation. We must give thanks to our blessed God and Creator who has dominion over all beings, for bestowing all these graces upon your dearest mother.

Your most loving father,
William Mompesson.

William placed his quill in the ink pot and read his letter through to give the ink time to dry before placing it between two clean sheets of paper in a desk drawer. Tomorrow, he would write to Sir George, as planned, but now his head truly throbbed and he desperately needed sleep. Whether or not sleep would take him was a different matter, however. As soon as he climbed into his lonely bed, memories of Catherine's smiling face, and the goodness that emanated from her, would fill his mind… and he would weep anew. The void her death had left inside him would never again be filled.

William Mompesson had become a mere shell of the man he once was.

He pushed himself to his feet, ready to climb the stairs,

but every muscle in his body was on fire. Could that be due to the exertions of digging Catherine's grave, or was it an early indication of something else?

William had hoped for a little longer before the symptoms of plague sank their wicked fangs into him. Yet should his death come soon, he prided himself on knowing that the Church of Saint Helen was ready for his successor to take over; the requisite paperwork and records were up to date and carefully stored away. But he was deeply concerned as to who would take care of him in his final days of plague. The kind and immensely capable Mary Hadfield had already spent many hours caring for members of her own family who had fallen ill or become prey to the pestilence. William couldn't bear the thought of burdening her with his constant cleansing and dressing.

He put such thoughts from his mind until certain he'd been stricken and headed upstairs to his lonely chamber to pray that his beloved Catherine was now at peace. It would not be long before they were together again.

—

The following evening, William visited Marshall Howe's home again as he had promised, relieved to see that Joan was clean and her lips appeared a little less parched. Yet it was evident to him that the woman would soon be with her Maker. In the deep sleep of the plague-smitten, her ashen face looked at peace. William ordered her callous husband to kneel beside him by her bed whilst he said prayers for her soul, beseeching God to forgive all Joan's transgressions and accept her into

Nineteen

Heaven for all eternity.

In the morning of the twenty-seventh day of August, Howe came to the rectory to report his wife's death at a little after midnight, and to ask permission to bury her in their small garden to the rear of their cottage.

William freely gave his permission, knowing that Joan had died of the plague and not from a beating by her husband.

'How is young William?' he asked the dour-faced sexton.

'Not too good, Rector. He's done nothin' but mope about since he got out of bed this mornin', saying he's got belly ache. I was goin' t' bring him 'ere with me, but 'e said he felt too ill to walk. I told 'im to get himself back to bed while I'm out.'

William sighed at the thought of yet another child stricken with this hateful disease. 'I'm truly sorry to hear that, Mr Howe. William is such a lovable child.' He glanced at the man, pleased to see the shamed expression on his face.

'I'll visit you this evening to see if your diagnosis is correct. If William does have the plague, you will need to stay home to take care of him, just as you did in your wife's last days.'

Howe averted his eyes from William's intense stare. 'I realise that, Rector. I promise I won't leave 'is side. William's my only child, and –'

'Then it's a pity you didn't treat him kindly when he was well. He needed you to be a good father and love him instead of beating him black and blue with your belt for the slightest transgression, or accidents with your prized vases and ornaments. William longed to hear you praise him for polishing your treasured objects so well. More importantly, he desperately needed to hear you say you loved him as much as he loved you.'

William took a few calming breaths. It wasn't his place to tell any father how to deal with, or chastise, their children – especially anyone of the Puritan faith. 'If your son does have the plague, he will need you more than ever to make sure he is as clean and comfortable as possible until the end.'

The big lead miner hung his head and stared at the ground. 'I'd best get back to 'im now, then. Joan's belly ache soon turned into the runs. And I've got 'er to bury this afternoon. William's already upset about his ma's death.'

'I'll be round to see William tonight, Mr Howe. Until then, like you, I have work to do.'

With that, William closed the rectory door and returned to his study.

—

In the late morning of the thirtieth of August, seven-year-old William Howe died of bubonic plague. An hour after noon, William arrived to say prayers and blessings over the child's lifeless body, just as he'd done for his mother. Although pleased to note that the boy was clean, as were his clothes and the bedsheet used as a shroud, William was saddened by his father's blatant lack of concern over the death of his only child.

'Let us kneel here, at William's bedside and pray for his immortal soul, Mr Howe, just as we did for Joan.'

'It'd better not take too long, 'cos then I've got t' bury him, and I've got Mary Abell booked for burial at three o'clock and Francis Wilson at six thirty. They both died this morning an' all,'

Nineteen

William glared at the man. 'Mr Howe, this is your only child we're talking about.'

'Aye, well, money doesn't grow on trees. Being village sexton's helped us a lot over the last couple o' months.'

'So I believe,' William replied, thinking of the heaps of household goods that seemed to have significantly grown since he'd first stepped into this house a mere few days' ago. Now, kneel beside me whilst I say a short prayer.'

Marshall Howe did as he was asked, his hands clasped together and head bowed as William recited:

Dear Lord, our Father,
give us assurance that although William has passed from our sight, he has not passed from your loving care.
Draw near to us in our sadness, bring blessing out of grief,
and help us to know that you bestow your love and healing, through Jesus Christ our Lord.
Amen.

Howe repeated the last phrase of the prayer and waited, evidently expecting William to leave now that his job was done. But William stood his ground as he thought things through, pleased that his constant glaring at Howe's face was disconcerting the man. He still struggled to read the lead miner's true feelings. If Howe had felt any love at all for his son, he certainly wasn't showing it, just as he hadn't at the death of his wife. No tears were shed nor emotion displayed, even as the words of the prayers had been said.

In truth, William thought it likely that Howe was glad that their upkeep – which came from his pocket – had come to an end. Then he chided himself for such uncharitable thoughts.

But still, he failed to find a single good thing to say about the rough and burly man, who bullied vulnerable villagers, beat his wife and child for no just cause other than his own explosive temper, and overtly avoided William's eye when they spoke.

He resolved to pray for the salvation of Marshall Howe's soul when the day came for the lead miner to meet his Maker.

Twenty

The cottage at Riley Farm had been devoid of joy and laughter for the past few weeks, the absence of six happy, boisterous children and a cheerful, constantly singing or whistling husband, all too evident to Elizabeth Hancock. With all seven of them taken by this merciless plague, Elizabeth had thrown herself into caring for tiny Katherine, the last member of the Talbot family now that old Bridgett had died.

In truth, Elizabeth's adopted daughter had given her little time to fully mourn the loss of her own family. The babe's crying and constant need of feeding were truly draining. But, not a woman to give up easily, Elizabeth persevered. The plague had taken everything she loved away from her, except for their eldest son in Sheffield. If old Bridgett hadn't pleaded with her to take little Katherine, Elizabeth would have been in Sheffield with Matthew three weeks ago. But now, she had a tiny daughter to care for, and would work hard to give the child a happy life.

The thirtieth day of August dawned dry and bright, as had most days for several weeks, and it seemed to Elizabeth that nothing she could do would stop the four-month-old infant from crying. Katherine would take little from a spoon, not even the bread soaked in warm goat's milk that she had seemed to enjoy to start with. It also became apparent that for the last two days the babe had felt overly hot and was bringing back most of the milk she did manage to swallow. On top of which, her clouts were regularly filled with particularly runny faeces. Memories of her own family battling against such symptoms flooded Elizabeth's mind, and she prayed to the God she'd forsaken not to inflict the same vile plague on this tiny babe. 'Let Katherine live, Lord, I beseech you!' she called out as the child continued to cry. 'She is innocent of all sin and will grow to be an honest, dutiful and loving woman.'

But by noon, Katherine's cries had turned into screams and Elizabeth agonised over how best to ease her discomfort. From the way the child's knees were rhythmically drawn up against her body, it was evident that the griping pains were intense. All Elizabeth could do was to keep the babe clean, hold her upright against her shoulder and gently rock her back and forth.

In the middle of the afternoon the screaming stopped, the infant's breathing telling Elizabeth she had fallen asleep. She laid the child in the wooden crib that John had so lovingly made for their own little ones, and washed the soiled clouts, tiny nightgowns and sheets before Katherine awoke. Elizabeth prayed that when she did, her pains would have gone.

It was late afternoon by the time Elizabeth had finished her chores, and having not heard a murmur from the crib, she assumed that the child's hours of screaming had worn her out. She poured some goat's milk into a pan ready to warm as soon as Katherine wakened, and leaned over the crib to check she was still asleep. The tiny girl looked so peaceful lying there, on her side, but when Elizabeth stroked her smooth cheek, she found it to be winter-cold.

The child was dead.

Elizabeth's loud wail reverberated around the room. Then she took a deep breath and held the little body aloft. In the throes of grief, she shrieked and howled at God, 'No, no…

this can't be happening again! I've tried so hard to take care of this babe. What have I ever done to make you take everything I love away from me? Does it please you to see those who worship you brought so low?'

For some time, Elizabeth sat on the edge of a chair, rocking little Katherine back and forth in her arms as tears of anguish rolled down her cheeks. When at length she composed herself, she washed the dear little body, redressed her in a clean gown and wrapped her in a small sheet.

As the late August daylight began to fade, Elizabeth carried Katherine along the hillside path to the deserted Talbot farm. Collecting the shovel from inside the outhouse, she headed to the meadow in which the rest of the Talbot family were buried. Katherine Talbot, daughter of Richard and Katherine Talbot, would be buried by Elizabeth Hancock who had loved her dearly for a mere three weeks. She would be buried beside the mother who had birthed her and loved her first.

Tomorrow morning, Elizabeth would walk down to the village and report the death and burial of the child to Reverend Mompesson. Then she would come home, pack a little food and the few clothes she owned and – the quarantine be damned! – she would flee to Sheffield to be with her son.

Just as she'd intended to do three weeks ago.

—

Tuesday, August 31 1666

Overcome with exhaustion and emotionally drained, William sank into his armchair in the rectory sitting room. Although his aching muscles had eased since digging Catherine's grave a few days ago, he felt as though all bodily strength had deserted him. Convinced he'd already succumbed to bubonic plague after tending his beloved wife, he quailed at the thought of suffering the disease himself. Resting his aching head against the back of the chair, his mind was engulfed by images of the ever-worsening symptoms until his ravaged body could take no more. By which time, he would sink into the fevered sleep from which he would rarely waken until he was finally taken by the Lord.

Added to William's fears was the knowledge that there was no one in his family to take care of him during those final days of appalling filth and bodily decay. How could he put Mary through all that again, especially for someone to whom she wasn't even related?

He had no answer to that.

August had proven to be the most harrowing month that William had ever lived through. Seventy-seven villagers had died, the last two being a man by the name of Francis Wilson, and Katherine, the four-month-old daughter of Richard and Katherine Talbot, who had been adopted by Elizabeth Hancock. It occurred to William that, like Mary Hadfield and one or two others, Elizabeth was one of the few people to have resisted the plague's wicked grasp, despite nursing several family members until the end.

Already fraught with anguish over losing Catherine, thoughts of the death of so young a child brought tears afresh to William's eyes. Certain that he, too, would soon be taken, he heaved himself from his chair and headed to his study to

Twenty

write the letter he'd intended to write a few days ago.

Once again, he placed an oil lamp at either side of his desk and arranged his writing paper, quills and ink pot in suitable positions. Satisfied he had all he needed, William sat before his desk, checked the letter he'd written to his children was still in the drawer awaiting postage, and picked up his quill to write to his patron, Sir George Savile:

Honoured and Dear Sir,

This is the saddest news that my pen could ever write. My beloved Catherine, my dearest dear, has been smitten with the plague and has gone to her eternal rest, endowed with a crown of righteousness. Had she loved herself as well as she loved me, she would have fled from this stricken village with our sweet babes and have remained whole and well.

Sir, this missive is to bid you farewell, and to convey my humble thanks for the many favours you have bestowed upon me over the years. I hope you will believe a dying man when I say that I have as much love as I have honour for you, and will pray to the God of Heaven that you, your dear lady and your children, will be blessed with eternal happiness.

Please allow your dying chaplain to stress this truth to you and your dear family: comfort and happiness can only be found in this harsh world by living a pious life. Never do anything for which you would first not ask the blessing of God for its success.

I hope you will not think ill of me, Sir, for having listed your name as executor of my will. I believe your good name and char-

acter will be of great comfort to my distressed orphans. I do not desire that they become great, but good, and are brought up in fear of being reprimanded by the Lord.

I am contented to make my farewells to the world and am hopeful that God will accept me into Heaven. I would be glad if you would choose a humble and pious man to succeed me as Rector of St Helen's. If only I could see you before I depart from this life, I would inform you of the ways in which my successor could live comfortably and happily amongst the good people of Eyam. It would give me some satisfaction to know that you had done so.

My dear Sir, I beg your prayers, and of those around you, that I may not be frightened by the powers of Hell and may find peace and rest when I come to die. With tears I beg that when you are praying for fatherless infants, you will remember my two sweet babes.

Please pardon the rude style of this letter. My head is a little discomposed as I wait for death to claim me, which I hope you will understand.

As always, you have my sincere thanks for your patronage and friendship.

William Mompesson

William read through what he had written again before addressing both letters for sending tomorrow via the recently improved mail service. He rubbed his aching head, too weary and downhearted to write to his Uncle John tonight, and headed upstairs to his lonely bed. And yet, as fatigued as he was, his restless mind refused to sleep.

Tomorrow was the first day of September and William

Twenty

prayed that the new month would see the beginning of the end to the disease in Eyam altogether. He also prayed for the courage to face his own death. A huge part of him had gone with Catherine when she died, and in his darkest moments William wanted nothing more than to be reunited with her.

But he put his trust in God and would face whatever was ordained for him with dignity and calm. Just as Catherine had done.

Twenty-One

Eyam: Early September 1666

Margaret Blackwell, née Merrell, thought her last day had come when she was forced to take to her bed. Coughing and sneezing and aching all over for the last two days, her brother insisted she must stay in her bedchamber, away from him.

'If I die of this plague, you will bury me in the garden, won't you, Simon? I don't want to lie in some strange place for eternity. I've lived in this house since I married Anthony Blackwell ten years ago.'

'Stop talkin' of dying, Margaret, you aren't that ill – not yet, anyways. You know how your Anthony looked before he died back in February, and our mam and dad. They all got the runs and started throwing up all over the place. Then they got those big lumps they call buboes. You haven't got any of them things, have you?'

'Then why are you telling me to stay in my room?'

'Because I don't want whatever you've got. And afore you say anythin', it sounds like yer've just got a bad cold in the 'ead. I wouldn't be able t' work at The Miners Arms if I got ill, would I? And Joe Wilkins wouldn't be pleased t' have to serve every customer himself. Not that we've had many customers since the plague started 'cos most of the regulars have already died. It's a miracle none of 'em have given me the plague.

'Anyways, you stay in that bed and try to sleep for a couple of hours. Yer'll probably feel much better after that. I'll get off

Twenty-One

t' work and see yer later. We've plenty of pie left for tonight's dinner, so yer've no need to worry about cooking.'

When the stomach pains started and her bowels became overly loose, Margaret felt so ill, she lay still for a while, waiting for the symptoms of plague to worsen and her end to come. By late morning she was sweating and feverish and in desperate need of a drink. Unable to wait until Simon came home, she would just have to struggle downstairs for some water before she died of thirst.

Once she'd heaved her well-padded frame out of bed, Margaret's head started to spin and her vision blurred. Confused and disorientated, she peeled a strand of dark hair from her sweaty face and shoved it back under her coif, then felt her way to the bedchamber door. On shaking legs, Margaret slowly made her way downstairs.

The living room still stank of the bacon her brother had cooked for his breakfast earlier, making Margaret's already queasy stomach feel even worse. On the table she noticed a mugful of milk that Simon must have poured for himself but forgotten to drink in his rush to leave for work. Hoping a long drink of milk would remedy her sickliness, Margaret picked up the mug and greedily drank.

The mug was almost empty before she realised it wasn't milk at all she'd drunk, but bacon fat. She'd been fooled by the cloudy, white appearance of it as it started to set. Now, the full force of the foul taste and thick, oily consistency hit her. She retched, managing to get through the door before spewing most of the greasy liquid across the garden outside. Her empty stomach still heaved and, after pouring a cup of water to take with her, Margaret returned to her bed to wait for the plague to claim her.

By the time Simon came home from work that evening, Margaret was up and about and busy cooking vegetables to serve with the beef and onion pie for their meal.

'I said you'd feel better after a few hours' sleep, didn't I?' Simon remarked, sitting himself down at the table, grinning in that annoying way he had when convinced he knew better than his older sister. 'I know what the symptoms of plague are, even if you don't.'

Margaret picked up the skillet and waved it menacingly in front of her scrawny brother's smirking face. 'Shut up and listen for once in your life! For your information, clever clogs, I know very well what the symptoms of plague are, and know for certain that I've had several of them today.'

Simon pushed the skillet away from his nose and hooted. 'Yeah, right, of course you 'ave! That's why yer're up and cooking this meal for us now. If you had the plague, yer'd probably be pukin' your guts up by now and wanting nothing more than to lie down and sleep.'

'Oh, I've puked all right, and had the runs, and this morning my whole body ached. I've also had the shivers and sweats, a spinning head and fuzzy eyesight. But I managed to get downstairs without breaking me neck, and once I'd had a drink, I puked it all up again.'

Simon gaped at Margaret as though she'd lost her mind, but thought better of saying so in case the hovering skillet connected with his head. As it had done on occasion.

'But the drink must have killed the seeds of plague,' Margaret continued, 'cos I felt all right after that. I did go back to bed, I admit, but I didn't feel like sleeping so I got up again.'

Simon scratched his dark head. 'So, you're telling me that a drink killed off the plague?'

'I don't *think* it did, Simon, I *know* it did.'

'Bloody 'ell. What did you drink… holy water?'

'Very funny. Can't you hear me hootin' at your pathetic attempt at a jest? I drank a full mug of what I thought was milk that you'd left on the table.'

'I didn't leave any milk on the table, just a mug of fat from the pan I'd cooked the bacon in that I 'ad for me breakfast…' Simon's eyes opened wide. 'You're not tellin' me you drank bacon fat, are you? Just the *thought* of that makes *me* want to puke.'

Margaret nodded. 'I told you, I thought it was milk. But even though the slimy fat made me vomit, it did get rid of the plague. I've no idea why, it just did, and I'm the living proof of it.'

Having no answer to that, Simon silently waited for Margaret to serve the meal.

A few days later, Simon came home from work at noon and barged through the door of the cottage he shared with his sister 'Have you heard about Uncle Humphrey?'

Margaret glanced up from her sewing. 'Heard what? And what are you doing finishing work so early? Your pay'll be docked if Joe Wilkins finds out.'

'I haven't finished; I'm going straight back. As a matter of fact, we only had three customers in, and Joe said I could pop out for a while. I just came 'ome to tell yer about Uncle

Humphrey, in case you wanted to go round and see him this afternoon.'

'Why, is he ill?'

Simon nodded. 'He came down with plague two days ago, so old George Butterworth said when he came into The Arms this morning. He reckons Humphrey'll soon get better 'cos he's got all his own 'erbal remedies to take.'

Margaret huffed. 'If our uncle's remedies were any good there'd be a lot more people alive in Eyam today. He might be an apothecary but I don't know a single person who says his potions work against the plague. Do you?'

'No, but I don't know everyone in the village, do I?'

'You know a lot more folk than I do, working at the inn.' Margaret shrugged. 'But let's not quibble about this. I'm just worried that Humphrey has lived on his own since Aunt Alice died and our senseless cousin, Andrew, took off to live on the moors with his cockerel.' Margaret shook her head at the thought. 'But it means that Uncle Humphrey hasn't got anyone to look after him while he's ill.'

Margaret was momentarily silent while she pondered on things. 'I'll go over to his house as soon as I've finished patching this shirt,' she declared, eventually. 'You'll just have to take care of yourself for a few days while I stay and look after him. I'll also tell him about my bacon fat cure. I'm sure he'll to want to try it when he hears how it cured me of the plague.'

It was mid-afternoon by the time Margaret managed to get over to Humphrey Merrell's house in the Townhead. Certain her uncle would want to try her miraculous cure for plague, she carried with her a cupful of the solidified fat from Simon's breakfast that morning. Realising Humphrey would likely be in his bed, she gave a cursory knock on his door and let herself in.

All was quiet and, since Humphrey wasn't around, she deposited her bags on the table and climbed the stairs to knock on his bedchamber door.

'Who's there?'

Humphrey's usual deep, mellow tones had gone, replaced by the reedy whisper of a man who was very sick. But having no fear of catching the plague now that she had such a potent cure, Margaret called, 'It's just me, Uncle,' then pushed the door open and walked in.

The sight that met her eyes was not a pleasant one, and the stench was even worse. Trying hard not to retch, she moved close to the bed. Although Humphrey was awake, he lay in a filthy state. Still wearing breeches and shirt, his chin and greying, dark hair were encrusted with dried vomit and the stink of emptied bowels emanated from beneath his blankets.

'Uncle, I've come to take care of you while you're ill, but first you must let me wash you and change your clothes and bedsheets. Will you do that?'

Humphrey nodded. 'Please… water…'

Knowing exactly how he felt, Margaret hurried downstairs to fill a jug from the water barrel outside the rear door and collect a cup from the dresser. Carrying them up to Humphrey's room, she contemplated the need to make a few trips to the water tough with the pails later on. She would need to heat a good deal of water to wash so many of Humphrey's clothes and bedsheets.

Hoping her uncle would agree to drink the bacon fat

and soon be well, Margaret realised that the fire in the living room had long since gone out. No clothes washing, heating the oven, or even melting bacon fat would be possible before she'd done that. So as soon as Humphrey had sated his thirst, she collected the kindling and logs from the outside store and set to, lighting the fire.

Once the fire was burning well, Margaret spent some time ensuring her uncle and his bed were clean. Baulking at the stench, she managed to wash the excrement and vomit from his body and change the filthy bedding before redressing him in a clean nightshirt. Satisfied he was now comfortable and no longer thirsty, she made to leave the bedchamber and start the rest of the chores, when Humphrey's voice gave her cause to halt.

'Please, fetch Water of Scabious, for sickness,' Humphrey's feeble voice begged. 'Warm Barberries in Wine… I'm so cold.'

Margaret nodded, noting that although Humphrey's body seemed to be sweating profusely, he was seriously shivering. She would fetch his potions, and cups from which to drink them, and hope they worked. If they hadn't done so by tomorrow morning, she would offer her bacon fat cure. Humphrey would be sure to give it a try.

The night seemed to last forever as Margaret kept vigil at her uncle's bedside by the light of a small oil lamp, offering regular sips of the potions he'd requested as well as water. Twice she needed to wash him and change his soiled nightshirt and bedding. Just before dawn, she noticed dark patches on Humphrey's body, particularly at the extremities. She silently wept, knowing that plague had taken a greater hold of her

Twenty-One

uncle's body. He would now grow increasingly weak until death claimed him.

The new day dawned and Margaret drew back the drapes, allowing warm sunlight to fall on Humphrey's face. His eyelids momentarily flickered before opening and Margaret gently raised his head with her hand and poured a few more drops of water through his lips.

'How are you feeling?' she asked, realising Humphrey would be unable to say a great deal, but to hear his voice would reassure her that he wasn't about to meet his Maker just yet.

Humphrey gave an almost imperceptible shake his head. 'Very ill,' he said, his voice quite clear. Margaret was pleased to note that her perseverance with water and potions throughout the night had, at least, eased his dry throat.

'Uncle…' she broached, tentatively, 'a few days ago, I had some of the symptoms of the plague and, like you, I felt so ill that I took to my bed. Simon was at work and I roused in great need of water…' Margaret continued to tell her tale, right up to the point where although the bacon fat had made her vomit, it had cured her.

She could see that Humphrey was listening, so she carried on, 'The plague symptoms I had, including sickness and runny bowels, just vanished. And since your remedies have done little, other than to stop your lips and voice from cracking, would you be willing to try my bacon fat cure?'

Humphrey's glowering face told Margaret precisely what he thought of her cure. 'No,' he said, adamantly, as his eyes closed again and he fell into an uneasy plague-induced sleep.

Although greatly disappointed, Margaret continued to

care for her uncle for the rest of the day, keeping up with the rigorous chores of fetching water from the trough and washing fouled clothes and bedding. By midday, grotesquely swollen red lumps appeared on his neck, and in his groin and armpits and she hurried downstairs to root through Humphrey's great store of herbal cures. Finding a balm labelled as being 'soothing to fiery bodily sores and skin complaints,' she followed the instructions and applied the balm on pieces of stiff material cut from an old doublet of her uncle's. Hoping it would bring him a degree of comfort, she remained by his bedside and continued to pour drops of water through his lips.

Humphrey rarely roused, but when he did it was for but a few fleeting moments, and by the time dusk was falling, he took his final breath.

For a while, Margaret could do no more than weep for the loss of a dear uncle. Humphrey had been a constant presence when she and Simon were growing up, someone to whom they could always turn for advice and words of comfort. As an apothecary and a knowledgeable man, he had been respected by everyone in Eyam, including Reverends Stanley and Mompesson.

Eventually, Margaret swept the tears from her eyes and washed and redressed her uncle's body ready for burial. Leaving him alone in his room, she damped down the fire, collected her belongings and, with a heavy heart, trudged back to her cottage so that she and Simon could make arrangements for Humphrey's burial. The only thing on her mind was the sad fact that her uncle might have still been alive if he'd tried her bacon fat cure.

Twenty-One

'We won't be using that awful Marshall Howe, for the burial,' Margaret declared when she got home with her news. 'I'm quite capable of helping you to dig the grave, or digging it myself, come to that. It would be quicker with the two of us doing it, though. Carrying Humphrey's body out to the grave would also be easier with two of us.'

Simon nodded. 'We'll bury him tomorrow in the field he bought behind 'is 'ouse. There's too much growing in 'is garden and I don't want to be diggin' up bushes and shrubs, or lots of 'erbs, come to that. We'd be best gettin' it done as soon as I finish work, while there's still some daylight. We can come 'ome and eat once we've finished.'

There was little left to say of immediate importance and to speak about who would inherit Humphrey's house and field seemed inappropriate at this time. But a thought entered Margaret's head. 'I imagine if Andrew Merrell ever comes back to Eyam, he'll want Humphrey's house. He is Humphrey's son, after all.'

'If 'e hasn't already starved or frozen to death out there on the moors, yer mean. I wonder if 'e's eaten his cockerel yet?'

That thought caused them both to smile as Margaret prepared a cold meal from whatever foods she could find. At least Simon had remembered to collect the supplies from the earl and the bread form Bubnell.

But he hadn't bothered to cook a thing for himself, other than bacon for his breakfast.

Twenty-Two

Eyam: September 10 1666

Mary placed a bowl of steaming vegetables on the rectory dining table and seated herself with William, ready to serve the meal they would share before she went home for the night.

'Am I right in thinking there have been considerably fewer deaths so far this month, Reverend?' she asked, carving him a few slices of roast chicken and passing him the vegetables before she served herself and they both tucked in to the meal.

William nodded. 'Only thirteen since the beginning of September, which is half the number we lost in the first ten days of August. That's a very encouraging drop, and it gives cause to hope that the numbers will continue to fall for the rest of the month. If a similar pattern emerges to that of last year, there should be even fewer deaths during October and hardly any at all over the winter. Whether or not the disease will return with the spring remains to be seen.'

'I was saddened to hear of Humphrey Merrell's death this morning,' Mary remarked as they laid down their knives and forks. 'He was such a nice man, and an excellent apothecary. His remedies helped us through many an ailment over the years. A lot of us in Eyam will miss him. Neither of the other two apothecaries in the village could match Humphrey's skills.'

William nodded. 'He was certainly a well-informed man. I've had several interesting discussions with him since I came here, and on a variety of topics, notably regarding the plague

Twenty-Two

in recent months. He readily admitted that none of his herbal remedies could cure bubonic plague, although some of his potions gave effective pain relief for some of its symptoms.'

'Yes, I found that when George Viccars and my own family were suffering.'

'As did I when Catherine was so ill,' William said as Mary cleared away the dinner plates and replaced them with bowls of blackberry compote. 'Now Mary, lest I forget, I must thank you for finding a new housekeeper for the rectory. Jane Hawksworth is such a pleasant lady and a very capable and reliable worker. I know she has suffered much heartache during the plague and seems pleased to be out of her own home for a few hours a day and have people to talk to.'

'Jane is my next-door neighbour, as you know, Reverend, and a lovely, caring person. I'm sure she'll keep the rectory as clean and tidy as she does her own home. And you're right, Jane has been very lonely since the deaths of so many in her family.'

'Why don't I ask her if she'd like to share the meal with us of an evening? I would be happy to do so, as long as cooking an extra portion wouldn't put you to too much trouble.'

'That's a wonderful idea, Reverend, and no trouble at all on my behalf. It would fill some of Jane's lonely evenings and she and I can walk home together afterwards. But I shall say nothing to her until you have offered the invitation.

'Oh, before I clear away the dishes, have you heard the funny little tale going around about Marshall Howe?'

William shook his head. 'I'm not sure what could be the least bit funny about that dreadful man, Mary, but I'm intrigued to hear what this story is.'

A Boundary of Stones

'Well, it seems that Mr Howe's skills as a grave digger were in great demand in August, when so many people were dying. So, aware of the need to get the bodies of plague victims buried as soon as possible, he took to digging a number of graves while sufferers were still alive, more often than not in their own gardens. Geoffrey Unwin, a near neighbour of Mr Howe's in the Townhead, was one such plague victim.'

William frowned. 'I have no record of anyone by that name dying. It seems I need to see Howe to ask for the date of Mr Unwin's death.'

'You might want to hear the rest of the story before you do that, Reverend. It's a rather strange one…'

William couldn't help laughing out loud as the scene unfolded. 'Well, I hope that taught the wretched man a lesson, although I can't help wondering how such an unfortunate incident affected Mr Unwin. Being almost buried alive could have a nasty effect on anyone. I can only imagine he'd been in a deep, plague-induced sleep and the bumpy journey down the stairs and across the garden roused him enough to realise how thirsty he was.'

'I agree, Reverend. It's also good to know that the poor man fully recovered from the plague, although he rarely leaves his house nowadays for fear of catching it again, and the same thing happening to him. Nor does he wish to come face to face with Marshall Howe. He has chosen to forget the event, which is why this story has only come to light now.'

'Oh, so why *has* it come to light now?'

Mary grinned. 'It seems Mr Unwin asked his daughter, Edyth, to say nothing about the event to anyone, not even her

Twenty-Two

closest friends. For a while she was happy to comply with his wishes, embarrassed at having pronounced him dead in the first place. But apparently, Edyth recently divulged the story to a close friend, in confidence – who confided in another friend, who confided in yet another friend. Eventually, everyone in the village was talking about it. You know how it is, Reverend.'

'Indeed, I do, Mary. Indeed, I do.'

On Sunday, the third of October, William held his usual service in Cucklett Delph. As he delivered his sermon, gazing down at the well-spaced groups of villagers from his elevated pulpit in the cliff, he admired the colourful splendour of what had commonly become known as Cucklett Church. A gentle breeze stirred the golden leaves clinging to the branches of trees, whilst those already carpeting the ground crackled as they tumbled and danced along. All poignant reminders that summer was gone and autumn was underway.

The congregation listened to William's sermon in praise of the glories of the Lord, and even his reminder of the need to pray daily for the forgiveness of their sins. Yet, as soon as he recited prayers from the Anglican Prayer Book which required responses, the only voice to be heard was his own.

As had become his norm, William finished the service with words of praise and encouragement for their compliance with the quarantine and an update on the recent trend in the death rate from plague.

'Brave people of Eyam, we have been through much together since bubonic plague found its way into our village thirteen months ago.' William swept round his arm to indicate them all. 'The depleted congregation I see before me lends proof to our losses. Some of you have buried many of your loved ones; others, like me, have buried only one, though I mourn the loss of every one from my flock. Death has walked amongst us and I have the highest regard for those of you who have coped thus far in your heartbroken, bereaved state.'

Several heads were nodding, though no one spoke, so William pushed on.

'Our decision to quarantine ourselves has proven successful in preventing the plague from spreading to neighbouring villages and, to the best of my knowledge, to any city, town or village further afield. All thanks to the valiant sacrifice made by every one of you.

'No one here needs reminding that the autumn days have already cooled but I can add that with that cooling, the death rate in our village has also fallen. Markedly so. In the whole of September, twenty-four people died of plague. And, although I agree that even twenty-four is twenty-four too many, it is a great improvement on the seventy-seven deaths during August and the fifty-six in July. The first two days of October brought another two deaths, and I pray that the rest of the month will see a continuing drop in numbers. Hopefully, we will see very few deaths from plague at all once we move into the heart of winter.'

The raised hand of grey-headed grandfather, Peter Hall, caught William's attention. 'You have a question about that, Peter?'

'Not about the autumn and winter, Reverend. What bothers me and, I imagine, most of us here, is the thought that the plague may come back again next spring.'

Twenty-Two

Murmurs of agreement filled the delph and William knew his answer would be a disappointment to all. 'No one can know what the new year will bring, my friends. All we can do is pray that in His infinite mercy, God will spare us from further grief. But should the disease return with the warmer days, as, indeed, it did this year, we can only act as we see fit at the time. I suggest we keep our everyday thoughts on the present, and leave the future to our prayers.

'Above all, do not lose hope. Plague will one day be gone from Eyam, and although the pain of our losses will be with us for some time, we will be blessed with greatly improved health and the return of normality to our lives.'

For a few moments William waited, until satisfied that no more questions were forthcoming, then went on to address his parishioners as he had planned.

'We are fortunate in having kind and generous people beyond our boundary who continue to provide us with foods and enable our quarantine to work so well. Amongst them, I name the Earl of Devonshire, who has fed us, at his own expense, since July. I am hopeful he will continue to do so until the plague has gone, and Eyam can function on its own again.'

Grunts and words of contempt swept through the congregation and William held up his hands for silence. 'Oh, I have heard the scornful gossip about Sir William's enormous wealth, and that he can well afford to feed us free of charge. I have also heard the tittle-tattle suggesting he only sends us food and firewood to ensure we remain isolated, thereby preventing the plague from reaching his eminently rich family in Chatsworth House.'

William swallowed his own misgivings regarding the motives behind the earl's generosity and held out his hands to the villagers below. 'Whether or not you believe such accusations, I tell you this: the earl is under no obligation whatsoever to send us free provisions. A less magnanimous member of the nobility may well have left us to fend for ourselves, as did a few noble and wealthy families I could name from here in Eyam.'

He paused to allow that fact to sink in. 'On a related matter, I have known of a meeting held in the market hall in the last week of August since the day after it took place. I believe the organiser was hopeful of inciting people to riot in protest of the quarantine and the closure of workplaces. On that occasion the outcome of a vote was to abide by the quarantine, which is why I chose not to remark upon the meeting. Until now.

'The organiser of that meeting passed away in mid-September, but it seems that others are hoping to fill his shoes.' He swept them all with a look of disapproval. 'Only two days ago I became aware of further grumbling of discontent and the likelihood of a second meeting with the sole aim of obtaining a vote in favour of mass protests against the quarantine.'

William held out his arms, his demeanour softening. 'We have come through so much together since plague came to Eyam so, *surely*, we can pull together a little longer, especially as winter is not too far away?

'Let me tell you this, my friends, should rioting and violence take place and the quarantine end, you will not only lose the sympathy and support of the Earl of Devonshire, but of our neighbours in surrounding villages. Their generous food supplies would cease, and the barricades of villages like

Twenty-Two

Tideswell and Bakewell would likely be strengthened to keep Eyam folk out.

'Thus, I ask you, which would be the more sensible course of action: to continue as we are until the plague is over, or to suffer violence on our streets and become alienated from friends and acquaintances beyond our village?'

William observed the shuffling feet and expressions of remorse, but he did not remark on it. 'Lastly, I must deliver a further reminder regarding our proximity to others during the plague. As I look down on you now, I am heartened to see family groups standing with distances of several feet between them. In so doing, you are adhering to a sanction intended to prevent the seeds of plague passing easily from one family to another. And yet, on the evening of that meeting, almost two hundred of you were crammed into the market hall, so close to each other that movement was barely possible. All I can say is that such proximity is tantamount to madness during this time of plague!'

William took a calming breath. 'Let us leave Cucklett Church today in the hope that the plague in Eyam is coming to an end. I entreat you to pray daily to the Lord for forgiveness of your sins and that, in His great wisdom and benevolence, He will soon bring an end to the suffering in our village.'

—

By the end of October, nineteen more Eyam folk had died of plague, only five fewer than during September. Although disappointed that numbers hadn't fallen as low as he had hoped, William knew that the Derbyshire winter would bring a substantial drop in the death rate. Bitter winds would howl across the moors and frosts would claw at fingers and toes, heralding the arrival of the first, heavy snowfalls. Unfortunately, the Derbyshire winter was not conducive to the wellbeing of the old and frail, nor anyone with existing health problems, or of a delicate constitution, like Catherine.

Once again William inwardly railed at his inability to realise just how harsh the winters could be in the midst of such hilly terrain and bleak, open moors. If only he hadn't brought his beloved wife to this place. Distraught and struggling to find the strength to carry on, he slumped at the desk in his study and wept as memories of Catherine engulfed him. He could not have loved her more, and was certain he would never love anyone so deeply and completely again.

In his state of grief and self-pity, William truly believed that too much of his life had revolved around 'if only'. And at this moment in time, his biggest 'if only' of all was, if only he and his family had not come to Eyam.

But what use was regret? It was easy for William to look back and wish his course through life had been different. Yet he knew that given the same choices again, he would still have chosen to become a minister in the Anglican Church; he would still have chosen Catherine as his wife, and still chosen to come to Eyam. The idea of converting the Puritan villagers to the Anglican faith had been something he relished. It was just unfortunate that, at the time the post was offered, he had no knowledge of just how deeply puritanism was rooted in the very fabric of life in Eyam.

Twenty-Two

Besides, he reminded himself, he was a man of the cloth, sworn to work in the service of God and to obey His will. God had guided him to Eyam for a purpose, and that purpose was to lead the people of this village through a pestilence, the likes of which they had never seen before. With the help of Reverend Stanley, he had guided Eyam folk through one of the most difficult and selfless courses of action to be made by everyday working people anywhere. Their courage had likely prevented the deaths of thousands of others, at enormous cost to themselves.

William longed for the day when he would be able to deliver all his services within the walls of St Helen again. Cucklett Delph had been perfect during the summer and autumn, but he could imagine few villagers venturing there in the depths of winter. He promised himself that if the November death rate proved to be lower than ten, normal services in the church would resume for the foreseeable future. And life in Eyam could return to the way it had been before the plague, albeit slowly and steadily.

William truly believed that God would want people to enjoy every day they were given. And yet, this year in Eyam, enjoying life had been impossible. Death lurked around every corner and there was no way of knowing how to avoid colliding with it. Caring for, and watching loved ones die in a state of disease was enough to make most people believe that they would be next and, for a couple of weeks, William had included himself amongst them.

And so, with bated breath, he waited to see what transpired in November.

Twenty-Three

On the first day of November, Mary was preparing the mid-morning cocoa when there was a knock on the rectory door. Knowing Jane would answer it she continued setting up the tray, but not wanting to carry it to the sitting room until the reverend was ready for it, she decided to start her preparations for the evening meal.

Ten minutes later, Jane popped her head round the kitchen door. 'You can carry everything through whenever you're ready, Mary. Reverend Mompesson will be in the sitting room in a moment.'

'Thanks Jane,' Mary replied, lifting the pan from the iron hook over the hearth and pouring the hot milk into the cocoa pot. 'Did you recognise who the visitor was? I hope it wasn't someone declaring another death.' She took a deep breath, releasing it as a long, weary sigh. 'We've all been praying that William Morten's death four days ago was the last.'

'Unfortunately, I think it was another of the Mortens, Mary, although I couldn't say which one. He looked a lot like Matthew from Shepherds Flat but, sadly, all his little family died in August.'

'Well, we'll find out, soon enough. If you'd hold the door open for me, we can make our way to the sitting room.'

William tried not to show his disappointment as the two women came into the room. Having had no plague deaths reported for the last few days, he had thought his prayers had been answered.

Twenty-Three

'Would you like a slice of Mary's wonderful honey cake, Reverend? She only made it this morning and it smells scrumptious.'

'How could I resist after such a recommendation? Besides, Jane, I can already smell the cake's glorious aroma.

'My visitor just now was Isaac Morten,' William said as they enjoyed their short break. 'He came to report that another of his cousins died early this morning. His name was Abraham.'

'I'm sorry to hear that, Reverend. I can't say I knew Abraham well, but I know he was a farmer, like most branches of his family. I truly feel for the Morten family; so many of them have gone.'

'Indeed, Mary. I believe Abraham's death brings the number to eighteen.' William shook his head at the thought. 'There are several formerly large families who have lost most, if not all, of their members. It is hard to think of such loss. But Abraham's death also means that the plague in Eyam has not yet come to an end for the winter.'

As the month progressed the days grew increasingly cold, bringing the first flurries of snow to the hills and moors. The people of Eyam went about their daily chores, just as they'd done since the beginning of the quarantine. The Earl of Devonshire continued to send his weekly supplies and the good people of Bubnell did not forsake their weekly deliveries of freshly baked bread. Nor did the people of nearby Foolow and Stoney Middleton, or the more distant Fulwood, cease their weekly treks to Eyam's boundary. William gave daily thanks to God for blessing their village with such kind and considerate neighbours.

By the end of November, William thanked God that no more plague deaths had been reported. It seemed that the death of Abraham Morten on the first day of the month had, indeed, been the last, and that the plague in Eyam was over.

On Sunday, the fifth of December, William held the first service in St Helen's since the end of June. Despite the icy conditions, he was pleased to see most of what remained of his congregation gathered here, although the absence of Marshall Howe did not escape him. He also noticed that despite the air of relief that the plague was over, few people smiled. The deaths of so many of their families and friends hung over them like an ugly, black cloud. As did William's loss of his beloved wife. Never again would he see Catherine's smiling face at the rear of the church, supporting him and urging him on, despite the reluctance of the congregation to accept his Anglican teachings.

William led his parishioners through the service, yet again hurt and disappointed by their continuing refusal to respond to the prayers and hymns from his Prayer Book. After everything they'd been through together, he'd desperately hoped they'd be ready to worship the Lord with him. Once again, he recalled Catherine's words on the matter:

They are just extremely devout Puritans and a faith so deeply ingrained cannot be dismissed or overturned in a mere two years.

So, the Church of England's Book of Common Prayer would remain an abhorrence to the people of Eyam for some time yet.

William tried to push such thoughts to the back of his mind, knowing that their rejection of the Prayer Book was partly his own fault. He had *allowed* his congregation to remain

Twenty-Three

silent during Anglican prayers and lessons, with neither chastisement nor persuasive words uttered by him. Added to which, at every service since his arrival in Eyam, he had permitted the recital of the villagers' own Puritan versions of the psalms.

He justified his actions in the belief that burdening them with constant demands to change their religious practises with the fear of plague hanging over them would have been far too unkind. And yet, whichever way he looked at it, he could not make that argument fit with the lack of authority he had wielded during the first year of his ministry in Eyam. Before the arrival of plague.

He brought his service to a close by delivering village news and information, just as he'd done in every service before and during those in Cucklett Delph.

'Words cannot express the depth of sorrow felt by everyone in our village. Two hundred and sixty of our citizens have been taken from us by the plague, so it is easy to understand how it overrides our relief that bubonic plague has gone. But I truly believe that although such loss has rendered us a smaller and sadder community, it has made us a more thoughtful and caring one. The enormous sacrifice you made in agreeing to the quarantine reflects your love for your fellow man. Your course of action will be recorded in history as a remarkable achievement. And people will marvel at it.'

He threw his arms out wide to embrace them all. 'I also believe that future generations will learn better ways of preventing the spread of such diseases from our actions. Plague, like typhoid, diphtheria, pertussis, smallpox, and other contagious diseases, will likely be around for some time. Let us hope that in years to come, people will look at the way we quarantined ourselves as an enormous – and successful – effort to stop the terrible bubonic plague from killing people throughout the land.

'Unfortunately, we cannot say for certain that the plague will not return to Eyam with the spring…' William waited for the words of concern to die down before adding, 'However, I believe we can increase our chances of seeing it gone from our village for good if, once again, we work together as a village. We must ensure that the seeds of plague are killed in every building in the village. And the only way those seeds can be destroyed is by fire.'

'We can't burn the whole village down, Reverend,' a male voice rang out. 'How would any of us survive a winter without shelter?'

Shouts of agreement followed, until William held up his hands for quiet. 'You misunderstand my meaning, Samuel; I am not suggesting we burn our houses down. But we do need to burn as many items from inside them that we can do without. By which I mean clothing and soft furnishings… like rugs, drapes, towels, cushions, pillows, blankets, bedsheets and upholstered furniture.'

Again, mumbles of unrest rippled around the church, prompting William to explain, 'As all of you, I have no idea where the seeds of plague come from, or how they find their way into our homes. But I do know that once they have done so, they stay there, resulting in the misery and death of occupants for a very long time.'

He paused, just long enough for those ideas to take root.

Twenty-Three

'We cannot ignore the possibility that those seeds could still be harboured in the very fabric of our houses –in our household goods, or even our clothes, and even the materials of which our homes are built. So, provided no further deaths from plague occur during the coming week, I hereby set the date for our great burning on Tuesday, the fourteenth of December. Once that has been accomplished, the Boundary Stones can be removed and the quarantine lifted. All of us can then return to the life we left behind before the plague arrived.'

William held out his hands and smiled round at them. 'I thank you all for attending our service today, and look forward to seeing you again next Sunday, when I will give you a few more details about the time and place of the great burning on the Tuesday.'

The following week passed by with no further deaths in Eyam and, as promised, at the end of his next Sunday service, William made his announcement regarding the great burning planned for the coming Tuesday.

'We will begin to congregate with the items we wish to burn on Church Street, immediately outside of Saint Helen's, at nine o'clock in the morning,' he started. 'The December morning will have lightened by then and I will have had time to lay the tinder for the bonfire. If the day dawns dry, I might have it already burning with some of the rectory's soft furnishings and most of my own clothing. If the day is too wet, I trust you will all realise that the burning will be cancelled until the first dry day.

'So, I ask you all to allow common sense to guide you. All I can say now is that I will pray to God for a rain-free day so that Eyam can take its first steps on the road to recovery form plague. Bring as many of the goods you wish to burn as you can carry. If you have further items, they can be collected once your first load has been devoured by the flames.

'Then, over the following days, we must scrub all inside walls, floors and wooden furniture with hot water and soap. Our homes must be spotlessly clean to discourage the seeds of plague from settling.'

For some moments, silence prevailed, then an uproar of angry voices echoed round the old church. William held up his hands for silence and gradually the commotion fizzled out, to be replaced by the ardent voice of old Jacob Ragge.

'You can't ask us to burn all our stuff, Reverend, especially our beds and blankets. If you think we're going t' sleep on the cold floor, you can think again!'

Pandemonium again erupted as villagers yelled their agreement with the old man.

'Jacob's right! I'm old an' all, and riddled with rheumatics. I need a warm bed t' sleep in – with plenty of blankets in the winter.'

'How d'you expect us to replace the things we burn, Reverend, especially now? Most of us have had no pay for months, and if it weren't for the free food we get, we'd have died from starvation months ago, never mind the plague!'

William nodded as he glanced round at the worried faces. 'I realise that many of you will not have the means with which to buy, or make, replacements for the clothes and furnishings you burn. Indeed, I could not afford to replace every carpet and item of upholstered furniture in the rectory. In which case,

Twenty-Three

what we must do is to fume and purify all items that remain in our homes. Just remember, no matter which means of purifying we choose, it must be thorough enough to kill the seeds of plague completely. I, for one, could not live with myself if I believed that any items of mine had been responsible for the plague recurring in the spring.

'I beg you to think on my words as you make your decisions.'

The morning of the great burning arrived. It was Tuesday, the fourteenth of December, and although the air was still and free of rain or snow, it was bitterly cold. A little before eight o'clock, William and the rectory's red-headed gardener, Joseph Taylor, began the first of many trips from the rectory to the middle of Church Street, their exhaled breaths momentarily clouding in the icy air. Feathery white hoar frost adorned the cemetery's trees and shrubs, glistening in the pale, yellow rays of the December sunrise.

Their first loads consisted of bundles of faggots and masses of brushwood that would form the bonfire's tinder, all heaped in Joseph's pushcart and wheelbarrow. Then came the first of several trips back and forth to collect the rectory's upholstered chairs, soft furnishings, bedding and clothes. William sighed with relief when their trekking to and fro was over and several pieces for furniture were stacked on top of the tinder. He shook Joseph's hand, greatly indebted to the gardener.

'Would you mind walking back to the rectory with me once everyone's gone home tonight?' he said, smiling at the gardener's kindly face. 'I have something I'd like to discuss with you, and it won't take long.'

Joseph doffed his wide-brimmed hat. 'Right you are, Reverend. I'm in no rush t' get home. Annie'll feed the two lads and keep some stew warm in the oven for me. Tom and Jack'll be ready for summat t' eat after lugging all our rugs and stuff out here.'

The church clock was striking nine as the first villagers arrived, their arms and a variety of hand-pushed carts laden with household goods and clothing. Soon, a substantial crowd had gathered and Joseph hurried back to the rectory to collect the lighted oil lamp and a long-handled torch. On his return, he used the lamp to light the strips of cloth soaked in oil that formed the end of the torch.

The flames sprung to life, writhing as they licked the cloth, and Joseph thrust it into the faggots and brushwood. It took barely moments to catch alight, the flames dancing and crackling as they devoured the brushwood. Soon William's soft furnishings joined the merry dance and before too long, heavy, wooden furniture glowed red, releasing grey-white smoke that drifted up into the still morning air, eventually to dissipate and disappear.

Folk held out their hands, welcoming the warmth of the roaring fire as William moved amongst them, controlling the order of items to be burned. Throughout the rest of the short, December day, a great bonfire roared on the dirt road, watched over by the old village church. As the hours ticked by, William was aware of people leaving, only to return with more barrow loads of goods. On several occasions he was quite overcome by people's willingness to help stop the seeds of plague from

Twenty-Three

returning in the spring.

As the early evening light gradually dimmed, the crowds began to filter away to their homes, in need of hot food in their bellies. William stood beside the fire until it became little more than glowing embers in the middle of the road which, without further fuel, would almost certainly burn itself away within the next hour or so. He thanked God that the day of the burning had been a great success and turned to thank his cheerful gardener, who had remained with him throughout.

'I owe you a great deal for all your help today, Joseph. Without it, I could not have managed some of that heavy furniture from the rectory.'

'You're very welcome, Rector. As I said this mornin', my two lads took care of the goods from our cottage, so it made sense for me t' help you.'

William took a final look at the smouldering embers as Joseph headed to the church gate, from where he picked up a wooden pail full of garden soil and hurled it over the remnants of the fire.

'Best be on the safe side,' he said as William wondered why he hadn't thought of doing that himself. 'You never know if anyone comes along here in a cart once it's dark, or some silly kids decide to sneak out and keep the fire burning. Who knows what damage even a few hot embers can cause?'

'You're right, and my laxity in overlooking that fact is shameful. Thank you for your thoughtfulness, Joseph. Now, shall we return to the rectory so I can tell you what's on my mind. I won't keep you long, then you can get off home to eat and rest.'

The worried look on the face of the usually cheerful gardener as they entered the study caused William to smile. 'I apologise for asking you to accompany me without telling you the reason, Joseph.' He gestured to one on the armchairs. 'Take a seat and I'll explain.'

William sat in the other chair, pleased to see Joseph looking a little more relaxed. 'I've lived in this house for almost two and a half years, and have always been impressed by the dedication you have shown to keeping the garden and churchyard looking so wonderfully neat, tidy and colourful, even during the harrowing months of plague. My wife sang your praises on many occasions, and you will know from the number of times she visited the garden to ask your advice on growing various plants and herbs, how much she valued your commitment and knowledge…

'What I am trying to say is that since my arrival here, you have always been a part of St Helen's and I realise how much I took your work as gardener for granted. I also noticed in the church records of expenditure that the yearly increase in your wage appears to have been overlooked for many years. Something I intend to rectify here and now.'

William retrieved a small but well-filled sack from his desk and handed it to Joseph. 'I think you'll find the coins in here will more than make up for the many increases in pay owed to you. There are also a few extra silver shillings from me as a thank you for your help today.'

Joseph forced his lower jaw to rise from where it seemed to have fallen and, for some moments, he struggled to find words to speak.

Twenty-Three

'I'm sure the coin will come in useful for replacing some of the household goods you burned today,' William added whilst the kind-hearted gardener wrestled with his disobedient tongue. 'But, of course, you are the best person to know what use you can put it to. Please know, my friend, that you have my greatest appreciation – and my admiration – for your work in the rectory garden, and my sincere thanks for your help today.'

'Reverend Mompesson… I don't know what to say. To be honest, I hadn't realised I was due any increases in my pay, but paying me now for all those missed years seems like finding buried treasure and I can assure you, me and Agnes will put it to good use. As for paying me for today, you had no need at all to do that. I knew you'd never manage to carry all that furniture out on your own, and I've lit more bonfires than I've had hot dinners. My help was freely given, with no expectation of payment.'

'Which makes me appreciate it even more. Now, I'm sure your family will be wondering where you've got to, so I'll see you to the door.'

Joseph shook William's hand. 'I can't tell you what your generosity means to me and my family. All I can do is thank you from the bottom of my heart.'

William smiled as the gardener headed to Church Street, on his way back to the arms of a loving family in their cosy cottage along the road. As he closed the door, he felt the solitude close in around him, and decided to connect with others through the written word. But first, he headed to the kitchen in order to placate his growling stomach.

After enjoying a bowl of beef stew left warming in the oven

for him by Mary, William felt the need to inform Uncle John that the plague in Eyam was over and, by the grace of God, he had lived through it. Once again, he arranged his oil lamps at either end of his desk in the study, retrieved his writing materials from the drawer, and started to write:

Dearest Uncle

You will doubtless be surprised to receive a letter from me, thinking me to have succumbed to bubonic plague along with so many others in Eyam. I can assure you that I am well, and display no symptoms of that wicked disease. Why that should be eludes me, but I give thanks to God that He chose to spare me, that I may continue to work in His holy name.

Thus, I was loath to worry you with a letter written by my hand, and to give you peace of mind I intend to request a friend to copy my words for me.

I know you realise that I have lost the kindest wife in all the world. I must tell you that Catherine's end was comfortable and she is now invested with a crown of righteousness.

Events in Eyam have been very sad and more terrible than any in history so far. Our village has become a Golgotha, the place of the skull, and had we not a small remnant of us left, we would have become like Sodom and Gomorrah. My ears had never before heard such doleful theatrics, my nose ever smelled such horrid smells, nor my eyes beheld such ghastly sights. Seventy-six families have been visited by the disease in our parish, from which two hundred and sixty poor souls have perished. I thank the Lord that since the first day of November, no more have died, and no one presently displays symptoms of plague.

We have recently had such a burning of goods, I declare, I have scarcely any garments left with which to shelter my body from the cold, nor any furniture left in the rectory. I intend to spend the next two weeks ensuring that all woollen clothes are fumed and purified for the safety of our village and, indeed, the safety of our country.

I know I am in your prayers, and that the prayers of good people have kept me from the very jaws of death. I have tasted the goodness of the Creator, who has eased my mind when grim thoughts of death did frighten me.

I always had faith that my children would fare well in your care, and you have my heartfelt thanks for the kindness and affection that you and my dear aunt have shown them. I know you concern yourself with my welfare and I am blessed with your love. I can assure you that during our troubles in Eyam, you have been frequently in my thoughts.

A line from your hand would be most welcome to your sorrowful and affectionate nephew,

William Mompesson

Satisfied to have eventually written all three letters he considered necessary, tomorrow he would ask Mary to copy out this last one before he sent it to Sheffield through the postal service.

As William lay in bed that night it occurred to him that he'd said nothing about George and Elizabeth returning to Eyam now that the plague was over. As he thought about it, he decided it might be a good idea for them to stay in Sheffield for the next few months or so, at least until life in Eyam had begun to return to normal and people felt able to smile again.

With those thoughts in mind, William eventually drifted off to sleep.

Twenty-Four

The day after the great burning, William pinned notices to trees and wooden posts all over Eyam to announce that the quarantine was over. He also asked that all those involved in placing the boundary stones would now remove them. As of next week, the lead mines and quarries would once more be open to Eyam workers; cattle that had roamed from their pastures could be retrieved and by the spring, crops could be sown in newly worked fields. Parents who had sent their children to stay with family or friends were now at liberty to bring them home and women could once again venture to the markets at Bakewell, Baslow and Tideswell, and gather at Eyam's own Friday market for fresh foods and a chat.

Yet the high death toll, along with the number of people who had fled during the plague, had left so many houses empty that Eyam had come to resemble a ghost town. William clung to the hope that some of those who had gained entry to other villages, or had survived the harsh months of living on the moors, would now return. He longed to see Eyam prospering again, though he realised it could take some years for that to happen.

Of more immediate concern to William was the number of villagers who had been unable to work at places beyond Eyam's boundary during the quarantine. As a result, many families had little or no coin with which to buy food until they'd earned at least a week's wage. He knew if he didn't find some means of helping them through the coming weeks, some of those with

Twenty-Four

explosive tempers would likely be inciting protests and riots. During which, innocent people would, doubtless, be harmed.

As William pondered on this, a possibility entered his head: a means of helping the villagers get by until the routine of working life had returned and people had coin to buy foods for themselves. With that in mind he retired to his bed a little more contentedly.

—

The following day, William rode out from Eyam to pay a second visit to Sir William Cavendish, Earl of Devonshire, at Chatsworth House. Unlike the warm day in late June when he'd last ridden out to this grand stately home, the December day was bitterly cold. The sharp wind penetrated his thick woollen coat and despite the leather gloves he wore, his icy fingers ached. The ride was far from pleasant but concentrating on what he needed to ask the earl, William tried to ignore his bodily discomfort.

His pull on the bell rope was answered by Anthony, the under butler who had opened the door to him the last time he'd called. 'Good morning, Reverend Mompesson,' Anthony said with a smile. 'I must say, it's good to see you again, if only to know that you are alive and well.'

William grinned back. 'Thank you, Anthony. I can tell you, it's a great relief to be able to be here alive and well.'

'Come in and take a seat, while I inform Sir William you are here. Let us hope he isn't too busy to see you.'

William seated himself in Chatsworth's sizeable hall and

waited, realising he should have made an appointment before simply arriving on the earl's doorstep. Just as he'd done on his previous visit.

'His lordship can see you in about fifteen minutes, if you'd be so kind as to wait in the drawing room,' the under butler said on his return. 'He is presently in the library, engaged in reviewing some legal documents and is determined to finish them this morning.'

'I'm in no particular hurry, Anthony, so I'd be happy to wait.'

'Then I'll show you to the drawing room and send one of the kitchen maids along with some cocoa for you.'

Twenty minutes later, Sir William Cavendish stepped into the drawing room and closed the door behind him. Garbed in an exquisite silk waistcoat of a golden hue interlaced with a silver thread, his aristocratic heritage was evident to see. 'My apologies for keeping you waiting, Reverend. I simply couldn't postpone dealing with those blasted documents a moment longer. It would make things so much easier if the people who wrote them did not completely confuse issues by using jargon unknown to anyone but themselves.'

William laughed as the earl directed him to an armchair and sat opposite to him. 'I know exactly how you feel, Sir William. I've felt the same about Church documents for years.'

'Now, Reverend, what can I do for you? Anthony tells me the plague in Eyam is over and I can see that you have come through it unscathed.'

'Though I and other survivors in Eyam may appear unscathed, Sir William, we have all lost loved ones, and our village

Twenty-Four

will take some years to become the thriving and happy place it once was. We buried two hundred and sixty people in little over a year. Grief is etched into every face I see, and others, perhaps, see it in mine.'

The earl's face creased in concern. 'If you have lost someone in your family, Reverend, you have my sincere condolences.'

'My wife, Catherine, died in August, and the weeks since then have been the worst I have ever known. But I am thankful our children are safe and well with my uncle and his family in Sheffield.'

'Yes, I can well imagine you are. And believe me, if I can assist you in any way, just say the word.'

William shifted in his seat, feeling like a child about to request some costly item from his father. 'As I said, Sir William, the plague has gone from Eyam and our quarantine has been lifted. I, and indeed, the thousands of citizens in villages and towns for many miles around, owe the people of Eyam a huge debt of gratitude. Their actions have ensured that the plague spread no further than our village boundary.'

Emboldened by his own words, William looked directly at the earl and worked his way towards his focal point. 'During the weeks of quarantine when workplaces beyond or boundary were closed to Eyam folk, most of our villagers were unable to earn coin with which to buy essential foods. I was, therefore, wondering if you could possibly extend the generous deliveries of foodstuffs for another three or four weeks. That would give the villagers time, not only to return to a life of some normality, but to save enough coin to resume purchasing goods for themselves.'

Sir William was silent for some moments and William had the feeling he was about to refuse his request. After all, he'd already been feeding Eyam folk for five and a half months. But the earl's answer took him by surprise.

'It is now mid-December, not the best time of year for people to be struggling to buy foods or obtaining firewood for themselves. I suggest that I continue with the weekly deliveries of foods and fortnightly deliveries of timber until mid-February. That will give people eight weeks or so in which to earn coin and feel able to visit the markets again. Would that be acceptable to you, Reverend?'

William's huge sigh of relief was evidently not missed by the earl.

'I'll take your answer to be a "Yes" shall I, Reverend?'

The two men laughed and William said, 'Your offer is more than generous and considerate, Sir William. Your kindness will not be forgotten by the people of Eyam, amongst whom I number myself.'

'Then the deal is sealed, and I can tell you that the sacrifices made by you and your villagers will be remembered by many of us for some years to come.'

The renowned Earl of Devonshire rang his little bell and shook William by the hand as they waited for Anthony to return. 'Now I must leave you and return to my cursed paperwork. It has been my privilege to give aid to your village, Reverend, and I wish you all well in the months and years to come. And before I forget, I must also apologise for the antics of that mindless carter from Bubnell back in August. He could have undone everything your villagers were working so hard to secure. He had a good dressing down from me, I can assure you, and the promise that I would never again offer him work. I believe he makes his living labouring on farmland nowadays.

'I wish you good health and happiness in future years, Reverend Mompesson. Having met you, I now realise why Sir George rates you so highly. You are a remarkably resourceful and courageous man, and a caring one. I await the day when Eyam once more becomes one of the most thriving villages in North Derbyshire.'

—

Rowland Torre of Stoney Middleton was both relieved and delighted to hear that the plague in Eyam was over and the quarantine lifted. At last, after months of being apart, he would see his darling Emmott and they could set a date for their wedding. Having not so much as cast eyes on her since the week before she missed their meeting in Cucklett Delph at the beginning of May, he was desperate to be with her again.

Emmott's failure to keep to their meetings had continued throughout May and into June, by which time the number in deaths in Eyam had risen dramatically and Rowland's family implored him to stay away from the village. Then, at the beginning of July, Eyam had isolated itself from surrounding villages and Rowland realised he would just have to be patient until the quarantine was lifted.

Not knowing if Emmott was dead or alive had been more than Rowland could bear, but he prayed constantly that his betrothed was safe and well. Now, in mid-December, with

Eyam's boundary once again open, Rowland was determined to walk to the home of the Syddall family and ask to see Emmott.

Eyam seemed unusually quiet as he headed towards Bagshaw House, the Syddall's family home on Church Street. His heart pounded as he neared, the sight of the boarded-up door and windows eliciting fears of possibilities so terrible he dared not contemplate. He continued to the rear of the house, only to see the door and windows similarly secured and not a single member of the family to be seen. Rowland gulped back a wail of anguish as his worst fears played in his head. But he clung to the hope that after losing so many of her family, Mrs Syddall had taken her young son, Josiah, and her daughter, Emmott, to stay with relatives in Bakewell.

Deciding the best person to ask would be Reverend Mompesson, Rowland crossed the road and headed to the rectory. He was surprised when Jane Hawksworth answered the door.

'I didn't expect to see you here, Jane,' he said, smiling at his cousin. 'Joan French was housekeeper here earlier this year, wasn't she?'

'I know you haven't been into Eyam for some time, Rowland, so you'll find a lot of things changed since before the plague. I'm afraid Joan and her husband both died in August… Is it the reverend you've come to see? I'll go and tell him you're here.'

It was evident that Jane didn't want to say more as she scurried away, her evasive action causing Rowland's heart to thump fast and loud again. By the time she returned to take his coat and lead him to the sitting room, he was convinced his worst fears had come true.

Twenty-Four

'Good morning, Rowland,' Reverend Mompesson said, gesturing for him to take a seat as he did the same. 'I hope you're keeping well, and there have been no more deaths in the Torre family since last year. It took some time for Jane to come to terms with her parents' deaths, not to mention, four of her siblings.'

Rowland nodded. 'The fact that they died from plague caused a great deal of panic in our village, Reverend, and many were convinced that Jane's mother had brought the disease to Stoney Middleton from Peter and Jane's house. But the family isolated itself, and friends and relatives in the village left food and milk on their doorstep and the plague went no further.

'You probably know that my father and Humphrey Torre, Jane's father, were brothers. Reverend.'

'Yes, Jane mentioned that you and she are cousins.'

'We are, and I am heartened to see that Jane didn't catch the plague.'

'Indeed, we've buried so many of our villagers since the plague took Eyam in its clutches. Jane lost her husband and two children, not to mention her family in Stoney Middleton. But, like several others I could name, by the grace of God, she has evaded the disease herself.'

'Reverend, I came here to ask if you know where the Syddall family has gone. I know Mrs Syddall has relatives in Bakewell.'

'The Syddalls didn't leave. I'm afraid that only young Josiah survived the plague and it pains me to tell you that Emmott died at the end of April.'

Rowland fought to stop himself from weeping, but tears still filled his eyes as the reverend continued, 'Barely a week before Emmott died, her mother married a man by the name of John Daniel. Did you know him?'

'I knew him from his visits to our mill to purchase flour over the years but not on a personal level.'

'Unfortunately, Mr Daniel died in July, and in the October, Elizabeth herself died, which left three-year-old-Josiah with not a single member of his family left alive. Thankfully, before Elizabeth died, she placed the boy in the care of a trusted friend who has pledged to raise the child as his own.'

The reverend poured a glass of water from a jug on the table beside him and stood to place it in Rowland's hand before sitting down again. 'I realise how hard it must be for you to take all this in, Rowland, and I'm afraid to say, I was loath to send word to you of Emmott's death for fear of the disease reaching your village again. Once the death rate started to rise in June, the quarantine was organised as a means of keeping neighbouring villages, and even distant towns, free of the plague.'

'Thank you for explaining all that, Reverend. We in Stoney Middleton are indebted to you for your thoughtfulness. We knew about the quarantine, of course, as many of us provided foods for your villagers at the Boundary Stone. And some of Eyam's residents have continued to leave orders for flour from my family's mill. But we had no idea of how many people were dying here, or who they were. All I could do was to pray that Emmott and the last of her family had survived.'

'You have my deepest sympathy, Rowland. Emmott was a lovely young woman and was mourned by many in the village.'

At that moment, Mary arrived with the morning cocoa.

Twenty-Four

'I'm sure you can manage a hot drink before you walk back to Stoney Middleton, Rowland,' she said. 'The wind is bitter out there today. Jane mentioned you were here, and I wanted to say how upset we all were when Emmott died, and how very sorry we are for your loss. We know how deeply you loved each other. Take comfort in the arms of your family and the fact that time does heal. Most of us in Eyam have lost loved ones, including Reverend Mompesson.'

'I'm sorry to hear that, Reverend,' Rowland said, sweeping the tears from his cheeks with his fingers. 'Forgive me for sounding so selfish in my grief. I had no idea that you were suffering the same.'

'I found the only way to prevent the grief of my wife's death from crushing me was to keep extremely busy. Thankfully, like several other families in Eyam, we sent our children to live in safety with relatives elsewhere.'

Mary made to leave, then turned back as the two men glanced up, expectantly. 'I almost forgot, I have a message from Jane for you, Rowland. She intends to visit all the family in Stoney Middleton on Sunday afternoon, if that's convenient.'

'Thank you, Mary. Would you tell her we'll all be at home and that I'll look forward to seeing her?'

'I'll do that,' Mary replied, before heading to the door.

The two men drank their cocoa in silence, then Rowland asked, 'Do you think you'll ever remarry, Reverend?'

Evidently taken aback by his question, Reverend Mompesson shuffled a little before replying. 'To be honest, Catherine's death is relatively recent and it's hard to imagine myself loving another woman as much as I loved her.'

'I shall never marry, Reverend. Emmott was the love of my life, and if I can't marry her, I shall remain a single man and wait to be reunited with my beloved in Heaven.'

'I understand how you feel and I share those sentiments. I suppose I should heed the advice I've given to most of those bereaved in Eyam and allow myself time to heal. But at this moment, all I can say is that when that time comes, I will still have no intention of looking for a wife. Yet none of us can predict what the future holds, and I place my trust in God to guide me along the correct path. As for the present, like you, Roeland, I have family to consider. Thoughts of being with my children again keep me from being engulfed by sorrow.'

Rowland stood and held out his hand. 'Thank you for taking the time to share your feelings with me, Reverend. They will be of comfort whenever I feel that life without Emmott has no meaning. The shock of hearing of her death has changed the course of my life and I must now find another route. I will try to take each new day as it comes, and wait for the time when my grief no longer feels raw.'

Twenty-Five

December 1666 – June 1667

The sense of relief that the plague was finally over was tempered by the heavy burden of grief and loss the villagers carried. Almost a third of Eyam's population had gone, taken in the cruelest of ways. But as the new year progressed, William was gladdened to see that broken hearts were beginning to mend, including his own. After fifteen months of plague, the village had embarked on its journey along the road to recovery, and people started to smile again.

Within weeks of the quarantine being lifted, the lead mine and limestone quarry were functioning fully once more and deserted farms were worked. Most of the stray cattle had been found and by the spring, fields were ploughed and crops were sown. Women resumed their visits to the local markets and enjoyed their little chats at Eyam's own, Friday market.

The great burning was proving to have been successful in destroying any remaining seeds of plague, and although many folk struggled to replace clothing and furnishings destroyed in the fire, none fell foul to the plague.

William would never forget the generous aid given to them by the Earl of Devonshire, whose deliveries of foods and timber continued until the end of February. Nor would he forget the kindness of neighbouring villages. Their gifts had prevented further deaths through starvation during the quarantine and

William gave constant thanks to God for the charitable actions of such caring people.

The gentle warmth of June gradually gave way to the fiercer heat of July. A year had passed since that fateful summer of 1666. Fruits swelled and ripened on trees and hedgerows along the lanes and grain crops in the fields gradually embraced their cloaks of gold. It would be a good harvest. Villagers chatted to friends and neighbours whilst purchasing goods at the Friday market, or congregating for weekly services in the Church of St Helen.

As he sat alone in the lovely old church, William made note of his thoughts relating to the recovery of the village for his service tomorrow. And, although it pained him to still be doing so, he would permit the congregation to recite their own Puritan versions of a couple of appropriate psalms. In turn, he would recite The Lord's Prayer, whether they joined in with it, or not. He had not completely given up hope of converting at least some of them to the Anglican faith.

Contemplating the wording of his service, William headed back to the rectory to write it out fully before any small detail eluded him.

As always, the church was packed on the morning of Sunday the third of July. Due to the warmth of the day, William was garbed only in his long black cassock and white surplice, having abandoned the black suit he usually wore beneath. On top of his dark head sat his usual little black hat.

From his place in the pulpit, he opened his arms out wide, a sense of elation embracing him as he gazed about the church.

Twenty-Five

'Good people of Eyam, on this beautiful July morning, let our hearts be light and full of love and thanks for our Heavenly Father and the bounties He provides for us. As the words of Psalm 23 tell us, the Lord is, indeed, our shepherd. Through Him we shall not want. He provides the foods to keep us fed, and water so that we may drink. It is a theme we have touched upon many times. Even throughout the plague, the Lord ensured that kind and thoughtful people kept us supplied with foods so that we may endure the hardships. For which we continue to give our heartfelt thanks.

'Today, I speak again of that disease, of which we are now free. We have all suffered sorrow and loss, some of us more than others. But what I wish to remind all of you now is that you have persevered. Each of you had the courage to do what you believed to be the right… the only… way to deal with the plague. The majority of you agreed that Eyam should be quarantined for the benefit of people from miles around. You had the courage to risk the plague yourselves in order to save the lives of countless others.'

Many of the congregation murmured agreement, others nodded their heads.

'Courage and perseverance are what you showed,' William went on, 'putting your trust in God to guide our village through the quarantine at whatever cost to yourselves. And my praises for all of you are boundless.

'I now ask Mr Morten of Shepherds Flat to step forward. He has kindly offered to lead you all in the recital of an appropriate psalm.

From his seat in the front row of pews, Matthew stood

and turned to face the congregation to lead them in their own version of Psalm 27:

The Lord is my light and my salvation; who shall I fear?
The Lord is the stronghold of my life; of whom shall I be afraid?
When evil men advance against me to devour my flesh,
When my enemies and my foes attack me, they will stumble and fall…

Following the recital, the congregation settled down to listen to William's sermon.

'Every one of you here today deserves praise for the way you pulled together,' his clear voice rang out. 'The reason for our village being smitten by plague in the first place is something we may never know. Perhaps all of us, or just a few, were guilty of wrongdoings in the eyes of the Lord. Or perhaps Eyam was simply unfortunate that the seeds of plague *somehow* found their way into our village. But it serves little purpose to ponder on that issue for long.'

William smiled at his parishioners, his pride in them swelling his heart. 'When the plague eventually left Eyam, we, the survivors, totalled but four hundred and twenty, a vastly lower sum than the original number close to six hundred and fifty. But over the last few months, the children who had been sent away to the safety of family or friends, returned. As did some of the adults who had fled in the early days of the plague. It is not quite seven months since the great burning and the end of the plague, yet already most of the abandoned houses are now lived in and our village is beginning to feel whole again.'

William gave them a moment to contemplate that fact before he resumed.

Twenty-Five

'One of the people I name as a returnee is Andrew Merrell, whom I see standing in the south transept with his cousins, Margaret and Simon. As you see, Andrew survived after he'd fled from Eyam to live on the moors with only the cockerel he took with him for company.'

William grinned. 'Perhaps if I ask him nicely, Andrew will explain how he lived through those months on the moors …

'Andrew, do you think you could come to the front and say a few words to us all?'

All heads turned towards Andrew in anticipation of a response. After a few moments Andrew squeezed between members of the congregation to stand at the foot of William's pulpit, the grin on his face suggesting he was happy to entertain them all with his tale.

'Well, Reverend,' he started, glancing up at William before focussing on the villagers. 'As you know, the plague 'adn't long started when I 'eaded out to live on the moors. I reckoned I'd 'ave a better chance of surviving out there. I knew the moors well and 'ad often snared rabbits and wildfowl t' take 'ome for the pot. There're many small streams, so I 'ad plenty of fresh water. In the winter when most of the streams froze, I melted ice in one of the pans I'd taken up there with me. I'd built meself a shelter t' sleep in a couple of years afore the plague came t' Eyam, from some of the rocks lying around and a few short planks of wood that Robert, the coffin maker, 'ad no use for. I took me bag of tools with me, a couple of pots and pans, and flints for lighting fires. I also took the blankets off me bed and a thick rug that pa'd thrown out. The rug came in useful for me, inside the shelter. Taking all those things meant I had t' make a few trips back an' forth.'

He glanced up at William for assurance he should continue, and William nodded.

'The shelter was just big enough for me t' keep food and other belongings in and for me t' sleep in at night. I blocked the entrance with some spare bits of wood while I was out hunting, or sleeping. And I didn't need t' persuade George – 'e's me cockerel – to come in for the night when the weather got cold.

'Anyway, I managed t' feed meself well all the time I stayed out there. I kept a fire going t' cook on, even in the winter. I made another shelter for it with a hole at the top for the smoke t' escape. I boiled most of the rabbits and birds I caught, and real tender they were, too.'

'It sounds as though you coped well on your own on the moors, Andrew,' William complimented. 'Tell us, how did you know the plague in Eyam was over when you eventually came home?'

Andrew shrugged. 'I didn't know it was over, Reverend. I 'adn't seen a soul on the moors in all the time I was out there. I'd probably have still been out there now if it 'adn't been for George.'

The congregation laughed and William fought hard not to do the same. 'I think you need to explain that, Andrew. In what way did George let you know the plague was over?'

Andrew pulled an indignant scowl. 'He didn't, Reverend. 'e can't talk, can 'e? He just disappeared one mornin' in April this year. I got meself in a bit of a panic wondering if someone walkin' on the moors could've grabbed 'im for the pot, or if 'ed been caught in one of me snares. But once I'd 'ad a think, I realised that it was spring, and George 'ad an eye for the hen birds, I can tell yer. I guessed 'e might 'ave flown from the moors to find a place where he could charm a few hens, like 'e did when we lived with pa in the village. So I came back 'ere t' look.'

'And was George here?'

'He was, Reverend, sitting on 'is old roost lookin' well pleased with 'imself. I thought it a bit strange that pa wasn't around, so I went t' see me cousins, Margaret and Simon. They knocked the 'appiness I felt at findin' George right out of me, when they told me that pa 'ad died last September. They also reminded me that the 'ouse was now mine, so I moved right in and stayed there. So 'ere I am.'

'Thank you for telling us all about your life on the moors, Andrew. Few people could have coped out there, on their own, especially through the cold winter months.'

Andrew grinned as he returned to his place beside his two cousins and William focussed once more on the congregation. 'It took courage and perseverance to cope with life on the bleak moorlands, as Andrew did. Yet, Andrew's courage must be seen in a different light to the courage shown by all of you who remained in Eyam throughout the plague, especially during the height of summer last year when plague deaths were at their highest.

'Many of you who left in the early months of the contagion will have had the courage to persevere away from your homes and, perhaps, learn to live amongst strangers, some of them hostile to people from Eyam. Whatever your stories, we welcome you back so we can all resume our lives and rebuild our village until it becomes the happy, thriving place of pre-plague days.

'Unfortunately, unlike our many returnees, the Bradshaw family has not returned and their once grand home, Bradshaw Hall, remains empty and untended. Let us hope the family found peace and happiness, wherever they went to.

'Almighty God has helped us through our darkest of times; times of suffering and immeasurable loss. So, to end our service today, I ask you to put your hands together as I say The Lord's Prayer by way of our thanks for His tender love and care during the plague and for evermore. You are all welcome to join in with the words.:

Our Father, who art in heaven,
hallowed be thy name,
thy kingdom come; thy will be done
on earth as it is in heaven…

William was pleased to hear a few voices adding to his own and rejoiced that after three years of his ministry, he had started to make progress in his mission to convert the staunchly Puritan villagers to the Anglican way of worship.

—

Eyam: Mid July 1667

It had always been Matthew Morten's habit to walk his faithful old greyhound, Gideon, at the end of each working day. Since losing his beloved wife and their children to the plague, almost a year ago, Gideon had become Matthew's constant companion, often accompanying his master during his daily work on his farm.

One of their favourite walks of an evening took them east along the Foolow Road, passing through the Townhead area of Eyam before the road turned south towards the entrance to Cucklett Delph. Gideon was an obedient and loving dog, and rarely ventured from Matthew's side, even when horses and carts, or groups of rowdy children, passed them by. But on this lovely, July evening, the old greyhound did something quite out of character.

As they entered the delph, Gideon suddenly bounded towards a young woman, who was quite unknown to Matthew. Seemingly lost in thought as she walked, she didn't see Gideon until he was circling her and wagging his tail as though greeting an old friend. But as he attempted to nuzzle her hand, she yelped, holding up her arms in front of her and backing further away as Gideon pursued his greeting.

'Come *here*, Gideon!' Matthew yelled, mortified that his dog could cause such panic in a person. Too late, the poor woman tripped backwards over a fallen branch and the delighted dog saw his chance to lick her face as though it needed a thorough washing, pushing her coif to the back of her head in the process.

By the time William had heaved Gideon's large frame away from the woman, her wavy, brown hair was in disarray and she was sobbing hysterically. As he opened his mouth to offer profuse apologies, he realised she wasn't sobbing at all, but laughing.

Now sitting on the grass, the young woman's hands alternately caressed Gideon's short, floppy ears and stroked his long neck as though she'd known him for years.

'I sincerely apologise for my lack of control over my dog, Mistress,' Matthew managed to say, knowing the woman would see the fault as his. 'Never before in the eight years I've had him has Gideon done such a thing.'

'He's a lovely animal so please don't scold him on my account. He just took me by surprise. Perhaps he thought I was someone else.' The woman pulled herself to her feet and held out her hand to Matthew. 'I'm Sarah, by the way, Sarah Hawksworth. And I happen to love dogs.'

Matthew took her hand, enjoying her easy smile and friendly chat after the months he'd spent avoiding people. 'Matthew Morten, from Shepherds Flat. I'm a farmer.'

'Are you related to any of the Mortens who lived in Eyam? I know the plague took many of them.'

Matthew nodded. 'We were a large family before the plague. I lost my wife and our three children last August.'

'I'm sorry to hear that, Matthew, and hope that time has helped to ease your pain.'

'I think it has, for most of the time. I don't dwell on my memories when I keep myself busy.'

'I imagine most folk in the village could say the same. And yet, I do believe that people are trying hard to put the past behind them and are working to make Eyam a happy and flourishing place to live again.'

'I believe that, too, Sarah. I suppose if I lived amongst them all, in the middle of Eyam, instead of out of the way at Shep-

Twenty-Five

herds Flat, it would be easier for me to forget my grief more often. A life of solitude lends itself to dwelling on memories…

'Forgive me for talking about myself. I've become so accustomed to being alone that my thoughts must have been bursting to be put into words.'

Sarah smiled. 'I can imagine how much you have longed to speak to someone about your losses. It does you good to share your sorrows with someone who understands. You will find me a good listener, as well as being someone who knows what it feels like to lose someone you love.'

'You lost someone in your family, too?' he asked, tentatively, hoping his question would not sound intrusive.

'My husband also died in August last year. William and I had only been married for eleven months and when he died, I was carrying his child. Elizabeth was born in early March and is now four months old. I give daily thanks to God that He spared my child from the plague, and me as well, so I could take care of her. My mother looks after her while I take a little walk of an evening.'

Matthew and Sarah continued to stroll around the delph, chatting like longtime friends as Gideon sniffed about, following the scent of one small creature after another. As dusk began to fall, they headed back into Eyam, arranging to meet here every evening for a stroll and a chat until the nights closed in with the autumn and the lack of daylight prevented a visit to Cucklett Delph.

The recovery of Eyam's working day continued in unison with the healing of its people. Small businesses, including the

A Boundary of Stones

cobbler, coffin maker and stonemason were once again fully open for trade and midwives no longer feared entering homes to help new life into the world. Marriages, christenings and funerals kept William busy, in addition to his weekly services.

In late November, when trees stood stark against the wintry sky, a young man with the surname of Talbot came to the rectory, asking to speak to Reverend Mompesson.

'Good afternoon, Mr Talbot,' William said, shaking the young visitor's hand and indicating he should take a seat when Jane showed him into the study. 'How can I help you?'

William waited patiently whilst the young man, evidently not a Puritan, tugged at the neck of the high-necked shirt he seemed unaccustomed to wearing. 'Me and my wife come from Bakewell. My name's Godfrey and I'm a blacksmith by trade. I was hoping to be able to take over Richard Talbo\t's place now he's… well, now that the place is empty. I'll be happy to pay the appropriate rent.'

'Are you related in some way to the Talbot's who lived there, Godfrey? Two blacksmiths by the name of Talbot is quite a coincidence.'

'Richard was my pa's brother, barely eighteen months older than him. They both grew up in Bakewell but my uncle came here to find work when he married Katherine, who was born in Eyam. My pa and Richard both became blacksmiths, and each wanted his own business, you see. There was already one smith in Bakewell and my pa made it two, so Richard was happy to stay in Eyam.'

William nodded. 'So, you followed in their footsteps and became a blacksmith yourself.'

Twenty-Five

'Never wanted to be anything else, but with my pa still working in Bakewell, I wondered if you were in need of a smith here.'

'I'm sure we are. I know of no one else in this village skilled in that trade. Did you know that the entire Talbot family died during the plague?'

'I did Reverend, and I was very sorry to hear it. Although we haven't seen each other for years, we children got along well when were young. It was the two eldest, Bridget and Mary, I knew best because they were only a little younger than me. But a busy life leaves little time for visiting, especially when you live almost nine miles apart.'

'Well, Godfrey, I can tell you that the house and smithy are definitely vacant, and considering Richard Talbot was your uncle, it's probable you can simply inherit the property. No one else has made claim to it, but I must tell you that before you move in, the house and outbuildings all need purifying.'

Godfrey's puzzled face prompted William to explain what purifying involved. 'You will, therefore, need to refurnish the house before you move in.'

'We have our own furniture, Reverend, including our beds and blankets, which we'd be bringing with us in any case.'

'Excellent. So, the only thing preventing you from moving in right away will be waiting for the burning and scrubbing to be done and the house to dry out. Unfortunately, at this time of year, drying could take at least a week.' William paused while he thought. 'If' I order a daily fire to be lit in the living room hearth once the scrubbing is finished, you could probably move in before the start of the new year. Weather permitting, of course.'

Godfrey stood to shake William's hand. 'That suits me fine, Reverend. And thank you for offering to purify the house for us. I'll pay what I owe you for that when we move in.'

Twenty-Six

Eyam: August - December 1668

At the beginning of August the following year, William decided to order the building of a tomb over Catherine's grave. He'd been intending to have one constructed in honour of her life since he'd buried her two years ago but so many other duties had taken his time. Now, he would delay no longer. It was time to visit the stonemason, whose trade had come to a halt when the demand for headstones had ceased during the plague.

Jake Glover's aged face wrinkled still further as the squinted up at the taller man in the August sunshine. 'What type of tomb had you in mind, Reverend?'

'I was hoping you could advise me on that, Jake. I had thought only of a simple rectangular structure of a few feet high with details of Catherine's life engraved on it. Nothing too ostentatious.'

Jake laid his chisel on the slab of stone he'd been engraving and scratched his balding head. 'Write down the measurements you want the tomb to be, along with the things you'd like people to know about Mrs Mompesson, and I'll see what I can do. I could engrave a few images to go with the writing, if you like.'

'That sounds perfect, thank you, Jake. I'll look forward to seeing the results of your labours.'

By October, the tomb was finished and placed over Catherine's grave in St Helen's cemetery. William's heart swelled with gratitude when he examined it; Jake had done a remarkable job. The tomb was an impressive, rectangular structure of local, grey stone, of approximately three feet high with a large, flat slab of stone resting on top and overlapping it. The slab had been artistically engraved with details of Catherine's life and familial connections in the county of Durham, in addition to the date of her death in Eyam.

Both ends of the tomb itself also exhibited engravings. At one end, an hourglass between the outstretched wings of a bird depicted the rapid flight of time, and the fact that Death can come to anyone when least expected. But it was the symbol and wording at the other end of the tomb that brought William peace of mind. It was an image of a resting death's head with the inscription, *Death is Gain to Me*. He exulted in his firm belief that Catherine's kindness and charity towards her fellow man had earned her eternal joy in God's Paradise.

The golden warmth of autumn gradually ceded to the cold, cheerless days of winter. Harsh winds and biting frosts kept the old and infirm by their firesides, whilst others pulled coats close about them as they headed to the lead mines, quarry, market or farm.

The first three weeks of December found William in dismal mood. It was Advent, when he should have been celebrating in preparation for Christmas. Yet once again, he was neglecting the tenets of his Anglican calling. Today was Friday, the twenty-first of the month, and he was seated at his desk, struggling to write an appropriate service for the coming Sunday. It would be the day before Christmas Eve, but he would not be delivering a Christmas service. Nor would he be doing so

Twenty-Six

on Christmas Eve, or on Christmas Day.

Praying for forgiveness did little to erase William's sense of inadequacy and guilt. The many times he'd allowed his congregation to recite their own psalms and prayers was probably enough to see him removed from his ministry in Eyam. But his failure to celebrate every Christmas and Easter since his arrival in the village would be deemed by the bishops as his greatest offence. For which they would likely dub him a traitor to his faith and have him ousted from the Anglican Church altogether.

William knew he had not been forceful enough to demand his parishioners accept the Church of England and its Book of Common Prayer. It would take a much stronger man than him to achieve that goal.

It was time he moved on.

Two years had passed since the end of the plague and Eyam was thriving again, which meant that William had no real reason to stay. Besides, he told himself, he should be seeking promotion in his chosen career. But promotion could only be gained after achieving success in a given parish.

He decided that once the Christmas period was over, he would write to Sir George, requesting a new living be found for him – one in an Anglican parish. Once he'd moved, he would collect his children from Uncle John's, something he had longed to do for many months. George and Elizabeth had never been far from his thoughts since they had left for Sheffield almost two-and-a-half years ago, and it was high time they came home. But he wouldn't want them settling back in Eyam only to be moved elsewhere soon after.

He stretched out his aching arms and wiggled his fingers in an attempt to bring them back to life. He'd been working on a suitable Sunday service since early morning and still hadn't written anything that would be of use. Several attempts had been crossed out before they were barely started. Now, as he stared down at his latest idea, he decided it would simply have to do. He'd spoken many times about the joys of three of the seasons, but never specifically about winter. And yet, the cold winter days had a beauty all of their own. He picked up his quill and wrote his title: *The Stark Beauty of Winter*.

Yet he still struggled to convey his thoughts to the paper and his attention drifted to the happy years he'd shared with Catherine. Tears filled his eyes as he thought of her loving nature and care for others. How sad it was that his lovely wife could only enjoy the beauty of winter through the windows of a warm room.

Through the glass doors of his study, William watched the snowflakes settling on the rectory garden. The snow had swept in during the night and paths, trees and flowerbeds were veiled in a blanket of glistening white. He recalled how the sight of it had always depressed Catherine. Pristine and white, snow drew her to it like a magnet, a force that she fought so hard to resist. To have been lured outdoors in the depth of winter would have meant risking her life. Her poor, infected lungs could not have coped with such cold, and Catherine would never have risked her life that way. Thoughts of leaving him a widower and their children motherless, were enough to keep his beloved wife indoors.

But he knew only too well that plague has no respect for

Twenty-Six

walls and doors. The devious disease effortlessly finds its way inside, often over thresholds with family or friends, or following neighbourly chats in the street. Though William suspected the source of his wife's infection, he kept it to himself. It served no purpose to lay blame at anyone's feet. Plague was a ferocious beast and few it embraced could counter its claws.

And yet, several of his parishioners had spent many hours amongst, or caring for, plague victims, but had not contracted it themselves. Mary and Jane were two such people, as were Elizabeth Hancock and Matthew Morten. More surprising still was the fact that Margaret Blackwell, Marshall Howe had Geoffrey Unwin had all survived actual attacks by this evil beast. Why that should be so completely eluded William.

He put aside his contemplations and decided to continue planning his service in the sanctity of St Helens, where he could always think more clearly, despite the cold. He donned his thick winter coat and headed to the church. By the time he'd finished he felt satisfied that no part of his Christmas Day service would offend his Puritan congregation.

He was returning his coat to the stand in the rectory's hall when Mary arrived back from the Friday market.

'Good morning, Reverend. If you have a moment, I have something to tell you. If not, it will wait until later.'

'From the look on your face, I take it you have good news to share. So perhaps you should tell me now.'

Mary nodded. 'I'm not sure if it's good news or not. It's just that John Coe has asked me to marry him.'

'Oh, I'm delighted for both of you. John is such a pleasant man and I'm sure he'll do his utmost to take care of you.'

William grinned. 'Not that I'm suggesting you can't look after yourself. I've met few women who can cope with as much work as you do and still wear a smile.'

'I haven't given John my answer yet. I just wanted to hear what you thought about his proposal. Knowing that you approve of him is heartening.'

'Mary, you deserve to be happy after what you've had to deal with over the last few years. If you care for John and he cares for you, I'm truly happy for you.'

'Thank you, Reverend, but if we do marry it won't be for some time. I've become accustomed to being on my own and intend to continue working here for as long as I am needed. I've told John how I feel and he says he's happy to wait a year or two.'

Mary paused and William could see she was deep in thought. 'When I was a girl,' she continued, 'I imagined marrying someone with whom I'd spend the rest of my life. Unfortunately, things didn't work out that way. Illnesses and diseases have a way of changing any plans we might have made.'

William nodded, knowing that only too well.

'You know, Reverend Mompesson, it would be nice to see a few more of the lonely people who lost loved ones to the plague marrying others in a similar position – just as Matthew Morten and Sarah Hawksworth did last year. In my case, John Coe is a widower, although his wife died some years before the plague came to Eyam. He's two years older than me and I've known him since we were children. It's funny how life turns out sometimes, isn't it?

'Now, Reverend, I need to get started in the kitchen. I've

got a nice shoulder of mutton to roast for tonight's meal, which I'll serve with a thyme and claret sauce. I know it's one of your favourite dishes.'

'My belly is rumbling at the thought of it, so by tonight I shall likely be slavering in a very ungentlemanly manner.'

Chuckling to herself, Mary disappeared into the kitchen.

Twenty-Seven

Eyam: May 1669

In mid-May, William received a long-awaited reply from Sir George Savile. It informed him that if he was still intent upon leaving Eyam, a new living would soon be available for a rector at the parish church in Eakring. As several other villages, Eakring was within Sir George's own estates of Rufford Abbey in Nottinghamshire, and the position would follow the retirement of the present incumbent on the last day of December this year.

William was delighted and decided to reply to Sir George immediately with his acceptance of the position as plans for the coming months filled his head. He and his children would spend Christmas with Uncle John and his family in Sheffield, before the three of them took the coach to Eakring at the end of December. He could hardly wait to have George and Elizabeth with him again and once they were settled in the new rectory, he would set about finding them a tutor.

Then William read the rest of the letter… twice… the second time aloud, needing to convince himself he hadn't misread or misunderstood Sir George's meaning:

Naturally, William, as a man of the cloth and, indeed, a rector and upholder of the law, it would be preferable if you were to undertake your duties as a married man.

But…William argued to himself… Sir George knows full well that my wife died during the plague. How could I possibly find a wife before December?

Concerned that his lack of a wife would prevent him accepting the new position, he read on:

Rest assured, I have found you the perfect bride – although, like you, she has been married before and is not a young girl. Indeed, I believe her to be five years your senior. One thing I can say is that she is an extremely attractive and accomplished lady, and is skilled in the management of a household and its accounts. Her name is Elizabeth Newby, a widow, and a great niece of mine.

You will therefore understand, William, that this post will only become yours once you have wedded this charming, intelligent and very able lady.

William couldn't decide whether he should be grateful to Sir George, or curse the man for interfering with his personal life. He could not deny that Sir George had always had William's interests at heart, and had done his utmost to find suitable employment for him since he'd graduated from Cambridge. But surely, finding William a wife was a different matter. As far as William could see, the only justification for doing so was due to a stipulation that the new rector at Eakring should be married. He could only wonder if a previous rector had been a single man with a roving eye for the ladies of that parish.

But since William had already made the decision to leave Eyam, he needed to inform Church officials of his intentions as soon as possible. That would give them a few months to find a suitable new rector for Eyam. It would also allow William time to collect George and Elizabeth from Uncle John's and head to Rufford Abbey to meet and marry Elizabeth Newby before taking up his new post the following January.

That evening, William sat at his desk to compose a gracious letter of thanks to Sir George for his kindness, and to accept his new living at Eakring.

—

Eyam: Friday, August 16 1669

'Come in,' William called in response to the anticipated knock on the study door as he replaced his quill in its pot.

The door opened a fraction and Jane peeped in. 'Reverend Henry Adams is in the hall. Will you see him in here, Reverend?'

'Yes, the study's the best place to start with, thank you Jane.'

Jane returned a few moments later to introduce a tallish man with collar-length fair hair, pleasant features and a genial smile. He was garbed in similar clothing to William, the black of his breeches and jacket broken only by the white cravat at his neck and the silver buckle of the black leather belt. And whilst he wore no cloak or coat on this warm, August morning, he had removed his wide-brimmed hat for Jane to place on the hatstand in the hall. William estimated him to be in his mid-twenties and absently wondered if he was married. Church officials had said very little about him.

William shook the young man's hand in welcome as he stepped into the room. 'Good morning, Reverend Adams,' he said, gesturing for his guest to sit in one of the two armchairs in the room as he sat in the other. 'As you know, my name is William, and I know yours is Henry, and since we are to work alongside each other for a while, I trust we can do away with formality and address each other by our Christian names?'

'Absolutely, Rev… I mean, William. I'll gladly toss formality to the wind.'

William grinned. 'So, now that we're done with the tossing, I ask if your journey from Leicester was a pleasant one?'

'It was actually very comfortable, particularly since we had an overnight stay in Matlock. We drove through some lovely scenery after that.'

'Yes, the hilly terrain is quite a draw to many people. Even in winter, the stark, white beauty of the hills and moors cannot be denied. But I hope you're a hardy man, Henry, and own a pair of strong, waterproof boots to cope with the snow.'

The young man laughed. 'I'm hardier than many folk, and yes, I have some very strong boots, and a thick warm coat, though I doubt I'll have chance to see a great deal of snow on these hills this year. Perhaps in sixteen months' time.'

'Sixteen months…? You'll likely see plenty of snow this coming winter. We've had snow every year since I came to Eyam five years ago, and I can't see that pattern changing.'

'It seems the bishops haven't explained my situation to you.'

William frowned. 'They have told me nothing, other than your name and that you hail from Leicester – and to expect you this morning. As far as I am aware, you are to join me in my daily work and church services for the next two weeks. I shall be leaving Eyam on Monday, the sixth of September and I imagine you will return the previous weekend?'

'That is only partly true, I'm afraid. Yes, I've been granted absence from my duties in Leicester for the next two weeks in order to observe you in all aspects of your work here. But you have not yet touched on the issue in question.'

'Then I'll continue; I may well have overlooked some important point. During those two weeks, you will be able to familiarise yourself with the routines I have adopted and could continue in that manner, if you so wish. Naturally, it will be quite understandable if you would prefer to adopt your own daily procedures, and the order of your services. But by accompanying me in my day-to-day work, you will come to know some of the congregation before you start here yourself.'

Before Henry could reply, William added, 'I don't know if you are aware that the people of this village have long been staunch Puritans, set in their ways well before I came to Eyam. My Church of England teachings and the prayers in our Book of Common Prayer, have still not been fully accepted, especially amongst the older members of the community.'

'I know a great deal about Eyam, William, and the faith of its residents. My father was rector here before your own arrival. I lived here, in this rectory, for several years when I was a lad.'

'Your father was Shoreland Adams…' William said, recalling Stanley's opinion of the man and feeling foolish for not having attached significance to the surname. 'He had died before I came here and another rector had been invited to fill the gap.'

'Thomas Stanley, you mean?' William nodded 'I remember him well. He really didn't like my father and the two of them were always arguing. I know Father was not as dedicated to the people of Eyam as he should have been, nor was he a Puritan, so I can see why Stanley objected to his ministry.'

Twenty-Seven

The knock on the door announced Mary's arrival with the morning refreshments.

'Thank you, Mary,' William said as she laid the tray on the small table between them. He gestured at his visitor. 'I'd like you to meet Reverend Henry Adams, who is to take my place as rector here in Eyam. Reverend Adams, meet Mrs Hadfield. Mary is the rectory's wonderful cook, as well as a dear friend.'

The two shook hands and Mary asked, 'You aren't Shoreland Adams son, are you, Reverend? I remember he had a son by the name of Henry who lived in Eyam before his university studies took him away. He'd probably be about your age now.'

'I am indeed, but I'm afraid I don't recall anyone by the name of Hadfield… although your face does look familiar.'

Mary smiled. 'My name would have been Cooper when you lived here, Reverend.'

'Now that name I do remember. Did you live in one of the four cottages on Church Street, a short way from St Helen's?'

'I did, and still do – but I'll leave Reverend Mompesson to explain about recent events in the village. Enjoy your cocoa before you go out.'

Mary left the room and Henry asked, 'Do you need to go out, William? If you do, perhaps your housekeeper could show me to my room so I can unpack?'

'I thought we could both go out, so I can introduce you to some of the villagers. It's market day, as you will know, and there will be many of the villagers about.'

'That would be excellent. I might even recognise a few faces, and some of them might even recognise mine.'

'Good. Then let us enjoy Mary's lovely Shrewsbury cakes

and cocoa before we go.'

As the two reverends walked along Church Street towards the market place, William continued to disclose a little more about what Henry's role would involve.

'I won't pretend your work here will be easy. The people not only cling to their Puritan faith, they are still recovering from fifteen months of plague. Although the disease left us at the end of 1666 and daily life and work are now back to normal, the plague took almost a third of our population. Many villagers still haven't fully overcome the grief of their losses.'

'That's understandable,' Henry said. 'I'll be sure to tread carefully and treat people with the care and understanding they deserve.'

William nodded. 'When you look in the parish register, you will see that some families almost disappeared altogether. In fact, there are a few families in which no-one survived.

'But, if you enjoy a challenge and, as you said, treat the people with care and understanding, without reprimand or scorn of their Puritan views, you will find them some of the kindest people you could meet. There are many I shall sincerely miss, although it's time for me to move on.'

'I look forward to the challenge, William. I like to think I'm an understanding man, and wouldn't dream of putting anyone down because of the faith they follow. I will try to continue as you have done to gain their trust, and gently persevere with our Church of England teachings.

'But it seems I need to clarify one issue about my appointment here. My position as rector here will not begin until the first day of January in 1671.'

Twenty-Seven

'Oh,' William said, confused. 'At least that explains your reference to enjoying the snow in sixteen months.'

Before either of them could say more on the subject, they turned into the green to come face-to-face with a group of women chatting away, baskets of provisions by their feet. At the unexpected appearance of two reverends at the market, their chatter abruptly ceased.

'Good morning, ladies,' William said with a smile. 'I have someone with me I'd like you all to meet.'

'He looks like an older version of a handsome lad I used to go to school with,' Margaret Blackwell remarked with a leering grin as the women gathered around William and Henry. 'But, for the life of me I can't remember who he was or where he lived.'

'I remember a good-looking lad who was a lot like 'im, too,' Ellen Percival put in. 'It must 'ave been a few years back when 'e lived 'ere 'cos I can't remember 'is name.'

A chorus of voices added agreement with Henry's handsome features being familiar, until an older woman by the name of Grace Townend yelled over the top of them. 'I know who 'e is… at least, I think I do. He's the son of that Anglican preacher, Shoreland Adams! But I can't remember 'is name either.'

William raised his hands to quieten the loud gabble of recognition and smiled round at them all. 'You are correct, Grace; my companion is, indeed, Shoreland Adams' son.' He gestured to the young man. 'As you see he, too, is now a man of the cloth. Allow me to introduce you to Reverend Henry Adams.'

Gabbled comments followed, while William and Henry

grinned at each other.

'Of course it's Shorland Adam's son! One look at that blond hair tells us that!'

'He's the same build as 'is pa, an' all.'

'I knew who he was, as soon as I saw him!'

'No, yer didn't, Margaret. You couldn't remember his name or where he lived.'

'But I knew I'd been to school with him, which is more than you did, Annie Swann!'

'Well, I knew whose son he was,' Grace Townend reminded them all, 'which is more than the rest of you did.'

Again, William raised his hands for quiet, as more village women gathered round to see what the commotion was about.

'Ladies, I am pleased that your astute powers of observation and memory have proven to be correct. Reverend Adams will be spending some time in our community over the next two weeks and I'm sure you can introduce yourselves at some point during that time. I shall be enlightening you all as to why he is visiting us during our service this Sunday.

'But now we must continue our walk, in order that my companion may re-familiarise himself with our lovely village. We wish you good day, ladies.

'Well, Henry, I didn't hear one word of criticism about your father, for which I'm thankful.' Henry nodded and William added, 'And they seemed quite impressed with your handsome, good looks.'

Henry laughed. 'Then I must hope their menfolk don't hold that against me.'

'They probably won't, unless you give them cause. But I

Twenty-Seven

think the sooner you're wed, the better.'

The two reverends continued walking along Church Street, heading towards the Townhead, as Henry reminisced about his years in Eyam. 'I loved my schooldays here, although the master, a Mr Ragge, was very strict. Like most people in Eyam, he was a Puritan and ruled his classroom with an iron rod. That suited me because I was keen to learn, and spent many hours poring over most of the books in the rectory's study. Other pupils weren't so keen on their studies and were frequently subjected to Mr Ragge's slipper on their backsides, or standing in the corner, facing the wall, for hours on end.'

'My schoolmaster was little different,' William admitted. 'But, like you, I was an avid learner and was rarely reprimanded. And by the way, Thomas Ragge died during the plague. I believe he was in his mid-seventies by then, although his mind was still razor-sharp.

'I imagine you know all parts of Eyam well, Henry,' William said as Church Street curved towards the north-west end of the village.

'I do. I know that this part is called the Townhead and that there's a well, or water trough, here fed by a stream that flows down from the moors. An apothecary, whose name I forget, lived over there with his wife and son, who was several years younger than me. And over there,' he said, his arm sweeping to indicate the opposite side of the road, lived a strange and quite nasty young man called Marshall something or other.'

'Marshall Howe still lives there and is probably the most unpleasant, and unpopular, man in Eyam. But I'll tell you about more about him later on. The apothecary you mentioned was Humphrey Merrell, another who died in the plague. His son, Andrew, has lived in the family house on his own since the plague came to an end.

'Now, I think it's time to head back to the rectory and have some lunch.'

As they ate their lunch of cold chicken with red beet and freshly baked bread, Henry explained about the delay to his starting date in Eyam.

'It's unfortunate that my present position in Leicester doesn't expire until the end of December next year. I suppose I should feel flattered that the bishops considered me worthy of waiting for in regard to the position here. And I do know they think extremely highly of you, which is why they wanted you to be the one to prepare me as your replacement.'

'Then we'll feel flattered together, Henry. I just wonder who they'll appoint to fill the gap between my leaving and you starting here.'

'Nothing was said about that, I'm afraid.'

'It seems I must be patient until the bishops decide to inform me. Now, about residing here, in the rectory. You will be free to make your own arrangements, of course, but I employ two very efficient and cheerful ladies to take care of the domestic arrangements, both of whom you have already met. Mary Hadfield is my cook, and an excellent one, too. My housekeeper, who keeps the rectory spick and span, is Jane Hawksworth. Jane also takes care of answering the door, as she did for you earlier. I also employ an excellent gardener by the name of Joseph Taylor. He keeps the rectory gardens looking wonderful all year.

Twenty-Seven

'I pay the three of them out of the stipend I receive and can say that the coin is very well spent, especially for a single man like yourself. Mary also has extra coin from me to cover the expenses involved in purchasing foodstuffs.'

'That sounds perfect, although by the time I start here in sixteen months, I'll be a married man. Ruth will be thrilled to know we are to have a cook and a housekeeper. It will give her time to attend to parochial duties, and any children we might have.'

William had instantly liked Henry, but felt it a pity he couldn't start his ministry in Eyam for over a year. A temporary cleric – worse still, a succession of them – could create a sense of insecurity in the village. After everything they'd been through during the plague, such disruption to their weekly worship was the last thing these people needed.

—

In the morning of Sunday, the eighteenth of August, Henry accompanied William to the church to be introduced to the people of Eyam. Garbed in black cassocks and white surplices, the two reverends stood at the church door in the warm sunshine, to welcome people to the service. William was pleased to see such a large turnout and many cheerful faces. Nor could he miss the looks of admiration cast Henry's way from many of the women.

'It seems that word has got round regarding your stay in Eyam, Henry,' William whispered. 'I'm guessing the ladies all want to gaze at you and their husbands are here to make sure they do not.'

Henry laughed. 'What an imagination you have, Reverend Mompesson. I sincerely hope they don't. Facing angry husbands would be a poor way to start my ministry here.'

They followed the last of the congregation into the church and William took his place in his pulpit while Henry sat on the front row of the pews.

William ensured he had everyone's attention and made a start, 'To open our service on this glorious August morning I will recite the first few lines of a hymn created by Martin Luther. It is based on the wording of Psalm 46, which is thought to have been written by the prophet Isaiah. I ask you all to contemplate the meaning of the words:

A mighty fortress is our God,
a bulwark, never falling;
our helper he, amid the flood
of mortal ills prevailing.
For still our ancient foe
Does seek to work us woe;
His craft and power are great;
and armed with cruel hate,
on earth is not his equal.

William held out his arms as he gazed round at the many faces. 'To me, the words in these few lines stress one overriding thing: not one of us could doubt the greatness of God. In times of peril and grief, who but God should we beseech for help? God is, indeed, a *bulwark*… a mighty fortress. It is to Him we turn when our *ancient foe*, whose power and guile are greater than anyone on Earth, seeks to wreak disaster and misery upon us.

Twenty-Seven

'So I ask you, just who *is* this ancient foe, who is filled with such *cruel hate*? I'm sure we all have our thoughts on that…?'

William watched as several hands were raised, and chose Thomas Hall sitting close to the rear of the church.

'It's the Devil, Reverend. He's the only one, other than the Lord, whose power is greater than that of anyone on Earth.'

'Thank you, Thomas, I believe that too. Does anyone disagree?' No hands were raised and William continued, 'It is through the Devil himself that all evil deeds are committed. Acts of cruelty, hate, greed and envy are but a few of the evils that people can inflict on others every day. All such deeds are possible to those who have allowed the Devil into their hearts and minds.

'So, in order to prevent Satan succeeding, we must constantly pray to God for the strength to keep Satan out. And, if our faith is strong enough, we will overcome.

'Now, I'm sure none of you will have failed to notice that I am accompanied today by a fellow clergyman whom many of you will recognise, even if you cannot recall his name.'

William signalled to Henry to come and stand beside him in the pulpit. A buzz of voices filled the church and William gave them a moment to air their views amongst themselves before raising a hand for silence. 'Yes, I heard the correct name mentioned several times just now. The man standing beside me is, indeed, the son of Reverend Shoreland Adams, who sadly passed away before my arrival in Eyam. Allow me to introduce you all to Reverend Henry Adams.'

William waited until the whispered buzz ceased.

'You may well be wondering why Reverend Adams is here,

and how long he will be staying. Perhaps he should answer that for himself.'

William twisted to face Henry in the confined space of the pulpit. 'Reverend…?'

'Thank you, Reverend Mompesson. I would very much like the chance to say a few words to everyone.' Henry flashed an engaging smile round the crowded church. 'Due to commitments elsewhere, I'm afraid that my stay in Eyam will be for a mere two weeks on this occasion. However, I can assure you that you will see a great deal more of me in the future, by which time I'll be a married man and my new wife will be coming with me.'

Comments again rippled around the church and Henry continued. 'Unfortunately, I am obliged to remain in my current position in Leicester for a further fifteen months. At the end of December next year, my wife and I will be packing our bags and coming to live in this lovely village.

'I greatly look forward to chatting with as many of you as possible over the next two weeks. I would dearly love to say 'Hello' to some of my old friends, as well as meeting new ones. I spent several of my childhood years in Eyam and, in all honesty, I can say that they were very happy ones.'

Henry glanced at William, who took his cue.

'It now befalls me to explain a few things regarding Reverend Adams' intended return to Eyam. Perhaps some of you have already guessed.' He glanced round at the mix of nodding heads and puzzled faces and took a breath.

'On the sixth of September, I will be leaving Eyam to take up a new position as reverend and rector in the village of

Twenty-Seven

Eakring in Nottinghamshire.'

The reaction was loud. Gasp of astonishment, calls of, "No… you can't leave us…' 'What will we do without you?' and "Why…?' almost brought tears to William's eyes.

'My friends, I have lived amongst you for over five years, during which time our faith in God and each other, have been sorely tested. Few standing before me today came through the plague unscathed, including me. My love and admiration go out to you all.

'But my work here is done. In truth, our survival during the plague was due to the strength of your own convictions as much as any persuasion or guidance by me or Rev… anyone else.'

William bit his tongue so that Thomas Stanley's name wasn't spoken in front of another member of the Anglican church and, as though the congregation understood his hesitation, no one commented on it.

'I have every praise for you all. You who have taken me into your hearts as much as I have taken you into mine. From shaky beginnings, when I was a stranger to you, and of a different religious calling, I have come to know you as generous, honest, hard-working and caring people. When I leave, you will all remain in my heart. My new congregation will be told of your courage, and the sacrifices you made for the good of people as far away from Eyam as Nottinghamshire, and even further afield.

'I now ask Reverend Adams to recite a few words from Psalm 18, a Psalm of David. David sang this song when the Lord delivered him from the hand of his enemies, and the hand of Saul. It is a story I'm sure you all know and, like Psalm 46, it praises God for giving us strength against our enemies, whether they be human, or otherwise… like the plague.'

'Thank you, Reverend Mompesson. I will gladly recite these few lines.' Henry held out his arms to encompass them all, and began:

I love you, Lord, my strength
The Lord is my rock, my fortress and my deliverer.
My God is my rock in whom I take refuge
My shield and the horn of my salvation; my stronghold.
I called to the Lord, who is worthy of praise
And I have been saved from my enemies.

'In Psalm 18, David gives praise to the Lord for being his strength, his shield, his stronghold and his salvation – or deliverance – from his enemies,' Henry explained. 'In many ways, this psalm gives the same message as the hymn, based on Psalm 46, which Reverend Mompesson recited to us earlier. Both refer to God as being a fortress… a stronghold. But, in Psalm 18, David starts by professing his love for the Lord. In addition, it does not refer to the *ancient foe* – the Devil.'

Henry gazed round at them all. 'From what Reverend Mompesson has told me about your quarantine during the plague, you all put your faith in God to bring you through what can only described as a great sacrifice. Future generations will marvel at the immensity of your strength and courage. I, for one, thank you for preventing the plague from travelling to Leicester. Reverend Mompesson's relatives in Sheffield will, doubtless, do the same. I look forward to working amongst such courageous and selfless people.'

Twenty-Seven

—

Over the following two weeks, William spent most of his time showing Henry where everything was located in the rectory, the church, and the village in general. The parish records proved both fascinating and horrifying to Henry.

'So many deaths in so short a time…'

William nodded. 'Indeed. As I mentioned on your arrival here, some families had no survivors. Their names remain only in our parish records, or scratched onto odd wooden or stone grave markers here and there. Those of us who have lived through the plague still strive to put those terrible months behind us. But I doubt that any of us will ever forget the wrath of the beast that ripped our village apart. As for me…' He sighed. 'When I leave Eyam to take up my new position, my heart will remain here, in the tomb of my beloved Catherine.

'Now, Henry, I shall take you on a delightful walk which I'm sure you will know well. It is particularly pretty in the spring and autumn, or on summer evenings when the sun is low in the sky and the air has cooled a little. It starts beside the church and goes up the grassy hillside…'

William's voice trailed away as his thoughts returned to his last walk with Catherine, when their delight in the August evening was so rapidly curtailed by those strange scents in the air.

—

Eyam: September 3 1669

When William knocked on Thomas Stanley's door, there was no response. He waited, feelings of relief and disappointment wrestling with each other in his chest, and then knocked again.

'Through here,' came a voice from the rear garden. William ducked around the side of the house and found Thomas deadheading his marigolds, a small knife in his hand. The old man smiled and gestured to William to sit next to him.

'You're leaving then?'

William nodded. 'To Eakring.'

Thomas stared at the pile of marigold heads on the path. 'When do you leave?'

'In a few days, once I've settled my affairs here. My replacement, Reverend Adams, won't be in post for over a year, so I must set things up for the interim ministers before I go.'

Thomas grunted. 'You know them?'

'Joshua Scargill I've met, though I wouldn't say we are well acquainted. He'll be here for nine months. After him is a gentleman called Morewood, whom I do not know.'

Thomas sighed and looked around his garden. 'I suppose I should make my own preparations for leaving.'

'Whatever for?'

Thomas smiled sadly. 'You saw how things were when you got here. If the Lord had not wished it otherwise, do you think I'd have been permitted to remain so long into your ministry?'

'Thomas, I said nothing to Henry about you still living in the village. I have asked Mary and Jane to say nothing, either, and my trust in them both is steadfast.'

'Thank you, I appreciate that. I have little time left in this world and if I should die before I have chance to move, my gardener, Daniel Lowe, has agreed to bury me in the common land behind my cottage. I have promised to leave the cottage to him by way of thanks for his loyalty to me over the years. He is to be married next year and I cannot think of a better use for the house in which I have felt such peace.'

'Then it's settled,' William said, watching the colourful flower heads bob and bow in the soft breeze. He stood, started across the grass, and paused, fiddling with his hat in his hands. 'I wish you well, Thomas. And thank you. For everything.'

Thomas rose, the few steps he took to close the gap between them showing a marked limp. William could see how much Thomas had aged in the three years since they had last met. His complexion had a grey pallor and his old bones were evidently causing pain. After a moment, Thomas took William's proffered hand, the veins on his own bulging through papery skin. William nodded and made his way across the garden.

'I was wrong to judge you on the faith you follow,' Thomas called, and William stopped and turned. 'Working with you over the quarantine gave me cause to reassess my previously rigid views of anyone who did not share my Puritan faith.'

William shook his head. 'Our country has suffered greatly over the years by those in power insisting that their faith alone is the true one. I have come to believe that all people should be free to follow whichever faith they choose without being persecuted for it. I was honoured to have you working at my side, Thomas. If not for you, I am certain the people of Eyam would not have accepted the quarantine. Your short sermon that day in Cucklett Delph filled me with admiration for you and your skills as a preacher, and I shall forever name you "friend". You will receive your just reward when God welcomes you to His Paradise.'

Thomas smiled. 'As will you, William. I pray that one day we may be reunited with all those we lost to the plague, if our God desires.'

William's smile came easily. 'Our God, Thomas?'

'I pray there is but one Heaven, with room for all those who have made such sacrifices as we have seen. I am honoured to have you as my friend, William, and am saddened by your leaving. I know that whatever you do, you will always have the welfare of your parishioners at heart. I confess, I have never heard of Eakring, and can only hope your ministry there will be a great deal easier than it has been here.'

'Thoughts of Eyam will stay with me for rest of my days.'

'And Eyam will oft think of you, sir.'

They regarded each other then, the two men of God whose actions had saved a flock and a nation. They shook hands again, then William turned and left the pretty cottage knowing he would never see Thomas Stanley again.

Other Books by Millie Thom

In the Sons of Kings Series:

One: Shadow of the Raven

Two: Pit of Vipers

Three: Wyvern of Wessex

Four: King of the Anglo Saxons

~

Stand Alone Books:

Take Height, Rutterkin

A Dash of Flash

A Second Dash of Flash

Printed in Great Britain
by Amazon